The Vintage Gardener: A Tale of Power and Betrayal.
by Stuart Walker

Table of Contents

Prologue

Alan's eyes snapped open, the oppressive darkness of his room doing little to quell the vivid memories that tore through his mind. The faces of his fallen foes, twisted and contorted in pain, stared back at him from the depths of his nightmares. He was trapped in a waking hell, a relentless replay of the battles that had etched scars on his soul.

The piercing screams from his nightmares echoed within him, their intensity magnified in the surreal realm of slumber, replaying in an unending loop that surpassed the horrors of his waking memories.

His clammy hands clung to the bedsheets, the fabric damp with the remnants of his torment. The pallor of the moonlight filtered through the window, casting an eerie glow on the walls. He could hear his own heartbeat, an irregular rhythm that mirrored the chaos within.

Turning to the bedside table, he reached for the whisky glass – its presence a physical link to the night before, though in truth, he had only stopped his drinking a mere three hours ago. It stood there, his most faithful companion, beckoning with the allure of temporary respite from the relentless torment of his past.

Alan lifted the glass to his lips, allowing the amber elixir to cascade over his tongue, its comforting warmth briefly pushing back the relentless grip of haunting memories. The whisky's sharp burn was a dual sensation – a reminder of his internal battles and a momentary distraction from the harrowing visions that plagued his mind. Stealing himself for the inevitable return to slumber, he braced for the opportunity to face his inner demons once again. The struggle against sleep was futile; sooner rather than later, its grasp would pull him back into the abyss.

The Package

The grey Prius glided to a slow, near-silent halt. Kevin Monroe's eyes darted around the dimly lit street, confirming the address and ensuring the package remained secure on the passenger seat. This moment was his shot at solidifying his standing in the family firm, a chance to follow in the esteemed footsteps of his father and beloved grandfather. Great Uncle Harry had labelled this job as "a special," a nod to Kevin's rising stock within the family legacy.

Kevin took a deep breath, his heart pounding like a drum. Through the frosted front passenger window, he focused on the dark blue door, the numbers "3" and "7" visible in the early morning light. He opened the car door with care, picked up the package, and stepped out onto the kerb. He decided against shutting the car door, despite the early hour minimising the risk of anyone hearing it. "It's all about planning, minimise the risks," Kevin reminded himself, echoing his grandfather's wisdom: "Planning is the bridge between ambition and accomplishment."

The chilly air outside bit into his skin, a stark contrast to the warmth inside the car. Kevin knew this was a straightforward task – deliver the package and drive away. He moved through the waist-high gate, mentally kicking himself for not planning to close it quietly; the noise was an unnecessary risk. Three strides across the damp grass brought him to the blue door. Kevin double-checked the numbers "37" and hesitated, package in hand, near the letterbox. It was too small. Then he noticed the cat flap. It was a stroke of luck, or perhaps a test of his initiative, something his grandfather would have praised.

Kevin smiled to himself, bent down, and gently pushed the package through the cat flap, watching as it settled inside. A sudden noise as the magnets secured the cat flap startled him. He glanced around, heart racing, but the street remained silent. It was still only 4:57 in the morning. "Take a breath, Kev," he whispered.

He closed the gate with precision, proud of his own carefulness, and slipped back into the car. The hybrid's noiseless advantage at low speeds made for a perfect getaway vehicle. Kevin pulled the car away from the kerb, hands gripping the steering wheel, nerves on edge. Every beat of his heart seemed louder than the car's electric engine. It would all be worth it. Great Uncle Harry would surely commend him to his grandfather – his stock was undeniably rising.

Alan Johnson

Alan woke with a jolt, aware of some noise in the bedroom but not alert enough to discern its origin. There seemed to be a lot of words, and someone was stomping about and, oh great, the curtains were opening. "I suppose you had a late night, did you?" More unwelcome noise. Alan pulled the duvet over his head. "Did anyone else stay over?" Alan closed his eyes, tightly. "I bet the lounge is a right mess?" Alan shut his eyes tighter. He knew he'd have to answer eventually, if only to make the noise go away.

"Is anyone in the box room?" That phrase again. Why did she call it the "box room", what was wrong with spare bedroom? "And when are you going to move this huge weight which is sat gathering dust?"

That was an exaggeration, the kettle bell was only 24 kilograms and Alan used it frequently, or at least he intended to.

"Good morning, Mrs. Kemp", or at least that's what Alan meant to say, but from under the duvet it was indistinguishable.

"You're alive then!" Sarah shot back, her voice dripping with sarcasm. Alan instinctively knew she was standing at the foot of his bed with her hands on her hips. He peeked out from under the duvet – yep, she was. Alan lifted himself up onto his elbows, squinting at the light.

"Why are you here, Sarah? And what time is it?"

"It's nine-thirty and I TOLD you I was coming today instead of Saturday," she snapped, her tone sharp. "I ALSO told you I'd need to come early because I have another client to see." Sarah always emphasised certain words when she was tetchy, and she was definitely tetchy right now. Alan wouldn't mention this though, history had proven this wasn't a wise move on his part.

"Ugh," he grunted, screwing his eyes shut again. "Please shut the curtains and leave me in peace. I'll pay you regardless, but right now I have a screaming hangover."

Sarah rolled her eyes but complied, walking over to draw the curtains closed. As she did, Alan couldn't help but steal a glance at her figure –

something even his hangover couldn't stop him from doing. She spun around quickly, catching him in the act.

"Right, I'll do the other rooms then." She stomped off, sweeping the empty whisky glass from his bedside table with a loud "tut".

Number 37 was small, an easy job for Sarah. The kitchen, a narrow galley-style space, was rarely used. The "box room" was only large enough to fit a single bed, between that and the main bedroom sat the one reception room, the largest room housing lounge and dining areas. The one bathroom was also small and that just left the hall. In the upstairs hall there was virtually nothing to clean apart from the cat tray, the apartment's own staircase led to its own front door area and Sarah didn't vacuum this on every visit.

Alan's bedroom was larger, one corner transformed into a makeshift boxing gym, complete with a 'heavy bag' and a 'speedball' hung from the ceiling. Some smaller weights were on, what looked to Sarah, like a shoe stand while the kettlebell had migrated towards the bed and was in her way. The furniture was dark and old, the sort which used to sell as antique but which nobody wanted anymore. "Dust gatherers," Sarah called it.

In the lounge, she threw open the curtains. "My DARLING Sarah, my picture-perfect nymph, silhouetted in the bright morning light. How are you my dear?" Max's voice, groggy and slurred, drifted over the back of the sofa. Sarah peered around it and saw him lying there, looking every bit as terrible as he sounded. As Max struggled to sit up, Boffin, the tortoiseshell cat, leapt off the cushions, her bright amber eyes flashing a reproachful look at Sarah.

Max reached down for his spectacles, almost knocking over a glass which looked like it held the dregs from last night's whisky bottle. Sarah estimated Max Moore's age to be about sixty, though she'd never ask. His thinning grey hair and round figure gave him the appearance of an ageing, overweight James Mason. This morning, he looked even worse – unshaven and generally unkempt.

"How are you, Max?" Sarah asked, bustling around the room, gathering empty beer cans, spirit bottles and glasses.

"All the more desperate for the warmth of a naughty nymph on this lumpy sofa," Max replied with a cheeky smile, though his voice lacked its usual energy. Adjusting his spectacles, Max endeavoured to sharpen his focus on Sarah. She couldn't help but smile fondly, observing how Max, in that moment, bore a striking resemblance to Penfold from the cartoon *Danger Mouse*.

"Yeah, sure, Max." Sarah smiled at the game they always played. She knew Max wasn't interested in women, and they both knew he didn't have the courage to come out. She felt sorry for him, not out of pity, but for all the opportunities he'd lost.

"What time did you two finish up last night?" she asked.

"Oh, my dear, it was gone three o'clock I think and there's no doubt I'm feeling it this morning. I'm not as young as I used to be, you know?" Sarah treated this as a rhetorical question and watched as Max finally sat upright. He was still sporting his waistcoat which was currently straining to contain his stomach.

Sarah groaned, possibly too outwardly. "Oh Max, honestly when will you boys ever learn? Please tell me you're not in court today?"

"Lord no, dear, not until Friday. I have a 10am at Brighton Magistrates," Max replied.

Sarah stood with her hands on her hips, trying in vain to adopt a disappointed motherly scowl, the glow of the morning sun streaming through the window behind her, her auburn hair forming a striking silhouette. "Max! It IS Friday!"

Max blinked, reaching for his watch in a panic, though it was no help. "Oh… well, I suppose I can't drive in this state, can I?"

"Nope, I'll book you an Uber." Sarah fussed. "Come on Max, get yourself washed and I'll make you a coffee."

Sarah dispatched the bedraggled Max, then returned to the lounge to finish cleaning. It had taken ages to clear the mess, but at last, the room looked tidy. As usual, she took special care around the antique chess set on the side table, a quiet fixture of Alan's home. Alan's one rule for her cleaning was to leave the board untouched; he and Max were in the middle of an ongoing game, each move studied, calculated, and never rushed. Chess was what had first bonded the two of them, and their matches had become almost ritual.

Satisfied with her work in the lounge, Sarah cautiously opened the door to the box room, peeking in to ensure it was empty. She sighed with relief – no unwelcome surprises. She'd tackle that room next.

Alan woke again, once more startled by the intrusion. "I almost forgot, this was waiting for you downstairs." Sarah threw the small box onto the bed next to Alan then left number 37, much earlier than she'd anticipated but pleased to have time to spare before her next job.

Sarah Kemp

Sarah Kemp stood at the sink, her gaze unfocused, drifting beyond the rain-slicked window to the modest courtyard garden outside. The soft patter of raindrops mirrored the heaviness in her chest. Forty-two years old and this was it? A two-up, two-down, no children, and a husband who had long since slipped into the category of "wanker" – was this really all she had to show for her life?

Her frown deepened as she caught her reflection in the glass, blurred but still enough to notice the changes. The years had thickened her figure, softened her once-sharp features. Her beloved Grandmother used to refer to her as being "handsome". She was never sure if she liked being referred to as handsome, it seemed too… male. "Pretty" would have been better, but right now, she'd take any compliment – handsome included. At least the grey strands didn't show in the dim light. What had she done wrong? Surely, she must have messed up somewhere, maybe even in another life. How else could she explain how things had turned out?

She wrapped both hands around her coffee mug, seeking solace in the heat radiating through the ceramic. The warmth was fleeting, though, barely cutting through the numbness. She brought the cup to her lips, then winced as the steam singed her skin – it was still too hot. She sighed, setting it down, frustrated at yet another small thing out of sync.

No more questions. No more daydreams or pointless wondering. She needed to stop staring out into the rain, stop wallowing in what-ifs. It was time to confront reality. Again.

Sarah turned to face her husband Peter, but she'd already lost him to his phone. "PETER!"

Peter slammed his phone down; his frustration had been palpable when Sarah had returned from her latest job earlier than expected. He had been banking on postponing any awkward conversation until much later that evening. "Apologies, it was work," Peter mumbled, his gaze lifting. "By the way, how was the 'Colonel'? Did he not detain you for long today?" Pointed questions, but at the very least, she had his focus now.

"Not this again Peter, deflection is a defence mechanism that people use to avoid their own guilt, now please shut up about Alan and please stop trying to change the topic."

"I don't have time for this. We both have work, remember?" Peter didn't linger for an answer. He abandoned his phone on the kitchen counter and ascended the stairs, presumably to fetch his coat. The phone emitted a soft ping, reminiscent of a distant clock chiming one. Covering the brief expanse of the kitchen to the breakfast bar which separated kitchen from living room, Sarah reached for the phone and unveiled the text message.

Naomi

Thanks again for an amazing night, can't wait for round 2!! Xxxxxx

Sarah looked up; Peter emerged seemingly dressed for the Antarctic, Sarah thought he should be just about warm enough for Brighton in May. What a dick. "NAOMI?" Sarah shook her head, exasperated, beaten, frustrated, but determined not to shed anymore tears. "Jesus Peter, you're old enough to be her father! NAOMI!! You're fucking NAOMI?!"

No response, just a startled look, the child caught with his hand in the sweet bowl.

"Will you say something Peter?"

Peter moved forward and snatched back the phone. "It's not what you think, and you shouldn't be reading my WORK messages anyway." As sharply as he'd moved forward, he backed off.

"Work messages? Is that what this is Peter?", it wasn't so much the weak response which tipped Sarah over the edge, more the puppy dog look, a look which said it wasn't his fault, like Sarah herself was to blame? "Fucking hell Peter, what a miserable pathetic stereotype you are. Fucking your secretary, does this make you feel bigger Peter, does it?"

The kicker. The ultimate insult.

"Fuck you, Sarah. If you must know we closed a big deal last night, half of a new development in Hove, and we're hoping to bag the other

17

half later. Now fuck off back to Colonel Alan and get your kicks. AND, she's not my secretary, she's my personal assistant," Peter turned on his heels and slammed the front door closed in his wake.

It was Sarah's (now deceased) Grandmother who had first called it out. Sarah and Peter had seemingly fallen head over heels in love but that made no odds to Grandma Boyce, she always called it as she saw it and what she saw was her granddaughter a good six inches taller than her chosen man. "A man should not be so much shorter than his wife!" It just wasn't right in her Grandma Boyce's book, and anyway Sarah was beautiful, she could do much better. It was an excuse, of course, Grandma Boyce disliked Peter with a passion for the fraud he was, regardless of his height, and Peter never quite got over it.

Sarah turned back to the window above the sink, her eyes tracing the slow, aimless paths of the raindrops as they meandered their way down the glass. She shifted slightly, studying her own reflection with a touch more scrutiny. *Be positive*, she reminded herself, as if the thought alone could lift her mood.

Her curves, once her pride, had mostly survived the passing years – though the battle to maintain them had become more exhausting. She could feel the creeping strain each time she dragged herself to the gym. Still, the occasional 'triple' – spin class, rowing, body pump – kept her in shape, even as her enthusiasm waned. It was the support of her ever-cheerful gym buddies that nudged her back on track, pulling her through when her own resolve faltered. Yet here she was, staring at her reflection, her face still locked in a frown. Glum. Irritated. As if she'd forgotten what it felt like to expect anything from life.

Hadn't she once loved Peter? Hadn't there been something in him that made her heart race, that made her believe in something beyond the grind of daily life? Now, it seemed that spark – whatever it was – had dulled, as if it, too, had slipped away with the years.

At five foot ten, Sarah was a full seven inches taller than Peter, though height wasn't really the point Grandma Boyce had been making. Her grandmother had sensed something deeper – she'd always known Peter wasn't right for Sarah, and she hadn't been afraid to voice it, even at the risk of upsetting her. Unlike Sarah's parents, who never rocked the boat. They wouldn't dare risk a confrontation, especially with their eldest daughter.

Maybe she should take some time away. Her parents were only down the road in Portsmouth. She could retreat to her old bedroom, but that was a depressing thought in itself. That room held too many memories of a blissful childhood – of nurturing parents who had showered her and her sister with endless love, who'd somehow juggled running a successful haulage business with boundless energy for their daughters.

Or she could stay with her sister. That was even closer. A quick train ride to Victoria, then half an hour on the tube, and she'd be there. But no. Sarah winced at the thought of walking into her sister's lavish London home, the immaculate décor, the successful husband, the two perfect children – all of it a glaring contrast to her own life. It would only magnify her feelings of failure, like a reflection she couldn't escape.

She needed to snap out of this. Alan crossed her mind for a fleeting moment – ten years her senior, and, despite Peter's cutting remarks, she didn't fancy him. She turned to her reflection and spoke the words aloud, as if convincing herself, "He's a depressive drunk with a gambling problem. *And* he has strange friends. *And* he's overweight, probably broke – and, well, there are loads of reasons why not." She let the sentence trail off, her tone laced with frustration.

Not that she owed anyone an explanation. Least of all Peter.

"Is that OK with you?" she muttered, challenging her reflection with a defiant glare. But no answer came. She could almost see the judgment in her own eyes, as though her reflection thought she was protesting too much.

The Hangover

Alan returned from the bathroom, dropped back onto the bed, and picked up his phone, he had one message:
Max Moore
Please thank the saintly Sarah for kicking me out so promptly this morning, I almost missed court. Catch up soon.
Alan collapsed onto his back, replaying the previous night in his mind. They'd met up at the Coach & Horses, a cozy pub just a mile or so from his apartment on the outskirts of Brighton. Alan usually preferred his own company, but he'd enjoyed the easy banter with some of Max's acquaintances. Max used the word "acquaintance" to describe people he'd represented in law, he seemed to have as few friends as Alan. Three of these acquaintances had come back to his after the pub closed for an impromptu poker school. One hadn't stayed long, citing work in the morning. The other two stuck around until the whisky ran dry, and good old Max had eventually passed out on the sofa.

Now, Alan rolled off the bed, reached for his wallet on the old mahogany dresser, and collapsed back onto the mattress, this time upright. Progress, he thought. Next, he'd attempt to stay on his feet for longer than five seconds. But there was no rush – first, water and paracetamol, key weapons in the fight to beat his hangover.

He explored his wallet tentatively; it revealed a lot less money than he'd started with. Alan frowned and rolled back to a horizontal position, consoling himself that the poker had lasted for three hours so at least he'd had some sport. As he swallowed the pills and chased them with a gulp of water, his attention drifted to the small box sitting on the other side of the bed. What was that again? He closed his eyes, waiting for the fog in his head to clear.

Languidly, Alan stretched his left hand out and groped for the parcel. He half expected it to contain a pair of children's shoes, the dimensions were about right. That was a dumb idea, why would anyone send him children's shoes? The package was sealed with tape to the point it was

20

almost impossible to break into. Alan deduced who it was from immediately. Only Harry sent him communication like this, hand delivered, handwritten, excessively wrapped in tape. Inside he'd find money and instructions for a job. The logic behind why Harry occasionally demanded such a shroud of secrecy was lost on Alan. He guessed Harry got a thrill from the clandestine nature of the packages. More often the jobs were discussed when Alan met Harry at his bar. The more significant jobs, however, arrived through these meticulously wrapped parcels.

Typically, the jobs were debt collection, although occasionally Alan was tasked with picking up packages from one location and discreetly depositing them to another. Alan had completed a handful of these assignments but had made it abundantly clear to Harry that he wanted no part in drug-related activities. Sometimes there were warnings to deliver. Alan didn't mind these, he completed them as a "neutral intermediary", devoid of intimidation or threat of physical violence, essentially just as the messenger. Alan didn't need the money, but he was grateful of something to fill his time, it brought a sense of discipline to his life. As an army veteran he missed the sense of purpose this often-clandestine work provided.

Alan resorted to using his teeth to tear at the package's edges, eventually gaining access to its contents. After some struggle, the package gave way, spilling its contents onto the bed. A collection of ten cash packets and a small, handwritten note lay before him. Inside were ten thousand pounds, an amount surpassing Harry's previous offers by some margin. Alan sifted through the packets, confirming their authenticity. As always, they originated from the casino on Brighton's seafront. Pre-prepared and meticulously sealed, each packet held an exact sum of £1,000, predominantly in £50 notes. These packets were designed for swift payouts to major winners at the casino, streamlining the process and sparing the cashiers the task of manually counting out the notes.

Alan was intrigued at what Harry was willing to pay ten grand for but also a little apprehensive as he reached for the short note.

Bruce Thompson

Bruce Thompson found himself well ahead of schedule affording him the time to enjoy the luxury of a leisurely breakfast. Full English, the works, and a pot of tea. The surroundings weren't great but in Bruce's opinion motorway services are much of a muchness on the M1, he'd tried almost all of them. This was Woodall Services. Somewhere in South Yorkshire, Bruce thought to himself, he was sure he was somewhere in Yorkshire. It had been three hours since Bruce had exited the M25 in his Mercedes 18-tonne refrigerated truck. Bruce still found it oddly satisfying playing that line back to himself, in his head of course, he wouldn't want anyone to think he was gloating about his 'ideal job'. He'd got his Heavy Goods Vehicle licence during his short time in the army, Bruce had yearned for the thrill of driving large vehicles. He relished the idea of work combining large vehicles and armaments, though such opportunities had proven rare.

However, his time in the armed forces was relatively short, spanning only two years before his own discharge. While the army wasn't his initial career preference, Bruce had long harboured a conviction that if his aspirations of becoming a racing driver didn't materialise, his path would inevitably involve cars, trucks, or motorcycles. This, coupled with his fervent dedication to martial arts, had dominated his formative years – a passion that, much to his parents' dismay, consumed a significant part of his upbringing.

This intense focus had rendered Bruce somewhat of a solitary figure, and once he completed his schooling, he encountered challenges in identifying the right occupation – one that could align with his distinct inclinations. Bruce's path to the military started on a whim, at a recruitment centre in Bristol. But that impulse was rooted in something deeper – a legacy passed down from his father. His father, discharged due to illness, had cherished his own time in the army, and his stories brimmed with admiration and pride. Though the discharge had left a scar, his father's memories remained untainted, shaping Bruce's image of military life. "Why not?" Bruce thought, feeling the pull of his father's legacy. If it had been good for Dad, maybe it would be good for him, too.

In the army Bruce had garnered admiration for two qualities. Firstly, his unparalleled knack for driving any vehicle regardless of its shape or size. Secondly, for his mastery of a wide variety of martial arts. However, that's where the admiration ended. Bruce hadn't fostered friendships during his service, he remained devoid of social airs and graces and nor did he try to develop them. His individuality was paramount, leading for him to resist the strict discipline and hierarchy of military life. However, the army had recognised his talents and for a short period Bruce found himself attached to Special Operations, but it was short-lived, Bruce was too renegade for their strict regime. He found some enjoyment in the experience, but it hadn't delivered the thrill he'd anticipated, there had been too much marching and schoolroom activity for his liking.

Upon his discharge from the army, Bruce promptly resumed his rigorous gym routine. He embraced the offer presented by a gym to instruct jiu-jitsu on a part-time basis. This arrangement suited Bruce well, serving as an interim solution that catered to both his fervent dedication to physical fitness and his financial needs.

Martial arts were Bruce's forte; he'd started the journey practically from the moment he learned to walk. While the specifics of which martial art he was teaching remained somewhat blurry over the years, his diverse martial arts experiences had gradually coalesced into a unified expertise. Although uncertain if what he taught was precisely jiu-jitsu, Bruce had unwavering confidence in his ability to impart effective self-defence techniques. His students and the gym management appeared content with the arrangement.

Several months into the job, a fitness trainer from the gym approached Bruce with an offer involving some "muscle work." Initially reluctant, Bruce's resolve waivered when he considered the attractive financial incentive. Ultimately, he conceded and decided to meet with the individual in charge.

Bruce had relished the motorcycle ride from Bristol to Brighton, especially on a sunny Summer's day, and found the address in Withdean Road easily enough, but initially he wasn't confident he'd come to the right place. All the houses along the road were palatial, many looked new although Bruce acknowledged his limited knowledge of property and architecture. Nevertheless, the address he'd been given landed him at just about the biggest house he'd ever encountered. It looked older compared to its neighbours. Standing at the imposing gate, Bruce removed his crash helmet and peered in, wondering how to gain entry.

A keypad situated to one side suddenly sprung into life, its small screen lighting up. "Mr. Thompson?" a voice enquired.

"Yes," replied Bruce.

The voice continued, "To speak with me you need to press the button with the ear symbol on, but that's not necessary right now," the gate made a sharp buzzing noise and then slowly opened, "please come to the front door," the voice instructed. Double gates groaned open providing a space large enough for two cars to pass through, Bruce wheeled his motorbike the 50 yards or so to the front door.

A rugged, tanned, well-built man, just over six feet tall, about 25 years old, dressed in a smart black suit, greeted Bruce at the entrance. "I'll show you through to Roland's office, he'll be with you shortly." The man in black closed the door behind Bruce and then led him through a narrow hallway into what resembled a compact waiting room. The walls of the small room were covered floor to ceiling in teak panelling, while four leather wingback chairs occupied the space. "Please follow me," Bruce was directed through a door opposite the one he'd entered entering what must have been Roland's office. The room was enormous, mirroring the teak panelling theme. Positioned closest to the waiting area was a substantial chestnut pedestal desk, with a Regency Chesterfield high back-office chair in a deep burgundy colour. On the other side of the desk sat three large but more traditional office chairs. Behind these chairs rested a dark boardroom table, capable of comfortably seating 16 people.

The room's expansiveness was such that it almost dwarfed the imposing boardroom table.

Stretching along the room's right side was an extended cabinet that practically spanned the length of the space. Within it a variety of cupboards could be discerned, some glass fronted. Bruce could just about make out several silver trophies and books nestled within. Beyond the long table was a large bay window, from which the dimly lit room appeared to crave light, desperately sucking it in. Along the left side was an imposing fireplace, remnants of the last winter blaze within its grate.

Flanking the fireplace hung two sizable paintings, each possessing a dark and whimsical aura, though they failed to resonate with Bruce's artistic sensibilities. Little did he know, these pieces hailed from the brushstrokes of the 18th-century virtuoso Fragonard and bore an incalculable worth. Despite their historical significance, Bruce found them mundane and unappealing, failing to perceive the depth and beauty woven within.

It's safe to say that Bruce had never encountered a room so grand in his entire life.

Several minutes later, Roland Monroe entered the room with a gradual gait. Standing at approximately five feet and eight inches, his hunch made him appear shorter. To Bruce, he seemed undeniably aged – remarkably old, in fact. His thin grey hair was swept back over his head, fully visible from his bent stance, he wore bib and brace trousers and a plain white t-shirt, they looked mud stained. Positioned at Roland's sides were two guards, one of whom had ushered Bruce into the house. The other guard, an older and larger individual of South Asian descent, also clad in the same black suit, sported a turban atop his head. His authority was enhanced by his bushy black beard, for him a gift from God.

Roland's left hand grasped the Chesterfield chair for support which steadied him sufficiently to look up at Bruce. "Mr. Thompson I presume?" The tone and inflection of Roland's voice exuded a notably calming quality.

"Um, yes. And you must be Roland Monroe?" Bruce muttered the words, unaccustomed to such a level of formality.

Leaning across his desk, Roland extended his hand for a handshake. To his own surprise, Bruce responded to the gesture with a willingness. "Please, do remove your leathers if you so wish and then take a seat, Mr. Thompson. I'm delighted that you could honour my invitation. Would it be acceptable to address you as Bruce?"

"Um, yes, of course," Bruce quickly unwrapped the leather motorcycle suit, draped it over a chair and settled into the middle of the three office chairs. "Excellent! Then you must call me Rollie," his smile radiating reassurance as he sunk into the embrace of the Chesterfield chair which seemed to engulf him.

The guards had now positioned themselves on either side of Rollie, stood erect and motionless. Bruce studied them briefly, mentally calculating how he'd incapacitate them should the need arise, he estimated he'd need less than ten seconds. "Are the bookends necessary?" he challenged.

"Bruce, please relax, their primary focus is my well-being. Sometimes they can be a little overprotective, but they mean you no harm." Rollie remarked, glancing at the guard on his left side and then the one on his right, "Gentlemen, you can leave us now please." The larger, South Asian, guard looked reluctant to leave Roland's side, but both made for the door from which Rollie had entered, their obedience leaving an impression on Bruce.

Rollie waited for the door to close behind the guards, "Do you tend a garden, Bruce?" Bruce wasn't sure how to respond, was this a trick question? "That's where I've just come from. I find gardening both therapeutic and rewarding, there's nothing comparable to eating something you've cultivated with your own hands. You really should try it if you haven't already. Of course, we have a problem with urban foxes in this area now. In the old days I would trap them, or even shoot them, but these days that's frowned upon. Too many think they're cute and endearing creatures, yet for us gardeners they can wreak havoc." Rollie looked at Bruce, his smile oddly reassuring.

"Would you like to take some vegetables with you when you depart?" Rollie inquired, not awaiting an immediate response. He seemed almost absorbed in his own discourse. "I've reaped a bountiful harvest of cucumbers and tomatoes this year, green peppers, and beetroot too. I assume you know how best to prepare beetroot. I'm afraid my strawberries have concluded prematurely; they were delightful while they lasted but I think the wet summer has curtailed the crop. I've even ventured into cultivating okra for the first time this season, I'm pleased to say they're quite the success." Bruce found himself drawn into Rollie's gentle narration; he spoke in a soothing tone with an occasional slight whistle in his voice. Normally, he'd be in uproar by now, urging the other person to get to the point or he'd leave. Yet the garrulous Rollie possessed a knack for mollifying and quelling Bruce's impatience.

A loquacious Rollie persisted in the same vein for another ten minutes or so, delving into topics such as thriving and less successful harvests, effective methods to manage snails and slugs, and mentally surveying the various types of rosebushes in his flower bed ("the Sunsprite roses look wonderful this year"). Yet still Bruce remained patient.

"Are you an angler, Bruce?" This sudden shift in subject matter finally roused Bruce from his reverie. "Um, excuse me, Rollie, did you want to discuss the job at all?" Rollie paused, as if a sudden realisation had dawned upon him. "My apologies, my dear boy. You've been patiently enduring my ramblings about gardening when there are more significant topics for us to cover." He paused once more, seemingly requiring some moments to transition into a work mindset. Bruce began to fret that this octogenarian across from him might never come to the point.

"Yes, of course, well first things first," another warming smile from his host to help put the guest at ease, "full disclosure from me." Rollie put both hands up in a consolatory manner. "I want to be completely transparent here. I've read both your military and MI5 reports, both classified as top secret, naturally." More smiles. This was taking an age, but Bruce was intrigued by the revelation of two previously unknown reports. "To put it succinctly, your mastery of hand-to-hand combat is exceptional, and you possess impressive skills in handling a variety of motor vehicles. However, the upshot is you're not a threat to national security and therefore not under surveillance." Rollie's tone carried a sense of admiration. "I also read that you scored an "E" grade at the driving range." Rollie's chuckle escaped quietly, clearly considering this last detail a way to break the ice. "Fortunately, you won't be requiring a gun for this role!" Bruce remained impassive.

"Yes, indeed, moving on. Now where was I?" Bruce interpreted this question as rhetorical, allowing Rollie to continue. It seemed Rollie was finally gaining momentum. "I'm taking a gamble at disclosing my business interests with you, however considering your current financial and work situation, I believe you're in need of a fresh start. The opportunity I'm about to present, and the excellent financial package which accompanies it, should be something you'll value."

"Bruce, I hold the position of CEO at Exotic Food Imports Limited. In short, we specialise in importing rare and unique foods. These items are then distributed through various resellers based in Brighton, London, and Bristol. Due to specific circumstances, which I won't delve into right now I've recently had to relocate my inward processing point to Edinburgh. My goods don't fly very well, so they arrive by ship and subsequently require transportation down South. Here's where you come in: I'm asking you to drive one of these vans from Edinburgh to Brighton approximately 25 times annually." Rollie slid a photograph of a white Mercedes 18-tonne refrigerated truck across the desk for Bruce to inspect.

Bruce couldn't help interjecting, "It's a lorry or truck, not a van." that was Bruce's only response.

"Indeed," Rollie responded, he had no concern for the specific terminology.

"The items will be loaded up in Edinburgh and offloaded once you reach Brighton. On rare occasions, I might ask you to make a drop in

29

Bristol, where, once again, the handling of the cargo will be taken care of. All I require from you is to drive the van, or rather the lorry, with one stipulation: never to leave it unattended when it's loaded." Rollie paused momentarily, as if gathering himself to reveal the next piece of information. "Most of the goods are refrigerated, some are frozen. The frozen compartment is situated in the middle of the cargo area, necessitating the removal of all refrigerated packages to access it." Rollie took another pause, as if hesitating to share the next point. "Within the confines of the legal frozen goods, there will be some illicit packages. These can only be reached by first removing the frozen materials around them. Remarkably, a sniffer dog would not be able to detect the concealed compartment, I'm confident you can travel without risk of detection."

"And I'd be journeying solo?" Bruce inquired, a trace of concern shadowing his features. "No security detail?"

"I believe you are the very safeguard this cargo requires, Mr. Thompson," Rollie's smile glimmered again, his eyes alive with assurance. "And besides, where might a wise man conceal a leaf?"

Bruce's brow furrowed, puzzled.

"Amidst a forest, naturally!" Rollie affirmed, a playful glint in his eye as he embraced the enigma of his own adage.

***

Back in the Woodall Services Bruce picked up the stainless-steel teapot but it was empty. He was making good time on his trip North so contemplated a refill. In the three years since he'd started employment with Exotic Food Imports Ltd, his regard for Rollie had grown, evolving into a genuine sense of trust. Rollie had proven to be a good benefactor to Bruce, and was munificent, providing him with a stylish apartment along the Brighton seafront and offering an astonishing salary.

Physical meetings between Bruce and Rollie were rare, but their phone conversations were frequent and meaningful. Rollie consistently demonstrated a keen interest in the lorry's progress and in Bruce's wellbeing. Bruce led a solitary existence, finding solace in his well-compensated job, this aligned perfectly with his preferences.

Bruce set his newspaper down and looked over at the queue forming for hot drinks. The length of the queue seemed to satisfy his sudden thirst. As his eyes swept along the line of people, they were immediately drawn to a specific group that stood out. Among them, his initial attention was captured by a woman. He estimated her height at around five feet and five inches, she had a rich coffee complexion and dark hair that cascaded over her shoulders. She was striking, early thirties, maybe a bit older. However, it wasn't her beauty that intrigued Bruce the most. It was the faint streaks of mascara under her eyes, subtle but unmistakable, that hinted she had been crying.

Beside her stood a younger, wiry man, just a few inches taller, short, cropped hair. He held her left wrist in a visibly tight and uncomfortable grip, evident from the pained expression she struggled to conceal. The trio was completed by the man positioned just ahead of them in the queue. This man was dressed in a smart blue suit, he had a portly build, and a short goatee beard. He exuded an air of arrogance, speaking loudly and apparently disrespectfully to the catering staff.

Suddenly, the man in the blue suit locked eyes with Bruce and mouthed the words "fuck right off".

The Heist

Having read Harry's poorly composed note about the upcoming "operation" Alan, initially at least, was quietly enthused. His military days had provided him with extensive knowledge of reconnaissance, and he knew he was good at it. Alan also welcomed the distraction, he struggled to motivate himself these days and Harry's occasional 'challenges' provided a purpose. Alan started planning straight away and eagerly anticipated the task of gathering information, analysing the terrain, collecting intelligence, and ultimately constructing a risk profile for the mission. However, the reality of scoping out a mansion on the outskirts of a city like Brighton provided a huge obstacle, namely the sheer abundance of CCTV coverage. The surveillance challenge came from both the council and, more significantly, the various villas and palaces lining Withdean Road. Alan was to learn it was almost as if they all had something to hide.

Alan boarded the number 27 bus for his trip to Withdean Road. He had given up driving since his accident. He walked the road's one-kilometre stretch, but the details he could glean were limited. All he could ascertain was that the mansion had a modest front lawn leading to a large bay window, while a gravel path to the right of the lawn connected imposing double gates from the street to the garages. The remainder of the building was shielded by a high brick wall adorned with numerous security cameras and lights. Even beyond the high walls, seen through the large double gates, various chrysanthemums and hydrangeas provided additional, natural privacy.

There was no point in Alan lingering around the target house for more reconnaissance, it would be counterproductive; he'd end up appearing as the star in numerous surveillance recordings. Back to the drawing board. Alan made a call to Harry. His response was typically helpful and gruff; "Just follow the bloody instructions." Alan asked whose house it was but got another brush off, "don't you worry about that; the less you know the better." Not very reassuring.

"Look, stop being a pork chop, get the job done and I'll double your pay day. Just show up at the exact time I've specified, and everything will go smoothly." Harry hung up.

And so, it unfolded... Despite his numerous reservations, the money was too good to turn down, Alan found himself dutifully following Harry's instructions. It was a Friday night, one week after receiving the note, and Alan, dressed completely in black attire, including a balaclava, was crouched behind an oak tree on Withdean Road, meticulously observing the target house from a discreet vantage point opposite. With just three minutes left until the clock struck 9pm, the time stipulated in Harry's instructions, he awaited his cue to move freely through the imposing double gates and across the small lawn area. To be fair to Harry; he'd kept his promise, the gates were indeed open. Alan had already resolved to go home if it hadn't been the case, he wasn't prepared to scale high walls or gates despite how good the money was.

At precisely 9pm, Alan scurried across the empty road from his hideout position. Except from a lone light above the front door to his right, the front of the house lay shrouded in darkness. The big bay window was round to the left of the house, Alan noticed it framed the scenic garden outside. As promised, a large sash window to the right of the bay was slightly ajar. Alan lifted the window further open, threw the black holdall he'd been guarding inside and attempted to climb through after it. That had been the plan, at least. However, the windowsill was much higher than he'd anticipated, and instead of slipping in gracefully, Alan tumbled awkwardly through the gap.

Following his rather unceremonious entry, Alan quickly surveyed the room. Positioned directly before him lay a long dining table, and beyond that, he could just about make out a huge antique desk. This arrangement again matched with Harry's directives. The room seemed to be adorned in a sombre dark wood, and the prevailing absence of illumination rendered further details shrouded in obscurity. There were doors at the end of both side walls.

Following Harry's instructions to the tee, Alan proceeded toward the antique desk, where he crouched down, assuring that he would be concealed from view unless someone walked around desk's periphery. His next instruction was one of patience, and he didn't have to wait long. Somewhere towards the rear of this long office come dining room a door swung open, casting forth a radiant stream of light the opposite side of the desk. Alan discerned the mellifluous strains of jazz music, possibly Thelonious Monk, resonating from a party elsewhere in the house.

"Brilliant!" The unmistakable gravelly timbre of Harry's voice resonated throughout the room. Harry was a lifelong smoker, a trait which etched its mark upon his vocal tract. Alan could perceive Harry's movements even if he couldn't see them, the shattering of glass provided a jolt to the almost silent scene. Harry then circumnavigated the desk, dropping a weighty object upon its surface. "Right. Give it five minutes and then get out of here. I've included some of those cigars you like as I'm generous like that. See you in the club tomorrow." With these words, Harry shuffled away, and the door was closed once more, immediately extinguishing the light source. A distinct clunk sound signalled the door was now locked.

Alan waited precisely five minutes before emerging from his prone position, he was glad to stand up as his knees had been protesting vehemently. He retrieved what, within the dimness of the room, resembled a sports trophy and added three cigars, each encased within their metal tubes, into his holdall. Back out through the open window his departure exhibited no greater grace than his initial entry, yet he soon found himself beyond the gates and making as swift a departure as his knees allowed down the street.

Bruce's curiosity was piqued, tinged with irritation that had successfully quenched his thirst. He discreetly maintained a vigilant gaze on the trio he had noticed in the queue, although he was primarily fixated on one individual amongst them. His target had already been mentally labelled by Bruce as a fat, indolent bully who, in all likelihood, derived pleasure from tormenting young women. Strictly speaking Bruce ought to let the matter slide, after all he was on the clock, and he knew that Rollie would not be pleased. However, he did have some time at his disposal, and he was particularly irked by the guy in the blue suit, the guy who had been unjustifiably rude.

The party of three exited the cafeteria, their backs turned to Bruce, who took the opportunity to leave his seat. He carefully folded his copy of the Daily Mirror newspaper; he tucked it under his arm and nonchalantly dropped his serviette on the plate. Bruce then started following the group towards the wide, well-lit corridor. He maintained a distance of about 50 yards, this seemed prudent he thought. There were still restrooms, an amusement arcade, and an M&S food outlet to walk past, so if the group paused at any of these points, Bruce could effortlessly secure another table, using the newspaper as a discreet cover.

However, the trio didn't need those services and proceeded toward the car park, the man in the blue suit carrying a white paper bag of takeaway café goods. As the automatic entrance / exit doors slid shut behind them Bruce observed the thin man gripping the woman's wrist once more. Now, he appeared to be almost dragging her along, and her reluctance was clear, but her fear seemed to outweigh her ability to resist significantly.

Bruce quickened his pace, prompting the automatic doors to part once more, although he remained a good distance behind. As he entered the car park, Bruce paused by a rubbish bin to lose his newspaper. He could now discern which car they were heading toward – a prestigious Audi, possibly an A8, although Bruce had little interest in the nuances of car models. It was discreetly parked away from the crowd, more importantly away from prying security cameras, not far from Bruce's own Mercedes lorry, a fact that suited him just fine.

A tall, imposing man of African descent occupied the driver's seat, and as the group approached the vehicle, he reached behind and to the left, opening the passenger door. The woman was unceremoniously shoved into the car, the door slamming shut with such force that Bruce was surprised she hadn't lost a limb in the process. The fat man unlocked and opened the front passenger door. Bruce decided to quicken his pace to close the gap; he had no intention of letting then drive away just yet. Bruce shouted, "Hey, hey you there in the big Audi!"

The fat man in the blue suit settled himself into the expansive passenger seat of the Audi A8. The seat provided generous leg room but standing at only about five feet and eight inches tall, he was unable to appreciate it. Nevertheless, he was the boss, and he had no intention of adjusting his seat forward to accommodate his stature. Clearly, he'd earned his right to the front seat and as much leg room as he wanted. His thoughts were interrupted by the sound of someone calling out, followed by hurried footsteps approaching the car. He hauled himself back out of the vehicle to investigate the commotion.

A man of similar height was attempting to open the door behind him, and the man in the blue suit could feel his anger simmering. Time had already been squandered deliberating over café orders, and now he simply wanted to get back on the road, deliver the woman occupying the back seat, and return to more important matters. He regarded himself as a significant player within his firm, far above the task of transporting this bitch from one town to another, and he intended to convey this message to his boss when they next met face-to-face.

As the rear door began to swing open, blue suit man forcibly shut it and wedged himself between Bruce and the car. His irritation was rising, "What exactly do you think you're doing?"

Bruce really didn't like this guy – sharp-suited, goatee-bearded, and now flushed with indignation. Bruce ignored him and turned his attention to the woman in the back seat, "Are you OK? Only I noticed that guy beside you was manhandling you earlier, and you look upset." The window wound down.

Blue suit pushed Bruce forcefully in the chest with both hands, causing Bruce to take a step back, albeit somewhat obligingly. The woman replied, her voice barely audible, and trembling with fear, "Please, I'm okay. Please, just go away. Nothing good can come of this, please."

Blue suit man was now apoplectic, "You absolute mother fucker! Who the fuck do you think you are? Listen to the bitch and GET LOST!" In a fit of rage, he lunged forward and pushed both hands against Bruce's chest once more.

This time, Bruce didn't comply but staggered back from the force of the push. As he stepped away his right heel caught on a high kerb, placed to separate parking spaces. He landed awkwardly on his backside, wincing at the sudden pain to his coccyx.

Blue suit man turned back to the car, "Did you see that?" His anger had transformed into amusement, and he burst into laughter, he was proving he was the king pin once more. He turned back to Bruce once more, "You fucking jerk!" With that he turned back to the car, "All right, enough nonsense, let's go." However, Bruce was already back on his feet, and a red mist of anger had descended upon him as he marched back towards the man in the blue suit.

"Do you need a hand, boss?" The resonant bass of the driver's voice rang out.

"No, stay put. Luke, come and sort this annoying fucker out for me will you," the man in the blue suit commanded. The door behind the driver swung open, and the wiry man named Luke sprung out of the car. Blue suit man turned his attention to the approaching Bruce, cautioning, "I really think you ought to…"

Bruce erupted with a primal shout as he thrust his clenched right fist into blue suit's face. Bruce immediately regretted his impulsive action; his years of training had instilled in him the wisdom of employing a closed fist only on softer targets like the nose or solar plexus. However, at times like this, self-indulgence overrode rationality, and in this instance, he had missed his intended target, connecting instead with a cheekbone. He knew he'd pay for it later, tending to his grazed knuckles, but for the moment, he had spared his left hand, preserving it for potential future use. All that said, it felt damn satisfying, so Bruce decided to indulge himself further. He delivered four more punches with the same fist, in quick succession, this time striking the targeted nose. Blue suit man staggered, falling backward onto the car before sliding to the ground, his broken nose pouring blood over his pristine white shirt, his expression now one of shock rather than indignation.

The guy now identified as Luke approached at speed, rapidly closing the distance between them. Bruce confidently retreated three steps, growing more attuned to the surroundings, most especially the step which had caught his heel. Luke leaned back and kicked out a headshot, a move that impressed Bruce, who recognised the style as Taekwondo. Luke was quick. Bruce shifted to his right, and then manoeuvred around some more, he was confident of dealing with his opponent but wouldn't be complacent. Luke pursued him, with the faith of a boxer controlling the centre of the ring. He attempted another kick, which, while impressively quick, felt too predictable to Bruce.

Bruce confidently continued to circle, gradually positioning his back toward the Audi. Luke persisted with his kicks, gaining confidence, but Bruce remained patient, waiting for the right moment. On the third kick, Bruce dropped into a crouching stance and executed a swift leg sweep beneath Luke, knocking out the supporting leg. Luke fell to the ground, and Bruce pounced with lightning speed. He leaped onto Luke's left knee with both feet, delivering a merciless stamp just before impact. The sound of the knee bone snapping under the pressure was gut-wrenching, and Luke let out an agonised scream.

Bruce swung his attention back to the car and was surprised to see blue suit man back on his feet, desperately attempting to deploy a switchblade, his vision clearly hampered by the extensive bleeding from his broken nose. Bruce approached calmly, grasping the wrist of the hand holding the weapon with his left hand. With a series of swift and relentless punches, Bruce battered the already bloodied face of the man in the blue suit. In a seamless motion, Bruce twisted the man's arm, compelling him to bend forward, and then delivered a powerful kick to the elbow, resulting in a sickening snap as the man's arm broke. The switchblade slipped from his grasp, and he lost consciousness, crumpling to the ground.

Bruce seized the blade and punctured the front passenger side tyre with a short jab. It was at that moment that he became aware of a colossal figure, a giant of a man, looming over him. Bruce looked up, but before he could react, found himself effortlessly lifted off his feet by a neck-crushing grip, the most astonishing display of strength he had ever encountered. Barely managing to hold onto the knife, Bruce thankfully noted that it exited the tyre with considerably less resistance than it had entered.

A colossal hand, massive and unyielding, wrapped itself around Bruce's throat, causing an overwhelming sensation of impending suffocation. With the knife clutched in his right hand, Bruce extended his left hand upward in a futile attempt to pry the vice-like grip away, but it was akin to attempting to move solid concrete. Bruce slashed at the hand with the knife, drawing a cut, but the grip remained unrelenting. Panic and nausea surged within him as he desperately struggled to maintain consciousness.

Bruce's legs flailed, and he kicked out, attempting to find purchase on anything that would help him break free. As his consciousness waned from the choke hold, he fought to suppress his rising sense of dread, he only had seconds to act before passing out. He slashed at the assailant's hand once more, and then again, this time horizontally, forming a trio of cuts akin to the markings of a noughts and crosses' board. A deep groan emanated from the giant, and, at long last, the iron grip released its hold.

Bruce collapsed to the ground; his relief mingled with breathlessness. Struggling to inhale deeply, he was acutely aware that he couldn't afford to stay still. Acting on instinct, Bruce hauled himself back onto his feet, although his legs felt as shaky as jelly. He thrust the knife forcefully at the leg directly in front of him, driving it deep into the muscular thigh with sheer determination. The giant staggered backward, almost growling, and clutching at the injured leg in pain.

Bruce swiftly withdrew the knife from the thigh, then, in one fluid motion, opened the rear door and reached down to plunge the blade into the rear offside tyre. "Let's go, come on!" Bruce was still gasping for air as he gestured towards his lorry. The woman in the back seat remained motionless. "Well, COME ON!" This seemingly stern command served as the extra motivation she needed. They both sprinted towards the lorry with all the speed Bruce could muster.

The Cleaner

Sarah had received Rollie's message early, inquiring if she could spare some time to clean up the broken glass in his office. She had promptly responded in the positive. As she made her way out of the bathroom, she unexpectedly ran into her husband of almost twenty years, Peter. She had slept in the spare room for longer than she could remember. "Where are you off to at this time on a Saturday?" he enquired.

"I've got a job for Rollie," she wearily responded, not interested in engaging in idle conversation.

"On a Saturday?" Peter questioned. Sarah ignored him and descended the stairs, leaving the bathroom clear for Peter.

Whenever the opportunity arose, Sarah was always willing to drop what she was doing to help Roland Monroe. He had consistently treated her well – generous with his money, kind words, never forgetting her birthday, and more. Sarah opened the drawer that held her work keys. Each key was identified only by a number, with only Sarah knowing which key corresponded to which client. Of the 25 available key spaces, Sarah used only five. She personally attended to two clients – Rollie and Alan – while her assistant managed the other three, she filled in for her assistant when she was away.

Fifteen years ago, Sarah had ambitious plans to conquer the domestic cleaning market across all of East Sussex, but it hadn't worked out. The problem wasn't Sarah, she was well organised and good at her job, a job which many people took for granted but few performed as effectively. No, the issue lay with people themselves; they were inherently unreliable. Sarah faced a revolving door of employees, numerous client complaints, and excessive time spent covering for mistakes or no-shows. Yes, she was paying minimum wage, but she always treated her employees respectfully, was always patient and tried to accommodate quirks and requirements, but ultimately it was a thankless endeavour. Most people were simply unreliable. She'd stumbled upon the Rollie job by chance, but it was a lucky break. Signing a non-disclosure agreement was a little strange and Rollie insisted that only Sarah could clean for him. The size of his house meant she was there often. Rollie paid her generously and offered unwavering support. She had even got to know many of Rollie's "support staff", though she only knew them by their nicknames, she wasn't allowed to know their real names. Rollie had been good to her, and she was happy to reciprocate, creating a simple but effective relationship.

The only other client Sarah exclusively catered to was Alan. She couldn't quite explain why she didn't let her assistant loose on his apartment, but once again, the pay was excellent, albeit it was a relatively small job, and there were no drawbacks.

Receiving a text from Rollie on a weekend was unusual but not alarming. Sarah knew he'd thrown a party the previous night, and besides, she had little else filling her day.

The Trophy

As Alan descended the narrow, worn stone steps into The Court Club, it felt as though the sunlight above was swallowed whole. The brilliant day outside dulled into a muted, nicotine-stained haze, like someone had dimmed the very sky. Inside, the air hung heavy with the smells of stale smoke, cheap cologne, and spilled beer. The jukebox softly played Bobby Darin's *Beyond the Sea*, a familiar tune that only added to the club's faded retro charm. Though Bobby Darin's music hailed from the '60s, The Court Club was firmly stuck in the 1970s – a relic of the past with its wood-panelled walls, cracked vinyl seating, and sticky, scuffed tables.

The ceiling above was a patchwork of old, nicotine-stained tiles, once white but long since yellowed by years of cigarette smoke. The smoking ban, enforced almost everywhere else, meant nothing in The Court Club. Harry never paid it any mind, and the police had long since stopped reminding him. Turning a blind eye to the Monroe family had become second nature for the local authorities, a quiet understanding that left the club's smoky atmosphere intact, even in a time when it should have been long gone.

Amber-tinted lampshades cast a sepia glow over the room, barely managing to pierce the haze. Mirrored tiles lined the back wall of the bar, reflecting warped images of the regulars, who, like the club, seemed untouched by time. Posters of forgotten rock bands and faded celebrities clung to the walls, curling at the edges, as if even they were too tired to hang on any longer.

The crowd was what Alan had come to expect – dropouts, miscreants, and the odd solicitor grabbing a pint between cases at Brighton's Magistrates Court, conveniently located across the street. The Court Club had always been a refuge for those looking to escape judgment, whether legal or personal. Trevor, the barman, was behind the counter, wiping down pint glasses with a rag that had clearly seen better days. His movements were slow, methodical, as if polishing the glass could somehow restore a semblance of pride to the place.

Harry, the club's owner, occupied his customary seat at the bar, tucked into the corner where he had a perfect view of the room. His shirt straining at the buttons as he lifted a glass of gin and tonic to his lips. His thick white beard barely concealed the wide grin that spread across his face when he saw Alan enter. Alan chose a seat two stools away from him, leaving a strategic gap – he knew Harry's habit of waving his arms animatedly whenever a story took hold of him, which was often.

Harry, ever the raconteur, had a near-inexhaustible supply of stories from "the old days." His tales, fuelled by bravado and nostalgia, invariably ended with some form of personal triumph – whether it was in a bar fight, a romantic conquest, or a shrewd business deal. He loved to talk, though his enthusiasm for listening was considerably less pronounced.

The club had a pulse of its own, a low hum of murmured conversations, clinking glasses, and the occasional burst of laughter from a shadowy corner. It was a place out of time, where the rest of the world didn't matter – and for a while, neither did the people who came here to disappear.

"Have you got it?" Harry's voice cut through the haze, his nicotine-stained teeth flashing in a grin that struggled to shine in the club's dim, smoky light. His smile widened, childlike, as if it were Christmas morning.

Alan set the holdall on the bar with care. "Is it valuable?" he asked, eyeing Harry's glee with a mix of scepticism and curiosity.

"Valuable?" Harry barked out a laugh, as though Alan had told the funniest joke he'd ever heard. "Not valuable, no. It's fucking priceless!"

Alan shook his head, half in disbelief, half in resignation. "Thanks for the cigars, by the way. Nice touch."

Harry waved it off, still beaming. "The least I could do, mate." He glanced down the bar and called, "Trev, get Big Al a Lagavulin on my tab." Trevor, the bartender, who was momentarily engrossed in whatever

44

was on his iPad, glanced up, startled, then shuffled off to fetch the bottle. "Actually, make it a large one, Trev. This man's earned it!" Harry leaned over and clapped Alan on the shoulder, the physical contact arriving early, even for Harry's standards.

Alan took the whisky, downing it in one go, savouring the sharp, smoky burn. He signalled for a refill, then turned to Harry, who was busy unzipping the holdall. "Harry, I've got two questions for you."

"Go on, Big Al," Harry replied, not looking up.

Alan cringed at the nickname but let it slide – he knew better than to correct Harry, who had a habit of rebranding people as he saw fit, like it gave him a sense of control. His name, however, remained untouchable.

Alan leaned closer, bridging the empty stool between them. "Why me? I mean, out of all the people you could hire to climb through a window and hide under a desk, you've got to have younger, more agile types on your payroll. So, why me?"

Harry didn't answer right away. His attention had shifted entirely to the bag as he lifted out a tarnished trophy, grinning like he'd just unearthed a long-lost treasure. Alan glanced at the object and blinked. "And why," he continued, lowering his voice, "were you so desperate to steal a bloody sports trophy?"

Harry placed the trophy reverently on the bar, admiring it like it was the FA Cup. In reality, it was a kitschy metallic dartboard with three oversized darts all striking the double three, the number awkwardly placed at the bottom of the circle of numbers. A banner, also metallic, linked the darts together with the number 180 emblazoned across it, though the score made no sense. The whole thing sat on a heavy, chipped marble base; the engraved plaque so worn that the lettering had faded into obscurity.

Harry gazed at the trophy with the pride of a king admiring his crown. "Well, Al," he began, clearly relishing every word. "Firstly, I needed someone I could trust. Someone reliable, who wouldn't cock it up or get greedy." He shot Alan another wide grin, his teeth showing more stain than gleam. "An old hand, like me. Not some cocky young idiot who'd take the job for granted."

Alan raised an eyebrow but kept silent, swallowing his pride at being compared in age to Harry.

Harry continued, still giddy as he admired the trophy. "And secondly," he said, tracing a finger along the faded engraving, "I'd have paid double for this beauty. You'll never understand how much this means to me."

Harry's laughter erupted, filling the space between them. Alan leaned back in his chair, taking a slow sip of his refill, knowing full well that he'd get no more information today. Whatever the hell this ridiculous trophy meant to Harry, it wasn't something Alan would ever fully grasp.

But that was Harry – full of mysteries that often didn't add up. And in this dimly lit, nicotine-stained refuge, that was just par for the course.

C-I-A-R-A

Bruce hastily shifted his white Mercedes Benz Atego 3 into first gear and sped toward the car park exit. He took a deep breath, attempting to slow his racing heart. The woman in the passenger seat had curled up, her knees against her face, sobbing into her jeans. Bruce knew he needed to focus on the getaway and control his own breathing; he was sweating profusely. Bruce was tough, even fearless, but the giant he'd just fought off had presented an exceptional challenge. He glanced back at the chaos he'd left behind, which was starting to attract attention. Bruce despised the modern kind of attention, with too many mobile phone cameras and excessive posting on social media networks. These were things Bruce didn't fully understand. The police would likely arrive at the scene soon, and Bruce wanted to be far away by then.

The traffic off the ramp onto the M1 was clear, and the motorway was flowing smoothly. This was a relief, and Bruce took the opportunity to shift through the gears and put some distance between himself and the Woodall Services as quickly as possible. The engine strained as Bruce kept his foot on the gas pedal.

"We're heading North."

Bruce was nearly jolted back to reality by the realisation that he had a passenger. He looked to his left. The woman hadn't moved from her huddled position, but her sobbing had subsided. She hadn't lifted her head, so her words were slightly muffled. There was a hint of an accent, although Bruce couldn't be sure. He also didn't know if it was a question or a statement.

"Uh, yeah. Well, I was on my way to Edinburgh when I stopped." No response.

Bruce concentrated on the traffic and his driving, weaving the lorry between the left and middle lanes, manoeuvring through traffic to make the most progress. Regular glances in the rear-view mirror showed no one in pursuit. "Are you okay?" Bruce had little else to offer the anonymous woman in his passenger seat. Still no response. Eyes back on the road. A few minutes passed. "Uh, do you need me to stop somewhere?" Another silent reply, with Bruce now in the slower lane, trying to blend in.

"You should drop me off at the next services." Finally, 15 minutes later, the woman's head emerged from her knees. The "off" had sounded like "ahff".

"Uh, you're Irish, right?" Bruce turned to face the passenger seat, she ignored the question. She was pretty, her tears had ceased, but her hair looked dishevelled, the mascara streaks had worsened, and there was swelling around her reddened eyes. "Did they hit you?"

"You really should drop me off at the next services." Her pronunciation of 'the' sounded more like 'da.' It was endearing.

"Look, I know you're scared, but I can't just leave you." More silence. Bruce was far out of his comfort zone, struggling to find comforting words. "Uh, I know a place just off the motorway." Bruce looked across, hoping for a reaction but received none. "Shall we stop and get a coffee or something? Give you a chance to catch your breath. It's, uh, it's out of the way, so they won't find us. Then we can maybe come up with a plan."

Another long pause. "Yeah, okay."

Bruce continued driving. He did know of a place where he could stop, a hotel he'd used many times, but he had forgotten how vast Yorkshire was. It was half an hour later when they exited the motorway just south of Leeds. Bruce was relieved but aware that he was still on a major road, exposed to automatic number plate recognition systems, various CCTV cameras, and perhaps even the occasional traffic cop parked in a layby with nothing better to do than watch for wanted white lorries. Maybe it was paranoia; surely, the police would have caught up with him by now if they wanted to. It was another half an hour before they pulled into the Gargrave Hotel, a full hour since their last exchange of words.

Bruce parked and turned off the engine. It was then that he realised how exhausted he felt. It had been quite a morning, and the adrenaline rush from the fight had finally caught up with him. Bruce released his tight grip on the steering wheel, feeling his hands and arms ache. He

48

leaned back gently, relaxing against the headrest, took a deep breath, and closed his eyes. Now, he had to think about how best to deal with the woman in the passenger seat. Maybe it would be best to drop her off somewhere, as she had requested, at a train station perhaps. He could do that with a clear conscience; after all, he had rescued her. She didn't owe him anything, and he didn't owe her anything more. Where would she go? What would she do next? It wasn't Bruce's concern, but that's where he could start the conversation.

"I meant to say thank you." The silence was broken.

"Uh, you're welcome." Bruce shifted slightly; eyes still closed. "There are some wet wipes in the glove compartment if you want to clean up a little. So are you Irish?"

"Thank you. Yes, I'm from Down."

"Uh, Down?" He cracked an eye open.

"County Down. Downpatrick, to be exact."

"Uh, that's nice," Bruce muttered, trying to break the awkwardness.

"Yeah, the east coast of Northern Ireland is very beautiful. Have you ever been?"

"Uh, no, well, I have been to Northern Ireland, but only Belfast." How had he gotten into this conversation, and why had he just revealed his military background?

"Ah, right. That's where you learned to fight. You're very good at it, by the way." She flashed a smile, something warm in it. Bruce thought it… endearing. That word again, endearing.

She opened the glove compartment and pulled some wipes from a pouch. "You've hurt your hand," she said softly, nodding at his bloodied knuckles. She reached over to Bruce's right hand, gently pulled it to her and dabbed at it with a wet wipe. Bruce hated being touched, but something in her tenderness disarmed him.

"Shall we go and get that coffee now?" Her accent softened, and Bruce smiled at the way she said 'dat'.

"Um, yeah, sure." Bruce unbuckled his seat belt, opened the door, and then turned back. "Oh, uh, what's your name?"

49

She smiled again, "Kee-ra," Bruce looked puzzled. "Spelled C-I-A-R-A."

"Oh, right, well, I'm Bruce."

In Flagrante Delicto

The mobile phone blared its antiquated ringtone, a relic from a bygone technology era. Harry picked up the phone and squinted at the screen. "Ha, you can bloody well wait." He pressed the red button with a phone symbol on it and set the phone back on the bar. "Trev! Another G+T," he called to the barman. The phone sprang into life once more, and Harry declined the call, sending it straight to voicemail. "Bloody nuisance," Harry muttered under his breath. His drink arrived, a gin and tonic with a bit of ice and a small lime slice. The phone rang again, its harsh tone filling The Court Club. Harry sighed but this time he answered, knowing he couldn't ignore his brother for long. He pressed the green answer button and raised the phone to his ear. "Yes, Rollie?"

"I'm not amused, Harold," came the unmistaken calm English voice of Rollie on the other end.

"Oh? And why might that be?" Harry was ready to be indignant.

"Harold, I have CCTV in my office, a camera which is separate to the main system, the system which you disabled last night." Only his brother called him Harold and it always sounded like an admonishment.

"Damn." The additional camera was news to Harry.

"Yes, Harold, well put, as always. Now, what are we going to do?"

Harry hadn't considered this scenario. He knew he'd be suspected in the robbery – after all, he was the only one with the motive, nobody else in the world could possibly want the trophy. He'd been at the party, so had the opportunity, and he was familiar with the security system. It all pointed to Harry.

"Well, what exactly have you seen?" Harry played for time, needing to think this through.

"I have a rather comical video," Rollie replied with a chuckle. "Let me put it this way, your Colonel Alan is not likely to win any awards for cat burglary."

Harry saw a potential escape. "So, Alan did it? Why are you calling me then?"

"Harold, old chap, I also have a recording of you helping yourself to some cigars from my humidor."

Harry's heart rate quickened; Rollie had seen him in his office.

"You made quite a mess of my Welsh dresser, but I'll overlook that. Nothing that can't be fixed. I'll forgive you for the cigars, too; you can make it up to me another time." Rollie's voice paused, and Harry could hear the rustling of papers. "However, old chap, I am not happy that you've deceived me, nor am I pleased that Alan broke into my office, and finally," another pause, "I am not happy that you stole *my* trophy." The emphasis on "my" annoyed Harry.

Harry stammered, attempting to mount a defence, but he was interrupted.

"This is what's going to happen, Harold. You will return my trophy as soon as humanly possible, no 'ifs' or 'buts.' You will demonstrate your remorse by dealing out some retribution on Alan. I don't care how you do it, but if you defy me, I will make trouble for you. I expect both tasks to be completed promptly." Another pause, this time on Harry's end. Would he dare say "no"?

"Yeah, okay. Is that all?" Harry didn't like the tone of this conversation, but he had little room to manoeuvre.

"That is all, Harold. Do not disappoint me again. Goodbye."

With a soft click, the call ended. Harry seethed. He was chuffed with himself for getting one over Rollie, but he despised taking orders from anyone, even his boss, especially when that boss happened to be an older brother. He smiled at the thought of Rollie having an extra camera in his office, he didn't like his brother but couldn't help being impressed. The robbery hadn't worked but he still had the trophy in his possession, and that meant it was nine-tenths his – isn't that what they said? Alan could take a little beating, Harry would make sure it wasn't anything over the top, but he wasn't about to spend a lot of money on this, and anyway, it wasn't in his interest to harm Alan, he'd want to use him again. Harry knew a group of young lads who would do the job on the cheap. "No time like the present," Harry said as he tapped into his phone's address book and made a call.

The Monroe Cup

Rollie pressed the off button on his desk phone to terminate the call and reclined in his Chesterfield leather chair. As he pondered how to handle the dilemma presented by Harry, he found himself humming the melody from 'The Sound of Music' – "how do you solve a problem like Harry". Rollie couldn't help but chuckle at the realisation that he was showing his age.

The darts trophy was more than just a relic – it was a Monroe family heirloom. For years, Rollie's father had organised a fierce annual competition, grandly named "The Monroe Cup." The competition was only open to the four siblings and their father to instil family values and a sense of healthy competitiveness. It wasn't about the prize, a modest silver-plated dartboard perched on a marble base; it was about winning their father's admiration. Rollie and his three brothers had thrown their hearts into the contest, each sibling vying for their father's approval as much as for the cup itself.

Harry, the youngest by seven years, had always been the odd one out. He was the rebel of the family, more interested in causing trouble than mastering darts. While his brothers practiced religiously, Harry treated the whole affair with indifference, often mocking the game and shrugging off the very trophy that had come to mean the world to Rollie. He was the poorest darts player, the least competitive, and ultimately the least concerned with earning their father's praise. But Rollie – Rollie was different. He lived for those competitions, for the rare smiles of approval that flickered across their father's face when he played well.

The cup had no significant monetary value, at least not to anyone outside the family. To Rollie, however, it was priceless – a tangible connection to the fondest memories he had of his father. After their father passed away, the brothers had tried, half-heartedly, to keep the tradition alive. But without the old man there to anchor them, the competition quickly fizzled out. The trophy gathered dust, but its sentimental weight only grew for Rollie. Every time he looked at it, he could almost hear his

54

father's voice, feel the intensity of those matches that once meant so much.

Harry, of course, never cared. He had always viewed the competition as a joke, and the trophy as nothing more than a cheap decoration. And that's exactly why Rollie knew Harry had stolen it. Harry didn't need the trophy, didn't even want it. But he knew what it meant to Rollie – he'd known all along. Stealing it was Harry's way of getting one over on his older brother, a dig at the past they shared but viewed so differently.

Rollie had never met Alan in person, but the moment he found out Alan was working for Harry, he'd looked into his background. Alan was just a hired hand, a pawn in Harry's game, and Rollie didn't have any personal grudge against him. But he couldn't let it slide. Alan had crossed a line, breaking into a place that still held meaning for Rollie, the office where that beloved trophy had been kept.

Now, Rollie had to act. It wasn't about revenge – it was about making a point. Alan might have been working for Harry, but Rollie couldn't allow his involvement in the burglary to go unanswered. Harry had gone too far this time, and Alan was caught in the crossfire.

Rollie felt unusually agitated, a stark contrast to his typically calm and calculated demeanour. He pressed a button on his desk phone, activating the intercom to one of the adjacent rooms. "October, come in please." His voice was steady, though a rare edge crept into it.

He had a peculiar system for his security team – each guard was named after a month of the year. It was an easy mnemonic, a simple way to avoid confusing their real identities or risking exposure. October, one of the most imposing of them all, entered the office swiftly and silently. Standing at 6'4", with a thick black beard flecked with grey, his presence was intimidating to most. But not to Rollie. October was more than muscle – he was loyal, precise, and had earned Rollie's complete trust.

"Thank you for coming in, October." Rollie looked up from his desk, meeting the guard's calm, steely gaze. "I need to bare some teeth. Nothing too aggressive, just a reminder." He leaned back in his chair, considering his next words carefully. "Send James to deliver a message to that Alan chap – Harold's guy. A light touch only. I want Harold, and this Alan, to understand who's in charge, but without causing a scene."

October nodded, his face giving nothing away. He didn't need further instruction; he instinctively understood exactly what Rollie wanted. James – Rollie's son – would know how to handle it. A firm but measured response. No mess, no unnecessary aggression. Just a calculated nudge to remind Harry who held the real power.

"That should do it," Rollie muttered, more to himself than to October.

Without a word, October turned and exited as discreetly as he had arrived, his heavy footsteps barely audible on the thick carpet. Rollie allowed himself a small, satisfied smile. Yes, that should suffice. He wasn't one to enjoy making these kinds of "statements," especially when it involved family, but sometimes, even with blood ties, a line had to be drawn. He understood the necessity of asserting his authority – quietly, but unmistakably. It wasn't about violence or threats; it was about reminding people of their place, maintaining the delicate balance of power that had kept him in control all these years.

There was a soft knock from the door opposite the one October had departed through, and Sarah entered. "Is now a good time to clear that broken glass, Rollie?"

"Yes of course, my dear," Rollie replied, glancing up with a gentle smile. "If you need me, I'll be in the garden. My cucumbers are in desperate need of harvesting. Any bigger, and they'll start to lose their flavour, I fear. Oh, and the chilli peppers! They're a brilliant red now, probably at their best." He trailed off into a meandering monologue about his vegetables, speaking for a good five minutes without a pause. Sarah listened with quiet patience, she didn't mind one bit.

The Gargrave Hotel

Bruce had never considered himself a "good listener." Conversations, especially those focused on people, often left him restless. He much preferred clear-cut exchanges of facts. He avoided talking about his own life because, to him, it was unremarkable. And listening to others go on about theirs was usually worse. Yet, sitting in the bar of the Gargrave Hotel with Ciara, he found an exception. Her voice had a soft, lilting rhythm, like waves lapping at the shore, and somehow it drew him in. The occasional glances he stole, noting how her eyes brightened at certain parts of her story, didn't feel out of place. He realised he wasn't just listening – he was enjoying her company.

As Ciara Logan continued, Bruce pieced together the fragments of her tumultuous upbringing. She was 31 but spoke as if she'd lived three lifetimes. Her parents had done their best, she stressed, though her childhood had been anything but easy. She'd started strong academically, her grades solid, but by her teens, school seemed pointless. Her hometown offered little but unemployment, and the idea of moving to Belfast didn't appeal either. So, she had set her sights on the mainland, though it turned out to be a far cry from what she had envisioned.

"I was always with the older kids," she said, a hint of mischief in her smile. "Fitted in like a glove, really. Too popular for my own good."

Bruce nodded slightly, his fingers drumming softly on his knee. He could tell from the way she spoke; she'd been in control for most of her life, even when things had gone sideways. Smoking, drinking – vices she toyed with but never let dominate her. As she explained her rise through the ranks of the local lap dancing club, from dancer to manager, Bruce felt a faint ripple of admiration, though he couldn't quite put it into words.

By 23, Ciara had mastered the club's business, from the finances to the intricate art of cutting corners where no one would notice. She spoke of a drug habit beaten and the hollow ache of losing her parents to illness. More than that, Bruce sensed the deeper hurt – her sister, lost to religious fervour, had been just as much a casualty.

When she mentioned the club's owner, the man who became her husband, Bruce's brow furrowed slightly. "Irish Mob?" he asked, more to clarify than judge.

Ciara chuckled softly. "Aye. Not your typical love story, huh? At 25, I was married and off to Boston. Funny how the 'mainland' turned out to be across the Atlantic rather than the Irish Sea."

Bruce nodded again, processing the whirlwind of her past. It was all so far removed from his life – yet he wasn't overwhelmed. Ciara's stories flowed like pieces of a puzzle he was keen to understand, even if they didn't quite fit into the orderly framework he was used to. And, surprisingly, he was okay with that.

Ciara paused her story and glanced around. "Do you think I could get a drink?"

Bruce, still absorbing every detail, blinked. "Uh, yeah, sure. Another coffee?" He noticed the subtle tilt of her head and quickly backtracked. "Oh, um, wine? Should I get some wine?"

Bruce wasn't one for alcohol – his gym routine was strict, and he liked to stick to it – but he was too absorbed in the moment to resist. He was about to stand when something clicked in his mind. "Wait… you don't have any luggage. Actually, you don't even have a handbag or a phone, do you?"

Ciara gave a soft shake of her head, her voice calm. "No. It's all in the car, back at those motorway services. Honestly, I don't care. I can start over. Not like I can call them to bring it here, anyway."

Bruce frowned slightly. "No, no, of course not." He thought for a moment. "I can book you a room here. I'll just sleep in the lorry. And… I'll see if they have, um, any spare clothes you can change into."

Ciara let out a quiet sigh, her head lowering as strands of blonde hair cascaded over her face. She looked down at the table, her expression hidden. Bruce's gaze followed, and for a brief second, he noticed how her dark blouse complemented her figure. It crossed his mind if she worked out as regularly as he did, though he immediately shifted focus, feeling a bit flustered by the thought.

58

"Well," Bruce continued, "I can't drive after wine anyway, so I guess we're staying put for the night." He hesitated, hoping for a smile. When Ciara did smile, soft but genuine, Bruce felt an unexpected rush of excitement. Like a schoolboy, he sprang from his seat and made his way to the reception desk.

Five minutes later, he returned, a touch breathless but clearly pleased with himself. "All sorted," he said, trying to keep his voice steady. "Most of the rooms are taken by a wedding party, but they know me here. Lucky for us, they had a no-show, so we got a nice room."

Ciara's smile deepened, and Bruce fumbled with his words again. "I mean... I got *you* a nice room." He ran a hand through his cropped hair, feeling a little embarrassed by his eagerness, but Ciara's quiet appreciation put him at ease.

Bruce offered a rare glimpse into his own life, something he wasn't usually keen to do. He mentioned his older brother, four years his senior, who had always been his role model. When his brother started Judo at eight, Bruce followed eagerly, hoping to impress him. What began as a way to connect turned into an obsession for Bruce – martial arts became more than just a hobby.

"Then, when he was 16, he got a motorcycle," Bruce said, his gaze briefly distant. "And of course, that became my thing too. But, no matter what I did, I never really got… well, the recognition I wanted." He trailed off, his words tinged with an old ache.

Ciara remained quiet, sensing there was more beneath the surface.

He shifted in his seat, his voice more subdued. "When I was 14, my parents died. Car accident."

Without a word, Ciara reached out, her hand resting gently on his arm. The simple gesture made his pulse quicken, but not with discomfort. There was an understanding in her touch that resonated deeply. She knew that loss, intimately. For a moment, Bruce found solace in her quiet empathy.

"I felt alone after that," Bruce continued, eyes still on the table. "My brother left for university not long after, and I stayed with my grandparents. But by the time I was 16, I'd had enough. I left. Thought I'd make it on my own."

Ciara hesitated for a moment, then asked softly, "What happened to your brother? Where is he now?"

Bruce's jaw tightened slightly. He didn't want to go there. Not now. "He's... around somewhere, we lost touch" he replied vaguely, his tone signalling that the subject was closed. Ciara picked up on it immediately and let the question drop. She'd learned quickly not to push Bruce on certain topics.

As the evening deepened, a meal arrived, accompanied by a second bottle of wine. Bruce, unused to drinking much, could feel the alcohol's weight pressing on him. A comfortable haze settled in, but it also sapped his energy. His storytelling started to falter, but before it did, he found himself awkwardly sharing details with Ciara – about Rollie, about Edinburgh, and even the lorry's hidden compartment. As soon as the words left his mouth, he realised he'd said too much. Still, sitting there with Ciara, the weight of those secrets didn't feel so heavy. In fact, letting them slip had brought an unexpected sense of release, something he hadn't realised he'd needed.

"I need to use the restroom," Caira said. Bruce gestured vaguely in the direction of the facilities, hoping to compose himself in Caira's absence.

As Ciara rose and walked away from the table, Bruce's gaze followed her, lingering on the way her form-fitting jeans accentuated her athletic build. It confirmed what he'd suspected earlier – she clearly kept in shape. There was something captivating about the way she moved, a certain grace in her stride, even across the thick hotel carpet. It was as if she was gliding, effortless and confident, a sharp contrast to his own growing clumsiness in the moment.

For a second, Bruce wondered if it was the wine clouding his judgment, but the thought quickly faded.

Ciara returned to the table, picking up where she'd left off, now with the additional wine she'd ordered. As she spoke, Bruce listened intently, despite the growing fog from the alcohol. Her marriage, she explained, had been solid, and her life in Boston was one she had cherished. She had lived in comfort, surrounded by friendships she valued, and often found herself heading to New York for wild nights out. Bruce, never having had the chance to visit either Boston or New York, couldn't help but mention how much he'd love for Ciara to show him around those cities one day.

Ciara smiled, but her expression dimmed as her story took a darker turn. Her husband's criminal ties had never been hidden from her. She knew her place within his world, and though her understanding of the organisation's deeper machinations was limited, her ambition drove her to contribute more. She'd proven herself adept at managing the drug and prostitution operations, drawing from her time running the lap dancing club. Her good looks, she admitted, helped open doors in a male-dominated underworld. Men underestimated her, and that worked in her favour.

Yet, despite her success, Ciara soon found herself in deeper than she had ever imagined. She had come to accept her husband's infidelities, though she loathed the mistresses – known as "gumars." It was just part of the life, and she tolerated it, all the while building her own financial escape plan. She saved diligently, never allowing herself to get too comfortable, because deep down, she knew her time in this world was temporary. Still, she was surprised the ride lasted as long as six years.

Then came the day that would unravel it all.

"A woman showed up one day," Ciara said, her voice lowering as her fingers traced the rim of her wine glass. "She told me she was my husband's mistress, but also… an FBI informant."

Bruce sat up straighter, sensing the gravity of what came next.

"She offered me a choice – work with the FBI or stay loyal to the Mob. I thought I could play both sides." Ciara's gaze dropped to the table; her voice laced with regret. "But you can't dance between two fires without getting burned. Eventually, the FBI got frustrated cut me off. And worse, they exposed me to the Mob."

Bruce could feel the tension rising as Ciara spoke, her words painting a vivid picture of a life that had spiralled out of control. Her husband was arrested, taking the fall for capital murder and drug trafficking charges, ensuring he'd spend the rest of his life behind bars. With him gone, Ciara became a target, fleeing to London in an attempt to escape the vengeance of the Mob. But they weren't far behind. The men Bruce had faced at the motorway services? They were en route to Boston, taking Ciara back to the US to deal with her once and for all.

Bruce's mind worked quickly, piecing together the situation. The man in the blue suit, Rob Gates, was the leader of the trio, aiming to climb the ranks and become a Captain in the Mob. Ciara was sure this botched mission would set him back, and she prayed she'd never have to see him again. The martial artist Bruce had injured – Luke – was new to the gang, and Bruce winced inwardly as he thought about the damage he'd done to Luke's knee. Then there was the giant – Goliath – a six-foot-seven wrestler from Ghana who had been a towering, imposing presence. Ciara knew him only by that name, and Bruce silently hoped their paths would never cross again.

As Ciara's story concluded, Bruce felt the weight of it all settling in. He had saved her once, but it was clear that danger still lurked around the corner. Yet, as he looked across the table at Ciara, there was something else – he sensed an understanding between them, a connection that he hadn't expected.

"I need a shower, Bruce," Ciara said, casually picking up the room key but purposefully closing the book on her life story. "Do you mind?"

Bruce, feeling lightheaded and a little disoriented, tried to focus. "Uhm, no, of course not. Maybe we should call it a night. I should head out to the lorry."

Ciara flashed him a look of amused disbelief. "No way, Bruce. Come on, you need a shower too. Christ above, I think you still have blood on you!" She gestured toward the remnants of their earlier ordeal, both of them having only managed a quick clean-up in the bar's restroom.

Her insistence was undeniable. "You take the key and shower. I'll get us another drink. You can always head to the lorry afterward."

Bruce hesitated, but when faced with Ciara's smile, he found himself nodding, surrendering to her charm.

As Bruce stepped out of the bathroom, a towel loosely secured around his waist, Ciara entered the room with a fresh bottle of wine in hand. Her eyes widened slightly at the sight of him – his muscular frame still glistening with droplets from the shower. The dim lighting of the room accentuated the hard lines of his six-pack and broad shoulders, though his biceps looked large whatever the light.

"You pour while I take my turn in the bathroom, okay?" she said, quickly averting her gaze and heading into the bathroom before he could respond.

"Uhm, yeah, sure, no problem," Bruce mumbled, trying to pull himself together. His head still felt heavy from the wine, and the warmth of the shower hadn't exactly helped his coordination. He wasn't even sure if his reply made sense.

He carefully made his way to a small table in the corner of the room, slumping into a small armchair. With effort, he retrieved the wine from the ice bucket, poured two glasses, and leaned back. The room felt hazy, the combination of exhaustion and alcohol overtaking him. Before he knew it, he had drifted into a deep, wine-induced sleep.

It must have been around 2 a.m. when Bruce awoke to the soft brush of Ciara's breath near his ear. Her voice was a whisper, carrying an unfamiliar vulnerability. "I'm scared, Bruce. Will you look after me?"

Still groggy and disoriented, Bruce blinked, struggling to reorient himself. He rose from his slumber directly into Ciara's arms. "I'm here for you," he muttered, the words escaping before he'd fully processed the situation.

As they embraced, Bruce felt the towel slip from his waist and drop to the floor. Ciara's arms wrapped around him tightly, her warmth pressing against him. His hand moved instinctively down her back, expecting to encounter resistance from the fabric of her clothes – but found none.

The Warning

At least he knew the address. Kevin Monroe clung to that thought as the rented grey Prius came to a quiet halt about 100 metres from number 37. The car was facing the right way for a quick getaway – just like he'd planned. His stomach churned, but outwardly, he was determined to stay calm. He'd been assured the key would work, though he might need to "wiggle the lock." His watch read 10:35 p.m., and the first-floor apartment was cloaked in darkness. It was time.

Kevin stepped over the low front wall, careful to avoid the creaky gate. His heart was pounding, each beat a reminder that this was his chance to prove himself. Crossing the small lawn, he fumbled with the key for a second, his hands slick with sweat. To his relief, the lock clicked open after a bit of wiggling, and he gently closed the door behind him. Silence. Only the faint hum of a fridge or freezer upstairs broke the stillness.

He was in.

The narrow hallway in front of him was barely eight feet by six, with a coat rack, a cupboard, and a staircase to his left. Kevin stood frozen for a moment, listening for any sound of movement. The place felt eerie, almost abandoned, but he couldn't afford to let his nerves get the better of him. His father had trusted him with this, and he wasn't about to screw it up.

Kevin crept up the stairs, each step measured, careful to keep his breathing under control. His palms were slick against the banister as he ascended, pausing at the landing to scan the apartment. Room by room, he checked – empty. Finally, he reached the lounge, his eyes flicking to the open door that gave him a perfect line of sight to the top of the stairs.

This was where he'd catch Alan.

It wasn't about violence – at least not tonight. His father had made that clear. It was about making Alan understand. You don't cross Rollie Monroe, or any member of the Monroe family, without expecting consequences. Kevin's task was to be the reminder of that. Someday, he'd have his own men doing this kind of thing for him, but for now, this was his moment to prove he could handle it.

He reached into his coat and pulled out the Sig Sauer Mosquito his father had lent him. It was small – a "peashooter" his dad called it – but enough to send a message. Kevin had been given strict orders not to use it unless absolutely necessary. The thought of actually firing it made his stomach turn. Sure, he'd practiced at his grandfather's range, but this wasn't the same. This wasn't target practice.

He clicked the safety on, his hands trembling slightly as he adjusted his grip on the gun. He didn't need to shoot; he just needed to intimidate. Alan would get the point.

Finding a spot in the darkened lounge with a perfect view of the stairs, Kevin settled in to wait. His heart thudded in his chest, the weight of the pistol cold in his hand. The quiet stretched on, the tension tightening around him like a noose. He tried to steady his breathing, telling himself this was just another step in the plan, a test to prove himself worthy of the Monroe name.

But his hands wouldn't stop shaking. His teeth chattered despite the warm coat he wore, a sign of the fear he desperately wanted to hide.

The George & Dragon

Alan relished the evening alone at the George and Dragon pub, but as the last orders chimed, he suddenly yearned for the comforts of home. Two hectic days had left him feeling weary. His thoughts turned to the substantial payment from Harry, not that he was in dire need of the money, but it promised a taste of future indulgence. With three properties fully paid off and one generating steady rental income, combined with a good military pension, a testament to the high rank he had attained, Alan led a life of comfort. His expenses were minimal, and the money from Harry was simply a bonus – money to spend freely, without a second thought.

As the bartender retrieved his empty pint glass and asked if he wanted another, Alan hesitated before 'reluctantly' agreeing to one last large whisky, despite knowing he'd already had enough. It all began with the dram Harry had bought him earlier in The Court Club. "One for the road," he muttered, a habitual refrain he couldn't resist. One of the charms of the George and Dragon lay in its strict observance of old licensing rules, calling time promptly at 11 pm. The hard stop suited Alan perfectly – without it, he knew he'd be too weak to refuse yet another "one for the road".

This particular bartender was a departure from the norm – likely middle-aged and experienced in the trade. It was a refreshing change from the usual transient workers in Brighton who bartended to make ends meet while in college. They often lacked the enthusiasm and dedication that this man clearly possessed.

Yet, there was a downside. The bartender seemed to assume Alan was lonely simply because he sat alone at the bar. Nothing could be further from the truth. Alan had chosen the pub for its proximity to home, its compact size, and the comforting anonymity it provided. Tonight, he was happy with his own company. He had scarcely moved all evening, contentedly enjoying his fish and chips at the bar, scrolling through various news feeds on his phone, happy to let the buzz of conversation from others exist around him. But in between serving other patrons, the bartender kept trying to strike up conversation, asking futile questions about Alan's background and marital status.

Alan, not wanting to be rude, responded but revealed as little as possible – a one-time marriage that "just didn't work out," no children, a local residence, and a life mostly dedicated to the military, which he half-jokingly referred to as his "true marriage." These vague answers were intended to deflect the bartender's persistent inquiries, though it did little to stop the man's efforts.

As the brass bell tolled again, signalling closing time, Alan stepped out of the pub and into the crisp embrace of the night air. He paused, adjusting to the shift from the warmth and bustle inside to the cool stillness outside. Above him, the sky stretched out in a dazzling array of stars, unusually bright against the dark canvas. His thoughts drifted to his ex-wife, whose encyclopaedic knowledge of the heavens once fascinated him. She could name every constellation, even pick out planets from stars. He missed those quiet moments with her, more than he cared to admit.

His apartment, fondly referred to as "number 37," lay approximately three-quarters of a mile away – just a "click" as they used to say in the army. It was the perfect distance for a reflective stroll, especially once you hit your fifties. Across the street, Alan stepped into St. Andrews' churchyard, guided by the weathered embrace of the old wooden gazebo at its entrance. Nestled beneath its timeworn rafters, small park benches stood on either side, quiet witnesses to countless joyful wedding pictures taken over the years.

In the darkness, the gravestones emerged from the ground like poorly maintained, uneven teeth. Hollyhocks adorned the fringes of the cemetery, standing tall on robust stems, reaching skyward in an earnest attempt to infuse the scene with nature's own glow – a semblance of floodlights illuminating a stadium in the quiet of the evening.

This church held a deep significance for Alan. Over the past three decades, he had attended various ceremonies here, from funerals to christenings, and, of course, his own wedding. The walk always stirred feelings of missed opportunities, lost friendships, and the road not taken.

As he invariably did, Alan cast his eyes toward the church steeple, its slight warping and crookedness still evident, particularly from this close vantage point. He couldn't help but wonder if one day he'd be startled to find it perfectly straight. Tonight, however, the steeple seemed to dissolve into the limitless expanse of the dark, infinite sky.

Emerging from the churchyard, Alan crossed a quiet road and entered a pedestrian lane. He had a particular distaste for the perpetually slick cobblestones that paved this passage, but it seemed dry enough tonight. The lane only stretched for about thirty yards, curving at a sharp 45-degree angle to the left around its midpoint. High walls flanked it, separating it from neighbouring houses. Soon, he would emerge onto another road, which would then lead him directly to his destination at number 37.

As Alan approached the bend, an unsettling feeling washed over him; there was a sudden, eerie presence behind him. They remained silent, too silent, deliberately silent. Alan quickened his pace, having been strolling leisurely until then. As he rounded the curve, the dim light from the entrance lamp dwindled, and he encountered two more figures. Both were cloaked entirely in black, their faces hidden beneath black balaclavas — imitating the attire he had worn the previous night, he noted with irony. They blended so seamlessly into the darkness that Alan nearly collided with them.

Coming to a halt, Alan could distinctly hear the person behind him do the same, indicating the presence of at least three individuals around him. "Yes?" Alan challenged, he stood about four feet from the two in front, both appeared small and of slight build, but they remained shrouded in silhouette. There was no reply, nor any movement; it seemed they had reached a point of hesitation, they weren't sure what to do next.

Recognising that this might be his only opportunity, Alan decided to take the initiative. He drew a deep breath and swiftly launched his right fist at the nearest figure in front of him. The impact was immediate, the first silhouette crumpled to the ground almost instantly, although Alan couldn't be certain if he had knocked them out. It was a promising start. The second figure fumbled, reaching into their jacket pocket. Alan reacted quickly, grabbing the top of their head and twisting balaclava, momentarily blinding them. In a burst of speed that surprised even him, he spun the second figure around, using them as a shield just as the third attacker struck. A small knife gleamed in the dim light, aimed at Alan's back, but the blade found the wrong mark – silhouette number two.

A strangled "No!" escaped from the second figure as they crumpled. Alan released his grip just as a fourth figure emerged from the shadows, similarly dressed in black. "They're cloning you," Alan muttered under his breath before springing into action.

He swung at the third attacker, the punch glancing off but enough to force them back. Number four stepped forward, brandishing a large kitchen knife with far too much misplaced confidence. Alan noted it was likely dull, probably borrowed from someone's mother, but he had no desire to test that theory. The fourth assailant lunged, a wild, untrained thrust reminiscent of a child playing at sword fighting. Alan easily dodged, sidestepping the blade, then delivered a rapid right-left-right combo to the figure's head. Number four dropped to the ground.

Alan swiftly picked up the fallen knife, feeling its weight before hurling it over the nearby wall. No sense in leaving it within reach.

Alan spun around, surveying the aftermath. Silhouette one was struggling to rise, while number two lay flat, groaning in pain. Behind him, numbers three and four had lost their resolve and were making a hasty retreat, or rather, a staggered one in the case of number four. Alan stepped toward the first figure, who was now on all fours, trying to stand. This hadn't been a random mugging, he needed answers.

He grabbed the person by the throat, lifting them off the ground and pressing them against the wall. Only then did he realise how slight his attackers were; this one weighed barely anything, almost childlike. Alan loosened his grip just enough to free his right hand and ripped the balaclava from their head, tossing it over the wall. The individual's hair seemed to come to life as it was freed from the confines of the balaclava, cascading free. It was a woman, barely eighteen by Alan's estimation.

"You're a woman!" Alan blurted in surprise.

"No kidding," she shot back with a sarcastic bite. "Now, let me go!"

"I will," Alan replied, his voice firm but controlled, "but first, you're going to tell me who paid you to do this." Silence. "What's your name?" he pressed, but again, she met him with nothing but a resolute glare.

Alan paused, recalibrating. "Look, I'm not going to hurt you, but you clearly have no idea what you're doing." She squirmed, trying to slip out of his grip, but he tightened his hold. "Did you even bother to research me? You don't bring knives to a fight without understanding the consequences." He glanced over his shoulder at the figure still groaning on the ground. "He's going to need an ambulance. Or is that a she?"

"It's a he," she finally muttered.

Alan caught the hint of cooperation and pressed further. "Who sent you?"

"Harry Monroe paid us to give you a warning."

Alan was incredulous, momentarily thrown. "What? Harry Monroe? Do you mean *Roland* Monroe?"

"No, it was Harry. He paid us tonight at The Court Club," she replied, defiant but still wincing from the pressure on her throat.

Alan struggled to comprehend this. "Why on earth would he do that?"

"How should I know?" she snapped; her voice laced with frustration rather than regret.

He released her throat and stepped back, half-expecting her to bolt. But she didn't. She stood there, rubbing her neck, glaring at him with a mix of defiance and uncertainty.

"Your cheekbone looks sore," Alan observed, "I might have broken it. You should go to A&E. And you'll need to call an ambulance for them," he pointed over his shoulder. "I'm not doing that for you."

She hesitated, then nodded, subdued by Alan's calm approach. "Okay. Thanks… and I'm sorry for tonight." She hesitated again, then added, "My name's Audrey, by the way."

71

Alan was taken aback. Audrey spoke clearly, albeit with a discernible tremble in her voice, betraying her nerves. "Okay, Audrey," he said, softer than he expected. "Next time Harry – or anyone, for that matter – asks you to do something like this, either don't do it or ask me first." He surprised himself with his own leniency. He *should* have been furious, but looking at her now, she seemed so fragile, as though one more blow would shatter her entirely.

Audrey glanced up at him, a mix of relief and fear in her eyes. "Thank you. I'll go, but I'll call the ambulance. And… I am sorry." She backed away before turning, scampering toward the churchyard. Over her shoulder, she called out, "By the way, my name's Audrey Hepburn!"

Alan stood there, momentarily speechless, watching her disappear into the shadows. He shook his head, muttering to himself, "Of course it is."

A Quiet Mews in Brighton

Sarah had returned home from Rollie's earlier than she'd expected. She'd cleared the broken glass quickly and, despite Rollie's warm protestations that she had already done enough for a Saturday, she had tidied most of the party detritus. She would have been even earlier, but Rollie wouldn't let Sarah leave without first providing a bag of produce from his garden, as he always did, and to regale her of a story about collecting grey squirrel tails to collect a sixpence bounty from the Ministry of Agriculture back as a child in the 1950s. It all sounded unlikely, but Sarah was happy to listen. Now, at her kitchen counter, Sarah unpacked the freshly picked cucumbers, tomatoes, beetroot, chilli peppers, and mid potatoes, savouring the earthy smell and the quiet act of kindness. Rollie's generosity never failed to bring a smile to her face, though it rarely lasted long after stepping back into the small marital home.

It wasn't that she disliked the house, it was quaint and had its charms. But it felt small, cramped even, especially considering Peter's success as an estate agent. "A successful professional estate agent," as he never failed to remind her. She'd assumed they'd have moved on to something more spacious by now. But Peter was always quick to remind her it was a great investment: a Mews house in a quiet cul-de-sac, in an unbeatable location, and the kind of property that rarely came on the market. He'd built their finances around it, meaning that leaving, or even thinking about it, was hardly an option. Not with both of their incomes propping up the large mortgage.

She spent hours curled up on the sofa, nursing her coffee and catching up on her favourite TV shows from the planner. These were "her" shows – reality and renovation programs, mostly American, that offered her a window into other lives, where problems were solved in a tidy forty-five minutes, with neat transformations and happy resolutions. But as she watched, Sarah's thoughts drifted back to her own life, and she felt a familiar, creeping sense of discontent.

Lately, she'd become all too aware of how self-focused she'd become, tangled in the monotony and frustrations of her own situation. Maybe it was time to stop waiting for change and take control. If she was serious about finding happiness – whether that meant giving love a second chance or building a new life – she'd have to be brave enough to act. Staying with Peter out of habit or financial entanglements would only keep her in limbo, and she was beginning to crave clarity.

Her gaze settled on a family in one of the shows, laughing together in their newly renovated kitchen. A pang of longing washed over her. Maybe it was time to reconsider the life she had, to think again about the children she'd long dreamed of. If her marriage was worth fighting for, if Peter could still be the man she'd once believed he was, then maybe this life, with all its imperfections, could still hold the future she wanted.

Almost absent-mindedly, she sent Peter a message:

Wifey

Hey hon, how about I make us dinner tonight and we open a few bottles of nice wine? We should give it one more try. You know I do love you. S. xx

The message felt both hopeful and uncertain, and a part of her instantly regretted it. Was she giving in too easily yet again? She knew Peter was deep into preparing for a crucial presentation. A prominent property investor had invited him to bid for exclusive rights to sell a new block of forty riverside apartments nearing completion in Shoreham. If he won the bid, it would be a career-defining achievement. And, of course, he'd been working on the proposal with Naomi – the "fragrant Naomi," as Peter had once described her. He had the knowledge; she had the PowerPoint skills; he'd said with a glint that Sarah tried hard to ignore.

To her surprise, she received a quick response:

Peter

That sounds great, I love you too and want to try harder. I'll be home about 8pm. Can't wait. P. x

Sarah received the message around 4 p.m., and with an unexpected buoyancy, she set to work. By seven, she'd prepped everything. She opened a bottle of Sancerre, set the dining table, and put on the playlist they used to enjoy together. She'd even ironed the good tablecloth, the one they rarely used. All that was left was to switch on the oven. As the evening wore on, she found herself glancing at the clock, watching the minute hand inch toward ten. Every time she thought she heard a car door, her heart leaped, only to sink back down in disappointment.

She considered sending him another message but knew it was pointless. The last four she'd sent had been read but left unanswered. Finally, she poured the remnants of the Sancerre into her glass, just a thimbleful, and raised it half-heartedly. She could feel the fragile hope she'd mustered at the start of the evening slowly slipping away.

Clowns

There were times when Alan cursed the limitations that age had slowly, almost mockingly, imposed on him. Tonight was undeniably one of those times. As he made his way home to number 37, he felt the weight of his years pressing down on him, especially in his right knee, which wouldn't give him more than ten yards at a run. The adrenaline of the attack was still humming in his veins, but it only served to drain him further. He was too riled to sleep, though, and all he could think of was the whisky waiting at home to help settle his temper.

Casting a quick glance over his shoulder, he confirmed that he was alone, though the alleyway encounter left him brimming with unanswered questions. "What the hell had that been about?" he muttered under his breath. It had been a calculated attack but amateurish – barely competent, really. "Bunch of bloody clowns", Alan muttered to himself. Still, that one line from the kid (a girl at that!) kept echoing in his mind: Harry had paid for it.

The thought of calling Harry right then and there crossed his mind, but he quickly dismissed it. Not tonight. He needed a clear head before that conversation, not one clouded by anger and booze. As his apartment came into view, he clenched his fists, feeling a cold resolve harden within him. Tomorrow, he'd get his answers – one way or another. If he had to drag the truth out of Harry himself, he'd do it, Monroe family name be damned.

Scorned

10:30pm. Sarah was seething.
Wifey
Where the fuck are you Peter? Answer my bloody messages!

11pm.
Wifey
Last chance Peter, where the fuck are you?

11:01pm. His reply finally came.
Peter
Sorry baby. Xxx

Six messages. No response for seven hours, save for those two flippant words. Fury surged within her, building from a simmer to a boil until, in a snap decision, she hurled her wine glass at the TV. The glass shattered, pieces spraying onto the floor. Miraculously, the TV was unscathed. She took a deep breath, trying to rein in the anger. "Calm down, Sarah," she muttered, looking at the shards glinting on the carpet. Breaking things wouldn't fix anything, it would just mean another mess that she would have to deal with.

Taking a shaky breath, she grabbed her phone, this time dialling Peter's number. She half-expected it to go straight to voicemail, but to her surprise, the call connected. Immediately, a chaotic mix of music and voices blasted from the other end, almost drowning her out. Heart pounding, she turned her phone around to shout into the microphone.

"WHERE ARE YOU?" she yelled.

A voice – feminine, muffled, and unmistakably drunk—came through the noise. "HELLO? WHO'S THAT?"

"WHERE ARE YOU?" Sarah demanded, her voice cutting through the tension, vibrating with barely restrained rage.

"WE'RE AT THE 'K CLUB'! ARE YOU COMING DOWN?" The woman's words were slurred, and the excitement in her tone only sharpened Sarah's suspicion. It had to be Naomi.

Sarah ended the call abruptly, her heart hammering. She slipped into her shoes, grabbed her car keys, and made her resolve clear: yes, she was indeed going down to the bloody 'K Club'.

<u>Safely Home</u>

Alan, exhausted, reached the front door of number 37. Fatigue was starting to overtake him. With one last glance over his shoulder, he confirmed that, as he had expected, no one was tailing him. Upon stepping through the door, Alan hung his jacket up, pondering his safety within his own home. He had been attacked by kids — children, of all things! His paranoia was growing, but he reassured himself that he was indeed safe here. Why had Harry done this to him? Alan had completed numerous shady tasks for Harry, and while he didn't particularly enjoy Harry's company, he believed their relationship was stable, one of necessary respect, if not friendship. Tonight's ambush felt deeply personal. And it had something to do with that house he had entered yesterday, and the absurd, cursed darts trophy.

The expense and trouble just to steal a darts trophy, it seemed sheer lunacy. Alan felt an ominous sinking sensation — the realisation that he had stolen the darts trophy from Harry's brother, the very man who commanded the organised crime syndicate Harry was part of. He had unwittingly become entangled in a foolish family feud with arguably the most dangerous family on the south coast. Alan cursed his own stupidity but made a resolute decision to set things right the following morning, even if it meant wringing Harry's neck. Alan started climbing the stairs, his anger towards Harry Monroe still coursing through him.

Alan ascended the staircase at a deliberate pace, his thoughts vocalised in a low mutter as he reached the top landing. However, he abruptly came to a halt, his mental alarms ringing with urgency. Two notable details seized his attention: firstly, a faint, unfamiliar odour that eluded his identification, and secondly, the subtle glimmer of light emanating from deep within the living room. Alan swiftly recognised the gravity of his misjudgement. Despite successfully having just fought off four unidentified assailants, he had allowed his emotions toward Harry to override his situational awareness, rendering him oblivious to potential dangers lurking within his own apartment. He'd broken a golden rule, against all his experience, he'd failed to stay alert.

Before he could react, he was struck with tremendous force on his left shoulder, the impact being so severe that it spun him 90 degrees to his left. In his peripheral vision, he caught a glimpse of a muzzle flash originating from the living room, and his shoulder blazed with searing pain. As the staircase receded behind him, the momentum from the strike propelled him downward. Desperately reaching for the handrail to his left, he managed to grasp it but lacked the strength to maintain his hold. He was falling.

In the ensuing fraction of a second, Alan was acutely aware that he was falling, backwards, down the stairs, he felt a profound sense of foreboding, and he had been wounded by gunfire. Survival became his paramount concern. His feet lifted from the top step, and as his body descended, his legs were thrust upward and over his head, initiating a backward somersault. Despite his frantic attempts to find purchase, he was unsuccessful in securing a grip on anything. His feet were now positioned behind him, and the descent continued to take shape. Upon the reconnection of his feet with the stairs, he deliberately relaxed his legs to absorb some of the impact force, resulting in a partial deceleration of his descent.

The imminent danger now lay in the concrete flooring awaiting him at the base of the staircase. While the stairs themselves were constructed from wood, the ground beneath was unforgiving concrete. Alan knew he'd cave the back of his head in if he failed to control his descent. He drew his arms tightly toward his body and, to the best of his ability, tucked his head into a protective posture. The collision with the concrete floor delivered a jarring impact to his back, momentarily robbing him of breath, but more importantly preserving the integrity of his skull.

The sudden and excruciating pain radiating from his shoulder eclipsed the discomfort in his back from the fall. Alan instinctively reached into his pocket, retrieved a handkerchief, and promptly applied it to the bullet wound. However, his physical stamina had been depleted. As Alan succumbed to encroaching unconsciousness, he discerned the sound of heavy footsteps descending the staircase, leaving him with the grim realisation of his impending demise and there was nothing he could do about it.

The K Club

Sarah pulled up opposite the 'K Club' on West Street, just around the corner from the Brighton Centre. The street was teeming with taxis and revellers, their laughter and shouts spilling into the night air, and there wasn't a spot in sight to park, not even to stop briefly. She noticed a line of police on patrol, keeping the Saturday crowd in check. After a bottle of wine, the last thing she needed was an encounter with them. She slipped her BMW 1-series back into traffic, navigating her way onto Marine Parade before finally finding a parking space in Regency Square. The square, once the epitome of Georgian prestige, now housed more student flats than luxury residences. Her parking permit didn't quite cover this area, but she had a permit nonetheless – she'd risk it.

It took her ten minutes to walk back, her steps measured and determined, yet as she neared the 'K Club,' uncertainty weighed on her. Across the road from the club, she lingered in the shadows, unsure of what she was even hoping to find. The club's roped-off smoking area allowed patrons to step out without rejoining the line, and from here, she had a clear view of the entrance.

She was about to give up her watch when Peter stumbled out of the club, struggling to light a cigarette. She instinctively stepped back, pressing herself against the wall. But Peter, barely able to steady the lighter, was oblivious to anything beyond his immediate task.

Moments later, Naomi emerged, radiating the careless joy of someone who hadn't a worry in the world. She was still half-dancing, enjoying the song playing within the club, her movements loose and uninhibited. She sauntered over to Peter, taking the cigarette from his hand, and expertly lit it. Teasingly, she held it just out of reach, her eyes flashing with mischief before she pulled Peter into a long, unhurried kiss. Sarah felt as if she'd been struck, the shock of the sight making her heart pound, and her breath catch. It was like watching a car crash, horrible but impossible to look away from.

Finally, they broke apart, Naomi still smiling as she placed the cigarette in Peter's mouth, then slipped an arm around him, her head leaning into his shoulder. They looked every bit the comfortable couple, wrapped up in their own world, oblivious to everything around them.

Sarah had seen enough. Heart pounding, she turned and quietly made her way back to her car, struggling to hold back the hot tears welling in her eyes.

Kevin's Exit

Kevin burst from his crouched position inside number 37, hurtling down the stairs, jumping over the prone figure of Alan. He pulled the door shut behind him, not entirely certain it had locked but unwilling to risk going back to check. His heart raced as he scrambled into his car, pushed the start button, and accelerated away as fast as the car allowed. The engine noise was the least of his concerns; all he needed was distance.

With trembling hands, he activated the speaker on his phone and dialled his father's number. It took five rings before the call was answered. "What is it son? How did it go?" Jamie's voice sounded composed and reassuring, a trait passed down by his own father.

"I've fucked up, Dad! I'm so sorry, but I've fucked up! What am I going to do?" Kevin's voice quivered with desperation.

"Son, calm down. What's happened?" Jamie's soothing tone helped steady Kevin's nerves a little.

"I've screwed up big time, Dad. I don't know what to do. I've really messed up!" Kevin sobbed into his phone.

"Calm down, son. You need to calm down. Breathe, Kevin, just breathe."

Kevin paused and gradually regained some control over his emotions. "I'm sorry, Dad."

"Now, what happened, son?"

"I've killed him." There was a heavy silence. "I thought I had the safety on, I was just trying to scare him with the gun, but it went off. It must have been a faulty gun, Dad!"

"The gun isn't faulty, Kevin. How do you know he's dead? Did you check his pulse? Where did you shoot him?"

"I shot him on the stairs, at the top. He wasn't breathing when I left." Kevin's voice started to waver as he spoke.

"I meant where on his body did you shoot him, Kevin, and what did you do with the gun?"

"I shot him in the chest, right through the heart, I think. And the gun, I don't know. I think I left it at the apartment."

"You THINK you left it at the apartment, or you HAVE left it at the apartment, Kevin?" Jamie's voice grew more deliberate and sterner.

"I have left it there, Dad. I'm sorry. I know…" Kevin's words were cut off, and this time, Jamie's response lacked the earlier calm.

"You are an idiot, Kevin. Lay low, keep your mouth shut, and leave it to me. I'll let you know when I've fixed it."

"I'm sorry Dad." Too late, the connection had been broken.

Somewhere To Sleep

Sarah glanced at her watch – 1:15 a.m. She'd spent the past two hours driving aimlessly before finally arriving at Alan's, only to find his place shrouded in darkness. The windows were tightly shut, curtains open, and not a single light on. Alan wasn't home. She muttered a quiet curse under her breath. She had no one else to turn to tonight. Over the years, her friendships had withered, her girlfriends drifting away one by one, partly because of Peter, who'd never made an effort with them. But she couldn't place all the blame on him; at some point, she'd become too absorbed in building her business, losing touch with everyone who might've been there for her now.

She checked her bag, though she already knew Alan's spare keys weren't there. The thought of driving all the way back home to retrieve them crossed her mind, if only to return and crash in his box room. But calling Alan might seem desperate, even if she felt desperate. Her exhaustion suddenly overwhelmed her. Leaning her head against the steering wheel, she closed her eyes, frustration swelling. How had it come to this? And where *was* Alan at this hour? The thought flickered that maybe he was in the Pier Nine seafront casino – she'd driven past it twice already tonight.

With a resigned sigh, Sarah decided to head home, pretending this never happened. The last thing she wanted was to reveal she'd tracked Peter or seen him with Naomi. She'd let the miserable charade continue, she told herself as she started the car and reversed to make a three-point turn. Her headlights swept across the row of houses, and she froze mid-turn. Alan's front door wasn't fully closed. She squinted, unsure if it was just a trick of the light – but no, the door was ajar.

Pulse quickening, Sarah shifted the car back into park, stepped out, and moved toward the darkened house.

The Poor Combination

Sarah peered around the front door and immediately spotted the motionless body of Alan sprawled on the floor. She screamed, and then turned the light on, rushing to his side.

"Please, Sarah, stop the bloody screaming," Alan managed to utter, his eyes squinting in pain.

Sarah reached into her handbag to grab her phone, but Alan shouted, "No ambulance."

"What? Are you bloody crazy? I'm calling an ambulance." Sarah's voice quivered.

"Will you please just listen, Sarah."

"You need the bloody hospital!" Sarah was on the verge of shock. Alan hoped she hadn't seen the gunshot wound and assumed he had merely fallen down the stairs drunk. He needed to manage this situation before it spiralled out of control. "Look at all this blood!"

"Stop and listen to me," Alan still couldn't get his eyes open, and the pain was intensifying. "Are you listening?"

"Please, I'm listening but you're losing so much blood." Slightly calmer Alan thought. "You need medical help – now!" Perhaps not he reflected.

Taking a steadying breath, Alan tried to sound in control. "You cannot call an ambulance. They'll notify the police, then there'll be all sorts of trouble. I need you to fetch the old brown suitcase from under my bed."

Sarah was confused, startled, and distressed but she knew the suitcase well; she had cleaned around it countless times. It never seemed to move. She needed to focus and retrieve the suitcase from beneath the bed. Alan heard her scream again.

"The combination is 4-3-2-1," Alan called weakly when she returned.

"There's a fucking gun in the hall upstairs!" Sarah fiddled with the case. "And what a shit combination number that is." The case clicked open. "Please, please, let me call you an ambulance, Alan."

He ignored her plea, "Just focus, Sarah, find the clotting gauze and unwrap it."

"What does it look like?"

"It's marked 'clotting gauze' on the packet!"

After some rustling, Sarah held up the gauze. "Take the handkerchief off my shoulder, rip open my shirt, press that onto the wound."

"ALAN, what the fuck are you talking about?" Sarah was bewildered but she followed his instructions and peeled back the handkerchief. It was nearly glued to his shoulder with dried blood, and she gagged at the sight. "Is this a gunshot wound?"

"Please, keep your voice down," Alan implored, acutely aware that time was of the essence. "Yes, it's a gunshot wound, but I assure you, with your help, I'll manage. Now press that gauze."

"Manage? How can you manage being shot?" Sarah's composure was slipping again. "Is the bullet still in you?"

"The round," Alan gently corrected, "yes, it's still in there."

"Oh my God!" Sarah gasped, the reality of the situation crashing over her in a wave of shock.

"Please, Sarah, the gauze." She finally followed his instructions. "No, press it down harder. Now get the compression bandage out and apply it tightly." She knew what a compression bandage was and complied but winced as she lifted him to get the bandage under his armpit.

"Now, go and get a pack of bottled water from the kitchen." Sarah stood and began to ascend the stairs again. "Oh, and bring the gun."

She hesitated, unnerved. "The gun, really?"

"Just do it," he murmured, his strength waning.

She seemed to take an age; Alan was slipping in and out of consciousness.

"Got it!" Alan woke up with a start, he was struggling to focus on his surroundings.

"Now listen carefully. There are vials of clear liquid in the case marked with an 'O'. Break one open and pour it down my throat." Sarah reached for the case.

"No, wait until I finish. There's co-codamol in the case; feed me two with the water. Wait, I need you to listen. There's an address on a post it note in the case; we need to drive there. You have to help me into the back of your car. Once the drugs kick in, I'll sleep, and you won't get any sense out of me. Wake me when we get to the address."

"Alan, this is unsane," she said, her voice softening, a mix of exasperation and worry in her tone. "Can't I just call someone? A doctor at least?"

"Sarah. Trust me. Please." He turned his head slightly and could finally see Sarah more clearly. "You look terrible, by the way."

"You don't look so great yourself," she managed a hint of a smile.

"What is that?" Alan nodded towards a hand towel on the floor.

"The gun, I wrapped it in the towel."

"Good idea," he had no idea why she'd done that. "Carefully unwrap it for me, please."

"Why?" Sarah questioned; her mind focused on the gravity of the situation.

"I want to check the safety catch is on," Alan explained.

"Of course," Sarah agreed, beginning to unwind the towel to reveal the small firearm.

Painfully, Alan shifted to get a better view of the gun. "See that small black tab near the hammer? Slide it down," he instructed.

"What's a hammer?"

"At the very back of the gun!" Alan clarified, his patience waning.

"Oh, I've got it," Sarah responded, securing the safety catch as instructed. "Why do you military types call it a 'round' and not a bullet?"

Alan found this a strange question in the circumstances, "Because it's round," he replied.

Sarah carefully re-wrapped the towel, treating it as if she were wrapping a fragile Christmas gift.

"Now please, let's get going, and don't forget to bring everything with you."

"Open up," Sarah poured the liquid. "What is it?"

89

"Oramorph."

"What's Oramorph?"

"Morphine!" Alan snapped back, growing increasingly impatient.

"Oh, right," Sarah said, not sure what to think in this growingly bizarre scenario.

Alan vaguely remembered falling across the back seat of Sarah's BMW 1 series. It was a tight fit, but he curled into the foetal position, trying to make himself as comfortable as possible. He heard Sarah mention an ambulance again and curse him that the address he provided was 150 miles away in Bristol. What was he thinking, etc.? Then he slipped into a deep sleep.

The Bridal Suite

Ciara quietly slipped out of bed, took a quick shower, and put her old clothes back on. Silently, so as not to wake Bruce, she slid out of the hotel room. The hotel, situated in the countryside with ample grounds, had rooms spread across two floors. Finding the premier rooms, including the bridal suite, proved to be an easy task. Ciara had already checked for CCTV, a habitual precaution she'd learned long ago. She was reasonably confident that the corridors lacked surveillance cameras, though she knew the reception and bar areas were well covered.

Ciara had a knack for creating her own luck. Following contemporary customs, she was convinced the newlywed couple would be enjoying breakfast, expressing their gratitude and farewells to their guests. These guests would continue to trickle in throughout the breakfast period, over the next few hours. Ciara also surmised that some of these guests would have already checked out, and the cleaning staff would already be at work, getting a head start on their day's tasks. Perfect timing.

Ciara spotted her foe quickly – a young male cleaner, possibly of Central European origin, who was just unlocking a vacant room to begin cleaning. His cleaning trolley held an assortment of white bed linens, white towels, and various shower gels and soaps. The coveted item, a master key with access all areas, dangled from a lanyard around his neck.

Switching from her Irish lilt to a polished English accent, Caira approached him with a warm smile. "Hi there! Oh Gosh, I am so sorry, but I've left my room key at breakfast. Could I please borrow your key for one moment? I have one last gift to give my husband while our families are still here," Her smile widened, her tone both innocent and charming. She reached for the lanyard casually, but the cleaner hesitated and stepped back.

"I'm... I'm not allowed to give this key to anyone. I'm sorry," he stammered, his eyes shifting. "Reception should be able to help you."

This man's resistance is futile, Ciara thought. She leaned in, her fingers lightly brushing just behind his ear. "Oh shucks, it would only take a second, promise," she murmured, a hint of vulnerability flickering in her eyes.

"Um, well if you're quick, I suppose it can't hurt," he conceded, his resolve melting away. Bingo!

With practised efficiency, Ciara unlocked the door to the bridal suite and slid her shoes into the doorway as a makeshift wedge. She handed back the key with a dazzling smile. "You're a lifesaver, hon. Thank you so much."

Back in the bridal suite, Ciara shut the door quietly and took in the chaos – scattered clothes, snack wrappers, and the aftermath of what looked like a wild wedding night. Perfect. It would buy her time; anyone noticing missing items wouldn't realise it right away.

In the bathroom, she spotted a near-empty Champagne bottle next to the jacuzzi tub. She tilted it optimistically, only to get a few lukewarm drops. She made a face – definitely not vintage. Shrugging, she scanned the bride's makeup stash next to the sink and freshened up with a quick swipe of mascara and a bit of foundation. "Cheers, love," she murmured with a smirk, she was enjoying this.

Moving to the wardrobe, she sifted through the groom's clothing first, only to find men's suits and trousers that were of no use to her. But a box at the bottom caught her eye. She slipped it out, peeling back the torn wrapping paper. Inside was a high-end watch and a card: *To our new life. Love, D. x* She fastened it onto her wrist with a grin. "Well, thank you, 'D.'"

The bride's side of the wardrobe was a goldmine. Ciara rifled through the clothes, found fresh underwear, a chic mustard skirt, and a sleek black sleeveless blouse, and changed quickly. As she turned, she spotted another, smaller box tucked at the bottom. She opened it to find a second watch, even fancier than the first. The note inside read: *Love you, my beautiful wife. T. xx* "Well, T, I don't mind if I do!" She slid it onto her other wrist.

A quick sweep of the room turned up a pair of designer sunglasses on the bedside table. *Perfect.* Not only stylish but also ideal for dodging the reception's CCTV. She slipped them on, checked her reflection with a satisfied smirk, and snagged a bottle of Christian Dior perfume, also from the bedside table. Not her usual choice, but she spritzed a generous mist, walked through it, and then spotted a small clutch bag on the bed. Tucking it under her arm, she stepped into her shoes and strolled out.

Outside, her young cleaning friend was still methodically working his way through the same room. She tossed her old clothes into his laundry sack, gave him a little wave, and sauntered down the corridor toward the exit. With her fresh look and shades, she felt like a whole new woman – and ready for the next challenge.

The Hotel Room

Bruce's head throbbed, his mouth felt like it had been scrubbed with sandpaper, and a dull ache pulsed in his right hand. Still, beneath the discomfort, he felt oddly euphoric. Sunlight poured into the hotel room, flooding the space with a bright, almost accusatory glow. He squinted as he opened his eyes, and his hangover flared up a notch. Alcohol was a rare indulgence for Bruce; he took pride in his disciplined approach to health, regularly working out and avoiding anything that dulled his senses. Hangovers were foreign territory for him, and right now, he remembered why.

He glanced around, searching for painkillers, and took in the state of the room. It was chaotic – definitely not his style. His military days had left him with a habit of keeping things in precise order, even in his civilian life. Yet, for once, the mess didn't bother him. The duvet lay tangled around his waist, his only shield of modesty. Nearby, a half-empty wine bottle sat in an ice bucket, the ice long melted into lukewarm water. A crumpled towel lay discarded on the floor, while the contents of his overnight bag were scattered haphazardly, as if it had been tipped off the armchair.

To his left, the bed was empty, and as his eyes scanned the room, he realised there was no sign of Ciara. Not a shoe, not a stray piece of clothing – nothing to prove she'd ever been there. Bruce vaguely recalled her slipping off his towel at some point during the night, yet now even that was gone, leaving him to question if his memory was playing tricks on him. His right hand throbbed slightly, a bruise blooming on his knuckles, a faint souvenir of the fight in the carpark. If it weren't for that bruise, he could have easily convinced himself he'd dreamt the entire encounter.

Alan stirred awake just as Sarah's car reached the M32, his low, sharp cry of pain cutting through the quiet dawn. She caught his reflection in the rearview mirror, pale and drenched in sweat, but resisted the urge to stop. They were nearly at his apartment, and Bristol's streets were mercifully empty this early on a Sunday morning. Despite Alan's intermittent protests from the back seat, Sarah pushed on, navigating the empty streets toward Hotwell Road.

Following the instructions Alan had given her, Sarah found the steep ramp leading to his building's private car park, slipping into space number '9' as dawn painted the city in hues of grey. A dongle attached to his keys had activated the gate, which clattered open as she pulled through, the same dongle opened the building door. Fortunately, his apartment was on the same level as the car park, but the real challenge was getting him inside.

With a blend of determination and gentle coaxing, Sarah half-supported, half-carried Alan into his apartment. She helped him to his bed, his face twisting in pain with each step. Once he was down, she carefully removed his clothes down to his underwear, following his whispered instructions to re-dress the wound. Alan gritted his teeth as she tightened the bandages, her hands steady but her mind racing. She gave him more co-codamol, then hesitated as she held up a vial labelled 'F.' Alan had muttered it was fentanyl, though she wasn't entirely sure. Regardless, he managed to mumble that it would help him rest and told her to get some sleep herself – "Five hours," he rasped, "then I'll see you."

Exhausted, Sarah paced the small apartment. A narrow hallway led to the bedroom, bathroom, and a compact lounge that combined a sparse kitchen and small dining area. She wished he'd let her take him to a hospital; she knew enough to help, but not nearly enough to feel confident. Her mind was foggy from the long drive, lingering resentment about her husband's betrayal, and the wine she'd indulged in last night to drown her frustrations. She wanted to sleep, but the anxiety of tending to Alan alone buzzed just beneath her exhaustion.

Finally, she slipped off her jeans and climbed into the bed beside Alan, her hand resting gently on his back to monitor his breathing. His bare skin was warm, and despite the pain, his breathing was steady, rhythmic. The hum of the traffic outside felt jarring, a reminder of the city's usual chaos, but exhaustion finally caught up with her. She closed her eyes, murmuring under her breath about how anyone could rest with so much noise outside, then drifted into a deep, fitful sleep beside him.

Remorse

Peter Kemp woke with a pounding headache and a gnawing sense of regret. The night before – and well into the morning – had blurred into a hazy fog of drinks and laughter, and now he was replaying fragments he'd rather forget. He'd lied to Sarah from the start, and a sinking feeling told him he'd blown everything. He could still see Naomi's skirt in his mind, too short and, last night, too tempting. Way too tempting. He'd spent the day watching her, taking every excuse for her to practice their presentation, his eyes lingering more than they should. When she suggested drinks, he knew he wouldn't resist.

They left work early, at five, sooner than he'd planned. Peter told himself he'd be home by seven-thirty, just in time for dinner with Sarah. But the drinks kept flowing, and with them, his focus on anything but Naomi slipped away. Sarah's messages came in bursts – each one sharper and more demanding – but they barely registered. In that moment, he wasn't up for another heated argument, but nor did he want to leave Naomi's side, he had to concede he was weak.

Then came the decision to hit the K-Club. Naomi, laughing and leaning in close. Naomi, still in that skirt, her attention fixed on him in a way that felt electric. He knew what she was after: the promotion, the recognition that came with working under his wing. "Leg up" was the term that came to mind, and Peter smirked at the irony – he'd certainly given her that.

Now, lying alone in bed, the thrill of last night had faded, leaving only the dull ache of self-loathing. Sarah, who'd stood by him through years of struggles and successes, deserved better. The thought of losing her clawed at him in a way he hadn't expected. He'd risked everything for a fling with Naomi, knowing full well she'd drop him the moment she got what she wanted.

And now, the house was silent. Sarah was nowhere to be found.

Nurse Sarah

Sarah sat in an unfamiliar apartment in Bristol, a city she'd never set foot in before, tending to a man with a gunshot wound – a task she'd never imagined herself handling. Just hours ago, her nursing skills had been non-existent; now, she was muddling through on sheer instinct. The gravity of the situation weighed heavily on her – if Alan's condition worsened, she didn't know if she'd have the skills or strength to save him.

Alan stirred, his face pale and drawn, and asked for a pan. She brought one from the kitchen just in time for him to retch into it. He let out a groan, and Sarah led him to the bathroom, helping him back to bed afterward. His shaky hand reached out for her, requesting more Oramorph, co-codamol, and water, along with a fresh bandage for his wound. She complied, feeling a growing dread with every medication she administered. Who was she to handle this? And what experience did Alan have to be doling out potent drugs to himself?

After he drifted back into a fitful sleep, Sarah wandered to the small lounge area, staring blankly at the passing cars on Hotwell Road. She could only think of one thing to do: call Max. Her voice cracked as she launched into a frantic summary of the morning's events, only stopping to stifle sobs. She barely noticed when Max cut in, his calm, steady tone anchoring her like a lifeline.

"My dear Sarah," he said gently, with a hint of admiration, "you really are a saint among mortals." His voice held the same grounded warmth she'd come to rely on over the years. "Now listen closely: if you turn left as you exit the building, you'll find an express supermarket about half a mile to the right. Go stock up on tea bags and milk. I'll be there in about five hours. Rest assured – I'll make certain everything is under control."

Sarah lowered the phone, surprised by the wave of relief that washed over her. She hadn't mentioned the address; Max hadn't asked. Somehow, he already knew where Alan lived and the layout of the area down to the nearest shop. His quiet authority, his confident assumption of control, soothed her panic.

A Double Take

Bruce did a double take as Ciara entered the room. She looked completely transformed – not just from the change of clothes, though those were stylish and unfamiliar, but in every detail. Her makeup was flawless, her hair was gathered into a neat ponytail, and she radiated a happiness that brightened the entire room.

"Where on earth did you get the outfit?" he asked, raising an eyebrow.

Ciara grinned mischievously and slipped into her native, but exaggerated, Irish accent. "Ah, ye should never underestimate de resahlve o' de iresh, so ye shouldn't!" Then, switching back to the accent Bruce recognised as more American than Irish (or English for that matter), she added, "Now, get up, lazy bones! We need to get you to Edinburgh."

Bruce hesitated, still lying naked under the bedsheet.

She gave him a look of mock impatience. "I've already had the grand tour, Bruce, *and* I like what I see. Now hop in the shower while I get you some coffee and painkillers." With a dramatic flourish, she whisked the bedsheet away, tilted her head for a better look, and exited the room with an upbeat "Nice!"

Bruce lay on the bed for a few moments, his heart skipping a beat. It was a strange feeling, as if, in that one playful moment, he was falling in love for the very first time in his life.

Looking After Alan

Peter dragged himself out of bed, his first order of business – a few painkillers – now accomplished. He shuffled into the kitchen, where last night's unfinished dinner preparations lingered. The countertop was strewn with chopped vegetables, and an empty wine bottle sat nearby. A pang of guilt hit him; Sarah, his wife of nearly two decades, had finished the bottle alone.

In the lounge, a shattered wine glass glinted ominously from the carpet. Peter crouched down, brushing his fingers over the fragments, a silent testament to the cracks in their marriage, reflecting Sarah's frustration as clearly as her silence.

She wasn't in the spare room, and judging by the undisturbed bed, she hadn't been all night. Part of him wanted to call, but instead, he took the less confrontational route, tapping out a quick message:

Peter
Hi hon, I'm sorry about last night. I promise to make it up to you. Where are you? xxx

The house felt eerily still, and he was startled by how much he missed her. Moments later, his phone buzzed with a response:

Wifey
Alan has had an accident, so I'm looking after him. I need some time to think. Be in touch in a few days.

Peter slumped into an armchair, rereading the message. It felt off. Sarah never signed her texts without a kiss, and her tone was brisk, almost final. "Looking after Alan"? He opened the key drawer to confirm: Alan's spare key was still there. That was odd.

Something snapped within him. Enough was enough. Gripping Alan's key, Peter resolved to go to the apartment. If he caught them "at it," his own actions with Naomi would feel justified. But if he didn't... well, he'd end things with Naomi and fight to win Sarah back. Either way, he'd take control.

Pulling on his jacket, he set off with grim determination, ready to confront whatever awaited him.

Edinburgh Bound

Bruce stole another glance at Ciara in the passenger seat, still amazed at her transformation. She looked stunning, radiant in the outfit she'd somehow acquired, and he couldn't help but marvel at her poise and presence. He'd already thought it to himself – more than once – but she truly was breathtaking.

Catching his gaze, Ciara returned his smile and reached over, lightly trailing her nails along his thigh. He felt a thrill shoot through him as her voice dropped to a husky whisper. "I had such a great night, Bruce."

The sultry tone sent a pleasant shiver down his spine, and Ciara could tell from his reaction. Over the years, she'd perfected a range of voices to suit any occasion, an ability that was as natural to her as breathing. Her hometown accent was rough, even a bit jarring to outsiders – a fact she'd been well aware of growing up. When she'd worked in the lap-dancing club, she'd experimented with a more refined English accent, one she thought sounded "professional," especially useful as she worked her way up to managing the club.

But her time in the States had sharpened her skills. She'd refined an accent that was now 75% American with a lingering 25% Irish lilt, giving her a unique charm. And when the moment called for it, she could slip seamlessly into a posh English accent, effortlessly changing her voice like she'd change an outfit.

Bruce found himself fascinated – not just by her beauty but by the layers she wore like armour, each crafted accent and persona a testament to the life she'd lived. He realised that, beyond her allure, he admired her for her sheer adaptability and mystery.

In fact, Bruce had been less than stellar the previous night. He had been fast asleep when Ciara emerged naked from the shower and had proven almost impossible to wake up. Ciara realised she'd fed him too much wine, but it had all worked out in the end.

Now, they were cruising north on the M1 in the white Mercedes-Benz Atego, Ciara stealing glances at him from the passenger seat. Bruce looked relaxed, clearly enjoying the drive, though he kept a vigilant eye on the rear-view mirror. She noticed that he'd often glance her way, a quick, approving smile sneaking across his face. Ciara still couldn't quite believe her good fortune. Here he was, her unexpected white knight, sweeping in to offer her a new opportunity. He had no idea yet what this meant for her, but she planned to let him in on it when the time was right. For now, she was content to enjoy the ride north.

The calm was broken by Bruce's phone, the speakers blaring an incoming call. He checked the caller ID and glanced at Ciara. "It's my boss. I have to take this, but he mustn't know you're here."

Ciara flashed a playful grin. "No worries, baby," she purred, watching as his eyes lit up at the word "baby." He returned the smile, then answered the call.

"Hello, Rollie, how are you doing?"

"Bruce, you're running behind schedule," Rollie replied, his voice as composed as ever. "I just wanted to check that everything's in order?"

"Yes, sorry, Rollie. I stayed overnight at that place in Yorkshire and got a bit delayed. But I'm making good time now."

"Good, good, though I see you're still south of Newcastle. Will you make the rendezvous on time?"

Bruce's confidence shone through. "Yes, I'll be there, barring any unexpected delays."

There was a brief silence, then Rollie's voice softened, almost ominously. "Indeed, Bruce, barring any unexpected delays. Best to hope for none. Keep me posted if you'll be late; they'll be expecting you."

With a final, professional "Will do," Bruce ended the call.

As he set the phone down, Ciara raised an eyebrow, suppressing a grin. "Someone sounds… particular."

Bruce gave her a knowing look. "Rollie's big on precision. Makes things interesting."

Ciara chuckled, her voice a low purr. "Well, lucky for him, you've got me keeping you on track."

Ciara glanced over, her expression mildly curious. "How does your boss know where you are?"

Bruce hesitated, choosing his words carefully. "He's just... thorough. Likes to keep things on schedule. There's a tracker in the cab." He added, as if to explain it all, "He's a decent guy, but a worrier. And, well, he's quite old." Somehow, that seemed justification enough.

Ciara raised an eyebrow, undeterred. "So, you pick up cargo in Edinburgh, then drive straight back to Brighton? That's a lot of miles in one go."

Bruce tensed slightly, realising she'd caught him off guard. He hadn't mentioned Brighton today, which meant it must've come out last night after a bit too much wine. "Uh, yeah, it is. But I'm used to it."

She nodded, and after a moment added, "And Bristol – how often do you drive there?"

This threw him completely. When had he mentioned Bristol? Had he really been that loose-lipped? He forced a casual shrug. "Not often."

Just then, his phone rang again, and he gratefully glanced at the screen, spotting an unfamiliar number. Anything to escape her questions, even for a moment. "Hello?"

"Hi, Mr. Thompson, it's Karen from the Gargrave Hotel here! How are you?" Karen's cheery voice came through, too upbeat for the situation.

"Hi, Karen," Bruce replied, trying to sound equally breezy. "I'm fine, thank you, though I'm driving right now. Can I call you back when I pull over?"

"Of course, Mr. Thompson! Just wanted to inform you we've had some reports of, well, items going missing from one of our rooms. Just checking to ensure you're not missing anything yourself."

Bruce felt his stomach tighten. A stolen glance at Ciara showed her reclining her seat, eyes closed, as if she hadn't a care in the world.

"Thanks for letting me know, Karen. I'll check and give you a call later," he managed, his gaze flickering back to Ciara's serene expression.

Ending the call, Bruce looked ahead, a knot of unease forming. Beside him, Ciara's breathing was deep and even, a sly half-smile at the corner of her mouth.

A Brainstem Break

Peter knocked on Alan's door but received no response, so he used the key to let himself in. The silence was thick, unnerving, as he stepped inside and called out. There was no answer. But at the bottom of the stairs, a dark stain caught his eye – blood, thick and alarming. Peter blinked, convincing himself it must have been from an animal. But as he moved up the stairs, he found more of it, smeared and sprayed down the steps. He called out again, his voice a little weaker this time. Still no response. The growing sense of dread gripped him, yet he climbed onward.

Peering into the main bedroom, he found it empty but unmade. The "box room" bed was meticulously made – Sarah's touch unmistakable. Was it possible she and Alan had slept in the same bed last night? Her message had said Alan had an "accident," but the volume of blood felt ominous, surely more than just an accident. His mind raced.

A sudden knock on the front door startled him, cutting through his thoughts. Bracing himself, Peter went down and opened it. Two men stood on the threshold, both in light blue boilersuits, baseball caps shading their faces. The man in front held a clipboard; his companion, a heavy-looking holdall.

"Hello," Peter managed, trying to mask his nerves. The man with the clipboard looked up, his eyes cool and assessing.

"You must be Alan Johnson, is that correct?" the man asked.

Peter hesitated but decided to play along. Something felt wrong about this situation with Alan, and he was determined to find answers. "Yes, I'm Alan. How can I help you?"

The man nodded, glancing at his clipboard. "A Mrs. Sarah Kemp called us. Do you know her?"

"Yes, I do," Peter replied, intrigued but uneasy.

The man continued, "We're professional cleaners. Mrs. Kemp said there's a... mess to be cleaned up, something on the carpets. We specialise in blood removal. That correct, Mr. Johnson? Or may I call you Alan?"

Peter forced a smile. "Yes, please call me Alan. Come in." He looked at them carefully. "What are your names?"

"I'm Jamie, and this is Josh," the man said, gesturing to his partner with a broad smile. "Well, let's get started, shall we?"

As they entered, Jamie scanned the blood with an almost clinical detachment, shaking his head. "Oh dear, this is quite a mess, but we'll soon have it cleaned up" he said, looking Peter up and down. "And more upstairs?"

"Yes," Peter replied, guiding them up, even as he felt a chill spreading through him. Jamie and Josh exchanged a brief look – a shared, silent message that sent a jolt of alarm through Peter. Boffin the cat, also sensing an unease, silently made his escape through the cat flap.

As they ascended, Jamie muttered to Josh, "The old man said he'd be six feet tall, ex-military," just loud enough for Peter to catch. Josh moved directly behind Peter, one hand dipping into his holdall.

Peter led them into the lounge, questions piling up in his mind. "When did Mrs. Kemp call you? What exactly did she say?" he asked, trying to mask his rising anxiety as he turned to face them.

But he never saw the hammer until it was too late. A sudden, blinding pain tore through his skull as Josh brought the tool down with ruthless precision. The blow pierced his skull, shattered his temporal lobe, and split his medulla oblongata. Peter felt his body buckle forward, but he couldn't reach out to break the fall. He sensed the hard impact of the floor but was strangely numb.

From his place on the carpet, his vision blurring, Peter noted the carpet needed a deep clean. He thought fleetingly about mentioning it to Sarah. He tried to speak, but no words came out. His vision dimmed, and everything slipped into darkness.

Hit Delete

Rollie squinted down at his desk phone, feeling a strange irritation at the sight of the bewildering array of buttons. These days he constantly found himself defeated by the modern contraption's seemingly endless functions. He'd been told the phone was capable of handling video calls, but Rollie had neither the desire nor the inclination to figure out how to use that function. Squinting at the screen, he saw an unfamiliar 11-digit number flash and answered the call, albeit with more uncertainty than his usual self.

"Hello?" Rollie inquired, tentatively.

"It's done. Unfortunately, we had to hit the delete button," a voice emanated from the phone's speaker, it sounded flat.

Rollie felt a flicker of recognition. He understood "delete button" well enough; it was code, a last-resort action reserved for operations gone wrong. Still, his attention was snagged by the unfamiliar number. "Jamie? This silly phone doesn't recognise your number – think it's acting up."

An exasperated sigh sounded on the other end. "I'm using a burner, Dad. It's untraceable, no GPS or anything." Jamie's tone was sharp, as though he was explaining it for the hundredth time. His personal phone, his "alibi," was safely stashed back home with his wife.

"Why did you have to delete?" Rollie asked, as though the malfunctioning phone were already forgotten.

"Not now, Dad. I'll call you later." Jamie's voice was tight, frustrated, before the line went dead.

Rollie lingered, holding the receiver as if it might offer something more. This wasn't how things were meant to go; he preferred order, meticulous planning, and control. The "delete button" was meant as an emergency measure, a contingency almost never used. The unexpected weight of it lingered, stirring memories he'd worked hard to bury. His own life had been built on carefully measured risk, and he had taught

Jamie the same principles. Yet Jamie was colder, clinical – even with him.

Setting down the phone, Rollie exhaled. Jamie was efficient, if detached, but he sometimes wondered if he'd raised his son to be too distant, too quick to sever ties when things went wrong. His gaze drifted back to the blinking lights on the phone. Each button, no doubt, had some function he didn't care to understand.

Sunshine On Leith

Bruce guided the white lorry off the A1, a journey that had taken just over three hours since leaving the hotel. Their destination was drawing near. Bruce typically varied his routes to the port, but this time he opted for the quickest path. He had joined the M1 just east of Harrogate and navigated the long road north, skirting the eastern edges of Edinburgh's city centre. The A199 had seamlessly taken over from the A1, and now, he found himself on the familiar Salamander Road, a sure sign they were closing in.

Throughout most of the journey, Ciara had been sound asleep, oblivious to Bruce's infatuated glances in her direction as they wound through the far northeastern reaches of England, eventually crossing the border into Scotland.

Bruce dialled a number, the ring tone emanating from the speakers within the cab, it was answered promptly. "It's Bruce, I'll be there in ten."

"About time. See you then," a gruff Scottish voice responded, ending the call.

The noise of the call stirred Ciara awake. "Wow, that's beautiful," she exclaimed, pointing to the milky waters of the Firth of Forth. The calm, glistening waters mirrored the tranquillity of the day. Ciara could just about make out an island seemingly sitting proud but alone within the waters.

"It is," Bruce agreed, his tone softening. "Important too, a major shipping route here. That island was heavily armed during the second world war to keep enemy ships from sailing into Rosyth." He glanced over, realising he was slipping into explanations. Something about Ciara made him want to tell her everything.

"And we're heading to Forth Ports, right?" her tone innocent yet curious.

Bruce couldn't recall revealing that information to Ciara, but they were nearly there now, and she might have spotted a road sign. "Yes, once the lorry is loaded, we'll be back on the road."

Leith turned out to be quite different from Ciara's expectations. She had heard of its reputation of being rough and gritty, reinforced by the Irvine Welsh novels she'd read, but the Leith she saw today looked charming in the sunshine, and she understood why the Proclaimers had sung about the 'sunshine on Leith'. Old industrial buildings had been transformed into chic apartments, trendy bars, and hotels. One gleaming building, now a vertical distillery, stood as a proud contrast against the Firth.

As the lorry rumbled along Leith's cobbled streets and approached the port area, it seemed as if they were driving into the sea. However, Bruce skilfully manoeuvring the vehicle, skirting a dock basin that extended into the Firth. Finally, they reached a cluster of squat industrial units, lockups that had yet to succumb to the wave of modernisation. They pulled up outside an oversized garage with the number '9' painted on it. Beyond the garage lay the port's waters.

The garage door slowly creaked open and upward, revealing nothing of its dark interior. Bruce expertly turned the lorry and backed it into the darkness, carefully using his wing mirrors to ensure precise placement before turning off the engine. The garage door immediately began to descend.

Bruce turned to Ciara. "You need to stay in the lorry, please. It'll take about half an hour, and then we'll be back on the road. Is that alright?"

Ciara nodded her agreement, and Bruce jumped down from his seat.

The team at the lockup operated with precision and expertise. Bruce unlocked the rear of the lorry and was pleasantly surprised to be offered a cup of tea. His role from that point onward was straightforward: he had to wait for two green lights. The first light signalled that the frozen compartment had been properly filled, and the second confirmed that the remaining goods were correctly loaded into the lorry.

The team comprised of two individuals and a forklift truck. Clad in parka coats to shield themselves from the frigid storage conditions, they immediately began their tasks. One team member operated the forklift, skilfully lifting boxes from a pallet, while the other diligently arranged

112

the cargo inside the lorry's trailer. Once all the smaller boxes were securely stowed, the forklift driver joined his colleague inside the lorry to assist with the more time-consuming manual handling and re-arranging.

After this meticulous process was completed, Bruce received his first "OK" signal. Without delay, he hopped into the lorry's cab, sliding a false door over the frozen cargo, and securing it with three heavy-duty padlocks. Although not a flawless disguise, it would only be detectable upon close inspection.

The subsequent step aimed to ensure that an inspection would be avoided at all costs. The forklift truck roared back to life, its task now involving the movement of larger pallets into the trailer. These specific pallets housed the legitimate (and lawful) merchandise. In the event of a potential inspection, it would be these boxes and pallets that would be scrutinised, all within the chilly confines of the refrigerated trailer.

Bruce descended from the trailer but was taken aback to find that the forklift had fallen silent. He made his way to the front of the lorry, where he could observe Ciara conversing with the forklift driver. Her hips displayed a slight angularity, her head tilted to one side as she playfully twirled her hair with her forefinger, sharing a giggle with the forklift driver over something he had just said.

"Come on, we're ready for you," Bruce urged impatiently, his tone revealing his eagerness to hit the road. Ciara had ignored his instruction to remain inside the lorry's cab, and it appeared she was becoming overly friendly with the perspiring forklift driver.

Ciara turned to Bruce and said, "Hey, sweetheart, I was just chatting with Tim, and he mentioned he could get me across the Irish Sea."

"Tim?! Who the hell is Tim?" Bruce pondered, glaring at a smug-looking man in a parka who was smirking back at him. Rollie insisted no names were exchanged and up until now, everyone had adhered to that principle. Bruce pushed aside the urge to disable the man and continued, "I thought you were accompanying me on the road." He couldn't help but feel a pang of neediness, a sentiment he was disappointed to detect in himself.

"No, darling, I need to return home for something, and Tim," she turned and flashed a smile at the forklift driver, "said he could assist a girl without any ID." She then directed her gaze back at Bruce, her tone softening. "Hey, once I'm back home, I'll give you a call. When I have my passport in hand, I'll hop on a flight and meet you in Brighton, alright, baby?"

Bruce silently seethed at the mention of Brighton; that was supposed to be a well-kept secret. He glared at the forklift driver, steadfastly refusing to acknowledge him as 'Tim.' "Get on with it, I need to hit the road," Bruce demanded, his confidence in his ability to neutralise 'Tim' in under ten seconds simmering beneath the surface. The forklift driver simply nodded, wearing a knowing smile, and strolled back to the forklift truck.

Ciara presented a faux sad look. "I'll be fine, Tim says he knows a fisherman he works with sometimes, occasionally runs goods into Ireland from Glasgow. It'll cost some but I'll find a way and anyway, you'll move faster without me in the cab." Ciara moved in close and softly kissed Bruce's ear, she ran her hand down his chest, across his taut stomach and lower. She whispered, "I'll see you very soon baby, and we can pick up where we left off this morning."

Bruce melted. "Yeah alright, but let me know as soon as you have a phone number, OK?"

Ciara kissed him full on the lips, lingering, then whispered. "Of course. And thank you so much again."

With a wink, she called to the forklift driver as he started the vehicle's engine. "Come on Tim, let's get a move on. You can show me the sights of Edinburgh before I head west!"

Fish & Chips

Jamie Monroe was still cursing his son. "How the fuck could he bungle this so badly?" he inquired of his assistant. But Josh knew better than to offer an opinion, keeping his eyes down as Jamie paced, fuming. "I should have known better than to entrust this job to Kevin. Sending a boy to do a man's work." Jamie seethed. He'd assumed Kevin would bring a more competent team member with him, he assumed it would be good experience for his son, an opportunity to learn, he assumed he'd just wave the gun around and intimidate this Alan geezer. However, he'd been proven wrong on all counts. "Never assume, it makes an ass out of you and me!" Josh didn't reply, choosing to fumble around inside his holdall as if he'd not heard.

Now Jamie was left with a mess, one he hadn't planned for. Blood everywhere – a reminder Kevin's shot must have hit someone, just not his intended target. Those questions would have to wait, though. Recriminations were a luxury he couldn't afford right now. They had a job to finish.

The priority now was dealing with Alan's body. The cleanup was tedious and unforgiving, but Jamie couldn't leave any traces behind. He doused the area with hydrogen peroxide while Josh followed closely, pressing paper towels against the stains, erasing every last drop. Before long, both men were on their hands and knees, scrubbing with microfiber cloths, inch by inch. It was slow, monotonous work, but it had to be flawless.

Jamie grimaced, replaying his father's warning. According to Rollie, this Alan was dangerous, someone to approach with caution. Yet Alan had been a pushover, barely putting up a fight. Jamie's jaw tightened as he worked. His father was losing his touch if he really thought Alan had posed any kind of threat.

After a final wipe of the floor, Jamie straightened and stretched, eyeing the wrapped body in the corner. To reward their efforts, he decided he'd take Josh for a quick fish and chips break – a brief moment to regroup before returning under cover of darkness to remove Alan's body. Their plan was simple: the body, wrapped neatly in a carpet, would be carried out and stowed in the van, taken from the nondescript apartment at number 37, with no one the wiser.

Max Arrives

Sarah flinched at the knock on the door, startled by the break in the silence. Before she could raise herself from the sofa, she heard the door being unlocked and swinging open.

"Max! Boy, am I glad to see you!" She rushed over and warmly embraced Max Moore.

"My dear," Max said, his voice typically gentle, though he looked weary, "I'm sorry I took so long. I'd quite forgotten how troublesome it is finding a parking space in the centre of Bristol." Max owned a much bigger brother to Sarah's BMW, and she could understand why it might be difficult to find a space. "How are you holding up? And how's our patient?"

Sarah wanted to ask how Max had managed to let himself in but was equally certain that news of the 'patient' took precedence. "Alan is... well I'm not quite sure. I've changed his dressing five times already, and I've been administering morphine, but he's just... he's completely out of it. I'm really tired Max, and, honestly, I'm scared. Why won't he let me take him to A&E?"

Max could see the strain etched on her face and rested a hand on her shoulder. "My dear, try not to worry. A doctor is arriving at any moment now. He's a friend of the family and has worked with Rollie's son who lives in Bristol."

This was all becoming too much for Sarah to take in, "Rollie has a son in Bristol?"

Max gave a brief nod. "Yes, the younger brother to Jamie."

Just then, his phone buzzed. He answered quickly. "Yes? ... Alright, I'll be right down." Ending the call, he turned back to Sarah. "That's Dr. Crawley. I'll go let him in. Could you put the kettle on, please?" He gave her a reassuring nod, hoping to keep her focused on something simple for the moment.

Sarah watched him head toward the door, her mind still a tangle of questions and worry, but finally reassured by Max's presence, but as she moved to put the kettle on, her hands still shook.

Father Christmas

The pawnbroker, a man in his sixties with a thick, white beard that could have made him Santa in another life, greeted her with a nod and gestured her in. His English accent caught her off guard, but she stayed quiet. She produced the two watches from her bag, sliding them across the counter to him. His eyes narrowed as he examined them closely through a loupe, inspecting every detail with the patience of someone who had done this a thousand times before.

He gave a low chuckle, glancing up at her. "So… didn't go quite as planned, eh?"

Ciara stiffened, uncertain. "I'm sorry?"

He flipped one of the watches to reveal the inscription on the back. "Noticed the little love notes. Maybe the marriage didn't stand the test of time?"

Ciara offered a thin smile, saying nothing, her eyes giving nothing away.

"From Ireland, are you?" he asked casually, eyes back on the watches.

"Yes, the south," she replied shortly. "I need a cash-only deal. No paper trail."

The pawnbroker smirked, a flash of stained teeth peeking through his beard. "Alright, then. Five grand."

She tilted her head, unimpressed. "Are we playing games here, or are you serious?"

"Alright, alright," he replied, his tone settling. He looked back down, holding the ladies' Cartier up to the light. "This one's a beauty – Cartier. Likely goes for around forty-five grand retail. The gentleman's TAG Heuer? Nice piece. Twenty grand, maybe. But here's the thing, darling: they're stolen, they're inscribed, and that makes them risky, *and* difficult to offload. Eleven grand, cash, no questions. Take it or leave it."

Ciara held his gaze, pausing before deciding to push back. "The backplates are easy enough to replace. I'll take fifteen, and I'll be out of your hair."

119

He chuckled, shaking his head. "Thirteen, and I'll throw in five hundred more for that Bottega clutch you've got there."

Ciara considered it briefly, then nodded. "Deal. But I'll need a carrier bag for the cash."

The pawnbroker laughed, a deep, throaty sound. "No problem, I charge ten pence for those!" With a final chuckle, he turned to his safe, counting out her money with practiced hands.

Dr. Crawley

Dr. Crawley entered the room, his presence immediately drawing attention. In his early fifties, he radiated a calm but watchful intensity, the kind that only years of experience could cultivate. His neatly cropped salt-and-pepper hair framed a face that was both sharp and composed, and his steady gaze seemed to take in every detail in a single sweep. Tall and solidly built, with broad shoulders and a strong posture, he moved with the efficient, measured grace of someone well-accustomed to situations under pressure. Though dressed in civilian clothing – a well-tailored jacket over a dark shirt – his bearing was unmistakably military, a quiet edge that spoke of discipline and control.

After acknowledging Max and Sarah with a confident nod, Dr. Crawley made his way to Alan, his gaze briefly lingering on the improvised setup. With efficient, careful movements, he began to examine the gunshot wound, gently peeling back the dressing and gauze. Alan stirred under his touch, roused briefly but still barely coherent. Sarah passed Max a cup of tea, then set another beside the doctor on the side table.

Dr. Crawley looked up at her. "What medications have you been giving him?"

Sarah unlocked the battered blue suitcase, flipping it open to reveal a neatly arranged selection of vials and supplies. She lifted a vial with clear liquid. "This one – I think it's morphine."

The doctor's brow furrowed. "It is morphine," he confirmed, examining the contents of the case with an experienced eye. After a pause, he asked, "Was Alan with the Royal Army Medical Corps?"

"No, he wasn't," Max replied, casting a sidelong glance at Sarah. "Most of his service record remains a mystery, I'm afraid."

Dr. Crawley gave a thoughtful nod, evidently intrigued. "Interesting. These supplies are standard issue in the Corps." He glanced back at Max. "What rank did he hold?"

"Lieutenant Colonel," Max said.

121

The doctor's expression shifted, a mixture of respect and curiosity. "Impressive. I served as a Captain in the Medical Corps." He turned back to Sarah, his tone firm. "No more morphine – and definitely none of these." He held up another vial, identical to the one Sarah had shown him. "This is fentanyl, highly potent. Even a small misstep with this could be lethal."

Sarah's face tightened, but she nodded. She chose not to mention that she'd already given Alan a dose in the panic of their journey to Bristol.

Dr. Crawley returned to Alan, resting a steadying hand on his shoulder. "I'll do my best for you, sir. You have my respect for your service." He began the painstaking process of removing the bullet, his movements confident and precise. Although the makeshift environment lacked the sterility of a hospital, his military training had prepared him well for field conditions.

An hour later, the procedure was complete. Dr. Crawley had applied a local anaesthesia, sutured the wound and applied a fresh, secure dressing, his expression turning to one of quiet satisfaction. "No more morphine," he reiterated, locking eyes with Sarah. "Alan's fortunate – the bullet was a small calibre, missed the bone, and caused minimal damage. He should recover well." He placed a few pill bottles on the table. "Ibuprofen and paracetamol, only. I'll leave antibiotics, steroids, and anticoagulants – enough for a week. Max, if anything looks off, you know how to reach me."

He stood, closing his medical case, and took a sip from his now-cold tea, unbothered by the temperature. "I'll take my leave, with the assurance that Mr. Monroe will tend to my fees," he said, casting a final glance at Alan. "Ensure his dressing stays dry."

"Thank you, Doctor," Max said, his relief evident as he extended his hand.

Dr. Crawley gave it a firm shake before heading for the door. He paused and looked back, his voice softer but just as steady. "Take care of him – and yourselves."

Low Battery Warning

Max wasn't the only one relieved; Sarah was equally happy that Alan had finally received professional care. Max empathised with her emotion. "I'm going to step outside and call Rollie, I promised him an update. Then I'm going to buy you an Indian meal and a bottle of wine. There's an excellent curry house just a stone's throw away. Does that sound good to you?"

Sarah managed a weary smile, nodding gratefully. "That sounds perfect."

As Max headed out to the car park, Sarah felt the tension of the last day finally start to ebb. Her mind drifted, for the first time in almost 36 hours, to Peter. She'd messaged him late last night, as she always did, but she was still annoyed at his indifference, his lack of concern for where she was or what she was dealing with. She reached for her phone, only to see a "low battery" warning flash on the screen. There was nothing from Peter.

"Oh, forget it, Peter," she muttered, tossing the phone back onto the counter. "If you can't be bothered, then why should I?"

Plugging it into a charger in the kitchen area, she took a moment to breathe, then made her way to the bathroom. She brushed her hair and splashed her face, eager to feel refreshed before the dinner. For once, she allowed herself to look forward to the small comfort of a good meal and Max's steady company.

Summons

Jamie had barely stopped through the door when his father's call came through. He answered with a weary, "Yes, Dad."

"Son, I need you to come into the office please," Rollie's tone was more of a directive than a request.

Jamie suppressed a sigh. "Dad, honestly, it's been a long day, and I just want to unwind in front of the television." He tried to keep the frustration out of his voice – what could the old bastard want now?

"I'll expect you in half an hour, son." Rollie replied, leaving no room for negotiation before the line went dead.

He's Awake

Alan awoke with a start, his senses in disarray, struggling to focus on his surroundings. He drew a deep breath, the heavy curtains successfully held back the light on the brightest of days, but Alan could sense the shroud of night. Though shadows clung to the room, the city's nocturnal vehicle symphony betrayed his location, he was in his Bristol apartment. His parched mouth resembled a desert terrain. Beside him, a lone bottle of water beckoned, and as his fingers brushed its surface, a searing pain coursed through his left shoulder. Awareness dawned, he knew where he was, and he'd now been reminded of why he was here.

He called out, "SARAH? ARE YOU THERE?" Echoes of silence answered him, the apartment concealed its secrets, leaving only the relentless traffic as a witness. With caution, he extended his right hand toward the water, his left side immobile. Clenching the cap between his teeth, a few drops graced his bare chest. Even that felt refreshing. He almost drank the rest in one gulp but stopped himself short.

His right hand traversed his chest, fingers tracing the marks of a skilled healer's artistry. An unsettling thought emerged – had Sarah enlisted professional aid? Weary and wounded, he rested his head upon sweat-soaked pillows, yearning for respite with a cleansing shower.

Once more, Alan closed his eyes, this time transported to the sanctuary of his childhood bedroom. There, an Airfix Supermarine Spitfire dangled gracefully from the ceiling. A tapestry of memories adorned the walls: the Rolling Stones' poster dominating one side, a contemplative Debbie Harry, her hair cascading in noir hues, presiding over a formation of toy soldiers, lined up in single file. In a corner, a cot cradled a few-month-old bundle – his younger brother. Resentment once brewed, the curse of sibling rivalry, but time had woven their hearts together. Why had they drifted apart? What had torn them asunder?

Abruptly, Alan's eyes flickered open, a desperate need to banish the dream, to combat the surge of nausea which clung to him. He sat upright, inhaling deeply, struggling to shake the decades-old reverie, one of the many dreams he wished to never revisit.

Two Glasses of Laphroaig

When Max and Sarah returned to the apartment after their Indian meal, their first thoughts were to check in on Alan. "Oh man, look at that?" Sarah exclaimed, pointing at the blue case on the bed. Max didn't immediately grasp the situation, and Sarah noticed his confusion. "He's taken more morphine!"

Max chuckled, shaking his head. "Straying from the path of virtue, even in his sleep!" He tried to lighten the mood, but Sarah didn't see the funny side. She re-secured the blue case, scooped up the empty morphine vial, and brought it into the living area, with Max following closely, gently shutting the bedroom door behind him.

"We'll have to hide this case. I'll put it in my car later." Sarah said, her irritation with the patient evident.

Max continued to chuckle to himself. "Yes, that's a good idea. Alan is a mischievous so and so."

Sarah shot him a look. "It's hardly amusing, Max. He needs rest, not more morphine."

Max's expression softened. "You're right. But he's always had a knack for doing exactly the opposite of what he should. Let's get that case out of reach before he decides he's his own nurse again."

During dinner, the conversation revolved entirely around Peter, Sarah's husband. She shared her concerns about Peter's affair, expressed her sadness over their childlessness, vented frustrations about their home, and finally, revealed her annoyance with Peter's lack of communication. Max struggled to offer Sarah comfort regarding her marital problems; having never been married himself and rarely experiencing deep emotional relationships, he felt ill-equipped to help. All he could do was listen sympathetically, which left him increasingly uneasy.

When Sarah asked about the apartment in Bristol, Max had assured her that he would share the details once they returned, ensuring their discussion remained confidential. Although he was being overly cautious, he adopted a 'belt and braces' approach to the situation.

When Sarah inquired about Max's own relationships, he hesitated, baulking at the topic and choosing instead to divert the conversation to the bottle of Chablis they were sharing – a subject he felt much more comfortable discussing, he considered his personal life as a taboo.

They settled down in the living room, where Max reached into a high kitchen cupboard, one Sarah hadn't explored yet, and retrieved a bottle of whisky. "You don't mind peaty, do you?" He inquired. "Something to help us both unwind, after today."

Sarah smiled, recalling her father's whisky lessons from her teenage years. "I don't mind at all."

Max poured whisky into two glasses and set them down on the coffee table next to a well-worn chess set, then took a seat beside her. While Max wasn't obliged to divulge anything to Sarah, he felt a sense of indebtedness toward her. After all, she had been unwittingly drawn into the world of his affairs when she discovered and subsequently saved Alan. They sipped in a comfortable silence before Max spoke, his tone taking on a more personal note.

"Alan has a strong affinity with Bristol, borne from the time his parents relocated from Brighton when he was around six or seven years old. His father seized a job opportunity at one of the prominent banks in the city centre, located very close to here in fact. His parents couldn't afford to live this close to the city centre, so they settled in a quiet idyllic village in North Somerset, some ten miles or so south of here." He paused to take a sip, eyes distant with memories.

Sarah listened quietly, realizing she was beginning to see Alan through Max's perspective. She hadn't known much about Alan's past, or about Max's deep connection to him.

Then, shifting gears, Max continued, "As you know, Rollie is CEO of Exotic Food Imports. What you might not know," he paused, glancing at her, "is that I'm his personal legal counsel."

Sarah blinked, surprised. "I've seen you at Rollie's place, but I never realised... I thought you were always off defending some dropout or layabout."

Max raised an eyebrow, slightly amused by her bluntness. "My dear," he said, almost chiding, "those so-called 'dropouts' often have nowhere else to turn. Many of them are living on the fringes, trying to survive with limited means."

Sarah's face softened, and she nodded apologetically. "I see. I didn't mean to judge."

"No need to apologise, my dear," Max replied, a warmth in his tone. "While I do represent the less privileged members of society, mostly pro bono, my primary employer, in fact, the one who provides the bulk of my income, is Rollie. The company does have its own legal counsel, of course; I'm not a contract lawyer. However, I serve as the intermediary between Rollie and his legal team." Another pause for whisky. "I also handle Rollie's personal legal affairs."

Sarah took a sip of her whisky, feeling its warm embrace as it flowed through her body. Max paused, letting her take it all in, before continuing. "Exotic Food Imports runs operations out of both Brighton and Bristol. Jamie, his eldest, manages the Brighton branch. Rollie's second son, Nigel, is based here in Bristol and oversees operations here."

As he spoke, Sarah couldn't help but notice his calm, unhurried manner, the same composed energy Rollie had. It made her wonder if this steadiness was something Max had learned from years of loyalty to Rollie.

"When I'm in Bristol, I often stay here," Max went on, gesturing around the apartment. "I have my own key, even keep a few clothes in the wardrobe."

The thought made Sarah smile, realising how embedded Max was in both Alan's and Rollie's lives. "I thought the chess set was a dead giveaway that you spent time here."

Max smiled, taking another sip. "Alan bought this apartment when it was newly built, using a small inheritance. It's one of three properties he owns."

Sarah's eyebrows shot up. "Three? I knew he wasn't exactly strapped for cash, but I didn't realise…"

Max chuckled. "Yes, he owns this place, number '37', and a three-bedroom terrace house in Brighton, which he rents out. He owns them all outright."

Sarah tilted her head, curiosity getting the better of her. "So where do you sleep when you're both here?"

Max patted the sofa. "This sofa pulls out into a double bed. A very comfortable one, I might add." He gave her a mischievous look. "So, where have you been sleeping the past two nights?"

Sarah let out a chuckle, covering her slight embarrassment with her whisky glass, from which she took a large sip. "Ha! Yes, I've been sharing the bed with Alan. I figured it was safe since he's been off his head on morphine. I could have had a party in that room, and he wouldn't have known!"

Max laughed, but then, after a quiet moment, he looked at her with a thoughtful expression. "Alan is a complex man. I don't suppose you knew he was once married?"

Sarah looked up, startled. "Married? I had no idea."

Max hesitated, his voice growing softer. "It didn't last. He's never quite forgiven himself, or… fully moved on."

A look of sadness crossed her face. "Oh… so she's passed away?"

Max shook his head, his gaze distant. "No, no, she's still alive. They just… couldn't make it work. He's a solitary soul, Alan."

There was more in his tone, a story untold, but Max left it there. Sarah sensed it was a wound he wouldn't reopen tonight, and perhaps one she wouldn't fully understand. They lapsed into a companionable silence, the whisky warm in their hands, both of them drawn into the quiet mystery that was Alan.

Nice But Tim

Ciara had resolved not to let Tim know the value of her spoils from the pawnbroker. On the surface, Tim seemed nice enough, but Ciara knew his mind was more on her body than her intellect. Ciara saw this as an opportunity, not a drawback. It provided her with the leverage she needed to maximise the benefits of what would undoubtedly be a brief and temporary relationship.

Out of the bulky Parka coat Tim seemed to be in good shape, maybe about the same age as her, moderate good looks underneath his short dark hair, she was sure he'd usually be a hit in the nightclubs on a Saturday night. However, Ciara had no interest in giving up what Tim desired. Her primary objective was to secure his contact in Glasgow, a necessary step for to get back to her hometown. This wasn't going to be a social visit; it was a mission to gain access to her safe deposit box, which held her alter ego – a passport, credit cards, cash, and even a mobile phone containing numbers she didn't readily have access to, but which would prove crucial for her immediate future.

Ciara tucked the carrier bag tightly under her arm, brushing off Tim's questions about her pawnbroker transactions. She knew Edinburgh boasted a Harvey Nichols store, but rolled her eyes when Tim suggested taking the tram. Ciara did taxis, not trams. However, as the tram glided smoothly up Leith Walk toward St. Andrews Square, Ciara marvelled at the location's sheer convenience. Harvey Nichols practically beckoned from just a stone's throw away. Stepping off the tram, she found herself facing the grandeur of St. Andrews Square, with its statue – a tribute to the Scottish statesman Henry Dundas, not Admiral Nelson, as Tim wrongly guessed – held its proud stance at the square's centre. Across the road, the Royal Bank of Scotland's neoclassical building was a timeless backdrop, flanked by statues, including a warrior standing in poise next to his loyal horse. Ciara couldn't help but contemplate how long it would be before this architectural gem would succumb to the burgeoning wave of bars and restaurants.

Inside the store, she directed Tim to the bar on the fourth floor and asked him to order her a Bellini in thirty minutes, assuring him she'd pick up the bill. In truth, Ciara doubted she'd need all that time to accomplish her shopping spree but better to make sure her drink was fresh. In no time, she managed to secure three complete outfits, an assortment of lingerie, a chic handbag, with a matching purse, and a stylish travel bag. After swiftly downing her Bellini, Ciara asked Tim to keep an eye on her travel bag and to order another Bellini while she slipped away to buy some shoes.

Fifteen minutes later, she returned sporting flat patent leather Prada shoes and carrying a box containing a pair of Gucci trainers. She promptly settled the bar bill, slipped the trainers into her bag, polished off her Bellini, and turned to Tim with a sly smile. "Where to next?"

Having traversed St Andrews Square, she made a deliberate choice to continue their evening in a bar called the The Dome, captivated by the opulence and grandeur of the architecture, from the marble-floored entrance that led to the splendid atrium crowned by a magnificent dome. Enormous vases brimming with lilies infused the expansive space with a heady, captivating perfume. The setting was as much a feast for the eyes as the cocktail list was for the palate.

Ciara wasted no time ensuring that both she and Tim indulged in a rapid succession of four distinct cocktails each. Unbeknownst to Tim, she discreetly added some extra potent spirits to his drinks. Tim, drawn in by her infectious energy, was enchanted by her agility as she darted between her seat and the grand circular bar, effortlessly delivering the next cocktail before Tim had barely sipped half of his previous one.

Tim's conversation was painfully boring, and his constant use of the word "ken" at the end of sentences was becoming increasingly irritating, but Ciara remained focused on her ultimate goal, "eyes on the prize" she kept saying to herself.

When Tim inquired about their dinner choices, she ordered some oysters, intrigued by the menu's claim that they were native to the Firth of Forth. "Is that it?" Tim had asked, disappointed.

"Yes, I'm quite full, thanks," she replied with a smile.

Tim chose the next bar, leading them further down the majestic Georget Steet to a bar named Westside. This venue exuded a notably different vibe to The Dome. More intimate, nestled in a basement, the bar pulsated with contemporary, unfamiliar music. Towards the back, pool tables beckoned to patrons. While the cocktails here didn't quite match up to the previous establishment, they were cheaper.

Ciara continued to lace Tim's drinks until he found himself resting his head on the bar. Seizing the moment, she ordered an Uber using Tim's phone, where his home address was conveniently pre-stored.

She was surprised at how far out of the city centre the Uber carried them. It felt like she had been transported to a completely different Edinburgh, far removed from George Street.

Tim's apartment was equally distinct. His ground-floor apartment was situated within a building that bore the unmistakable aesthetic of a 1970s prefab structure. As they stepped inside, it became evident that Tim hadn't planned for company; the place was unkempt, almost neglected.

She found some cheap vodka and fed, an already compromised, Tim some more. From this point, she was strictly water only.

She helped him stumble to his bed, having first stripped him naked. She slipped out of her clothes, down to her underwear. That's as much as Tim was going to get out of her, but it didn't matter – by now he was unconscious. In the morning, she could spin him whatever story she liked, and he'd have no memory to dispute it.

Mistaken Identity

August swung open the grand front door of the Withdean Road mansion, gesturing for Jamie to enter and head straight to the office. Jamie frequently pondered the origins of his father's remarkable security personnel. August, hailing from Greece, possessed only a rudimentary command of English. His striking shock of blond hair and meticulously chiselled features were complemented by the obligatory black suit, leaving an indelible impression as yet another extraordinary figure seemingly unearthed from the depths of obscurity.

Inside, Rollie was already settled at his desk, seated comfortably in his Chesterfield chair, his attention fixed on the laptop before him. Jamie was relieved there'd be no waiting this time. Sighing, he slouched into the chair across from his father. "It's late, Dad. Can we just get on with it."

Rollie glanced up from the laptop, arching an eyebrow. "Good evening, James. You seem rather… impatient."

Jamie stifled an eye roll. "It's been a long day, Dad. Can we skip the pleasantries?"

Rollie ignored the jab, leaning back in his chair. "As you know, I celebrated my 84th birthday last week. I won't be around forever, son. I've even surpassed the age of the oldest US President now, even they don't go on for as long as I have. I need to pass the reins to someone I can trust, someone who I know is up to the task. That person needs to be a pedagogue, not a dictator."

Jamie simmered with irritation. "I'm tired, Dad. It's been a long day." Rollie's lack of focus grated on Jamie's nerves. "And why can't you just call me Jamie, Dad?"

Rollie raised his eyes from the laptop once more and languidly reclined into his oversized leather chair, causing it to flex backwards. "You were christened James, son." Rollie replied, detecting his son's impatience. "Now, please, tell me what happened at Colonel Alan's."

Jamie let out an audible sigh, mentally preparing himself to give the bare minimum. "What's there to say? I brought Josh along. Colonel Alan opened the door, clearly injured. We finished the job, cleaned up, rolled him up in an old carpet, and disposed of the body. Then I went home for dinner, which you interrupted."

"What kind of injury did he have?" Rollie's patience remained steadfast.

"He'd been shot, Dad. What do you think his injury was?" Jamie's patience was wearing thin.

"Did you personally see the gunshot wound?"

Jamie began to suspect that his father possessed information he didn't. "I don't know, Dad. Believe it or not, I didn't perform a post-mortem. Do you want me to fish him out of the English Channel and find out for you?" Weariness had consumed Jamie, and he had had enough of this exchange.

Rollie's voice remained calm but firm. "My instructions were clear: you were only to warn Colonel Alan, not to kill him."

Jamie interrupted, defensive. "I know, Dad. That was Kevin's doing. He got carried away – I'll deal with him. There's no real damage done."

But Rollie's tone turned sharper. "Everyone makes mistakes, that's why they put erasers on the end of pencils, but James, I entrusted you with the job, and you delegated it. You need to take responsibility for that."

Jamie recognised the futility of arguing but replied with more impatience. "Fine, Dad. I understand, whatever you say."

"Did you retrieve the gun?" Rollie asked, still holding his son's gaze.

"No. We looked everywhere, but it was gone. My guess is that Kevin picked it up without realising it." Jamie waited, hoping this answer would satisfy him. Rollie just sighed, shaking his head, but then gestured for Jamie to come around the desk.

"I need to show you something." He motioned toward the laptop.

Reluctantly, Jamie walked around the desk and stood behind his father, leaning over his shoulder. "What am I looking at?"

His father wriggled the cordless mouse, trying to start the only application on the screen but the mouse pointer was running too quickly for his coordination. "Let me do it," more impatience from Jamie. He started the application and could immediately see a blurry black and white figure falling through what appeared to be the bay window at the far end of the office. "What am I looking at?"

Rollie responded, "That's a security camera I've had hidden on that shelf for years. It's not connected to the main system." He pointed to a high shelf on his right.

"How crafty," Jamie thought aloud. "Judging by the quality of the picture, it's been up there since 1980. I can't make out any details."

"Just keep watching, son." Rollie urged, still exuding patience.

Jamie continued to watch. The shadowy figure had vanished, and soon Jamie could unmistakably identify his Uncle Harry entering the frame. Harry walked over to the trophy cabinet and broke open the darts trophy. "Cheeky bastard!" He found it amusing as the scene played out, showing the shadowy figure exiting the window with his holdall. "So, what am I supposed to gather from this?" Jamie asked, shifting his gaze from screen to the actual bay window. "Hang on a moment." He took the long walk to the window and examined the frame. "I see." The figure exiting the window in the video was indistinguishable, but noticeably taller than the Alan they'd removed in the carpet.

Returning to the office chair, Jamie sat down and stated firmly, "That's a different person."

"No, it's not," Rollie replied. "Colonel Alan is in Bristol, nursing a gunshot wound to his shoulder. Max and Sarah are with him. So, tell me, son – exactly who did you dispose of?"

Jamie's face registered a flicker of shock. "I don't know, Dad."

Rollie nodded, his expression as unreadable as ever. "Neither do I."

To Kiss or Not…

Silently, Sarah slipped into the bedroom, her every move calculated to avoid waking Alan. His rhythmic breathing reassured her that he was sound sleep. Gently, she pulled back the duvet and nestled beside him in the bed. Alan lay with his back to her, carefully positioning himself to avoid any pressure on his left shoulder.

With a heavy heart, Sarah reached for her recharged phone, the absence of a message from Peter weighing on her. She began typing:

Wifey

I'll give you a call tomorrow. We need to talk. I hope you're OK. X

She hesitated before adding the kiss, but the reality of her crumbling marriage made it easier to include. The kiss no longer represented an affirmation of their love, it had transformed into a wish for Peter's well-being.

Sarah lay there, her gaze fixed on Alan's bare back. She had thought that a combination of wine, whisky, and a hearty meal would ensure restful sleep, but she had been wrong. With four fingers, she gently traced the contours of his rhomboid muscles, surprised when Alan stirred. She had assumed he was deeply under the influence of painkillers.

"That's nice," he murmured, his voice a soft whisper.

"I thought you were asleep," Sarah replied, a smile tugging at her lips.

"I will be again in a moment. You managed to get me a doctor?" Alan inquired, his eyes still closed.

"Yes. He said you were very lucky. The bullet was low calibre, and you'll heal just fine. He wasn't thrilled about all the self-medication you've been doing, though."

"I was lucky it was only a .22 calibre! I'm not sure being shot in your own home counts as lucky. Which reminds me, what did you do with the gun?" Alan asked, his tone casual.

"It's in Max's car," Sarah responded.

"OK, good. Well, the doctor did a fantastic job on my scapula," Alan observed. Sarah could sense he was fading back into slumber.

"Scapula! Listen to you, acting like a medical expert! Just stop taking the bloody morphine, Alan. What makes you think you're such an authority on these things?" Sarah teased lightly, but the conversation faded as he drifted into deeper slumber. Not long after, Sarah surrendered to sleep as well, the weight of the day finally pulling her under.

Laurence Olivier

Ciara had an early shower; it would have been even earlier if she hadn't spent so much time locating a clean towel. She dressed in new clothes – jeans and a sweatshirt – chosen specifically to cover as much flesh as possible, she wanted no distractions and as little attention as possible. The jeans were still designer, of course. It took her a while to rouse Tim from his drink-addled slumber, but when she did, she complimented his "incredible performance" from the previous night. However, no, there was not time for a repeat performance, she was already showered and dressed. Yes, she promised to look him up again, who wouldn't want another night with such a "super stud," like him?

She handed Tim a bottle of water infused with a strawberry-flavoured electrolyte replacement tablet, assuring him it would help invigorate him for the upcoming drive across Scotland. The promise of a full Scottish breakfast ultimately provided the motivation Tim needed to get out of bed and embark on the journey.

Traffic on the M9 was more congested than usual, stretching a routine drive to Ardrossan into a nearly two-hour ordeal. Ciara could have tolerated the delays more if Tim hadn't talked about himself incessantly. She was certain his ambitions would never be realised but maintained a façade of impressed and encouraging responses. His monotonous self-absorption was becoming increasingly tiresome.

As they entered the small town, she spotted castle ruins perched atop a hill. They followed the signs to the ferry terminal in search of the harbour. The fishing boat was already docked and appeared to be ready to sail. Tim spoke to the captain for about five minutes before summoning her from the car. The captain demanded £5,000 for the crossing, and without hesitation, Ciara handed over the cash, leaving Tim momentarily speechless. The captain was suitably impressed. She kissed Tim on the cheek and told her he'd see her soon. Despite Tim's protests, it was too late, as she followed the fishing captain over to his boat.

"It's mah boat and ye'll do as I say lassie!" That was Ciara's best guess of what the captain grumbled. The instruction was fine with her, what she knew about driving a boat wouldn't fill the back of a postage stamp, she was fine to keep out of his way. He led her onto the deck of the 60-foot *Laurence Olivier* and pointed her toward the cabin. The captain himself couldn't have looked or sounded any more different to the popular mid-20th century actor.

He sported a vibrant yellow sou'wester on his head, and his face was framed by a long, wild beard that looked as though it had weathered as many storms as he had. At first glance, Ciara would have guessed his age to be around sixty, but upon a more careful observation, it was evident he was much younger, a testament to the toll a life at sea can take. The stereotypical look of a seasoned fishing captain had momentarily misled her.

He regarded her with an unusual intensity, prompting her to draw her coat tighter around herself. "I've no interest in what lies beneath that coat any more than you would in another lassie," he asserted dryly, accepting her instinctive need for privacy. She nodded, appreciating the unspoken understanding.

Inside, the cabin offered two battered chairs, one of which she used for her travel case, the other for her backside. "Dinnae move," the captain commanded.

The boat stank of fish and diesel fumes, and the day seemed to be fading into a dull dark grey hue much faster than Ciara would expect. Disorientated, she found it difficult to distinguish shapes on the shoreline. As she squinted, trying to discern the shoreline through the mist, the fishing captain chuckled. "You won't see much through the mizzle – that's the North Atlantic drift ye're lookin' through." The term 'mizzle' was new to her, and she knew even less about the North Atlantic Drift, but she nodded anyway, keeping the conversation amiable. She had no reason to irritate the man steering her across the choppy seas.

The captain navigated the *Olivier* out through the Firth of Clyde and into the Irish Sea, where there was little other maritime traffic, she guessed it was getting too late to set sail. Unbeknownst to Ciara, the Firth of Clyde boasted one of the deepest sea-entrance channels in Northern Europe, capable of accommodating even the largest 'capesize' vessels and super tankers. The captain of the *Olivier* possessed the skill to navigate this intricate waterway, carefully charting a specific course out of the river Clyde to evade any unwarranted attention.

As they proceeded. the mainland to their left and the Isle of Arran on their right, the sea became increasingly turbulent. Ciara gripped the bolted-down chair, grateful for its stability as the boat lurched to the rhythm of the waves. The cold, damp air mingled with the smell of fish and fuel, and her initial adrenaline gave way to fatigue and nausea.

Seemingly hours later, Ciara found herself on the edge of a catatonic state, struggling to shut out the unpleasant smells and unpredictable motions of the boat. "How long to go?" she eventually shouted over the roar of the diesel engines. They had actually been sailing for three hours, she had totally lost track of time. She felt queasy, exhausted, and her backside hurt.

"As long as it takes, lassie!" the captain bellowed from the wheel. He remained as steady and unflinching as the vessel itself, seemingly impervious to the noise, the smell, and the darkness that had swallowed their path.

Eventually, and without warning, he raised his arm and pointed ahead. "That's the Isle of Man!" he shouted, his pride evident even in the dark. She strained to see, but through the pitch-black outside, she could barely discern a shape.

"Aye!" she responded with feigned confidence, hoping her acknowledgment was sufficient.

"Starboard in forty minutes," he called back. True to his word, forty minutes later he made a sharp right, revealing the rugged but beautiful coastline as it emerged from the shadows. Half an hour later, they finally docked at a small pier in Ballyhornan Bay.

Finally, Ciara stumbled onto solid ground, taking a moment to reorient herself. The familiar landscape gave her a surge of relief; she knew she was only about eight miles from town. The captain offered a terse nod as he climbed back aboard the *Olivier*, presumably preparing to head back across the Irish Sea, frankly Ciara didn't care what plans he had. Watching him disappear into the night, she felt a fleeting moment of gratitude for his skill and discretion, but more than anything she was pleased to be off his boat. She could now turn her focus toward the next steps of her mission.

The Sardine Tin

Alan's attempts to rise from bed stirred Sarah awake. He gave a quiet apology, his voice strained as he struggled to steady himself. Sarah pulled the duvet up to her chin, stifling a smile at his wobbling. "It's nothing I haven't seen already," he muttered, a slight grin playing on his lips.

"You haven't seen mine!" she teased, but Alan, focused on reaching the door, merely chuckled before slipping out of the room. She watched him, noting his unsteady movements with concern.

"Are you feeling any better?" she asked, sitting up. "Want a hand?"

"No, I've got it, thanks," he replied, closing the door a bit harder than intended. She winced, certain the impact had nearly knocked him over.

Sarah got out of bed and quickly found a pair of shorts and a T-shirt in the wardrobe. In the narrow hallway, she heard the bathroom door click shut, so she headed for the kitchen to make coffee. There, she found Max at the sink, his usual flair dulled slightly by his Hawaiian-print boxers and white socks. He turned as she entered, his beer belly jutting comically in her direction.

"Was that Alan up already? I'll get the coffee going," Max said, seemingly oblivious to his dishevelled state.

"Please do. And Max? Some clothes wouldn't hurt!" Sarah rolled her eyes, grinning.

"Oh, pardon me, dear!" he laughed. "Imagine, the mighty Kallos meeting Silenus himself at the crack of dawn, brewing coffee in boxer shorts!"

"If you say so," she replied dryly, shaking her head, she had no idea what he was talking about. She moved away to give him a moment to dress, pulling out her phone to check her messages. Still nothing from Peter. Worse, her message from last night remained undelivered. A feeling of unease crept in as she tapped his number, but it went straight to voicemail. "Please call me, Peter," she murmured before hanging up.

The morning dragged on, filled with quiet conversation and more coffee than any of them likely needed. Alan, looking pale but stubbornly resolute, was settled back on the bed by midday. Sarah had changed the bedding and arranged the sheets neatly beneath him, transforming the bed into a makeshift meeting spot. Max declared he needed to head back to Brighton for urgent business with Rollie, and Sarah shared her own plan to return as well, hoping to sort things with Peter, but also to tend to her own business.

Alan gave a nod of relief. Having three people in his small flat had felt a bit like living in a sardine tin, and he assured them he would manage on his own. He even promised to keep his diet sensible and stay off the morphine – or worse. They agreed to take Max's car for the journey, planning to return by Friday afternoon. Alan mentioned he'd book a table at the local Indian restaurant, eager to treat them to a meal on their return.

As they left, he saw them to the door with a wave and a smile, watching until the car disappeared down the street. Then, his hand slipped into his pocket, pulling out a vial of morphine he had discreetly lifted from Sarah's bag. He swallowed it quickly, leaning back onto the bed and feeling the familiar warmth take over, pulling him gently into much-needed sleep.

Ballyhornan Bay

Ciara trudged up the narrow, gravel-strewn path from the dock, her limbs leaden from the bone-chilling boat ride across the Irish Sea, dragging her case behind her. After hours of relentless, choppy waves, even the sight of the small bed and breakfast near Ballyhornan Bay felt like a haven. The place was simple but clean, with a warm light glowing through the curtains, and she felt the tug of sleep as soon as she saw it.

She paid in cash, thanked the innkeeper, and politely declined the offer of a meal, too drained to even think of food. The room was modest, with creaky floorboards and faded wallpaper, but she felt a strange sense of comfort in its anonymity. Collapsing onto the bed, she let exhaustion pull her under almost immediately.

It had been only five days since she was sprinting through crowded London streets, every step shadowed by the fear that she'd miscalculated her safety there. London, bustling and impersonal, had seemed like a place she could disappear in – but her pursuers had reminded her how fragile that illusion was.

Now she was in the quieter, windswept edges of eastern Ireland, as anonymous as she could hope to be. Tomorrow carried its own unknowns; there was the lingering threat they might have traced her safe deposit box, but she clung to the hope of staying one step ahead.

Although she couldn't relax fully until she'd successfully visited her deposit box, for tonight, her only goal was some rest.

Tomorrow, she'd start fresh and early, mentally laying out the new strategies she would need to stay safe and stay hidden.

Shower Gel

Max pulled up outside Sarah's home, the rumble of his BMW idling as he waited to see her safely inside. With a small wave, she closed the door behind her, listening as the car's engine faded into the distance. The house was silent, yet an unsettling feeling hung in the air.

Sarah moved quickly through the downstairs rooms, casting a careful eye over everything. Nothing seemed disturbed. She then climbed the stairs and checked both bedrooms and the bathroom. The familiar signs of Peter were scattered around: his half-empty shower gel sat on the side, never quite making it back to the basket, and a trail of clothes lay tossed across the bedroom floor. Typical Peter. And yet, something felt off. She had the uneasy sense that he hadn't been home for several nights.

The second bedroom was exactly as she'd left it, the bed made up and untouched. She crossed to the window, peering out at the street below, half-expecting to spot Peter's distinctive, orange-liveried VW Golf. But the spot where he usually parked was empty.

Growing more anxious, Sarah called him again, her stomach knotting as the phone went straight to voicemail. She left a message, her voice tense and edged with exasperation. "Peter, I can only assume you're staying with Naomi. Will you please have the decency to call or message me? Thank you." She sighed, noting that her previous message, sent almost a full day ago, was still showing a single blue tick.

There was nothing more she could do tonight. Tomorrow, she had work lined up – one of Rollie's scheduled house cleaning days. It wasn't how she'd planned to spend the day, but at least it would keep her busy. She resolved that if Peter hadn't called her by then, she would go straight to his office and confront both him and Naomi. The thought fuelled her, pushing back the creeping sadness with a simmering resolve.

Krug & Canapés

Ciara picked up two business cards from the B&B's tiny reception desk, scanning them for local taxi numbers. She hit the jackpot with her first choice; the driver would be ready to pick her up in ten minutes. Though she couldn't access her deposit box until the bank's 10 a.m. opening, she was determined to leave the B&B well before any morning small talk might start. Showering early, she changed into yesterday's "safe and discreet" outfit and quietly slipped out just after 8 a.m., bypassing the clinking breakfast sounds from the dining area.

The twenty-minute ride to Downpatrick was blissfully silent, with a driver who kept his thoughts to himself. Ciara welcomed the peace. In Downpatrick, she found a coffee shop on Market Street almost directly across from Ulster Bank and claimed a window seat. She pulled out a pen and paper she'd taken from the B&B, setting her mind to work.

Over the next hour and a half, Ciara meticulously transcribed everything she had recently uncovered. She began with what Bruce had told her, delving into the logistics and inner workings of the operation, each detail significant. Then she moved on to Tim's unwitting contributions; he hadn't given away much directly, but his offhand remarks had painted a clear picture of the operation's scope and hinted at key departure points. His casual talk might prove to be the most valuable piece of the puzzle.

Ciara was toying with the idea of a second Danish – they were excellent – when she noticed a couple exiting the bank across the street. She hadn't realised it had opened. "No rush," she thought with a faint smile. Today, for once, she had time.

Inside the bank, however, accessing her safe deposit box required a small hurdle. After answering a series of security questions and supplying two separate passcodes, she finally retrieved what she needed: two credit cards, her passport, a thick stack of Euros, and a mobile phone. A surge of control washed over her; Ciara had never struggled with confidence, but holding these items felt like regaining something personal, something powerful.

From a nearby shop, she picked up two pay-as-you-go phones for backup, along with a more professional notebook to organise her thoughts and notes. Then, after a quick visit to the town's solitary taxi rank, she set off for the Ballynoe Resort & Spa.

An hour later, Ciara found herself stretched across an indulgent bed, flipping through the resort's glossy pamphlet of spa treatments. She'd booked a full week – an extravagant move that felt deliciously self-indulgent. But this time wasn't just for rest; it was for resetting, planning, and savouring a taste of freedom she hadn't felt in years.

Staring up at the ceiling, she ran her calculations once more, drawing on the pieces she had gathered from Bruce and Tim. The numbers didn't seem real. The number of pallets on the lorry, bricks per pallet, shipments per year – her calculations hinted at an annual revenue stream close to £180 million. Could that really be true? Even when she factored in substantial operating costs, she estimated a possible profit near £90 million. She blinked, stunned, the magnitude sinking in.

"THIS IS HUGE!" she exclaimed to her empty suite, the sound bouncing back with a sharp echo.

There was still so much she didn't know. How did the distribution routes from Bristol and Brighton work? Why didn't they utilise Edinburgh for distribution? What were the safeguards that kept the operation under the radar of both the authorities and their rivals? And then, the money laundering process: was it being funnelled through legitimate businesses in addition to the food distribution company or obscured in some other way? For now, though, those questions could wait.

Ciara picked up the phone by her bedside. "Yes, I'd like to book a full-body massage, please. Then, could I reserve exclusive use of a hot tub, and could you bring a bottle of Krug with your seafood canapés? That sounds perfect," she said, a broad grin lighting her face as she hung up.

I Can't Stand the Rain

Sarah almost forgot that she'd left her car in Bristol. The hassle of parking two cars in the congested road was a constant annoyance, but now she found herself with none. Fortunately, her Uber ride was en route and wouldn't take too long, ensuring she'd still make it to Rollie's at the appointed time. Rollie had always been understanding about punctuality, as long as she eventually showed up during the day.

Raindrops tapped gently on the windowpane, a sound that had become synonymous with being at home, a rather disheartening association and a somewhat cheap metaphor. She snatched her coat from the hook and reached for keys in their designated drawer. She plucked Rollie's key from the drawer, but it was the conspicuous absence of Alan's key that caught her eye, leaving her perplexed.

Her phone chimed, alerting her to the Uber's arrival. She shut the drawer with a quiet sigh, pocketed Rollie's key, and ventured out into the rain-soaked world beyond. As she stepped outside, the cool drizzle met her face, grounding her for a moment. There was so much hanging in the air – unfinished conversations, missed messages, and an odd, hollow silence that seemed to follow her now, even in the rain.

The Key to #37

Max had finally concluded his lengthy meeting with Rollie, a session that had stretched well beyond two hours yet yielded only two pages of scribbled notes in his small notepad. As usual, a significant portion of their time had been consumed by Rollie's impassioned tales about his garden allotment and his relentless war with the local fox population. Max, with his limited knowledge of horticultural matters, had little to contribute.

As he made his way through the ante room and into the hallway, just steps from the front door, Sarah seized his arm, her expression anxious. "Alan's key is missing from the drawer!" she exclaimed.

"I'm sorry?" Max replied, baffled by her alarmed tone.

Sarah reiterated with urgency, "The key to Alan's place – number 37 – it's vanished from my work key drawer. Do you have a spare?"

Max hesitated, still trying to make sense of her concern. "Yes, I have a key," he admitted, sensing there was more to the issue than he understood.

"Can you come to my place as soon as possible?" she asked, practically pleading.

"I'll be there in about an hour," Max promised, as a new tension settled over him. He wasn't sure why Alan's missing key mattered so urgently, but he had a feeling he was about to find out.

The Fauxpology

Alan cherished the solitude of his apartment, a sanctuary against the outside world. The steady hum of traffic had long since faded into white noise, part of the background tapestry of his life. Earlier, he'd managed a simple cheese on toast, carefully favouring his right hand to spare his injured shoulder. Now, he was savouring a freshly delivered pepperoni pizza, generously tipping the delivery person to bring it straight to his coffee table. In the background, the television murmured with an afternoon quiz show, barely audible, setting a relaxed tone.

Max had thoughtfully left a bottle of whisky on the table – a temptation Alan intended to indulge; despite knowing it didn't play well with his medication. He trusted himself to enjoy it responsibly. For a brief moment, he'd nearly forgotten his phone, which had been charging overnight in the kitchen. When he finally powered it on, he saw no messages – not that he'd expected any. Aside from Max, Alan rarely spoke to anyone and was used to weeks of silence.

He was halfway through his pizza when his phone suddenly vibrated, startling him out of his reverie. Seeing Harry's name on the screen, Alan let out a weary sigh, then reluctantly tapped the answer button and switched to speakerphone.

"Alan, mate! How's the shoulder?" Harry's voice crackled through the line, his tone coarse from years of chain-smoking, the word "mate" hitting a particularly raw nerve.

Alan's patience wore thin. "Why the concern, Harry? Thinking about sending someone to finish the job?"

"Come on now, don't be like that, mate," Harry replied, attempted to sound affable. "I'll admit to sending those kids as a warning, but listen, mate, I had no choice. And I picked a group least likely to pose a threat. I was right; they couldn't even get close to a pro like you!"

Alan remained unconvinced. "They came at me with knives."

"Yeah, but they were clumsy with those knives. As I said, they never stood a chance against a pro like you, mate. Anyway, about that shooting

– it was a colossal mistake, but not my doing. I didn't instigate it, so not my fault, no point blaming me for that. I'm calling on behalf of the Monroe family to apologise. Can we make amends?"

"No, Harry, we can't. I could have been killed! It was a bloody close call!"

Harry sighed. "Look, two things. First, when you're back in Brighton, I'll make sure you're compensated for the injury. Second, my nephew Nigel's in Bristol, and he wants to apologise on behalf of Rollie – my brother's mess, not mine."

"You want me to meet your nephew?" Alan's voice was laced with scepticism.

"Exactly, mate. As part of making amends. Plus, he'd like to take the gun back. It's quite valuable. That solicitor bloke, Max, has all the details; he'll arrange everything and drive you over to meet Nigel next week. Does that work for you?"

"No, Harry, this does NOT work for me!"

Harry's tone turned dismissive. "Talk it over with Max when he's down in Bristol tomorrow. Don't make a fuss, Alan, stop being a pork chop. Accept the apology and move on. These things happen. See you back in Brighton soon. And take care of that shoulder, yeah? I've got some work lined up for you."

Before Alan could respond, the line went dead. Seething, he poured himself a generous measure of whisky, ready to drown the bitter taste of Harry's so-called apology.

Naomi Knocks

Sarah stood once more in her kitchen; eyes fixed on the bleak garden outside. She hadn't found the time to plant out her pots this year and obviously the useless Peter wasn't going to bother. Too interested in his little floozy, she thought bitterly. She watched the rain cascading upon the sombre courtyard, hues drained, and puddles danced upon the ashen paving. A cold draft whispered through the slightly ajar window, a stark contrast to the earlier warmth that had embraced the room before the rain arrived. Watching the rain, Sarah almost wished it would swell into a river she could skate away on, leaving all this behind.

She glanced at her phone; the message she'd sent to Peter was still marked undelivered. His phone went straight to voicemail, as it had for days. There was no point in trying again; another message would only sit in the queue, unanswered like the first. Three days of silence now – a solitary, waiting vigil.

An almost overpowering urge flared within her to storm into Peter's office, to confront him – or better yet, them. But she forced herself to wait for Max. The missing key to number 37 must be with Peter, she reasoned; he was the only other person who had access to it. Why he'd taken it, though, she couldn't fathom. Was he following her somehow? The thought seemed absurd, but in this twisting uncertainty, almost anything felt possible.

The doorbell's sudden chime jolted Sarah from her restless thoughts. She shook herself, recognising the need to snap out of her melancholy. But as she opened the door, her breath caught – standing there wasn't Max but Naomi.

"What the fuck do you want?" Sarah practically spat, her resentment flaring into sharp, biting words.

Naomi flinched, her confidence visibly crumbling. "I – I'm looking for Peter…" she stammered, intimidated by the force of Sarah's glare.

"Oh, I'd suggest checking your own bed," Sarah retorted coldly, venom lacing her voice.

Naomi cowered on the doorstep, her initial resolve unravelling. "Look, you've got it wrong… about us, I mean. I haven't seen Peter since the weekend, when we worked on that presentation together. We were supposed to deliver it today, but he never showed up. Please, Sarah," she added, desperation creeping into her tone, "do you know where he is?"

A flicker of uncertainty broke through Sarah's rage. Was Naomi actually telling the truth? But she forced herself to stay firm, her voice icy. "I don't believe you. You're both playing some sick game with me."

Naomi's eyes widened, her voice urgent. "No, Sarah, I swear. No one at the office has heard from him. His phone's been off."

Sarah hesitated, wavering. But her anger surged back. "Just fuck off my doorstep," she snapped, slamming the door in Naomi's face, trying to silence the strange, unsettling doubt Naomi's words had stirred.

A fierce, unforgiving blaze of loathing surged through Sarah – a passion she hadn't known herself capable of. Yet, as the initial wave of anger subsided, a chilling question crept in: could Naomi be right? Was Peter actually missing? Her urgency to reach number 37 grew, every unanswered question gnawing at her.

The doorbell rang again, slicing through her thoughts. Steeling herself for a fight, she yanked the door open. "Are you joking with me? What part of 'FUCK OFF' didn't you understand?"

But instead of Naomi, there stood Max Moore, drenched to the bone, a silvery key glinting in his outstretched hand. He blinked in surprise, momentarily cowered by her ferocity.

"Oh," she breathed, deflating slightly, realising her mistake.

The Carpet Cleaner

Max stepped over the threshold, only to have Sarah toss a hand towel at him before launching into a ten-minute tirade. Her words poured out in a fierce, unbroken stream, and Max couldn't help but wonder how she managed to breathe amid the onslaught. He caught the essentials through the storm: the key to number 37 was still missing, and Peter was her prime suspect; Peter, by Sarah's estimation, was a total bastard; Naomi's audacity in showing up on her doorstep had left Sarah livid ("What a fucking cheek!"); and Peter had vanished from both home and work (a "total bastard" twice over). Above all, there was an urgent need to get to number 37.

Finally, Sarah paused, gasping for breath, and Max seized the brief silence. "Shall we go?"

Without another word, they stepped out into the rain, the tension between them more charged than ever.

As they pulled onto the street leading to number 37, Sarah suddenly commanded Max to stop the car, prompting him to slam on the brakes. He was beginning to worry his nerves might never fully recover. She jumped out and inspected an orange VW Golf parked nearby. Returning to the car, she declared with conviction, "That's Peter's car, without a doubt."

Inside number 37, Max settled uneasily into Alan's sofa, joined by a purring Boffin who he gently stroked, while Sarah conducted a room-by-room inspection. Soon, she returned, leaning over him, her expression intense, and inhaling deeply. "Can you smell that?" she asked.

Max, bewildered by the cryptic observation yet again, shook his head. "No, I can't detect any scent."

Sarah pressed on, "Fine, but can you at least see this section of the carpet? It's cleaner – noticeably so."

Max squinted down but shrugged. "Absolutely not. To my eyes, the carpet looks uniform. My dear, enlighten me – what are you perceiving?"

Sarah pointed insistently. "This part has been scrubbed down with a powerful cleaner, much more than the rest of the carpet. Same on the stairs."

Trying to lighten the tension, Max joked, "Maybe if you'd been more thorough in your cleaning before –" He was cut off as Sarah fixed him with an intense glare. "Apologies, my dear. What precisely, are you trying to say?"

"I'm serious, Max. If a forensic team tested here, they'd likely find blood. Someone's tried to clean it up."

Max felt a chill. "Blood? Who, exactly, is 'someone'?"

"Whoever was here," she replied, her voice tight with frustration. "Possibly Peter himself. Although it's too good a job to be him!"

Max tried to piece it together, still struggling. "So… it's Alan's blood, then? That makes much better sense. But who would have covered it up?"

Sarah's face darkened. "Or maybe it's Peter's blood," she said quietly. "We need to return to Bristol and speak with Alan again – soon."

Max nodded. "Actually, I have an errand in Bristol for Rollie that involves Alan. I'll feed Boffin then take you home now, and we'll head out first thing in the morning. Nine sharp?"

Sarah agreed, her gaze lingering on the suspiciously clean carpet.

Bruce's Embarrassment

Rollie had invited Bruce over under the pretence of a casual catch-up, though his true motives were more probing. Word had reached him that Bruce had shown up for the recent pickup in Leith with an unexpected companion – an attractive Irish woman who'd arrived alongside him in his lorry. Coupled with Bruce's slightly delayed arrival at the port, Rollie felt he was owed an explanation.

Bruce, intent on minimising the incident, admitted it had been an oversight. He explained that he'd met the woman at a hotel in Yorkshire, where she mentioned needing a lift to Edinburgh. Out of courtesy, he'd offered to bring her along. Though he acknowledged he'd found her attractive and felt a passing interest, he was firm in insisting that nothing improper had happened between them. He expressed an embarrassment about the whole episode, an error of judgement he wouldn't repeat.

Rollie eyed him, doubt flickering in his gaze, but ultimately let it go and concluded their chat. As the rain had cleared, he led Bruce out to his garden, casually pointing out his various vegetables and flowers. Bruce, though naturally reserved, listened with polite attentiveness, accustomed to Rollie's rambling discussions about horticulture.

Yet Rollie could sense that Bruce's thoughts lingered elsewhere, perhaps on the woman in question. For now, he knew he wouldn't get any more from Bruce. But he had a hunch that this wouldn't be the last time her presence came up in their conversations.

Theories and Models

Sarah and Max arrived in Bristol by early afternoon, but navigating the M32, central Bristol, and finding parking stretched their journey well into mid-afternoon. They made a quick grocery stop before finally reaching Alan's apartment, a subdued yet determined tension in the air.

The hours that followed were consumed by intense conversation, analysis, and speculation. Alan, now free of morphine's haze, recounted the events of the night he was shot with careful precision: the quiet walk home from the pub, his fateful encounter with four young assailants, and the brief moments inside number 37. He described entering, hanging up his jacket, climbing the stairs – and then, the gunshot. Everything went black until Sarah found him later that night.

Sarah then laid out her own account: the messages and voicemails to Peter that went unanswered, Naomi's unexpected visit, and her chilling discovery of Peter's car parked on the same street as number 37. The freshly scrubbed carpet in the living room, in her mind, all but confirmed her suspicion that Peter's blood had been cleaned up from that spot. Though Max and Alan hesitated to fully endorse her theory, the gravity of her conclusion lingered, unsettling them all.

Max then shared details of his recent meeting with Rollie, mentioning the tense "truce" they'd managed to establish and his upcoming meeting with Rollie's son, Nigel. Nigel's close proximity – living less than a mile from Alan's Bristol apartment – cast a shadow of potential relevance that none of them could ignore.

With all this information laid out, Sarah broached a theory that made even Max shift uneasily. Could Rollie be involved, directly or indirectly, in Peter's possible disappearance – or worse? Max and Alan immediately dismissed the idea as premature, and Rollie's motives felt unclear. Yet privately, they both recognised an unsettling plausibility, even as they assured Sarah that her suspicions were purely speculative.

At last, Sarah suggested taking what they knew to the police. Max pushed back strongly; warning that doing so could unleash a storm they weren't prepared to handle. "We have too many unknowns, and if the police get involved too soon, we could lose control over this entirely."

But Sarah was quick to counter, pointing out that Naomi would almost certainly report Peter missing if she hadn't already. Their secrets, she argued, might unravel sooner than they thought, and with or without their cooperation, police inquiries could soon disrupt everything.

Realising they needed time and leverage, Max promised he would reach out again to Rollie the next day, hoping to learn more from their tenuous alliance. Yet privately, he was hatching a different plan – a plan that would involve having Peter's orange VW Golf discreetly removed from the street near number 37 and finding a way to replace the suspect carpet in Alan's apartment, effectively erasing what traces of Peter might still remain.

As the evening wound down, Alan treated them to an Indian meal across the street, his first venture out since the shooting. It was a small celebration of his recovery, and a way for Alan to say, "thank you", yet an underlying tension remained. Each of them knew that the theories they'd begun weaving could have far-reaching implications – and that the truths waiting to be uncovered might change everything.

Max Dances with the Devil

Max suggested a nightcap, hoping to let their rich Indian meal settle. He reached for an unopened bottle from Alan's collection, selecting an 18-year-old Glenlivet. Sarah, her mind still spinning from the intense conversations of the evening, welcomed the chance to unwind before bed. Alan, however, excused himself; the strain on his shoulder was evident, and he needed his painkillers and rest.

"I don't understand how we ended up here, Max," Sarah murmured as she took a sip of her whisky, the smooth warmth of the Speyside gradually easing her tension. "Mmm, lovely choice." She raised her tumbler a little to acknowledge her satisfaction.

"Nor do I, my dear," Max replied. "But here we are, and all we can do is navigate this as best as possible. Know that I'll do everything in my power to keep you safe." He reached out, resting a comforting hand on her shoulder.

She leaned into his touch, letting her head fall softly against his hand. "Thank you," she whispered, a quiet gratitude in her voice.

After checking in on Alan, who was deeply asleep, Sarah returned to the sofa beside Max. They shared a companionable silence, each savouring the calm, until Sarah finally spoke. "How did you ever get involved with Rollie in the first place?"

Max hesitated, glancing down at his glass before answering. "I'm willing to tell you, but...it may colour your view of Rollie – and perhaps even of me – in a less favourable light."

"I'm not completely blind to Rollie's business dealings so I doubt that" Sarah replied gently. "Please, go on, Max."

Max exhaled slowly, his gaze distant, as he began recounting his story, his words flowing as if he were telling it more to the room than directly to her.

Rollie recruits Maximilian Moore

"I was running a modest one-man legal practice, scraping by but doing work I believed in. Then, out of the blue, I received an unexpected call inviting me to a business meeting at Rollie's place on Withdean Road. I hadn't realised it was Roland Monroe I'd be meeting. If I'd known, I likely would have declined on the spot; I'd heard enough stories about him to know he was trouble."

Max paused, the memory clearly unsettling. "Rollie was charming, though, engaging even. He'd read up on my work and praised my abilities as a criminal defence lawyer, offering to retain my services. He said he could provide cases he thought I'd enjoy and wanted me as his personal lawyer – available anytime he needed, at his beck and call so to speak. Although flattered, I declined, explaining that I preferred working independently, I didn't want to be incumbent of anyone. I even believed I could be of more service to society that way. Money didn't motivate me; as long as I could keep my BMW on the road, I was content. But truthfully, Rollie's reputation also unnerved me."

Max leaned back, exhaling deeply. Sarah poured more whisky into his glass.

"Rollie didn't take 'no' for an answer. He thanked me for meeting him, saying most people would've made excuses. He asked me to reconsider over the next week. I agreed, knowing full well I wouldn't change my mind but not wanting to appear impolite."

Max took a sip before continuing. "Later that night, I got another call from someone claiming to be 'from the office of Rollie Monroe.' At the time, I often worked as a duty solicitor for clients who couldn't afford their own representation, so calls from unknown numbers were common. They asked if I'd do Rollie a favour and represent a young chap he knows who had got into some trouble. They said Rollie had given him a second chance and would appreciate my help but would understand if I couldn't take it on. I saw no harm and agreed. They provided the young man's name and said he'd be before a magistrate at 10 a.m. the next morning. I had no time to prepare, but they ended the call before I could protest. Of course, I couldn't leave the young man stranded."

Max paused, the weight of what happened next visible in his expression.

"I arrived at court early, hoping to meet my client beforehand. When I finally met him, I wasn't impressed – Ben was a scrawny, inauspicious, pockmarked young man who greeted me with, 'I'm shit out of luck.' I told him we could make his defence sound more sympathetic. But I sensed something off from the start. The prosecution had a solid case: Ben had been caught with a large amount of Ketamine and Xanax – enough to fuel a party for the whole of Brighton for a weekend, if you can believe it. The Crown Prosecution Service were confident and had presented charges for 'possession with intent to supply.' The prosecution's confidence was palpable. Frankly, he was bang to rights, as the old saying goes."

He rubbed his hands together as if reliving the tense moment. "We waited for hours to appear before the judge. Ben, increasingly jittery and agitated, was struggling. Of course, I couldn't judge; my own morning tremors were a familiar companion, making me empathetic to Ben's situation. In my mind, I was already planning on how I could support this young man's rehabilitation, I knew of government-funded programs designed to help him overcome his addiction. Eventually, our turn came. Just before he went up, he pulled a small packet from his pocket and asked me to hold it. I told him I couldn't. But in one swift move, he slipped it into my jacket pocket. I tried to hand it back, but I was too slow, he was ushered to the dock."

"I remember the judge reviewing his notes, removing his glasses, and calling the case number. He greeted me with a smile, expressing pleasure at seeing me again."

"I recall I replied, 'The privilege is always mine, your Honour,' and then focused on my notes. Behind me, I heard determined, heavy steps, akin to a march. The Judge removed his glasses and, glancing behind me, inquired of the police officer if this matter could wait."

Max paused, clearly reliving the moment. "The judge looked on, perplexed, as the officer suggested that I was in possession of illegal substances – substances I might be planning to supply to my client."

Sarah's hand flew to her mouth in shock.

"Of course, I protested, explaining Ben had just slipped the packet into my pocket. But the officer searched me right there and then and pulled out a small bag of white powder. I was mortified. It was a perfect setup. The judge was livid. I was arrested on the spot for possession and contempt of court. I was horrified by this invidious claim."

"In the holding cell, shock coursed through me. Once a champion of lost causes, I now found myself confined in a cell, with a parade of police officers passing by to gawk and mock me. My reputation seemed shattered, and my livelihood in jeopardy. The events had unfolded so swiftly that comprehension eluded me."

Sarah refilled his glass, her hand resting on his for a moment.

"They left me in that cell for five agonising hours before finally the door creaked open, and in walked Detective Superintendent Richards. I'll spare you the details of this character, but suffice it to say, he held the highest rank among the local detectives at that time and was conveniently available. He explained that they had found cocaine in my pocket. Horror washed over me, and I tried to assert my innocence, but he silenced my protests. He expressed his willingness to vouch for me, recognising my competence in my profession. He referred to the wrongdoers as 'scrotes' and stated they needed someone like me to represent them. I was appalled, struggling to grasp what he was implying. He offered to replace the small bag they had discovered in my pocket with one containing washing powder. He assured me it would be dismissed as a grave error, a mere misunderstanding, and my reputation would swiftly be rehabilitated. Basically, all my problems would simply disappear. He then asked if I wanted him to do this favour for me. Ashamedly, I jumped at the opportunity, saying yes, but I questioned his motivation. He walked towards the open cell door, glanced back at me, and said, 'Rollie expects to see you in his office at 10 a.m. tomorrow.'"

"I felt an intense sense of embarrassment for what had transpired. The Desk Sargeant took a perverse pleasure in the situation and made no effort to conceal his amusement at my fate."

Max slumped back, a mixture of shame and frustration on his face. "I dutifully went to see Rollie the next day, ready to give him 'what for,' to decline his offer despite his dirty tactics. I waited alone in his office for more than half an hour, absolutely determined to reject his offer. But when he arrived, he seemed oblivious to the entire affair. He thanked me for coming, almost as if he'd not me before, he chatted about his garden, providing a disquisition on crop rotation, he even offered me fresh vegetables to take home. His charm was disarming, and somehow, he made me feel like the meeting was my idea. In that moment, I gave in. I agreed to his terms."

He looked away, pained. "I felt like I'd sold my soul. I'd gone against everything I believed in – a fair legal system, independence. The devil in the guise of Rollie had won, and I was bound to him from that day on. I had compromised my principles and made a Faustian bargain."

Sarah placed a comforting hand on his shoulder. "Hey, at least you got to meet me," she said softly, a sympathetic smile on her face.

Max's expression softened. "That's true, and I am grateful for that, my dear," he said sincerely, cherishing her presence.

He rose to stretch. "I need the bathroom and then I'll check on Alan. Fancy one last whisky? One for the road?"

"Absolutely," Sarah replied, knowing sleep was still far from her mind. "I'll pour."

Richards

Max leaned back, swirling the whisky in his glass as he gathered his thoughts. Sarah filled his glass, sensing this next part might weigh heavily on him.

Breaking the tranquillity, Sarah turned to Max with a thoughtful expression. "Perhaps I shouldn't ask this, but I know Rollie's operation doesn't strictly operate within legal boundaries." Max's face tightened, apprehending what she was about to ask next. "No, don't worry, I'm not delving into the ins and outs of his business enterprise." Max looked relieved but a hint of caution remained. "But how does he manage to fly under the police radar, not just here in Bristol, but also in Edinburgh and Brighton?"

Max deliberated, lost in contemplation. Eventually, he spoke, "Well, my dear, he has numerous police associations. I'm not entirely sure about the mechanics here in Bristol, but I know it's overseen by his son, Nigel, and it involves considerable financial investment. In Edinburgh, they employ the strategy of 'hiding in plain sight' and operate under a legitimate import licence. Brighton is a different kettle of fish and remember that was where the operation started. The key lies with the officer I mentioned earlier – Detective Superintendent Richards."

Sarah interjected, seeking clarity, "So he's essentially bought off this police officer?"

"That's correct, but as is often the case with Rollie's affairs, there's more to it than meets the eye."

"Richards," Max began, his voice taking on a contemplative tone, "was an ambitious officer, and, eventually, thanks to Rollie, known for his quick rise through the ranks. Brighton was, and still is, a city with more than its fair share of crime – drugs, gang-related violence, organised theft. Richards made it clear he was the man to tackle it, especially when it came to cracking down on high-profile offenders. That was how Rollie spotted him."

Sarah listened closely; her gaze fixed on Max. "So, Rollie saw an opportunity in Richards' ambition?"

"Pour me another glass and I'll tell you a brief tale about Richards," Max proposed.

Detective Richards and Barry the paedo

Max settled into recounting the tale, though Sarah noticed a slight faltering in his voice, likely a mix of the whisky's effect and fatigue. "When Rollie first encountered Richards, he had just earned his promotion to Detective Sergeant. This was, oh..." he hesitated, calculating the years. "Some twenty-five years ago. Given that, he must be nearing retirement soon." He took another sip of whisky, nodding in agreement with his own calculation.

"Richards wasn't exactly a standout star in the police world at that time; his career had progressed only steadily. Rollie's brother had recently expanded their business beyond legality, and at that juncture, they were using Shoreham harbour for imports. Rollie managed the Shoreham operation, leveraging the contacts he'd established through the legitimate food import business. Richards was called in by Brighton CID to investigate a human trafficking ring potentially operating out of Shoreham, they met, and he and Rollie hit it off from the beginning."

"While delving into the human trafficking operation, Richards inadvertently came close to exposing Rollie's illegal activities. It was accidental. Rollie struck a deal with Richards: he'd assist Richards with resources for his investigations, and in return, Richards would turn a blind eye to Rollie's imports. In addition to making Richards into a hero, Rollie would also grease Richards's palm."

"The revelations themselves were horrifying. It was human trafficking at its worst, involving children, some not even teenagers, who were later distributed across Europe. Rollie played a crucial role in unveiling the shipments, using his resources to diligently track many of the ships and their cargo entering and leaving the harbour. The slippery head of the enterprise, Barry Ali, remained elusive. He was an accountant by trade, and he used that as his cover quite successfully. The police had identified him easily enough but lacked enough evidence to apprehend him."

Sarah interjected, seeking clarification, "Barry Ali? Was he of Asian descent?"

"No, no," Max clarified, shaking his head. "He hailed from a quaint little hamlet in West Yorkshire. It's a peaceful, unassuming place, a most unlikely place to harbour a criminal. I happened to pass by once, running an errand for Rollie; the nearby train station is called 'Steeton and Silsden', which always struck me as a perfect moniker for an old-fashioned music hall comedy duo."

"Ah, I see," Sarah replied, absorbing the information. "And, yes, very drole, Max."

"Anyway," he pressed on, "Barry Ali remained untouchable; they couldn't pin anything on him. This is where Rollie came into play." Max paused, as if working out what he should or shouldn't reveal. "Let's just say Rollie 'arranged' for Barry to get caught," he emphasised the word 'arranged.' "I'm not entirely sure of the specifics, but I know this Barry Ali had a particular weakness for young boys, the outcome was that Rollie orchestrated Barry's capture. The upshot was, they removed a major — probably the biggest in Europe — human trafficking and paedophile ring from operating. They had successfully taken an exceptionally vile individual off the streets."

"Sergeant Richards became a hero, receiving a medal, a promotion, and the admiration of his superiors. His connection with Rollie was solidified for time immemorial."

Max pondered further, musing, "Without Rollie, that same vile operation couldn't have been dismantled. What he'd done was illegal but for the greater good."

Max's recounting of Rollie's complex, morally ambiguous past had left Sarah with a lot to process. Rollie had skirted legality and relied on Richards's compliance, yet his actions had led to the dismantling of a notorious human trafficking ring. It was a reality Sarah found both disturbing and oddly compelling.

Curious, she inquired, "Why did the imports stop coming in through Shoreham? I mean, it's obviously much closer to Brighton than Edinburgh."

Max explained, "That was an unfortunate consequence of Richards's success. He accepted a DI role in Bristol, a move that, I believe, marked the beginning of the company's connection with the city. Anyway, Rollie thought Shoreham too small a harbour when their imports grew, he felt they stood out." He took another sip of whisky, "Initially, they attempted Hull, but they couldn't secure the necessary contacts and support there. Edinburgh, with the Firth of Forth, provided the requisite scale, and being a busier shipping lane, inclusive of military vessels, allowed them, as I mentioned earlier, to 'hide in plain sight'."

Sarah let out a yawn, not due to any lack of interest in Max's narrative, but from a sudden wave of exhaustion that washed over her. She managed one final question, "So, this Richards is now a Superintendent, back in Brighton, and in Rollie's pocket?"

"That's right," Max affirmed. "Brighton desperately wanted their hero back and it was only a year or so before they offered him another promotion. Rollie was thrilled to have his old pal back. Over time, Richards became one of Rollie's most loyal allies. Rollie made sure he was more than compensated – financially and with favours that only someone like Rollie could offer. Richards was living well above his means, driving a new car every year, taking exotic holidays. And eventually he was promoted to Detective Superintendent, in charge of CID for the area."

Max glanced at Sarah, gauging her reaction. "The sad part is, Rollie was careful to keep his hands clean with Richards in many ways. On paper, they never directly interacted after those early years, and yet Richards remained one of Rollie's staunchest protectors. Even as Rollie expanded his business, Richards was a constant behind the scenes, making sure Brighton's police force didn't look too closely at certain activities."

Sarah shook her head, the extent of Rollie's manipulation both astonishing and troubling. "So, all these years, Richards has been indebted to Rollie, and his career was built on Rollie's machinations. And now he's nearing retirement?"

"Indeed," Max confirmed, his tone tinged with irony. "Richards will probably retire with a nice pension, his reputation intact. Meanwhile, Rollie has groomed others to take his place – just in case. Richards is an asset, but Rollie never relies on one person alone. If it weren't Richards, it would be someone else."

Sarah sighed, feeling a pang of sympathy for Max, who was equally caught in Rollie's web. "You'd never think Rollie could be so... well, tough! He always seems so affable. I guess it's hard to imagine an escape from someone like Rollie, isn't it?"

Max gave her a weary smile. "Hard, yes. Impossible? Perhaps. But for now, it's best to play along and avoid stepping on his toes."

"I bet!" Sarah enthused. "Thank you, Max. I appreciate you taking me into your confidence."

"You're always welcome, my dear," Max responded. "But now," he stretched his arms and let out a yawn, "I believe it's time for me to put my head down."

"Me too, Max," Sarah said, draining the dregs of whisky from her glass and standing up. "Hopefully, Sleeping Beauty is still sound asleep!"

As she retreated to Alan's room she felt a surge of sympathy for Max, caught as he was in Rollie's shadow. Alan lay sprawled on his right side, his breathing deep and steady. Sliding into her familiar spot behind him, she wrapped her arm carefully around him, mindful of his injured shoulder, and allowed herself to unwind in the comfort of his presence.

Yet her mind churned with questions. Rollie's actions walked a fine line between villainy and heroism, making it hard to categorise him. His ruthlessness in orchestrating Barry Ali's downfall had exposed a hidden ugliness in the world, but it had also ensnared Richards, complicating his loyalties as a police officer. Could she really trust Max's impression that

Rollie had been acting for a greater good, or was that just how Max had learned to justify Rollie's choices over the years?

The room was silent but for Alan's breathing, a calming rhythm that grounded her. Her thoughts drifted to Peter, her vanished husband. The search for him had lost the urgency she once felt, as if the questions she now faced were more pressing than those that had once plagued her. She fought back a sense of guilt for not making her missing husband her top priority.

Lulled by Alan's warmth, Sarah's questions began to fade, her exhaustion winning over her curiosity. She felt herself drifting, hoping that with the morning light, answers might become clearer.

Bermuda in Bristol

Alan glanced at his phone to check the time; it was 7:15 a.m. Good, he thought – he'd managed to sleep through the night again, a crucial step in his recovery. Feeling the familiar weight of Sarah beside him, he carefully sat up, mindful to keep pressure off his left side. On an impulse, he leaned down and planted a gentle kiss on her head, noticing her hair was a bit tousled and catching a faint hint of whisky lingering in the air. That explained the quiet snores and her deep slumber.

As he shifted to stand up, Sarah, still half-asleep, reached out with her arm and mumbled, "No, come back to bed, please." Her arm fell as quickly as it had lifted, and Alan stifled a chuckle at her sleepy protest. She must be feeling a bit worse for wear, he thought.

From the bathroom, he decided to let her rest a while longer and slipped quietly into the lounge. Expecting to find the curtains drawn and Max snoring, he was surprised to see the room filled with morning light. Max lay on the extended sofa bed, his beer belly extending over his Bermuda boxer shorts, finishing a call on his mobile.

"That was Rollie checking up on us." Max informed him as Alan nodded and filled the kettle, switching it on to boil. "He confirmed our meeting with Nigel for Tuesday at 9am." Max's voice turned serious. "We need to return that gun."

Alan shook his head, his anger surprising him as he snapped back, "The gun they used to try and kill me you mean?"

"Yes, Alan," Max tried placating him, "that very gun. Look, I know it's hard, but you're going to have to get over it. They've called a truce, and you'll get compensated. Please, just take the deal. It's the best for everyone. You cannot win against the Monroes".

Alan ignored him, pouring hot water over the tea bags. "We'll see, but either way I don't trust them."

Max hesitated, sensing the tension, but continued cautiously, "I've also informed Rollie about Sarah's husband's car in your street. He'll arrange to have it moved as soon as possible. Apparently, Peter's Estate

171

Agent's office has been in touch with the police about his disappearance, but they're not acting on it yet. They can't be held back for long, though. We'll need a story for Sarah for when she gets back to Brighton."

Alan shook his head, more to himself than to Max. "Poor Sarah. How did she ever get mixed up in all this?" He knew the question was rhetorical, but it weighed on him all the same.

Missing Person

Jamie orchestrated the discreet removal of Peter's car under the cover of darkness and the police investigation was 'allowed' to commence. Brighton CID contacted Sarah, who explained she hadn't heard from her husband for over a week. She underscored her suspicions of Peter's extra marital affair with Naomi and explained she'd be back in Brighton on Tuesday night, available for an in-person interview.

Meanwhile, Max and Alan had grave concerns over Peter's whereabouts and wellbeing, though they masked their concern when speaking with Sarah. She remained genuinely baffled by the whole situation and had begun to believe that her husband might have experienced a nervous breakdown and chosen to disappear overseas. Desperate for a plausible explanation, Sarah clung to this theory, which Max and Alan cautiously supported, hoping it would bring her some comfort – and perhaps buy them more time.

Barramundi and Giant Scallops

Max and Sarah agreed there was no need to rush back to Brighton before their meeting with Rollie's son, Nigel. Instead, they opted to explore some of Bristol's tourist attractions, including a visit to the nearby SS Great Britain. They strolled along the harbourside, enjoying a break from the cramped apartment, which was particularly stifling with all three of them cooped up inside. Alan's wound was healing well, allowing him to initiate some gentle physiotherapy to gradually regain mobility on the left side of his torso, but the work was painful.

Back in the apartment that evening, the three discussed their approach for the meeting with Nigel. Max, having moved his car to adhere to Bristol's harsh parking enforcement, had also picked up some wine and beer along the way. They were now relaxing with drinks and another takeaway pizza.

Sarah had carefully brought the gun in from Max's car, bringing it in for Alan's attention. Only Alan was qualified to empty the gun's magazine. He held up the small gun, carefully inspecting it from all angles.

"Can you put that thing down, please?" Sarah said, exasperated. "It's not a bloody toy."

Alan looked at her with a hint of disappointment. "It almost is, though. This is a Sig Sauer Mosquito – semi-automatic. A testament to German engineering, top quality, but if it had been a larger calibre, I'd probably be dead. I spent nearly two decades dodging bullets in the army, much bigger ones at that. And yet, this little thing is what caught me, and in my own home." He paused, counting out eight rounds, which he set down beside a pizza box. "In a strange way, I suppose I *should* feel lucky."

"Sarah's right. Put it down and eat your pizza," Max interjected.

Sarah took a swig of beer straight from the bottle, then glanced at Max with a puzzled expression. "So, tell me, how did Rollie – or, I guess, the whole Monroe family – end up in all this? I mean, I know Rollie isn't an innocent, but they hardly seem like your typical crime family."

Max set his own beer down, reclining on the sofa with a thoughtful look. "Rollie honestly believes they aren't part of organised crime. Sure, he knows importing drugs is illegal and maybe even morally wrong, but he's convinced himself it's just business. He's satisfying a genuine demand with a supply. After all, he'd say, he's not dealing in human trafficking or guns." He chuckled, adding, "As if that somehow makes it all respectable."

He paused, then continued, "I'll give you the condensed history, as much as I know. And if it stops Alan from fiddling with that bloody gun, all the better." Alan, sufficiently chastised, returned the gun to the table, focusing instead on his pizza.

A Potted History of the Monroe Brothers

Max started his monologue. "Rollie came from a family of four boys: Robin, the eldest by six years; Les, about eighteen months older than him; and Harry, the youngest, about eight years his junior. Their father was, well, what years ago, people might have called a 'spiv' – today we'd probably label him an entrepreneur, albeit one who liked to dance around the edges of the law. He ran a respectable butcher's shop in Brighton and made a decent living from it, but it was never enough, he was always hungry for more. He tried his hand at other ventures, thinking he was destined for bigger things, but none of them ever took off. The butcher's shop was his only true success, his only constant and steady source of income."

Max went on, "Robin, the eldest, had a sharp business sense. He was the only one of the brothers to take the eleven-plus seriously. It wasn't that he was the smartest amongst them, he just tried harder. As soon as he was old enough, he joined their father and quickly expanded the business from a single shop to three, all of which turned a solid profit. Robin was the driving force behind everything that followed – without him, we wouldn't even be discussing Rollie's story."

He leaned forward, emphasising, "Robin's vision extended to supplying local restaurants and pubs. Back in those days, it was rare for pubs to serve food, and there weren't nearly as many suppliers as there

175

are now. He practically cornered the market around Brighton. It started small, but as his reputation for quality spread, the business gained real momentum"

"Les and Rollie were always inseparable, and always mischievous," Max said, leaning back as if reflecting on the past. "Once they left school, they found a way to support the family business by directly sourcing the produce themselves. They ran a fleet of small fishing boats, hauling in their own catches, and they'd buy up seafood stocks cheaply from other local boats. But it wasn't just the standard stuff. Les and Rollie were bold enough to deal in venison, game, and trout – often acquired through a bit of 'creative sourcing.'" He grinned. "In other words, they poached it, or they paid people to poach it for them, even stealing from the Duke of Norfolk's estate in Arundel. You could say it was Les and Rollie who first took the business across the line into outright illegality!"

Max paused to take a sip of his beer, clearly amused by the brother's audacity. "But they were sharp. They realised they could fetch even higher prices for more unique foods, like fresh lobster. Horse meat too – it's unthinkable now, but back then, it was just another affordable option. Their real breakthrough, though, came when they started eyeing overseas markets. They had a knack for finding exotic foods that nobody else was bringing in yet, and eventually, they laid the foundation for the company that exists today: Exotic Food Imports Limited."

"Les and Rollie spent time abroad, travelling to forge partnerships and secure rare, sought-after foods. They started with imported meats – zebra, crocodile, kangaroo, and ostrich – and ventured into seafood not readily available in the UK, like barramundi and giant scallops. They even went into unique vegetables: Ghanaian corn, New Zealand oca, Chinese pak choi. Today, it sounds like the offerings of a specialty supermarket, but back then, these foods were unheard of in the UK. The brothers were fearless, they were both determined to succeed through sheer audacity."

He leaned in, emphasising the era. "You have to remember; this wasn't long after World War II. Rationing was still fresh in people's minds, and the country's palate hadn't expanded much beyond basic staples. The idea of flying in exotic foods wasn't even questioned back then – 'food miles' weren't on anyone's radar." Max chuckled, shaking his head. "Les and Rollie were ahead of their time, both daring and unbothered by the legal grey areas they operated in. And it was high end, those who could afford it were willing to pay a premium, the margins were high."

"Rollie even gave the company a slogan," Max said, pausing as he tried to recall the exact words. "Ah, yes, here it is: 'Shattering the crust of local habits by introducing the expansive ideals of international haute couture.'" He chuckled, shaking his head. "Of course, it never caught on. Nobody knew what the hell haute couture even meant back then!"

Max's laughter softened as he added, "But that was Rollie. Always a touch grander in vision than the times allowed. He believed that just like in fashion, food could have style, and he wanted to bring a taste of the world to people who barely looked beyond the English Channel. He truly was ahead of his time."

Sarah couldn't help but ask, "How on earth do you know all this, Max?"

Max grinned. "I've had a peek at some of the old records kept by their accountant, a Mr. C.C. Langsford. He's as old as Rollie and just as full of stories. But I'll save his story for another time!" He took a sip of beer and continued, "And, as you've probably noticed, Rollie's a natural storyteller. Some of his tales from poaching with Les are downright hilarious. He got caught by the duke plenty of times – Rollie had this habit of calling him 'Bernie,' which didn't sit too well with the duke. And then there were the mishaps. He and Les managed to sink a few of their own boats over the years, too."

Max smiled, almost as if he'd lived through those antics himself, immersed in the memories as though he'd been part of every wild escapade.

Alan asked, "What about Harry? You haven't mentioned him yet."

Max nodded thoughtfully. "True enough. Harry was the youngest by some margin and always a bit of an outsider, even in his own family. Unlike the others, Harry fancied himself a villain – a real tough guy – and seemed set on a path of trouble right from the start. They tried to bring him into the family business, but he became more of a liability than an asset. By the time he was eighteen, Harry was in and out of prison every few years for the better part of the next twenty. Mostly petty crimes, but enough that they couldn't afford to have him close to the business. They feared he'd bring it down."

Max paused before continuing. "Eventually, Harry grew up a bit, but that sense of being an outsider never left him. Even now, he's constantly running little schemes, and side hustles the rest of the family doesn't learn about until it's too late. Loan-sharking, for instance – that's one venture no one else wanted a part of. But Harry's resentful. He feels overlooked, still nursing a grudge that he wasn't given the CEO role. He believes it's his birthright, overdue by years. Ironically, Rollie's eldest, Jamie, feels exactly the same way."

Sarah asked, "What about their mother?"

Max shrugged. "She's almost a ghost in the records – and in Rollie's stories too. It's as if she was always in the background, keeping things together but rarely acknowledged. From what I gather, she passed away just shy of her 70th birthday, a long time ago now. Their father, though – he was a different story. He was a tough old character, lived to the age of 91. His sons rarely included him in the running of their business, but he never wanted for anything."

"That is a real shame about their mum – a huge gap in their story," Sarah remarked. "So, if things were going well, why did they make the switch to drug running?"

Max pondered his words. "Well… the world was changing. Some of the exotic foods they imported started falling out of favour, and some items even became protected. The global food market was shrinking; people's tastes were evolving. Added to that, Chinese, Thai, Indian, and many other restaurants had opened and sourced their foods from their own suppliers. And then there was the rise of 'food miles' – consumers wanting locally-sourced foods, demanding transparency about where their food came from. The Monroes had overextended themselves just as demand for their niche imports declined, and profits began to dwindle."

Max added with a wry smile, "And it didn't help that Rollie and Les were notorious lotharios, they had women in every port. Rollie especially had a thing for women from far-flung places, and he married a few too many of them! Between all that, their focus often strayed from the business."

"That clarifies a lot!" Alan interjected, the pieces falling into place.

"Indeed," Max continued, "but by then, the brothers had built valuable connections – and even friendships – for example, at Shoreham Harbour, where their operation was thriving. That's when they took the plunge into drug running. It was a major shift that brought a surge in profits but also far more danger. Rollie and Les had already made enemies with their monopolisation of small fishing boats across the Southeast, and they had profited off the boat owners, which didn't go unnoticed. But once they added drug importing to their portfolio, things took a darker turn. Robin, as sharp a businessman as he was, was no gangster, and his security measures were woefully inadequate. Tragically, he was assassinated about 25 years ago."

Sarah nearly choked on her beer. "That's horrible!"

Max nodded sombrely. "It was a terrible blow. Robin had been too young to command the army, but it had aged him terribly. They'd crossed into territory that was beyond them, *terrae incognitae* so to speak. After Robin's death, Les, as the next eldest, took charge. Together with Rollie, he scaled down the operation dramatically, putting their focus back on food imports while still discreetly handling contraband. They returned fishing rights to the boat owners, no longer charging them but instead securing loyalty in exchange for protection and surveillance. They even sold their three butcher shops, reinvesting heavily to boost security. It wasn't long before the model worked, and once they felt established, they expanded the contraband trade again – but this time, with far more caution."

Max shook his head, almost as if he could hardly believe the history he was recounting.

Alan interrupted again, "They're still importing food today. Is that profitable on its own?"

Max shook his head with certainty. "Absolutely not. The legitimate food side of the business is nothing more than a front – a money laundering operation for the illegal activities behind the scenes. Rollie set Harry up with five bars in and around Brighton and Hove, all of which serve the same purpose, though he's never really involved in any of them beyond The Court Club. Harry may claim ownership and management, but the books are kept entirely separate from him. Rollie also set up his sons to handle the distribution side of things, bringing a younger, more cautious approach to the operation."

Sarah raised an eyebrow. "What happened to Les?"

"Les is still alive," Max replied. "But he never wanted the CEO position. It was too public for him. He held the role for about a year but was more than happy to hand it over to Rollie. Now, he prefers to stay behind the scenes. He's got children and grandchildren of his own, but none involved in the business. As Rollie once told me, Les always felt like there was a sword of Damocles hanging over him, constantly expecting the authorities to knock on his door. It made him a nervous wreck. Rollie, on the other hand, is confident that they've put enough layers between themselves and the law to avoid prosecution. He believes their legitimate business ventures provide enough cover to mask the illegal side of things."

Alan smiled wryly. "And what about you, Max? Aren't you worried about what could happen if it all unravels?"

Max smirked, unbothered. "Not at all. I know nothing!"

Underfall Yard

When Max had told Alan and Sarah the location of the meeting with Nigel was close, neither of them had expected the car journey to take only five minutes. In fact, it had taken longer to navigate out of the car park and onto the busy Hotwell Road than to reach Underfall Yard. They were packed and ready to return to Brighton, just needing to stop for Sarah to retrieve her car on the return trip.

Underfall Yard was a rugged tribute to Bristol's maritime heritage. At first glance, it looked chaotic, with boats, parts, and equipment scattered around, but as they stepped out of Max's BMW, Alan and Sarah began to see the purpose in the apparent disorder. Workshops and heavy machinery were clearly in place to service the various boats that passed through the yard. Since the area was closed to the public, it appeared eerily empty, with only the distant hum of equipment breaking the silence. Alan took note of the sluice gates, essential for managing the harbour's depth and water flow, as he walked towards the main building.

As they approached, Max spotted a group of three men stepping out from behind the building and moved forward to greet them, gesturing for Sarah to wait in the car. Max shook hands with Nigel, who was flanked by two men. "Nigel, good to see you again. How's the family?" he asked, his tone light.

Nigel, who Alan quickly identified as Rollie's second son, nodded with a forced warmth. "All's good, Max. And this must be Alan?" He gestured vaguely in Alan's direction, barely making eye contact. Max confirmed, and Nigel's expression shifted as he addressed him brusquely. "You go on and sit in the car, Max, while I have a word with your mate here."

As Alan drew closer, Max took a step back but paused, glancing at the two men behind Nigel, each holding a baseball bat. "Nigel, what's with the muscle?" Max asked, a wary edge to his voice.

Nigel smirked, dismissing the question with a casual wave. "Relax, Max, it's just in case your mate here got any ideas. Now go park your jacksy back in the BMW and stop fretting." He turned his back on Max, effectively dismissing him.

Facing Alan now, Nigel forced a friendly tone. "Alright, Alan? Come over here, mate; I've got something for you." He reached into his pocket and produced an envelope, thick with cash, holding it out with a grin that didn't quite reach his eyes.

Alan approached Nigel, offering a handshake in a gesture of goodwill. Nigel, bearing a strong resemblance to a younger, leaner version of Rollie, gave him a hard, arrogant look. Unlike his father, he lacked any hint of warmth. Behind him, the two henchmen – large, bearded, and heavily tattooed – stood watchfully, exuding a threatening presence.

Ignoring Alan's outstretched hand, Nigel simply pressed the envelope into it, staring him down with a cold glare. "My father's gone soft, making peace with you," he sneered. "If it were up to me, I'd be battering you right now." Alan kept his composure, feeling the tension mount. He gripped the envelope, but Nigel held onto it just a moment too long, forcing Alan to tug it free.

"Thanks," Alan replied calmly, though he felt his pulse quicken. "But if you're upset with anyone, it should be your uncle Harry. It was his idea, not mine." He turned to walk away, his focus set on reaching the car. Suddenly, he heard movement behind him.

In an instant, he spun around, instinctively raising his right arm just as a baseball bat came crashing down on his forearm. Pain radiated up his arm, but he barely had time to react before the second thug struck high on his left shoulder. Agony tore through his gunshot wound, and he fell to the ground, gasping. Another blow slammed into his ankle as he curled up, arms over his head, bracing himself against the assault.

Sarah's scream pierced the air. "STOP! JUST STOP!"

To Alan's astonishment, the assault actually ceased. Blinking through the pain, he looked up and saw Sarah standing next to the BMW, her stance firm, both hands gripping a gun aimed squarely at Nigel and his men. Her hands were trembling, but her voice carried unmistakable authority. "Drop the bats!" she ordered. The two henchmen exchanged uncertain glances before letting the bats clatter to the ground.

Nigel's face twisted in anger and disbelief. "Who the hell are you, and why are you pointing my brother's gun at me?" He took a step toward her, defiant. "Hand it over and stop wasting my time."

Alan tried to get to his feet, only managing to push himself onto his hands and knees. He heard Sarah's voice, louder and more desperate this time. "Stop right there or I swear I'll shoot!"

Her tone was fierce, but Alan could see the tension in her eyes. She was holding her ground, but she was out of her element – and Nigel knew it.

Nigel hesitated, sneering as he taunted Sarah. "It's not loaded," he muttered, resuming his approach, though now with a hint of caution. Meanwhile, Alan staggered upright, teeth clenched against the fiery pain radiating from his shoulder wound. His patience had run thin, but he was snapped from his rising anger by the sound of a gunshot. He looked up to see Nigel crumpled on the ground, his bravado shattered.

The two henchmen flanking Alan wore expressions of shock and horror, frozen in place. Alan didn't waste a second; seizing both bats, he swung them hard in a wide arc, landing a blow to the man on his left, who dropped to his knees with a howl of pain. Alan quickly redirected, catching the second man in the legs. He too collapsed with surprising ease, leaving Alan with both men sprawled at his feet. He gripped the bats tightly, ready to end this encounter.

Alan stepped closer to the shaken Nigel, who flinched at his approach. "Oh my God, did I actually shoot him?" Sarah's voice quivered, her hands trembling as she gripped the gun. Alan worried she might accidentally fire another round.

Nigel, unscathed but visibly rattled, spat out, "That crazy woman nearly killed me!"

Alan raised the bats one last time in one swift motion, bringing them down on Nigel's prone torso, who let out a pained cry. Alan stared down at him with a smirk. "You're not shot, just a coward," he said, tossing the bats aside.

Turning to Sarah, Alan gently lowered her aim and engaged the gun's safety before easing it out of her hands. He slipped his arm around her shoulders and led her to the back seat of Max's BMW. As he opened the door, he called out, "Max, it's safe, you can come out now – get the car running!"

Settling into the seat with a satisfied sigh, he glanced over at a pale-faced Max. "Well, I'd say that went rather smoothly. Take us back to Brighton." From the back seat, Sarah's quiet sobs filled the silence. "Sarah can't drive, so we'll leave her car here."

Police Interview

The journey back to Brighton was smooth, with no surprises. Just south of Crawley on the A23, close to home, Rollie called Max. His voice boomed through the car's speakerphone, thanks to Bluetooth.

"Maximilian, is that you?" Rollie's voice was as distinct as ever.

"Yes, it's me, Rollie," Max replied quickly. "I'm in the car with Sarah and Alan, and you're on loudspeaker," he added, hoping to avoid any offhand remarks from Rollie about his fellow passengers.

"Good, good." Rollie's voice softened, followed by his trademark pause. Max silently hoped he wouldn't launch into his usual talk about his garden allotment.

Instead, Rollie's tone shifted to something more serious. "I need to apologise to your passengers. Nigel acted entirely against my consolatory wishes – he had no right to behave as he did. He has an overdeveloped sense of rectitude, and an undeveloped sense of humour," he said. Then, a hint of warmth returned to his voice. "Sarah, dear, you certainly gave him a fright waving that gun around! But in all seriousness, I hope you're well, and I trust this incident won't sour our relationship."

Sarah responded with an edge of humour, "No, Rollie, we're fine. Just keep your sons away from me in the future."

"Message received, loud and clear," Rollie replied. "But you really should drop by the house. I've got a bag of goodies for you – some delightful strawberries, since I know how you enjoy them. And Alan," he continued, "I hope there are no hard feelings. I know Harold was the real scallywag behind the theft, not you. Let's put this behind us, shall we?"

Alan responded in his calm, measured way, "That's fine with me, Mr. Monroe. But I'll still need a word with Harry."

"Go easy on him," Rollie said, almost pleading. "He may be grown, but he still thinks he's a kid – and sometimes acts like one. Besides, he speaks highly of you."

Max steered the conversation to a conclusion, "Thank you for calling, Rollie. I'll be round tomorrow morning to collect the goodies for Sarah."

"Perfect, Max. I'll make sure there's something for you and Alan too. See you then." Rollie concluded before signing off.

Fifteen minutes later, Max pulled up outside number 37 to drop off Alan, then continued to Sarah's mews cottage. A police car was stationed outside, occupied by two female officers. Though visibly exhausted, Sarah offered to handle the situation alone, but Max was firm.

"I'm coming in with you," he insisted, leaving no room for argument.

Sarah welcomed the two officers into her home and offered them tea. Although both officers recognised Max, he didn't recognise them, and they seemed curious as to why Sarah needed legal representation. Max clarified, insisting they were just friends and that his presence was purely coincidental, though the officers remained suspicious.

The officers conducted a thorough inquiry about Peter, gathering various details, including his physical description, recent photos, medical conditions, known associates, habits, and any potential risks or vulnerabilities. They mentioned that they had already taken statements from Peter's colleagues, including Naomi, and had requested tracking information from Peter's phone from the telecom's provider. They explained, however, that contrary to what she might have seen on TV shows, obtaining this data might take weeks. Media alerts, they added, would only be considered once more information available.

After an hour of questions, Sarah completed her statement, and Max carefully reviewed each detail she had provided, ensuring nothing had been overlooked.

Finally, the police departed, Max inquired, "Shall I make us some more tea?"

"No, Max," replied a weary looking Sarah, "I'm opening a bottle of red wine!"

New Carpet

When Alan returned to Number 37, he was taken aback to find the living room, hallway, and stairs transformed with brand-new carpeting. The fine wool, in a tasteful light grey, gave the place a fresh, polished look. "Thank you, Mr. Monroe!" he called out to the empty room, grinning at the unexpected improvement.

Boffin wove around Alan's ankle, purring loudly. "Well, I'm happy to see you too!" Her lively presence and bold demands filled him with a quiet, genuine joy.

Alan put fresh cat food down and then attended to his latest bruises with a mix of ice packs (in the form of frozen peas) and Arnica cream, his tried-and-true remedy, an old standby from his boxing days. As he looked at himself in the mirror, he noted his haggard appearance, he'd lost weight since the shooting incident and appeared to have aged about twenty years. Determined to bounce back, he vowed to dedicate the next few weeks to sleeping, eating, and drinking beer, "That should set me straight!" he declared to the silent apartment, his voice echoing slightly in the freshened space.

The Storyteller

"What do you think has happened to Peter?" Sarah asked Max, seeking a direct answer. They had spent the last hour discussing the ongoing police investigation, and now Sarah stood at the sink, opening a second bottle of red wine.

"Do you want a hand opening that bottle?" Max offered, attempting to steer the conversation away from Peter's whereabouts.

She glanced over her shoulder, her movements deliberate. "Max, I'm tired, but not so much that I've forgotten how to use a corkscrew." Her words carried a sharp edge. "You've been dodging this question for over a week now. I appreciate everything you've done with the police, but I need the truth."

Max shifted uneasily, adjusting his glasses. He was skilled at weaving narratives, especially in courtrooms, but outright deceit wasn't his forte. "Sarah..." he began, his hesitation louder than any words he might have chosen.

"Max," she interrupted, her voice firmer. "Please. Enough with the deflections. What do you really think?"

He leaned forward, resting his elbows on his knees, and ran a hand through his hair before pushing his glasses up to his forehead. For a long moment, he stared at the floor, as if searching for the right words in the worn pattern of the rug. Finally, he exhaled, his voice low but steady.

"Sarah, you have to prepare yourself for the possibility that Peter isn't coming back."

Sarah was coming to the same conclusion, grappling with a mix of emotions. Peter was her husband – her supposed life partner. But hadn't he proven time and again to be unreliable, uncaring? In truth, a complete shit. Her throat tightened as tears threatened to spill. "Yes," she asked quietly, "but what do *you* think happened to him?"

Seeing Sarah on the verge of breaking down, Max softened. He walked over, wrapping her gently in his arms. "Sarah, my dear," he said, his voice calm but sincere, "I don't know what happened to Peter. I wish

I did. But I *can* tell you this: Rollie will look after you. I will look after you. And even Alan – grumpy as he is – will look after you."

A broken laugh escaped Sarah, muffled against Max's shoulder, before giving way to quiet sobs. He held her for a moment longer, then gently took the wine and corkscrew from her hands. "Let me handle this," he said, offering a small distraction as he opened the bottle.

As the wine flowed, so did Sarah's words. She poured her heart out – recounting the highs, the lows, and all the moments in between that had defined her life with Peter. Max listened, attentive and steady, interjecting only when he felt it was expected.

By the time the second bottle was nearly empty, and Sarah was out of tears, she sighed and set her glass down. "I don't want to talk about him anymore, Max. It's too depressing." She looked at him, wiping her eyes. "Tell me about yourself instead."

Max shifted in his seat, clearly uneasy. "What do you want to know?" he asked cautiously.

"Oh, I don't know," Sarah said, her tone lightening. "How about how you first met Alan? And how that led to him working for Harry?"

Max leaned back, smirking faintly. "Ah, now there's a story. But you know the rules – what I share stays between us. And I'll definitely need to open another bottle of wine for this one."

When Max Met Alan

Max leaned back, settling into storytelling mode as Sarah reclined further into the sofa, curling her legs beneath her. "I met Alan by chance," he began, his tone reflective. "Or maybe by bad luck, depending on how you look at it." He adjusted his glasses, rubbed his eyes, and took a generous sip of wine. Sarah, her inhibitions softened by the alcohol, couldn't help but think he was delivering a performance, though one grounded in truth.

"Alan was... broken when he left the army," Max continued, his voice tinged with sympathy. "I still don't fully understand everything he went through. What I do know is that he spent an unusually long time in the field. Most officers are rotated out of active duty after four or five years.

Alan? He stayed for nearly fifteen. And much of that was solo work, operating behind enemy lines."

Sarah tilted her head, intrigued. "You mean like a spy?"

Max nodded slowly. "Something like that, though I doubt any of us will ever know for sure. The last few years of his service were quieter, at least on paper. They promoted him out of regular duty and put him on the reserve list. I suppose it was meant to ease him out of the army gracefully, but it had the opposite effect. He turned to drinking instead." Max paused, his gaze distant, before adding, "Have you noticed Alan never drives? Refuses to, actually."

"I had noticed," Sarah replied, frowning slightly. "I thought maybe he didn't have a license?"

"Oh, he has one," Max said, swirling his wine thoughtfully. "He lost it for two years after a bad accident, but he got it back ages ago. Still, he swore he'd never drive again."

"What happened?" Sarah asked, leaning forward slightly.

Max sighed, setting his glass down. "He was drunk – had spent an afternoon in the pub and decided to drive home. Ran his car off the road. He was only six feet or so away from hitting a mother and her child." He hesitated, letting the weight of his words settle. "Alan was mortified. When I first met him, he was adamant about facing prison time for what he'd done. He felt he deserved it, believed it was the least he could do to atone."

"Oh my God, that's terrible. Was anyone hurt?" Sarah asked, her voice a mix of horror and relief.

"No, thank goodness," Max replied, shaking his head. "Well, Alan gave himself a nasty knock on the head when he hit the steering wheel, but that was it, and you know what they say – no sense, no feeling. No one else was hurt. Still, the gravity of what *could* have happened – and his overwhelming guilt – made him almost impossible to defend. He was like a man determined to dig his own grave. But I could see there was a good man buried under all that misery, and I wasn't about to let him go down without a fight, without proper representation at least."

Max paused, swirling the wine in his glass before continuing. "I put together a solid defence, but the prosecution was baying for his blood. It was clear they wanted to make an example of him, and the judge seemed all too willing to oblige. To make things worse, the prosecution stretched the truth, claiming Alan missed the mother and child by inches. That was an outright lie."

Sarah frowned, leaning forward. "What happened next?"

"Then," Max said, his tone growing quieter, "something unexpected happened. An army officer turned up in court – unannounced, no less – to vouch for Alan's character. He was the real deal, and you could see the respect he commanded. But that wasn't the strangest part. The officer handed the judge a letter, and whatever was in it... well, it changed everything. I wasn't allowed to see it – no one was – but it was clearly significant."

"What did it say?" Sarah asked, her curiosity piqued.

"I have no idea," Max admitted. "All I know is that after reading it, the judge abruptly ended the trial. He suspended Alan's license for two years, fined him, and made him pay £5,000 in costs, which is a considerable sum in the circumstances. That was it. No jail time, no long speeches. The prosecution was livid, of course, but it was a done deal. Case closed."

Max took a sip of his wine, his gaze distant. "Whatever was in that letter saved Alan's life – literally and figuratively. I'd never experienced anything like it before or since."

"And you two hit it off right away?" Sarah asked, curiosity laced with amusement.

Max chuckled, shaking his head. "Not exactly. Most of our early meetings were at The Court Club, and let's just say our 'bromance' took a little time to blossom. At first, getting Alan to talk was like pulling teeth. But then, somehow, we landed on the topic of chess. He mentioned he'd played a bit at university, and since I love the game, we decided to give it a go. It's a game which encourages long silences, it suited us well."

"Is he any good?" Sarah asked, raising an eyebrow.

"Well... at first, he was awful," Max admitted with a grin. "But even then, I could tell there was something there. Without realising it, he played some classic openings. He'd memorised the King's Indian Attack without even knowing what it was."

Sarah tilted her head, her expression a mix of amusement and confusion. "Should I know what that means?"

Max laughed. "Not unless you're secretly into chess. It's a strategy used by high-level players. Clearly, Alan had once been quite skilled, though he'd probably forgotten most of it." He paused, taking a sip of his wine. "Anyway, after plenty of practice – mostly at my expense – he's now better than me. Just don't tell him that!"

Sarah smiled. "Sounds like chess isn't the only thing you two bonded over."

"No, it's not," Max said, his tone softening. "I suppose we're kindred spirits, in a way. Connected through our shared experiences... and maybe our mutual appreciation for a good drink."

"There's an overwhelming awareness of mental health these days, and from what you've said, it sounds like Alan might be dealing with PTSD," Sarah remarked, glancing curiously at Max.

"Alan almost certainly has PTSD," Max replied, a wry smile tugging at his lips. "But he's not *from* these days."

Sarah refilled their glasses, careful not to spill. She wasn't entirely sure she'd be able to stand if she drank much more, but the wine felt like a necessary companion to the conversation. "Poor Alan," she said, swirling the dark liquid in her glass. "He's never opened up about any of this. He seems so... alone. Does he have any family, Max?"

Max leaned back, his expression thoughtful. "As far as I know, he has a brother he hasn't spoken to in over thirty years," he said. "But he's only mentioned him once, in passing. His parents died around the same time he became estranged from his brother, but beyond that, I don't know much." He took a sip of wine, as if punctuating the sentence.

Sarah frowned, the weight of Alan's isolation settling over her. "That's so sad."

Max nodded solemnly, then added, "As for how he became involved with Harry... well, you can blame me for that."

Sarah blinked; her curiosity piqued despite her tipsy haze. The room seemed to blur and sharpen all at once as she listened, her mind almost transported to the past Max was beginning to describe...

When Harry Met Alan

Alan stepped into the dimly lit haze of The Court Club, the thick scent of stale cigarettes and spilled whisky meeting him like an old adversary. The muffled sounds of laughter and chatter from the alley outside had misled him, suggesting a lively crowd within. Instead, the bar was nearly deserted.

Harry, the ever-present owner, was conspicuously absent, leaving the place in the hands of Trevor, the long-suffering barman. At the counter, three men held court, their boisterous celebration cutting through the otherwise subdued air. Alan didn't need to guess they had been in court – they reeked of courtroom triumph and cheap cologne. Their voices were loud, slurred, and full of self-congratulation, driving away most of the regulars.

Alan gave Trevor a curt nod and ordered a pint, his voice barely audible over the trio's raucous laughter. Taking his beer, he retreated to the shadowed corner of the room, as far from the noise as possible. He sank into the Formica chair, its surface cracked with age, and stared into the amber depths of his glass.

From the corner of his eye, he noticed the three men glance his way, their hushed murmurs laced with laughter. Alan ignored them, refusing to give their drunken banter any weight. He was too weary to care, the hangover pounding at his temples a reminder of yesterday's indulgence.

The smoke from an abandoned cigar curled lazily under the low-hanging lights, adding to the oppressive weight of the room. Alan glanced at the door, hoping Max would appear soon. His friend had promised to meet him after finishing court, and the thought of escaping to a quieter place felt like the only relief from the noise and the dull ache in his head.

Max entered The Court Club, immediately greeted by the oppressive din of the trio at the bar. He hesitated for a moment, his unease palpable, before making his way to Trevor. "Two gin and tonics, please," he said, his voice low but firm, hoping to avoid attention.

Alan, seated in the corner, watched as the ringleader of the rowdy group – a tall, broad man with a cocky swagger – fixated on Max's order. With exaggerated bravado, the man grabbed both glasses as they were placed on the bar, raising them high like trophies. "To justice!" he bellowed, before downing both drinks in quick succession.

The bar erupted into raucous laughter and cheers, the sound echoing off the smoky, low ceiling. Alan closed his eyes and took a slow sip of his pint, muttering under his breath, "Not yet. Just wait."

Max's face flushed, equal parts embarrassment and frustration. He leaned in closer to Trevor, his voice more insistent this time. "Two more gin and tonics and bring them to the far end of the bar," he said, pointing to a spot well away from the drunken trio.

Trevor hesitated, casting a wary glance toward the group, but nodded and prepared the drinks. As the glasses were placed at the designated spot, a loud, mocking "BOO!" erupted from the men. The ringleader strutted over with exaggerated steps, his cronies egging him on. With a grin that dripped arrogance, he picked up the drinks and downed them again, one after the other, to a fresh round of cheers.

Max stood frozen, his discomfort now unmistakable. He glanced toward Alan, who set down his pint and rose slowly, his movements deliberate. As Alan approached the bar, the laughter from the group subsided slightly, curiosity mingling with the tension in the room.

"Gents," Alan said, his tone calm but carrying an edge of warning. He raised his hands in a placating gesture, his eyes locking on the ringleader. "You've had your fun. Now let my friend have his drink in peace."

The air grew heavy, the cheerful bravado of the group tempered by Alan's quiet authority. The ringleader smirked but didn't immediately

194

reply, his expression shifting as the moment stretched uncomfortably long.

The ringleader's demeanour shifted, shedding the veneer of courtroom decorum as he shrugged off his jacket and loosened his tie, tossing them onto a nearby stool. He rolled up his sleeves with deliberate precision, revealing powerful forearms marked with a tapestry of tattoos. Alan's eyes flicked briefly over the ink – West Ham emblems, a sprawling George Cross, and other symbols best left uninterpreted. The man's sturdy build and roughened hands suggested a life of manual labour, but his movements were practiced, as if he thrived on intimidating others.

Bald, with a goatee that stretched unnervingly long, the ringleader presented a peculiar sight. Alan found himself momentarily distracted by the sheer effort required to maintain such a beard. Surely, he thought, if one were going to commit to such grooming, a full beard would make more sense.

The man's bloodshot eyes locked onto Alan, struggling to focus through the haze of alcohol. "Are you this poof's *bum* friend?" he slurred, his tone dripping with insinuation.

Behind him, his cronies erupted in another round of whoops and jeers, their drunken mirth amplifying the slur's underlying intent. Alan felt a spark of anger flare in his chest but kept his face impassive.

The labourer stepped closer, his bulk casting a shadow over Alan. He jabbed a finger into Alan's chest, the gesture both confrontational and clumsy. His breath reeked of cheap gin as he barked, "Three more G&Ts, Trevor – and these *poofs* are paying!"

Another cheer erupted from his entourage, their boozy camaraderie fuelling their bravado. Alan held his ground, his calm exterior betraying none of the quiet rage simmering beneath. He glanced briefly at Max, whose discomfort was palpable, before fixing his gaze back on the ringleader, steady and unflinching.

The tension hung heavy, the room's smoky air thickening as if even the walls were holding their breath. Max was scared and wanted to run but he was taken by Alan's apparent calmness.

Alan took a half step back, his gaze drifting upward to the ceiling, once white but now speckled with age and stains. The labourer, momentarily confused by Alan's stillness, blinked in irritation. "Well?" he demanded, his voice rising, but Alan remained silent, his eyes fixed on the tiles.

"I want a gin, *gayboy!*" The labourer's patience snapped, but still, Alan did not react.

A moment passed, the air thick with anticipation. Alan let the silence stretch, letting the tension build before finally lowering his gaze. The builder, along with the two others, followed Alan's line of sight, craning their necks to see what had so captivated his attention. Even Max, his discomfort visible, glanced upward.

With a smooth, deliberate motion, Alan stepped forward. His fist, a tight ball of controlled power, swung through the air and collided with the labourer's exposed throat. The impact was precise and forceful, carrying the weight of Alan's entire body behind it. The labourer's eyes bulged in shock, his body crumpling immediately as he dropped to his knees and then collapsed onto his side, gasping for air, clutching at his throat.

The second man, already unsteady from drink, charged forward in a drunken blur, a misguided attempt to capitalise on his friend's sudden fall. Alan sidestepped effortlessly, using the man's own momentum to guide him into a nearby table, sending chairs scattering across the floor with a sharp crash.

The third man, stunned by the turn of events, shook his head, his disbelief almost comical in the situation's gravity. Alan's eyes locked onto him with unnerving calm.

"That noisy breathing your friend's making? It's called stridor," Alan said coolly, his voice low but cutting. "It means his airway's blocked. He'll be in respiratory distress soon if you don't get him help. When the paramedics arrive, tell them it was a stupid prank between the three of you."

He advanced, closing the distance between them in a few long strides. Grabbing the third man by the collar, Alan pulled him forward, his face inches from his own. "This bar is owned by the Monroes," he growled. "You get your friends out of here, and you make sure you never come back."

The man's breath hitched, his eyes wide, and Alan released him, shoving him backward.

Alan then turned toward the fallen labourer, still gasping for breath on the floor. With a casualness that belied the tension of the moment, Alan reached into the man's back pocket, retrieved his wallet, and tossed it across the bar to Trevor. "Make sure his tab's settled," he instructed, his tone detached, "and charge him for any damages."

Alan's eyes returned to Max, his expression hardening. "Right," he said, with a quick glance at the wreckage around them. "We should probably find another bar."

***

Sarah's expression was one of disbelief. "Alan did all of that? I honestly didn't think he had it in him. So, he does actually use all that boxing gear in his bedroom then?"

Max nodded, his lips twitching with amusement. "Yes, I wouldn't have believed it either if I hadn't seen it myself. It was all over in less than a minute! And yeah, I think he still trains occasionally. He told me he was an accomplished amateur boxer back in the day. I asked him, right after the whole scene, where he found that kind of courage…" Max paused, frowning slightly. "I told him he should give some of it to me, I lack both courage and fortitude, Alan has both in spades."

Sarah chuckled, though her tiredness was creeping in. "Don't be silly, Max. You've got plenty of skills of your own, and your own courage in court has helped more people than you probably realise, *including* Alan."

Max watched as Sarah stifled a yawn, her eyes fluttering closed. "Sorry, Max…"

He smiled softly before continuing. "Anyway, his response was something. He said he'd done a 'risk assessment.' Talked about it like it was some kind of financial investment he was weighing. He said if the labourer had been sober, he'd never have even tried to attack. Alan figured the guy was too drunk to fight properly – he called it a 'monkey dance,' like some awkward display of dominance. He said even though there were three of them, they wouldn't fight as a team. They'd just be too uncoordinated."

Max let out a laugh, shaking his head. "He said, in terms of him losing, 'the likelihood was very unlikely,' and the severity was 'negligible.' What a way to analyse a pub brawl."

Sarah mumbled something incoherent in her sleep, her soft breathing deepening. Max continued, though, speaking more softly now, as if sharing a secret.

"Alan always says that when it comes to fighting, people are quick to think they can win. But the moment pain enters the picture, they start second-guessing everything. He believes fighting's all fun and games until someone punches you in the face and makes you cry. Naturally, Harry heard the entire story from Trevor the barman and immediately wanted to hire Alan. To this day, I still don't quite understand why Alan got involved with Harry in the first place. But then again, sometimes I think Alan isn't truly content unless he's finding himself in some sort of mischief."

Max glanced at Sarah, her eyelids heavy, already drifting into sleep. He smiled to himself before gently extending her legs and stretching them out on the sofa. After a moment, he retrieved a duvet from the main bedroom and covered her with it. Quietly, he made his way upstairs to the spare room, slipping into bed, the night wrapping around him as the sounds of Sarah's slow breathing filled the silence.

Portobello Beach

It had been a month since Rollie had first spoken to Bruce about the hitchhiker he'd taken to Edinburgh. Since then, Rollie had made a point of catching up with Bruce on a weekly basis, even inviting him round to the house twice during this time, but the topic had gone cold. Rollie still wasn't convinced it wouldn't resurface at some point, but for now, he had to put it aside, especially considering Bruce was still fulfilling his courier duties impeccably.

Bruce had made the latest drive from Brighton without stopping and was hours ahead of schedule for his next pickup in Leith. He decided to give the hotels in North Yorkshire a wide berth for the time being. Seeking a place to pause near his destination, he opted for Portobello Beach, he'd read about its Victorian charm and figured it would be a good spot to unwind.

Strolling along the promenade, Bruce watched swimmers braving the chill and windsurfers cutting through the waves. The beach was picturesque, just as described, but its quiet beauty didn't quite hold him. After a short walk, he grabbed an ice cream from a kiosk and headed back to his lorry, thinking he'd do an hour of bicep curls before moving onto Leith. Bruce wasn't impressed by Portobello Beach.

As he settled in, his phone buzzed with a call from an unknown number. He ignored it, assuming Rollie had told him all he needed to know. But then the voicemail alert flashed. Curious, Bruce picked up, absently gazing over the, now familiar, Firth of Forth as he played the message.

"Hi, baby."

The unexpected voice jolted him, nearly making him drop his ice cream. It was Ciara. "It's Ciara here. I'll be in Brighton a week Saturday for a few days and wondered if you're free to catch up? I'm just about to board a plane, so ping me a message to let me know if you're around. Speak soon, babes!"

The message ended with a soft click. Bruce played it again. Then once more, relishing every lilting note of her Irish accent. Her voice, with its musical cadences, seemed to reach right through the phone, filling him with a thrill he hadn't expected.

He saved the number and quickly sent her a message, letting her know he'd be there. As he hit send, he realised that he was actually starting to like Portobello Beach.

Succession Planning

A week had passed, and Alan's condition had notably improved; he'd even started working the heavy bag again, though only with his right hand. Now, seated in The Court Club, he waited for Harry, who had been persistently calling him – a barrage of calls Alan had ignored until now.

When Harry finally breezed in, he immediately flagged down Trevor, the bartender, demanding drinks even though Trevor was busy serving another customer. Used to Harry's self-importance, Trevor barely flinched and continued his work. "Bring them over, mate," Harry instructed dismissively, before sliding into the seat across from Alan with an air of entitlement.

"I've got a job for you," Harry said casually, as though nothing had happened since their last encounter. "You're looking better, by the way."

Alan's expression hardened. "No thanks to you or your brother, Harry. What on earth were you thinking, sending those kids to frighten me? I could've been seriously hurt – or worse, I could've hurt one of them!"

"You *did* hurt one of them, Big Al," Harry replied with a smirk. Alan winced at the nickname. "You put the poor sod in the hospital – cost me a bit extra, that did. But don't worry, I won't charge you." Alan could hardly believe Harry's audacity.

The drinks arrived. "Thanks, Trev," Harry said, downing half his glass before turning back to Alan. "Alright, now, don't be a pork chop about it. Let's bury the hatchet and call it a truce, yeah? After all, you've still got all that cash from Nigel. All in all, you've done alright out if this mess."

Alan felt more disappointed than angry. "You mean the truce your brother called, Harry. This isn't good enough –"

Harry waved his hands dismissively, cutting him off. "Sure, sure, Al. Just move on, yeah? Stop harping on about it, and stop being a pork chop."

Alan held back the urge to snap, to tell him he'd only mentioned it once – and to stop using "Al" and "pork chop." But he knew it would be pointless. Harry was too wrapped up in himself to listen.

Alan took a slow sip of his drink, letting Harry carry on. "Right, Friday at midday. We'll grab a cab from here to Rollie's. He's called a board meeting, and attendance is mandatory. Even my nephew from Bristol has to be there. I want you by my side – no arguments. And of course, I'll pay for your time."

"Harry don't be ridiculous. Rollie's sons have a beef with me, and my being there would just provoke them, it's a stupid idea. Besides, I'm *not* on the board of your company," Alan replied, trying to keep his patience.

"Yeah, but I've just decided I'm grooming you as my successor – just in case, you know, I get hit by a bus or something." Harry gave him a grin, his yellow front teeth visible through his white beard. "Plus, it'll wind up my brother. Win-win."

Harry didn't pause long enough for Alan to get a word in before announcing, "Alright, that's settled. Midday on Friday." He turned toward the bar and called out, "Trev! More drinks, and this time, make them proper large ones!"

Trevor sighed, casting an apologetic look to the lady he was currently serving before nodding to Harry's demand.

Alan didn't linger at the Court Club. Instead, he hailed an Uber to the George & Dragon, the local pub near his home where he still managed to keep a low profile. Once there, he sent a quick message to Max.

Alan

Max, Harry wants me at his board meeting on Friday, will you be there? I'm at the G&D if you fancy a pint.

Max's reply came quickly.

Max Moore

Yes, I'll be at the board meeting, so I'll see you there. How mischievous of Harry inviting you! Can't make it tonight – heading to see Sarah as the police are coming by to discuss Peter. Wish me luck.

Alan did just that and wished Max luck. As he settled in, he couldn't help but wonder. If he didn't know better, he might almost suspect something was happening between Max and Sarah. An amusing thought, really – what an odd couple they'd make.

Alan had dinner perched at the bar once again, deciding on an early night. However, he still didn't leave the pub until the call for last orders echoed through the room.

On his way home, he followed his usual route through the churchyard. It was his first time crossing the cemetery since the attack, but his logical mind assured him the risk was no different than before. Shadows clustered behind trees and monuments, but he reminded himself it was just a natural trick of the mind.

Turning the final corner to number 37, Alan noticed a small figure sitting on his doorstep. He paused, slipping into the shadows and narrowing his eyes to make out who – or what – was waiting for him. Whoever it was didn't appear threatening.

Crossing the road and opening the gate, he watched as the figure rose to greet him. "Hello, Audrey Hepburn," he said with a bemused smile. "To what do I owe this pleasure?"

The FLO

Max had dealt with countless criminals over the years, but missing persons cases were new terrain for him. He spent the late afternoon and early evening supporting Sarah through her third interview, this time with two female officers. One introduced herself as a Family Liaison Officer – an 'FLO,' as they called her. While Sarah understood the FLO's role as a bridge between her and the investigation team, she found the officer's relentless empathy grating, almost cloying. Still, she maintained a polite front, knowing it was necessary under the circumstances.

The case had been escalated to the UK Missing Persons Unit, a team the officers assured her were experts in such matters. Max, ever the pragmatist, pressed for information about Peter's mobile phone tracking data. His question made the lead officer visibly uneasy. After a pause, she disclosed that the data confirmed Peter had left their shared home. Her careful phrasing aimed to cushion the blow.

Peter had driven to Alan Johnson's apartment, stayed there for several hours, and then made his way to Shoreham Harbour. At this revelation, Max nearly choked on his tea. The Monroe family, with all their dysfunctions, were nothing if not professional.

The officer continued, reading from her notes. Peter's phone had been powered off at Texaco Wharf, a remote part of the harbour. That was the last signal detected. Sarah's stomach tightened as the officer explained that CCTV footage from the harbour was under review.

The tone of the room shifted when the officer added, with pointed deliberation, that during Peter's visit to Alan's Brighton apartment, Sarah and Alan had been together in Bristol. Sarah gave a solemn nod, feigning discomfort at the implied indiscretion.

The officers concluded the session by classifying Peter as a high-risk case. They assured Sarah they were leveraging international contacts to aid the investigation, stressing that Peter couldn't have left the country without detection. They were confident they would find him.

Sarah signed her statement. The FLO touched her shoulder with what was meant to be a reassuring pat, promising to stay in touch. As the officers left, Sarah maintained her composure, her mind racing with the implications of what had just been revealed.

After they had gone, Sarah turned to Max. "Shoreham Harbour?"

"Yes," Max nodded affirmatively, "Perhaps he chartered a boat to cross the English Channel?" He turned it into a rhetorical question by adding, "I'll open some wine."

Lagavulin

When Audrey Hepburn asked if she could come in for a drink, Alan hesitated briefly but felt a sudden urge for a whisky himself. "Why not?" he said, inviting her in, then fetching two tumblers and a decanter of Lagavulin. He placed them on the coffee table and sank into the sofa, while Audrey took the armchair to his left.

"Do you drink whisky?" he asked, glancing over. She nodded, so he removed the stopper and poured two generous measures. "I can't keep calling you Audrey Hepburn. What's your real name?"

"My real name *is* Audrey Hepburn," she replied smoothly, her expression unchanging. Under the sharper light of the living room, Alan could make out her features more clearly. She wasn't quite the teenager he'd assumed; likely in her early twenties, though she carried herself with a confidence that belied her age, and she *did* resemble the film star Audrey Hepburn.

Alan chuckled. "Well, the real Audrey Hepburn was a polyglot. Are you a polyglot, *Audrey?*" he asked, deliberately repeating the name to catch her off guard.

"*Je sais ce qu'est un polyglotte, et merci pour le whisky,*" she replied, her French flawless and spoken with a subtle, refined accent.

"*Très bien, mademoiselle Audrey Hepburn!*" Alan laughed, surprised and amused. "Where'd you learn French?"

"In France," she answered dryly, then tossed back her whisky in one smooth gulp.

Still Missing

After the police left, Sarah found herself more shaken than she had anticipated. Over the next hour, she wrestled with a torrent of thoughts. "The police will need to talk to Alan," she muttered, one of many fragmented reflections flitting through her mind.

Max, ever steady, tried to reassure her. "Yes, they will. But don't worry – I'll brief him first. Everything will be fine."

Sarah exhaled sharply, her voice tinged with frustration and weariness. "I just want closure. I want this whole ordeal behind me, behind us!" She hesitated, her gaze drifting to the floor. "Even Peter," she added softly, as though testing the weight of her own words. "That makes me a terrible person, doesn't it?"

Max shook his head firmly. "Not at all, my dear. I understand completely. Your feelings are natural and entirely reasonable."

The hours stretched into the night as they nursed their drinks. Sarah, weary but still probing, circled back to her perennial curiosity about Max's past. "Max, you're like a brother to me, but one of these days you're going to let me in. I know you're not ready yet, but..." She paused, studying him. "You deflect too much."

Max smiled faintly, avoiding her gaze. "Did I ever tell you why Harry recruited Alan?" he asked, steering the conversation away from himself with practiced ease.

Sarah sighed but played along, tucking her legs under her on the sofa. "No, you didn't. Actually, I don't even really know what Alan does for Harry. I mean, I assume it's got something to do with those idiots he handled at The Court Club?"

Max leaned back, his voice taking on the tone of a storyteller. "Harry is, among other things, a moneylender. Not huge sums, but enough – five figures, mostly – to warrant a collector. That's where Alan comes in. He doesn't resort to violence, but the possibility of it. That's always there. And yes, Harry knew about what Alan did at The Court Club, but he already had a collector at that point."

Sarah tilted her head, intrigued. "So why Alan?"

Max gave a small, enigmatic smile. "Harry values loyalty and competence above all else. Alan ticked both boxes."

***

The police did, in fact, visit Alan, but their efforts yielded little. Even without Max's coaching, Alan was adept at steering a narrative.

"Yes," he admitted with a composed smile, "Sarah and I were in Bristol, and, well... it's true – we're in a relationship. How awkward for you to find out this way." His tone carried just enough self-deprecation to seem genuine.

"Is this a long-term relationship?" one of the officers asked.

"Yes," Alan replied evenly, projecting an air of earnestness. "We've been together for some time now."

"And were you aware of Peter's potential involvement with someone named Naomi?"

Alan arched an eyebrow, feigning surprise. "Naomi, you say. I can't say I've ever heard that name before."

The officers exchanged a glance before one of them gestured toward the room. "Is this a new carpet?"

The innocuous question hit Alan like a jolt. His heart quickened, but he forced himself to remain calm. If they pressed for details – where he bought it, when – it could lead to questions he wasn't prepared to answer.

"Yes," he said lightly, willing his voice to stay steady. "It is. I thought it was time for a refresh."

"Very nice, I like the smell of new carpet," the officer remarked, their interest seemingly superficial.

The conversation soon shifted back to more mundane matters, the carpet momentarily forgotten.

By the time the police left with Alan's signed statement, they appeared satisfied. The inquiry, at least for now, seemed to be leading nowhere. Alan saw them out, his calm façade unbroken, but once the door clicked shut, he exhaled deeply. Luck had been on his side this time.

Whisky and Cigars

Audrey poured herself another generous measure of whisky, the amber liquid glinting as it splashed into the heavy tumbler. "Which whisky is this?" she inquired, her tone casual but her eyes sharp.

Alan, still taken aback by her sudden appearance, found an almost surreal amusement in the situation. "Lagavulin, 16-year. A taste not for the faint of heart." He paused, letting his gaze settle on her. "Why are you here, Audrey?"

She raised her glass to her lips, ignoring the question, and took a slow, deliberate sip. "From the island of Islay," she replied, pronouncing it perfectly as 'aye-lah.' Alan's surprise deepened, and a flicker of admiration crossed his face.

"You don't look like someone who'd know her way around a whisky bottle, especially one from Islay," he said, unable to keep the edge of disbelief from his voice. His eyes flicked briefly to her cheek. "And I see the bruise healed nicely. I'm glad."

Audrey's fingers traced the faint shadow on her cheekbone, a remnant of their last encounter. "As I told you, Alan, I'm older than you think," she shot back, her voice steady, yet there was a hint of steel in her words.

Boffin curled up at Audrey's feet, her purring soft and contented. Audrey leaned down, offering the cat a gentle stroke. Alan watched, surprised – it was unusual for his cat to favour a guest over him. Perhaps Boffin sensed something about Audrey's character that Alan was about to discover.

Alan let out a low chuckle, settling into his chair and lifting his tumbler to his lips. "Seems to me, you're here with an agenda. What's really going on, Audrey?"

She glanced at him, her posture poised, almost too poised, as though bracing herself. "Are you that eager to be rid of me?" she replied, her voice cool, though he sensed the tension beneath her calm exterior.

Alan studied her, his gaze unwavering. "Not eager, no. Curious, definitely." He tilted his head slightly, scrutinising her. "People don't tend to show up at my doorstop for no reason, especially not people like you."

A small, enigmatic smile tugged at the corners of Audrey's mouth, though her eyes remained guarded. "Maybe I just wanted a change of scenery." She took another sip, her gaze holding his as if daring him to probe further.

"A change of scenery?" he echoed, a hint of amusement colouring his tone. "Or maybe a distraction?"

Her smile faltered for just a moment, an almost imperceptible crack in her composure. She set her glass down, running a finger around the rim. "Sometimes a distraction is exactly what one needs, Alan."

He leaned forward slightly, catching her eye, the intensity of his gaze unrelenting. "Well, if there *was* something on your mind, you can just say it."

A flicker of something vulnerable crossed her face before she quickly masked it, but Alan had caught it. She looked away, the guarded edge in her voice softening ever so slightly. "Perhaps I just wanted to be around someone who doesn't expect anything from me."

Alan's expression shifted, a trace of sympathy breaking through his practiced stoicism. He knew that feeling, the weight of expectations, the loneliness of never quite fitting into others' moulds. He took a sip, allowing the silence to linger between them, thick with words unspoken.

"Let's just sit in silence for a while and enjoy the Lagavulin," Alan suggested. But his silence held for only about ten seconds. "She was way before your time, anyway."

"Who was?" Audrey asked, arching an eyebrow.

"Audrey was," Alan clarified, as if that explained everything.

Audrey looked amused. "Audrey who?"

"Audrey Hepburn. I assumed that was the origin of your name," Alan said, watching her closely.

"How do you even know Audrey Hepburn was a 'she'?" Audrey's question threw him off-balance.

"What else would she have been?" he asked, genuinely perplexed.

"A 'they,'" Audrey replied, her tone firm but patient. "As in non-binary. My gender is non-binary," she added, holding his gaze confidently.

Alan blinked, caught off guard. "Audrey Hepburn wasn't non-binary. That term didn't even exist back then!"

Audrey gave a small, knowing smile. "How can you be so sure? Do you think gender diversity is a new concept? If Audrey Hepburn were alive today, they might very well identify as non-binary, just like me. It's not a simple binary question."

"No, it's a non-binary question." Alan replied.

"You don't know what you're talking about," she countered.

"You're right there," Alan conceded.

Alan was silent for a moment, realising he'd underestimated her conviction. "So, what is it you choose to identify as?" he asked, feeling pleased with himself to have phrased it well.

Audrey tilted her head, meeting his eyes. "I identify as Audrey Hepburn," she said simply, as if it were the most natural thing in the world.

Alan let out a huff of laughter, but there was a faint tension in his smile. "But you can't know she would have identified as non-binary!"

Audrey's eyes sparkled with the hint of a challenge. "You mean 'they,' not 'she.' Please try to get it right."

Alan studied her, a little exasperated and wondering if she was now teasing him, or perhaps making a deeper point. Frankly, he was baffled and not quite sure how to respond.

Alan groaned loudly, then ambled over to his small wooden humidor. He selected a cigar, clipped the end with practiced ease, and lit it, the faint scent of smoke curling into the air as he reclined back into the sofa. "Alright then," he said, exhaling slowly, "I identify as a cigar." He grinned, clearly pleased with himself.

Audrey smirked, leaning forward with a twinkle of mischief. "Oh, is that because you think you're 'shhmoking'?" she teased in an exaggerated American accent. "Or just because you regularly stink up this apartment?"

Alan raised an eyebrow, feigning offense. "Very clever," he replied dryly. "But I'll have you know; this is the scent of sophistication."

Audrey chuckled, leaning back. "If by 'sophistication' you mean a smoky old gentleman's club, then yes, you're spot on."

The Ballad of Billy Brown

Sarah cradled her wine glass, swirling the deep red liquid as Max refilled his own. "Do you remember hearing about Billy Brown? Must have been about four years ago," he asked, settling back into his chair.

Sarah furrowed her brow, searching her memory. "No, I don't think so," she replied.

Max nodded, adjusting his spectacles and pushing them onto his forehead. He leaned back into the sofa, his tone shifting to that of a storyteller. "Alright, let me start from the beginning. Billy was raised in a solid family. They didn't have much money, but his parents worked hard and they owned their council house, and managed two weeks in Spain every year. He had a younger sister, and between the four of them, life was steady. Billy didn't want for anything. He was a good kid – studious, polite."

Max paused, as if recalling the turning point. "But somewhere early in senior school, Billy started going off the rails. At first, it was just fighting. He wasn't a big lad, and not particularly skilled at fighting, but he had a knack for intimidation. And he was fearless. Didn't care about losing a fight – he'd just keep coming back, again and again, until people thought twice about crossing him."

Sarah sipped her wine, listening intently as Max continued.

"Then there was the stealing," he said, shaking his head slightly. "At first, it was petty – sweets from the corner shop, a CD or two from bigger stores. It got him into trouble, sure, but his parents stayed lenient, hoping he'd grow out of it. They couldn't see the bigger picture yet."

Max glanced at Sarah. She was still awake, her eyes fixed on him. "In his mid-teens, Billy had something of an epiphany," he began. "First, he realised he was wasting his life, always in trouble over petty nonsense. But more importantly, he recognised he was… different. It wasn't just bravado that set him apart. It was the fact that Billy felt *nothing*. No fear, no guilt, no hesitation. He was willing to take risks that even the boldest of his friends wouldn't dare."

Sarah tilted her head, her brows knitting. "A psychopath, then?"

"Exactly," Max replied, a faint smile tugging at the corner of his mouth as he took another sip of wine. He reached for the bottle. "Top-up?"

Sarah waved him off, covering her glass with her hand. "No thanks," her gesture seemed to say.

Max settled back into his story. "Billy left school as soon as he legally could. No GCSEs, no plan – just odd jobs and a carefree existence. He eventually got married, had two kids, but settling down? That was never in the cards. He carried on a string of affairs, barely making an effort to hide them. Sometimes he'd even bring these women home, right under his wife's nose. He didn't care – not about her, not about the kids. The man was utterly devoid of compassion."

Sarah interrupted again, leaning forward slightly. "How do you know all this, Max?"

Max sighed, swirling his wine before answering. "Sorry, my dear, I should have explained. I represented him many times as his solicitor. I got to know him well – though not by choice. He wasn't an easy client. Frankly, he was intimidating."

"Did he ever do time?" Sarah asked, her tone curious but cautious.

Max nodded slowly. "He did, but not as much as you'd expect. Most prosecution teams were too scared to press charges, and with good reason. I represented Billy on multiple occasions, and I can't say I enjoyed it. There was always this unspoken fear of retribution if things didn't go his way. But oddly enough, he treated me fairly. I suppose I respected me – at least as much as someone like Billy could respect anyone."

Max leaned back, his voice lowering as he continued. "I thought he'd found his niche when he landed a job managing security staff for a company that ran most of the nightclub doors in East Sussex. They held group meetings in the evenings before shifts, and Billy would always attend. It was fascinating – and unnerving – to watch. He was smaller than an almost all of the bouncers, most of whom could easily overpower him in a fight. Yet they all feared him. It was like watching a Rugby Union referee scold towering players twice his size. Billy had this aura – this ability to control a room through sheer menace."

Max paused, his expression darkening. "But, of course, Billy always knew how to push people's buttons. One night, he went too far. A doorman – a big, tough guy and a martial arts expert – finally snapped. Whatever Billy had said, it must have been something vile because the man gave Billy a proper beating. Billy didn't stand a chance. He wasn't a fighter in the physical sense, but he knew how to provoke.

"Later that same night, Billy showed up at the club where the man was working. He didn't say a word. Just walked straight up to him in the middle of the crowd and slit his throat – clean across, ear to ear."

Sarah gasped, sitting upright as if jolted back to life. "Oh my God! And you had to defend him in court for that?"

"Yes, indeed," Max replied, his tone steady. "But don't forget, my dear – everyone deserves representation, no matter how heinous the crime."

Sarah frowned, clearly struggling with the concept. "I understand the principle, Max, but... when the crime is so blatant, I don't know how you do it."

Max leaned forward slightly, his voice firm but calm. "Because I have an unshakable belief in the law. A fair justice system is essential, even for those we despise. Without it, society crumbles. More often than not the guilty just want someone to tell them it's not their fault. Well, I'm good at telling them it's not their fault even if I don't believe it." He paused, letting the weight of his words settle. "And, as unbelievable as it sounds, that night's drama didn't end there."

He took a generous sip of wine before continuing, his tone laced with incredulity. "After slashing the man's throat, Billy didn't flee. Instead, he immediately switched into first-aid mode. He shouted for bar towels and did his best to compress the wound until the paramedics arrived. The guy – bleeding profusely and in shock – was yelling at Billy to get off him, demanding someone arrest him. But Billy ignored him and held on, doing everything he could to stop the bleeding."

Sarah stared at Max, her wine glass frozen mid-air. "You're joking," she whispered.

"Not at all," Max said, shaking his head. "Incredibly, Billy's actions actually saved the man's life. The paramedics were so impressed they even recommended Billy for a bravery award."

Sarah's jaw dropped. "You're kidding me."

Max's expression darkened as he delivered the final twist. "Of course, when the police reviewed the security footage, they saw exactly what had happened. Billy was promptly arrested for attempted murder."

Max paused, a wry chuckle escaping him. The absurdity of it all still baffled him. "Billy was nothing if not deviously clever. He persuaded me to appoint two independent doctors to assess his mental state, insisting it was the best course of action. I advised against it, convinced he wouldn't pass their rigorous evaluations. But, of course, he did. Both doctors confirmed he was insane at the time of the attack."

He shook his head, recalling the moment. "The judge had little choice after that. Billy was found not guilty by reason of insanity. Instead of prison, he was sent to Ashworth Hospital, near Liverpool."

Sarah's brow furrowed with concern. "Those places sound just as bad as prison. Are they?"

Max met her gaze, his expression thoughtful. "Not quite. If you're compliant – and Billy was – they're far less harsh than a maximum-security prison. The staff aren't there to punish but to rehabilitate. Four years later, he walked out of Ashworth, allegedly cured of his insanity, and a free man."

He let out a bitter laugh, shaking his head in disbelief. "Truly remarkable."

Max continued, "Harry knew all about Billy's reputation and thought he'd make use of it, so he offered him a job. Billy, of course, jumped at the chance."

"That sounds like a disaster waiting to happen," Sarah said, raising an eyebrow.

"And it was," Max admitted with a sigh. "Rollie warned Harry – told him in no uncertain terms to steer well clear of Billy. But you know Harry. If Rollie says black, Harry says white. He hired Billy just to spite his brother. You have to understand, Harry's antipathy towards his brother isn't just theoretical or ideological, it's visceral and personal."

Max leaned back, his tone growing reflective. "At first, it seemed like Harry had proven Rollie wrong. Billy did his collections, followed the rules, and kept everything running smoothly. For a while, all was well. But Billy couldn't help himself. He got bored, and boredom for Billy meant trouble. He started taking liberties – hurting people unnecessarily, purely for the thrill of it."

Max's voice lowered as the story darkened. "Things escalated. Billy began selling drugs on the side, targeting the very people who were borrowing money – vulnerable, desperate people who were already in over their heads. When Rollie found out, he was furious. Apoplectic, actually. He demanded Harry deal with it. No excuses."

Max paused, glancing at Sarah to ensure she was still engaged. "That's where Alan came in. Harry didn't want Billy eliminated – it wasn't his style, and Alan wouldn't have agreed to it anyway. Instead, Harry turned to Alan's expertise in surveillance. The plan was simple: set Billy up, frame him, and make sure the authorities finally put him away for good."

Sarah leaned in, completely captivated. "How on earth did Harry manage to set that up?" she asked, unable to tear her eyes away from Max.

Max's expression darkened as he spoke, his tone grave. "Harry went all in. He orchestrated a massive drug deal for Billy – one that personally cost him about £20,000. I couldn't believe it at first. Harry's usually so tight with his money, but this was different. It showed just how far he was willing to go to get rid of Billy."

He paused, letting the weight of his words settle before continuing. "Harry arranged for Billy to buy a stash of drugs at a bargain price, a deal that promised to net Billy a pretty substantial profit – something like forty grand. He knew Billy would take the bait. The plan was for the deal to go down after the clubs had closed, in one of Billy's favourite spots: an abandoned building in Hove. It used to be a tool shop, now just a quiet place, ideal for after-hours transactions."

Max shifted in his seat, his eyes focused as if retracing the steps. "Alan rented an apartment just across the street from that building. One of those short-term holiday rentals. He set up two hidden cameras pointed at the old tool shop, then he waited."

Max finished his glass of wine and immediately topped it up, the bottle emptying at a rapid pace. "The kicker," he continued, his voice low, "was that Harry had arranged for the police to show up instead of a real buyer. Harry knew Billy would be caught red handed with a huge quantity of drugs *and* some kind of weapon. Alan was sitting in the dark, watching the front of the building on his laptop. Billy showed up on time, set up as planned, and everything seemed to be going smoothly. But then... nothing. No buyer. No cops. Apparently, the police had paid little attention to Harry's arrangements – they didn't take him seriously. By 4:30 a.m., Billy had started consuming his own product."

Max paused, his gaze distant as he recalled the scene. "Alan watched as Billy paced around the car park, shouting at shadows, slapping himself across the face. He was losing it. Then Billy disappeared into the building for about ten minutes, and when he returned, he was carrying a gun. Alan tried calling Harry, but there was no answer – Harry was fast asleep, unaware of what was happening."

Max leaned forward, his expression darkening. "Then, disaster struck. Two police officers came into view. Alan could see them, but Billy couldn't. They'd just finished their shift in the city and were heading back to the station. The senior officer – he'd been on the force for fifteen years, had a family – was mentoring a young female officer, still new to the job."

"He approached Billy to ask what the shouting was all about, completely unaware of the drugs or the gun."

Sarah was riveted now, "Oh no, I think I do remember reading about this story in the Argus."

Max's expression grew sombre as he continued the story. "By this point, Billy had completely lost his grip on reality. He pulled the massive gun from under his jacket and shot the officer point-blank through the head. The officer dropped like a stone; he was killed instantly. The female officer froze, unable even to press her emergency button. Billy started shouting at her – look what she'd made him do, why had she made him do that, and so on. He raised the gun at her, but suddenly pointed it down and shot her through the foot. I don't think he meant to shoot her through the foot, he just had terrible aim. She survived physically but I doubt she'll ever recover mentally. Billy shouted at both officers again, blaming them for his actions. Then he put the gun in his mouth and blew his own brains out."

"Holy crap!" Sarah exclaimed, a phrase she'd never used before but found fitting for the moment.

"Indeed," Max responded, his tone sombre. "Alan quietly packed up his gear and slipped away the next morning, and Harry had to lay low for a while." Max poured the last drops from the wine bottle, the clink of glass echoing in the quiet room. "The news spread like wildfire; it made all the national press – especially since Billy had used a 'Dirty Harry' gun. A .44 Magnum, I think it's called. A massive, intimidating weapon. God only knows where he got it. Harry called it a 'hand cannon,' a term I always found a bit too crass."

"Yeah, I remember that now," Sarah said, recalling the details.

"And here's something the press never revealed," Max continued with a wry smile. "Billy's real name wasn't even Billy. It was Jacob, though his family called him Jake. One of his many girlfriends once told me she was at a pub with him when he walked in, a razor blade between his teeth. She called him 'Psycho Billy,' and – surprise, surprise – he didn't mind. The nickname stuck."

Sarah shook her head in disbelief, her eyes wide as the story sank in. "One more bottle of wine?" she asked, the weight of it all settling in. Max nodded, a knowing glint in his eye.

Brighton When It Sizzles

Audrey and Alan settled into another comfortable silence, the kind that seemed to stretch easily across the room. Alan finished his cigar, exhaling one last plume of smoke before stubbing it out. Audrey remained poised on the edge of the armchair, unmoving, like some timeless figure set apart from the world. They had dimmed the main light, leaving only the soft glow of a single lamp, casting warm shadows across the room and adding an intimate, almost dreamlike quality to the space.

The low light and the steady warmth of the whisky left Alan feeling pleasantly woozy. He glanced over at Audrey, whose slender, statuesque figure seemed to blur the line between memory and reality. They shared the refined elegance of the Audrey from the films – the same almond-shaped eyes with a soft, playful sparkle under gracefully arched brows, and that hint of a smile at the corners of delicate lips, radiating a quiet confidence.

Audrey's clothing was a seamless blend of black and white, classic yet understated, perfectly suited to the ambiance, enhancing their natural allure without demanding attention. In that moment, Alan couldn't help but feel he was in the presence of an Audrey who belonged to another time – a figure who had somehow stepped from a black-and-white film into his dimly lit apartment, bringing with them the elegance and mystery of a bygone era.

Alan blinked, realising he needed to shake off the haziness clouding his mind. This wasn't the real Audrey Hepburn, he reminded himself – just a trick of too much whisky and low light. Suddenly, a phone on the coffee table burst to life, shattering the silence with the opening notes of *Moon River*. He hadn't even noticed it lying there, but of course, he thought with a smirk – what else would Audrey's phone play?

Audrey glanced at the phone as it rang but made no move to answer. The call eventually went to voicemail, leaving the room silent once more.

"That was my father," they said, their expression unchanging, voice steady.

Alan thought he noticed a tension but decided against probing further. Instead, he gestured to the cigar stub in the ashtray. "Do you smoke?" he asked, half-offering.

"No," Audrey replied, their tone clipped. "And neither did they."

"Yes, they did," Alan countered, raising an eyebrow. "Hepburn was often photographed with a cigarette holder – a long, opera-length one, if I remember right."

Audrey dismissed it with a wave. "A fashion accessory, Alan. The cigarette was never lit."

Alan eyed them, amused but unconvinced. Audrey seemed resolute, however, and he let the matter drop. Against his better judgment, he poured another finger of whisky, swirling the glass thoughtfully, wondering what else this Audrey might reveal if the evening stretched on just a bit longer.

***

Alan teetered on the edge of consciousness, the ebb and flow of awareness tugging at his senses. Audrey's voice cut through the haze, jolting him awake. He had almost forgotten they were still lingering there.

"Do you fancy some coke?" Audrey's words danced in the air, provocative and tinged with temptation.

"I've only got diet, it's in the fridge, you'll need to help yourself. Christ, you'll want ice with it next." Alan quipped; his sense of humour miraculously intact despite teetering on the edge of unconsciousness.

"*C'est drôle!*" Audrey replied.

"No, thanks, I don't do that." Alan replied, his eyelids heavy as he rubbed his eyes, grounding himself back in the room. "I doubt they would have gone for it either."

"They would have, trust me," Audrey retorted, "Living for today was their mantra."

"Not this again," Alan chuckled, shaking his head with a mix of amusement and disbelief. "And how, exactly, do you know *that*?"

Audrey met his gaze, a hint of mischief in their eyes. "Because I embody their essence," they said with quiet conviction. "And I'm about to indulge. If you don't mind?"

Alan gave a reluctant nod, a fleeting look of hesitation crossing his face. Audrey reached into a small handbag, pulling out a transparent bag of white powder. "You're content enough to drink yourself into oblivion and risk lung disease with those cigars," they pointed out, eyebrow raised.

Alan let out a soft laugh. "When did you get so cynical? And at such a young age, no less."

"I've told you before, I'm not as young as I look." Audrey pulled the coffee table closer, tapping the bag so a fine dusting of white powder fell onto its surface.

Alan's resolve wavered as he watched, the alcohol dulling the voice of reason in his mind. "Alright," he murmured, "I'll join you." He watched, transfixed, as Audrey carefully arranged the powder into a precise, narrow line. "You don't use a banknote to sniff that?" he asked, curious despite himself.

Audrey glanced up, momentarily pausing, an ironic smile playing at their lips. "It's snort, and no, the new plastic notes are too thick – they'll slice your nose open. Anyway, who carries cash these days?" They reached into a pocket and pulled out a small, metallic straw. "Metal works best."

"So, I see," Alan murmured, his voice a mix of fascination and caution, as he observed the meticulous ritual unfolding before him.

***

Alan basked in the initial euphoria, feeling a rush of energy coursing through him with a potency that took him by surprise. For a moment, everything was sharper, clearer; his senses felt electrified, his thoughts quick and luminous. But as the minutes ticked by, the high began to shift, turning hazy around the edges. About half an hour later, his once-clear thoughts grew muddled, the thrill giving way to a creeping sense of disorientation, as if he were sinking slowly into an unsettling mental fog. The high that had initially lifted him was now pulling him toward a dark, dissonant place, blurring the line between clarity and chaos.

Meanwhile, Audrey had consumed more, their demeanour growing more assertive. They locked eyes with Alan, their determination apparent. "I want you to teach me how to kill my father."

Alan was taken aback, caught off guard by the sudden gravity of their request. "Why?" he managed to ask, struggling to comprehend the motives behind such a statement.

"Because I want to kill him," Audrey shot back, their words sharp and unapologetic.

Alan took a moment to steady himself, searching for the deeper reasoning behind their desire. "No, I mean, why do you want to kill him?" he inquired, hoping to unveil the root of their pain and anger.

"He's been mean to me," Audrey's words held less impact than Alan had expected.

"I guessed that much, but what has he done to warrant the death sentence?" Alan pushed for more information, concerned yet empathetic.

"He abused me." For the first time that night, Audrey's emotions surfaced, catching Alan off guard. In that moment, they seemed fragile, young, and small.

"Why not go to the police?" Alan inquired, treading carefully.

"It's my word against his, and anyway, that would hurt my mother," Audrey replied, their voice reflecting a deep dilemma.

"And killing him wouldn't hurt your mum?"

"She would be relieved," they admitted, exposing the depth of pain and torment they had endured.

"Well, either way, you're not killing him." Alan insisted.

"Can you kill him." Audrey persisted.

"Could I kill him? Yes. Can I kill him. No. Do you live at home?" Alan replied firmly.

"No, I've moved out," Audrey replied simply. In reality, they had left their family home at eighteen, drifting between temporary places over the last four years. Yet they'd returned many times – sometimes out of a lingering, misplaced sense of duty to protect their mother, other times because they'd run out of options. Despite everything, a part of them found a strange solace in the familiarity of that home, even though their relationship with their father had soured beyond repair.

"Good," Alan said, visibly relieved. He was glad Audrey had removed themselves from that toxic environment. "So where are you living now?"

Audrey hesitated, a faint glimmer of vulnerability breaking through. "I was thinking... maybe your spare room?"

The suggestion hit Alan like a jolt. He sensed a certain hope in Audrey's voice, as if they saw in him a possible escape – a saviour of sorts. But he kept his tone steady, firm. "Bad idea," he replied, without hesitation.

Audrey's expression didn't shift, but Alan saw a flicker in their eyes, as if the wall they kept up had just cracked, if only for a second.

Audrey waved off the setback with a flick of their hand. "Will you hurt him for me? Will you just make him leave me alone?"

Alan hesitated, but the question lingered in the air. He knew he should pause, think it through, but somehow he couldn't bring himself to deny the request. "Yes, okay." The words slipped out before he could fully consider the consequences.

Audrey's shoulders relaxed, a slight sense of relief creeping into their voice. "I'll give you the address later. Thank you, I think you're a good person."

Alan, still feeling the weight of his decision, let out a rueful laugh. "I hope I'm not going to regret this," he muttered. He was acutely aware that agreeing to this – whatever it entailed – was rash at best. "But you can't stay in my spare room."

Audrey's brow furrowed, surprised by the rejection. "Why not?"

Alan's words faltered as he searched for a reason, any reason. "Well, because…" His mind struggled to articulate the deeper hesitation, the unease settling in his gut.

Audrey, seemingly oblivious to the hesitation, quickly changed the subject. "Let's do some more coke," they suggested, retrieving the transparent bag from the table once more, their tone light, almost too casual.

***

Audrey's sudden question caught Alan off guard, snapping him back into the moment. "Why aren't you married, or don't have a girlfriend?"

It took him a few moments to process the question, his mind sluggish from the haze of coke and whisky. "How do you know I don't have a girlfriend?" he asked, genuinely puzzled, trying to make sense of Audrey's insight.

Audrey tilted their head and gestured around the room, a playful smirk tugging at their lips. "Look around. You *definitely* don't have a woman in your life."

Alan glanced around, taking in the unremarkable space – empty, save for a few scattered items. The chessboard sat alone on the dining table which had been shoved tight into the corner of the room. The pieces had been placed randomly on the board, likely moved by the carpet fitters. With a resigned shrug, he conceded. "Fair enough. I was married once, but it didn't work out."

Audrey's eyes sharpened. "Is that because of your military service?" Their tone was casual, but there was a probing edge to it.

"How do you know about my military service?" Alan asked, genuinely baffled.

Audrey's laughter was almost mocking. "Look around," they said again, as though it was obvious.

Alan's gaze fell on the mantelpiece where his medals were displayed on a small stand. He had nearly forgotten they were there. It had been Sarah's insistence to keep them on show, driven by a strange attachment to polishing them, as if they were trophies rather than reminders of a past that was better left undisturbed. "Oh, right," he muttered, suddenly feeling the weight of the room close in on him. The alcohol and coke were making it hard to think clearly, and the conversation was becoming more uncomfortable by the second.

Audrey's voice grew quieter, more intense. "Have you ever killed anyone?"

The question hit Alan like a punch to the gut. His response was too quick, too cold. "Yes, loads."

Audrey didn't flinch. "Anyone up close and personal?"

Alan felt a knot tighten in his chest. The memories, sharp and vivid, threatened to surface. He wasn't ready to face them, not now, not here. "Yes," he answered simply, a chill in his voice.

"Tell me about it?" Audrey pressed, leaning forward, eyes fixed on him with a mixture of curiosity and something darker.

Alan's jaw clenched, and he looked away. "No." His tone left no room for argument, shutting down the conversation before it could go any further. He didn't want to revisit those memories, not for anyone.

***

"You look tired," Audrey observed, their tone flat, without any emotion.

Alan's eyes struggled to focus, the room spinning slightly. He tried to muster a response, his words slurring a little. "I am hammered."

Audrey didn't seem to notice his struggle, rising smoothly from the chair. "I'll get you to bed."

"I can manage," Alan insisted, though the determination in his voice was a little weaker than he'd like to admit.

Audrey chuckled, a dry, almost pitying laugh. "You really can't." Their gaze locked onto him, and despite the haze clouding his thoughts, Alan felt a subtle challenge in their eyes, as if they were daring him to argue.

***

While Alan's physical presence remained anchored in the quiet apartment in Brighton, his mind drifted – unmoored, unbound by time or place. He was no longer in the here and now. Instead, his consciousness was whisked away, transported fifteen years into the past, far from the familiar coastal air of England to a place where the atmosphere felt heavier, and the weight of memory pressed upon his chest like an invisible hand.

It was as though the past had crept up on him, silently pulling him into its grasp, forcing him to confront long-buried moments – fragments of himself that had been hidden away.

Alan had long since perfected the art of compartmentalisation. His psychological training, forged over years of rigorous preparation, kept him grounded in moments of extreme duress. While physical prowess had its place, it was the mental acuity – shaped by years of discipline and focused detachment – that truly defined his effectiveness. The mental edge was what allowed him to perform under pressure, walking that fine line between empathy and psychopathy, where one's humanity was both an asset and a liability.

His training had thrust him into trauma at varying intensities, pushing him beyond his limits time and again. With each trial, his resilience grew, until it was less about survival and more about precision. He had become an instrument of execution – a high-functioning killer with the rare, bitter gift of empathy. But no one had warned him about the shadows it left behind. The nightmares, the haunting presence of memories that never truly faded, lingered like ghosts.

Now, Alan closed the blue metal gate behind him, the sharp creak of its hinges reverberating in the night. He was wearing the olive-green fatigues of the National Army of Guatemala, and the three solid gold bars on his epaulette marked him as *'Capitan Segundo'* – Second Captain – his rank in this distant world that was no longer his own.

Though he wasn't really in Guatemala City, and certainly not 36 years old, his mind had carried him back to that precise moment, fifteen years ago. The path ahead was familiar – the one that led toward the sentry. Alan's eyes instinctively lifted toward the office window on the first floor. The lights still burned bright against the darkness, a lone beacon of purpose in the oppressive night air. His target was there, just beyond that window.

The sentry challenged him, "*Parar! Quién va allí?*" [Stop. Who goes there?]

"*Buenas noches. Vengo a ver al General Parr.*" [Good evening. I have come to see General Parr.] Alan replied, hoping his Spanish would hold up to scrutiny.

The sentry noticed Alan's insignia, lowered his rifle, saluted, and stood at attention. "*Lo siento, señor, no lo reconocí. Todavía está en su oficina, por favor proceda.*" [Sorry sir, I didn't recognise you. He is still in his office, please proceed.] The sentry had never met Alan, his rank had given him all the authority he needed to move forward without further scrutiny.

The hallway lights cast a dim, flickering glow as Alan entered, the door left ajar, allowing the guard to benefit from the air conditioning in an attempt to counter the stifling, humid heat. Alan nodded as he passed, murmuring, "*Gracias,*" while the sentry, now at ease, acknowledged him.

Climbing the short set of stairs, Alan felt a low, simmering tension start to rise. This quiet, unremarkable approach belied the extensive months of preparation, training, and precise resource-gathering – a monumental undertaking. He noticed how well the olive-green uniform fit, its tones close to those of his British fatigues, though not quite identical. Still, there was something oddly comforting about its familiar weight.

He paused outside General Parr's office, his fingers brushing the door handle, steadying himself for the next move.

Alan knocked twice on the office door. "*Entrar!*" came a shout from within. Alan stepped through. "*Pensé que era el único que seguía trabajando…*" [I thought I was the only one still working…] General Parr looked up from the paperwork on his desk, and a jolt of recognition struck him like a slap. His expression froze. "Captain Johnson? What in God's name are you doing here?"

"Major Parr, or should I say *General de brigade* Parr?" Alan replied, stepping in front of the desk and eyeing the man he had once known well. Parr had aged, but his thin, dark-haired features were unmistakable, though now drawn with anxiety. The animosity that surged in Alan felt as fresh as the betrayal itself. "That was quite the promotion, you treacherous dog."

Parr shifted in his chair, his shock giving way to alarm. "What do you want, Alan? Why are you here?"

Alan smirked, letting a sharp edge into his tone. "Isn't it interesting how your Geordie accent, still so strong, all but disappears when you speak Spanish?"

Parr's face contorted as he regained some composure, though his eyes betrayed his unease. "Answer me. What do you want?"

"You deserted us, Parr," Alan seethed. "Switched sides for a foreign cause. Sold yourself out for rank, for power – willing to trade British intelligence to line your pockets."

Parr's fingers clenched his papers as if to ground himself, his voice tight with denial. "I don't know what you're talking about."

"Oh, don't you?" Alan's voice rose, laced with barely controlled fury. "You're a traitor, feeding intel about Belize to the highest bidder. You're jeopardising the lives of former comrades – men who trusted you, who would've stood by you in the worst of it."

Parr's façade cracked further, and his eyes flickered toward the door in a momentary, useless glance. "You're in over your head, Alan. You think you're some avenger for the crown, but you don't understand what it's like here. You haven't seen what I've seen. You don't know what I had to –"

"Spare me the excuses." Alan cut him off, his voice razor-sharp. "The only thing you had to do was stay loyal. You didn't just betray your country; you betrayed every last soldier who believed in you."

Parr swallowed hard, but his gaze hardened, and he forced out a defiant sneer. "So, what's your plan, Captain? Kill me in cold blood and call it justice?"

Parr didn't wait for a response. "Look, Alan, please, sit down. Let's talk things through." He gestured to the chair across from him, reaching down into the drawer on his right. "I've got some whisky in here – I know you're partial. Let's be reasonable about this."

But Alan's instincts flared, adrenaline pulsing as he read the real intent behind Parr's calm words. He knew he'd overplayed his hand, letting his anger lead him into a pointless dialogue when he should have kept his focus. The intel had been clear – the general's pistol was usually hung on the coat rack. But tonight, the rack stood empty.

Alan sprang forward, but Parr was faster. His hand came up from the drawer gripping his service revolver, and in one fluid motion, he fired twice. The rounds slammed into Alan's chest, propelling him backward. Alan hit the floor hard, his body sprawled, breath knocked from his lungs. Rolling onto his stomach, he lay prone, pain radiating as his mind struggled to process the shock.

Parr stepped around the desk, looming over Alan's prone figure. "This is how a Geordie speaks, *pet!*" he sneered, emphasising the last word with a taunting familiarity. "I may be a treacherous dog, but I'm a *rich* treacherous dog." He grinned, levelling the gun at Alan's head. "You brought a knife to a gun fight, you complete idiot!" Parr's laughter distracted him from his cause.

In those days Alan was agile, and he wasn't beaten yet. In a flash, he rolled to the side and, with all the strength he could muster, tackled the distracted Parr at ankle level. The impact was forceful, and Parr stumbled backward, firing another shot that sailed wide, embedding itself in the visitor's chair. Parr crashed to the floor, and Alan focused every ounce of his remaining energy on wresting the gun from Parr's grip.

In a swift, practiced motion, Alan drew a stiletto from his trouser side pocket and drove it into Parr's right arm just below the elbow. Parr let out a piercing scream as pain shot through him, and the revolver slipped from his grasp, skidding under the desk.

Alan scrambled up Parr's body, pressing his left hand over Parr's mouth to silence him, then scrambling onto his knees, pinning Parr to the floor. "These are your true colours, Parr, you piece of shit." Parr tapped Alan's arm and pointed at the hand covering his mouth. Alan released his hand, "What excuses do you have now?"

Parr was desperate, "Please, mate. Please, I've got money. I promise I'll disappear." He realised he was getting no joy from Alan, so he screamed "HELP!" as loudly as possible. He only got one shout away before Alan covered his mouth once more. Emotions had overtaken Alan, clouding his judgment. Seeing Parr in such a vulnerable state, having lost control of his own bodily functions, amplified Alan's disgust. "I always knew you were a coward," he sneered, unable to hide his contempt.

Alan swung the bloodied stiletto round with his right hand and stabbed Parr in the neck. Blinded by a rage which surprised even himself, he repeated the action two more times. Blood poured from the neck wounds, and Parr made a choking noise. Alan released his left hand from Parr's mouth and reiterated, "You piece of shit."

Within the confines of his dream, Alan felt an urgent compulsion to desist stabbing, driven by an unrelenting desire to escape the oppressive building. Every thrust of the blade spurred on another, urging an ending, a step towards freedom, a desperate attempt to break free from the clutches of the dream's suffocating hold.

Guns had not been part of the plan; Alan had intended to conduct the operation in relative silence. Parr had ruined that.

Time was critical now. Alan seized Parr's revolver, rushing to the office door, but as he pulled it open, he was met by the startled face of the sentry standing just outside, his rifle prone. Instinctively, Alan fired, the bullet striking the sentry's abdomen. He aimed to incapacitate, not kill – buying himself precious minutes while leaving the soldier a chance for survival if medical help arrived quickly. Yet, a part of him knew the risk he was taking. Bleeding out was a real possibility for the young soldier, and in this fleeting, intense moment, Alan registered a pang of regret.

"I hope you survive!" Alan shouted, but only in his dream.

Alan bolted from the building, diving into the backseat of his getaway car. "You were right about the bulletproof vest," he muttered to the driver.

As the engine roared to life and the vehicle shot forward, he was suddenly jerked awake. His eyes snapped open, heart hammering in his chest. Panic clenched at his throat, making it feel like he couldn't breathe. The room was pitch black, save for a sliver of moonlight filtering through the edges of the curtain. It had been fifteen years, but the memories still gripped him, haunting him even here, in Brighton, far from the streets of Guatemala City. His mind replayed the contorted faces frozen in time, and he felt the sting of tears as they slipped down his cheeks.

He struggled to steady his breathing, forcing himself to inhale deeply and exhale slowly, fighting the weight of the past that refused to release him.

The room seemed unfamiliar in the darkness. He couldn't remember how he had gotten into bed, or when he'd undressed down to his boxer shorts. How long had he been lying here, lost in the grip of his memories? He lay awake, eyes wide, wrestling with the spectres of the past, trying to avoid the pull of sleep, but exhaustion and intoxication soon dragged him back into unconsciousness.

***

In the depths of slumber, Alan was jolted awake by an abrupt burst of bright light, brief, and searing, before being swallowed once more by darkness. The bedroom door had opened, exposing the bedroom to a fleeting encounter with the bright light from the hallway, and then closed, back to black.

He blinked his eyes shut, trying to return to the solace of sleep, but felt a subtle shift in the duvet, as though someone had moved it aside. Consciousness wrestled with dreams, caught in the space between, as the fabric of his boxer shorts slipped from his legs, gliding away like a whisper in the night.

Confusion enveloped him. What was happening?

A presence materialised – Audrey. Their form moved with eerie silence, climbing atop Alan with an unsettling certainty.

"No, I don't want this." Alan groaned, his voice barely audible.

"Shush." Audrey's voice was calm, soothing, almost musical, seeking to still his unease.

"I thought you were non-binary?" Alan murmured, a faint, disoriented attempt to make sense of it all.

"I am. I didn't say I'm asexual," Audrey whispered as they settled, upright, into place, their connection deepening, unspoken and undeniable.

"No, I don't want this," Alan breathed again, his voice just a touch louder, though still veiled in quiet tension. His hands reached upward, forward, but encountered only the softness of their breasts, diminutive, unadorned, fragile.

"Shush," Audrey urged, the word a soft plea, reassuring him as they adjusted their position above him. Alan's resistance started to fade, slipping away like the last embers of a dying fire.

A symphony of muted sighs filled the space between them, the act of union dissolving as gently as it had begun. Audrey, like a spectral wraith, slid the duvet back into place, her presence fading.

Then, a second burst of brilliant light flooded the room, intense and ethereal, before it dimmed, sinking like a star falling from the sky. The bedroom door clicked softly shut, sealing him back into darkness.

Had it all been a dream? The question lingered, suspended in the silence, unanswered.

And then, deep sleep claimed him once more.

***

Daylight pressed insistently against the thick bedroom curtains, heralding the arrival of a new day. Had the previous night been nothing more than a long dream? Alan stirred from slumber, rising with languid grace, slipping into shorts and a t-shirt.

He opened the bedroom door, and the hallway greeted him with the warm, tantalising scents of coffee and fried bacon. Moving into the lounge, he sank into the sofa, still tethered to a foggy sense of reality.

Audrey materialised, radiant and wrapped in the comforting aroma of freshly brewed coffee. They set the mug down on a coaster in front of him. "Breakfast?" they asked.

Reality seemed to pulse with uncertainty, and Alan, caught somewhere between sleep and waking, managed a half-hearted, "Yes, please," his words more an acknowledgment of the surreal moment than a genuine request.

Audrey returned with a bacon sandwich, the sizzle of the bacon lingering in the air. "Where did you get this?" Alan asked, his voice hesitant. It was a feeble inquiry – he had far more pressing questions – but it was a start.

"Well, I bought the bacon at the mini supermarket around the corner and then I cooked it," Audrey replied, a flicker of amusement in their eyes as they observed Alan's lack of focus.

"Thank you," he said, though his mind was elsewhere. He had more important things to ask, but for the moment, the simple act of sipping coffee and biting into the bacon seemed almost grounding, a small but necessary escape from the haze that still clung to him.

***

"Was I talking in my sleep?" Alan asked, having finished the coffee and bacon. Audrey had reappeared, now dressed in a different outfit that still carried the timeless elegance of the 1950s, in classic black and white. They suited the style, Alan thought.

"I wouldn't know," Audrey replied, their attention focused on the contents of their small handbag, meticulously rearranging its contents.

Alan, determined to steer the conversation toward more pressing matters, asked, "Didn't you come into my bedroom last night?"

Audrey, absorbed in their task, replied without looking up, "Only to help you into bed. Then I slept in your spare room." They paused for a moment, considering their words. "By the way, that bed is quite comfortable." Alan nodded, his mind still clouded with questions. "When I helped you to bed, you were mumbling something about Guatemala and Belize bilateral relations. It didn't make much sense to me. Was that something you worked on while in the army?"

Once again, Alan was taken aback by their perceptiveness. He fumbled for a response. "Um, yes, I did." He cleared his throat, feeling uneasy. "So, you didn't come into my bedroom?"

Audrey stopped fussing with their handbag and met his gaze, a smile playing at the corners of their lips. "I'll get you another coffee. You clearly need it!" Their grin was soft but knowing, as if they could see right through him.

As Audrey brought the fresh cup of coffee, Alan fought the urge to confront them about the events of the night. But before he could voice his thoughts, Audrey, sensing the shift, spoke first, their voice smooth and gentle. "You should try and get more sleep. I'm off."

Alan blinked, caught off guard. "Where are you going?" he asked, his curiosity peeking.

Audrey turned, their mischievous grin widening. "Are you the possessive type?" They asked, their tone playful but edged with something more elusive.

"Oh, no, sorry," Alan stammered, feeling his face flush under their teasing gaze. "I don't know why I asked."

Audrey simply shrugged, then walked out of apartment number 37, leaving Alan to wrestle with the strange mix of confusion and intrigue that lingered in the air. As the front door closed shut behind them, Alan returned to the bed, the questions about the night's events swirling in his mind. Had he revealed more than he intended? Had the harrowing Guatemala story, a nightmare he'd buried deep in his subconscious, slipped past the veil of slumber and into reality?

As the effects of caffeine wore off, exhaustion took its toll, and Alan finally succumbed to sleep once more. When he awoke, the soft, diffused light filtering through the bedroom curtains signalled the lateness of the day. The room felt heavy with the aftermath of his restless mind.

In the living room, Alan grabbed his phone from the coffee table. The screen blinked with a new notification, pulling him out of his groggy state. A message from Audrey. How had they gotten his number?

He opened it: *"Here's my father's address, he'll be home tonight."*

The words hit him like a jolt. The hazy memory of his reluctant promise from the night before surged back. He hadn't thought about it in hours – hadn't wanted to. But now it was real again, the weight of the commitment hanging over him, the echo of Audrey's voice urging him on.

A Spark

Ciara
Hey babes, looking forward to seeing you next Saturday, I'll call you about midday to let you know where to meet. C. xxx

Brucey Babes
I can't wait! See you then. Bruce. Xxx

A frisson of excitement jolted through Bruce as he read Ciara's message. Grinning, he swung open the creaking wardrobe doors in his compact seafront apartment. He frowned, surveying the uninspiring rows of clothes. It was painfully clear his wardrobe needed an overhaul. Meeting Ciara was just the push he needed – and after many years of dodging the task, it was long overdue.

Keeping a Promise

Alan was glad of the short walk to the George & Dragon; he needed the time to clear his head. Curiously, he never took the path through the churchyard on his way to the pub, saving that route exclusively for the journey back home. Tonight was no different, he opted for the slightly longer path along the main thoroughfare.

Once inside, he settled onto a barstool, carefully placing his phone and house keys on the counter. He found comfort in the presence of the now-familiar bartender. Typically, he frequented this pub for the anonymity it provided, but tonight was different – tonight, he sought not just solace but an alibi, just in case.

Reluctance and apathy held Alan in its grip as he hesitated to leave the bar, acutely aware that a second pint would quash any chance of progress tonight. His motivation was dwindling rapidly. Signalling the bartender, he mentioned his plan to step out to buy a cigar, leaving his keys and phone in the bartender's care, while requesting another pint in about ten minutes. The bartender nodded agreeably and returned to drying glass wear fresh from the dishwasher.

Luck favoured Alan upon his departure from the pub. A white and aqua taxi with a bright, almost neon, orange light on its roof cruised by at a leisurely pace. He had barely waited thirty seconds before securing his ride. Providing the address, he asked the driver to "wait and return". The driver pointedly informed him that the meter would keep running, a concession Alan accepted.

The ride was short, no more than eight minutes. While the driver prattled on about local traffic and football scores, Alan stared out the window, his mind locked on the task ahead.

The taxi came to a halt in a quintessential British cul-de-sac. Alan informed the driver he'd be about ten minutes and stepped out of the cab. The street was comprised of six detached bungalows, each an exact replica of the others. Alan's target lived in the third house, almost perfectly centralised. These were modern, smart houses, boasting a wide drive leading straight into an attached garage. The front door to the house was situated to the right of the garage.

The garage of the target's house was slightly open, spilling light onto the short driveway from under the 'up-and-over' garage door. Alan could only hope Audrey's father was inside, dreading the possibility of encountering their mother.

Alan raised the garage door, revealing a man in a dark blue boilersuit bent over the open bonnet of a car. The mechanic barely glanced up; his focus fixed on the engine. After stepping inside, Alan let the door fall back down, leaving a gap of about twelve inches at the bottom.

The mechanic straightened, wiping his hands on an oily rag. He was probably younger than Alan, but a similar build, his stance casual but wary. "Yes? Can I help you?" he asked, his accent carrying the clipped tones of Southeast England.

"I'm looking for the father of Audrey Hepburn," Alan said evenly.

"You've found him," the man replied, his voice sharp and guarded.

Alan stepped closer, narrowing the space between them to just a few feet. The mechanic shifted slightly, the wrench in his right hand catching the light.

"I've got a message for you," Alan said, his tone firm.

The man smirked, his laugh short and mocking. "Mate, who the fuck are you?"

Alan's expression hardened. "I'm not your mate. I'm a friend of Audrey's – they came to me for help."

The mechanic chuckled again, this time louder, as if relishing a private joke. "A friend? You're probably older than me! Don't tell me you're shagging her." He didn't wait for an answer, his words tumbling out like a sneer. "That girl is such a slut. Mate, you're just the latest in a very long queue."

Alan's stomach twisted. He took another step forward, his voice rising. "You're talking about your own child! And *they* are not a 'she' anymore." His disbelief and anger spilled over.

"She's pretty good between the sheets, isn't she?" the man sneered, letting the oily rag fall to the floor while tightening his grip on the wrench. It was a deliberate provocation, his eyes locked on Alan's.

"You're disgusting," Alan replied, his voice low and deliberate. He took a step closer, emphasising each word as if delivering a final warning. "Keep. Away. From. Them. Or. Else."

Audrey's father burst into laughter, the sound harsh and mocking, cutting through the charged air. "Get fucked, you old pervert. Close the garage door on your way out."

Alan hesitated, weighing his options. He had no desire for a physical confrontation, but he wasn't about to back down. The man's sneer deepened as he studied Alan, testing his resolve. "What's the plan, old man? Want me to make you leave?"

Alan remained unmoved, his expression unreadable. He should have felt the weight of the threat – the heavy wrench in the man's hand, the obvious advantage of sobriety compared to Alan's lingering fatigue from the night before. Yet, inexplicably, he felt no fear. He stood his ground, his calm unnerving in the face of the man's aggression.

After a tense standoff, Alan broke the silence. "Are you going to leave them alone, or do I have to make you?"

Audrey's father didn't answer. Instead, he swung the wrench with a ferocity that Alan barely had time to counter. He raised his left arm instinctively, absorbing the full force of the blow. Pain radiated through his side, a sharp reminder of the gunshot wound still healing there. Alan gritted his teeth, cursing both his lingering injury and the limitations of age. He knew he'd pay for it later.

The man came at him again, but this time Alan was ready. Audrey's father was a bruiser, used to bullying his way through situations, but he lacked the discipline to face a trained fighter. His movements were sloppy, leaving his left side wide open. Alan stepped forward with precision and drove a right hook straight into the man's jaw. The impact was solid, snapping his head to the side.

Alan restrained himself from following up with a combination – his left side wasn't ready to throw a punch yet. Instead, he pivoted, closing the distance, and delivered a punishing right uppercut. The wrench slipped from the man's grasp, clattering onto the concrete floor. He staggered backward, collapsing against the car he'd been working on before sliding to the ground.

Alan didn't let up. Moving quickly, he dropped to his knees, pinning Audrey's father to the ground in a hold reminiscent of what American police often referred to as a 'knee-on-neck' technique.

"Are you going to leave Audrey alone?" Alan growled, his frustration boiling over. His words were deliberate, sharp with the annoyance of being dragged into this fight.

"Fuck you!" Audrey's father managed to respond, the struggle to speak evident under the pressure.

Alan increased the pressure of his knee against Audrey's father's neck, feeling the futile attempts to break free and the garbled attempts at speech. "If I press my knee any harder, I'll completely cut off your oxygen supply, creating a high risk of positional asphyxia." Alan dug his knee in even harder before releasing it slightly, allowing Audrey's father to take a breath.

Audrey's father gasped for air in short, desperate breaths. Alan leaned in close, "I can do this all night, but I doubt you'll last that long. Are you going to leave Audrey alone?"

"Yes!" Audrey's father gasped, struggling to produce even that one short word. Alan applied more pressure with his knee and heard a strangled, "No, please stop!" escape from him.

"Let me be clear," Alan stated, maintaining the pressure. "If I have to return, I won't be as lenient."

Alan stepped back into the waiting white and aqua cab. "Back to the George and Dragon, please," he said, settling into the seat. The driver gave a silent nod, pulling away from the cul-de-sac. Sensing the gravity of the situation, the driver wisely kept the conversation to a minimum. Alan appreciated the silence, grateful for the space to gather his thoughts.

When they arrived at the pub, Alan handed the driver £100 – well beyond the fare. "I'd appreciate your discretion about this trip," he said, locking eyes with the driver.

"No problem, mate," the driver replied, his voice steady but wary.

Alan paid him and made his way back inside, taking his place at the bar. He grabbed the freshly poured pint and took a long, steadying gulp. The cool beer helped to dull the tension still gnawing at him. As he massaged his left forearm, the bartender caught his eye, clearly curious.

"So, where's the cigar?" the bartender asked, raising an eyebrow.

"They sold out," Alan replied flatly, offering a slight shrug.

He picked up his phone and saw a new message. He unlocked it and read:

Audrey Hepburn
Thank you. x

He couldn't help but wonder how they had gotten his phone number – or how they'd managed to add themselves to his contacts so seamlessly. Even more perplexing was how they'd known so quickly that he'd visited their father. These imponderables swirled in his mind, a mixture of disbelief and admiration for Audrey's resourcefulness. He chuckled softly, still amused by their ingenuity.

Glancing up at the bartender, he grinned. "Can I get a Glenlivet with this, please?" he asked, gesturing toward the top shelf with his right hand, casually letting his left arm relax on the bar.

<u>Made in Denver</u>

Alan stood in front of his wardrobe, uncertain about what to wear for the unexpected "board meeting." The surprise invitation had him questioning its true purpose. Harry's gesture of nominating him as a potential "succession plan" seemed, on the surface, generous. Yet Alan couldn't shake the feeling that there was an ulterior motive at play. In the end, he settled on the only suit that still fit – a sombre, dark grey ensemble. Even then, doubt lingered. The jacket felt just a bit too tight. It was time to update his wardrobe but there was no time to think about that now.

He arrived at The Court Club at 11:30 a.m., a full half hour before the scheduled time. "Where have you been?" Harry asked, his voice without a trace of irony. To Alan's surprise, Max was already seated next to Harry at the bar. With a dismissive wave, Harry gestured for Alan to move away from the stools. "No time for a drink. Max is driving us to the meeting now." Harry stubbed his cigarette into an ashtray and slid off his barstool.

Alan knew arguing about his punctuality was pointless. Despite being early, Harry seemed intent on rushing them along. But before they left, Trevor, the bartender, handed Alan a generous shot of Glenfiddich. Alan knocked it back in one smooth motion, feeling the warmth spread through him. Without a word, he turned and walked out to join Harry and Max in Max's sleek BMW.

As they neared Rollie's house, the front door swung open with customary precision, just before they reached it, courtesy of October, the ever-watchful security guard. They were ushered inside, and after a brief nod from Rollie's assistant, Harry and Alan were led to Rollie's office while Max disappeared down another corridor.

Alan's eyes roamed the space, taking in the room's sheer opulence. Memories of hiding under the massive desk, of nearly tumbling through the grand bay window brought a faint flush of embarrassment. The room's grandeur seemed to unfold further in the light, its details that had once been hidden by shadows now laid bare. Dark, polished wood panelling lined the walls, lending the space a stately, almost solemn air. It wasn't to Alan's personal taste, but he couldn't deny the weight it carried, like the room itself was a piece of history.

For the first time, Alan noticed a small writing desk tucked near the rear of the room – an escritoire, he thought it was called. He studied the two paintings hanging above it, their lush, Rococo style unmistakable. "Yes, they're real," Harry whispered, as if reading his mind. Alan froze, his breath catching. The paintings were the kind of masterpieces that belonged in a museum, not an office. They must be worth a fortune.

Rollie's desk, as always, remained unusually uncluttered – just the polished surface of dark wood, reflecting the room's heavy air. His large Chesterfield office chair sat in repose, awaiting his return, while three chairs stood in front of the desk, clearly for visitors. Behind them, about twenty feet away, six more chairs were arranged in pairs, almost as if the room were set for an audience, each seat angled toward Rollie's desk with deliberate precision.

Harry and Alan took the nearest pair, settling into the velvet upholstery. Alan couldn't help but feel a little out of place in the vast room, as though every element, from the furniture to the paintings, had been carefully orchestrated to remind him that he was not quite in his element.

The next to arrive, some ten minutes later, were Rollie's sons. As they entered, Harry stood to greet them with an expansive gesture, "My beloved nephews, great to see you both!" He embraced them both warmly, but Alan sensed the unease that lingered beneath their seemingly heartfelt greetings.

Turning toward Alan with a playful grin, Harry gestured to the pair. "I think you've both met Alan before, haven't you?" A mischievous chuckle escaped Harry's lips, but it was clear that his words carried an edge – like a setup for something unsaid. "Alan, this is Jamie and Nigel."

Alan rose, extending his hand to Jamie first. Jamie's grip was firm, almost calculating, as if trying to make a point by asserting his dominance from the start. "Nice to meet you, Jamie." Alan's eyes

245

flickered over to Nigel, who stood slightly behind, his posture rigid. Alan reached for his hand. "And nice to see you again, Nigel. I didn't get the chance to thank you for meeting me in Bristol. I appreciate that."

Nigel, the shorter and more reserved of the two, hesitated before shaking Alan's hand, the discomfort clear in his eyes. The past encounter in Bristol hung between them like a cloud. His grip was limp, as though unwilling to revisit their previous dealings.

Harry, ever the mediator, was enjoying the tension but moved to smooth things over, his voice upbeat but carrying a slight edge. "No hard feelings, though?" His question hung in the air like a challenge, aimed more at Nigel than anyone else.

Nigel's forced smile did little to mask his discomfort. "No, no," he muttered quickly, his words almost too hurried, too dismissive. "It's just business."

Alan scrutinised his face, sensing the lie behind the casual dismissal. The forced ease in Nigel's tone only amplified the tension. But for now, Alan let it go, accepting the words at face value, though his doubts lingered like a shadow in the back of his mind.

Alan didn't recognise the next person to enter. An elderly man, stooped with age and leaning heavily on a walking stick, made his way into the room with slow, deliberate steps. He shuffled over to the third pair of chairs, his movements and breathing stiff and laboured, and settled into the seat with an audible effort. Jamie and Nigel immediately rose to greet him, addressing him with the familiar term "Uncle," confirming that he was another Monroe brother, though one whose presence seemed less significant to Harry. Harry merely muttered a curt greeting, barely lifting his head, and didn't bother to rise in respect.

As the elderly man adjusted his position, October re-entered the room, offering him a glass of water, which the man accepted with a quiet nod of gratitude. Alan, who had been preoccupied with the ongoing introductions, now took in October's imposing presence. The man was far taller than he had originally realised – at least six feet three, with broad shoulders and a physique that suggested regular, intense workouts.

His turban, perched perfectly atop his head, only added to his already formidable stature, making him seem even more commanding as he moved around the room.

October took his customary position at Rollie's side of the desk, settling slightly off-centre with a casual nonchalance that only someone of his imposing size could manage. His all-black suit, stark against the dark wood-panelled room, made him stand out, despite the room's otherwise subdued lighting.

The door swung open, and Max entered, his suit as usual a bit too tight, the fabric stretching across his frame. Just behind him, a man in an immaculate suit followed, his striking blonde hair almost glowing in contrast to the dim room. Alan's eyes were immediately drawn to the man's chewing gum, which seemed to be rolling around his mouth with such exaggerated movement that it almost appeared to be trying to escape. Behind the man trailed a woman, striking, with near model looks, her slender figure moving with effortless grace. Her skin tone, somewhere between caramel and bronze, seemed to glow under the muted light. She wore a knee-length grey skirt, a perfectly tailored jacket, and a crisp white blouse that completed her sophisticated look.

Alan couldn't help but notice Nigel's subtle gesture – a slight pat on his brother's arm, his eyes widening in a silent, almost playful nudge. It was clear that he wanted to make sure Jamie noticed the woman's beauty. Harry, on the other hand, was less restrained. He muttered, "Very nice, I would," in a tone that was just a bit too audible, his eyes lingering on her a little too long as he scrutinised her appearance.

The three took the seats nearest to Rollie's desk. October broke the silence that hung in the room. "Rollie's on his way. He's been in the garden all morning and wanted to clean up before the meeting."

The man with striking blonde hair leaned back in his chair, his resonant voice carrying an easy confidence. "Take your time, big guy. We're not in a rush. So, what's your gig with Mr. Monroe?"

October's expression didn't flicker. He stood like a statue, silent and imposing, refusing to acknowledge the question. Across the room, Alan's sharp ear caught the faint traces of a non-rhotic accent in the blonde man's speech – a telltale sign of New York origins.

The door swung open with practiced precision, and August, the steadfast security guard, stepped aside to allow Rollie Monroe to enter. Rollie moved with the measured grace of someone who refused to let age diminish his presence. Each step was deliberate, neither hurried nor hesitant. His slicked-back grey hair was still damp from his shower, catching the light as he approached his desk.

As Rollie settled into his chair, August resumed his post standing sentinel behind the boss's left shoulder, his eyes scanning the room with quiet vigilance.

Without hesitation, Rollie extended his hand to the American visitor, his smile warm but calculating. "I'm Rollie. It's a pleasure to meet you."

The American stood, his movements broad and deliberate, and grasped Rollie's hand in a firm shake. "Denver Hume!" His voice carried a booming authority that filled the room, though Alan suspected it was more habit than intent. The woman seated to Denver's left remained composed, her expression unreadable.

Rollie's gaze shifted subtly toward her, his tone inquisitive but calm. "And this is?"

Before she could answer, Denver cut in with a laugh. "This is Ciara – but don't mind her, she's just here to be my eye candy!"

Ciara's posture stiffened for the briefest moment as she sank back into her seat. Her face betrayed nothing more than a flicker of disappointment, quickly masked by a professional calm.

Rollie let the crude remark pass without acknowledgment, leaning back in his chair with an air of easy authority. His tone was smooth, almost casual, as he turned to October. "Would you mind bringing Mr. Denver an ashtray?"

Denver erupted into raucous laughter. "Haw haw! It's *Hume*, Mr. Hume! Denver's my first name!" He gestured expansively as though correcting a class of schoolchildren. "And don't worry – I don't smoke indoors, Rollie. Mind if I call you Rollie?"

Rollie studied him for a moment, his expression unreadable, before replying with a faint smile. "Of course, you can call me Rollie." As he spoke, October silently placed the ashtray on the desk in front of Denver. Rollie's smile deepened, but his eyes remained sharp. "The ashtray is for your chewing gum."

Alan stifled a chuckle, while Max smirked, recognising the manoeuvre as vintage Rollie – a subtle assertion of control that both disarmed and assessed. Denver's laughter rang out again, louder than before. "Haw haw! Well played, Rollie, well played!" He plucked the gum from his mouth and dropped it into the ashtray with an exaggerated flourish.

Rollie's eyes lingered on Denver for a beat longer. "Your surname is Hume?"

"Haw haw! Sure is!" Denver replied, his laughter erupting once more, seemingly unprovoked. "You know, I think my parents named me Denver because that's where I was conceived – if you catch my drift! Haw haw!"

The room remained silent except for the faint clink of the ashtray as Denver's gum hit the glass. Max looked back and exchanged a knowing glance with Alan, silently appreciating Rollie's ability to keep the upper hand in even the most absurd encounters.

Denver watched as October silently retrieved the ashtray from the desk. His wide grin revealed impeccably white teeth as he leaned forward. "Where do you get your security, Rollie?" he asked, his tone playful but probing. Without waiting for an answer, he added with a loud laugh, "Guantanamo Bay? Haw haw!"

Denver glanced over his shoulder as if expecting a chorus of chuckles, then repeated the punchline. "Guantanamo Bay? Haw haw!" When the room remained silent, his grin didn't falter. Instead, he shifted tactics. "Anyway, why are you called October? I mean, this is England –" he exaggerated the word as "Ing-ger-land," his delivery reminiscent of a boisterous football supporter. Rollie's lips tightened slightly; the affectation grated on him. "Wouldn't you want to be one of the summer months instead?"

October, now standing silently at Rollie's right-hand side, maintained his stoic demeanour. Denver's grin widened as he gestured toward the turban. "What's under your hat, buddy? Is that where you store your lunch?"

Before Denver could continue, Rollie's voice cut through, calm but laced with quiet authority. "Mr. Hume, my security team's names are chosen by me with care to protect their anonymity, and I expect them to be treated with respect. That is not a hat – it's a turban. Among the followers of the Sikh faith, it represents equality and holds profound spiritual significance. October calls it by its proper name: a *pagri*. I'd appreciate it if you showed him the same respect."

For the first time, Denver paused, his grin flickering slightly before bouncing back. "Oh, right, sure, I get it," he replied, brushing off the reprimand. "Still, I reckon you'd want to be one of the summer months. August sounds better, eh?" He pointed to the guard standing on the opposite side of Rollie, then leaned in conspiratorially. "So, is there a September hiding in the back somewhere? Haw haw!"

Rollie paused, a faint crease forming between his brows as he rubbed the spot just above his eyes. The desire to end this conversation simmered beneath his calm exterior. Finally, he spoke, his voice measured. "Mr. Hume, did Maximilian take the opportunity to show you around?"

"Maximilian!" Denver's booming voice seemed to bounce off the wood-panelled walls. "Haw haw! You mean Maxy-boy here!" He gave Max a playful punch on the shoulder, eliciting a flicker of discomfort from Max, who shifted awkwardly in his seat.

"Yes, he did," Denver continued, undeterred. "And what a lovely place you've got, Rollie! Real nice. Those rosebushes outside are something else. Have you ever tried using spent coffee grounds as fertiliser?"

Rollie inclined his head in acknowledgment, a faint smile brushing his lips, but before he could respond, Jamie's voice cut through the room from the cluster of five seated at the back. "Don't get him started on his garden, Mr. Hume. You'll be here all week."

The temperature in the room seemed to drop a degree as Rollie's sharp gaze locked onto Jamie, silencing him with a single look. Jamie sank back into his seat, any notion of speaking further at the meeting clearly extinguished.

Returning his attention to Denver, Rollie's tone remained composed. "I've heard about using coffee grounds," he said, "but I haven't tried it myself yet. Are you a gardener, Denver?"

"Me?" Denver's surprise was genuine, his booming voice dropping a notch. "I don't have the time for that sort of thing, though I've got a little garden back at my place in Boston. Nothing fancy."

Rollie leaned back in his chair, studying Denver with the faintest hint of curiosity. "A shame," he said smoothly. "A garden teaches patience, Mr. Hume. It rewards those who know when to nurture and when to prune."

Max smirked faintly at the subtle edge in Rollie's words, the underlying message clear.

"Do you have trouble with foxes in Boston, Mr. Denver? Ours have become diurnal; they're a constant nuisance," Rollie asked, once again blending first and last names.

Denver had come pre-armed with the question about the rosebushes but had no further horticultural knowledge, he blinked, unsure if it was a genuine question or a veiled jab. "Uh, no, I don't think so." His brow furrowed, and he added, "And it's Mr. Hume. Denver's my first name. Please, just call me Denver."

As he spoke, Denver reached for his phone. October shifted slightly, his sharp eyes narrowing momentarily, but relaxed once he saw there was no threat. Denver scrolled through his photos with exaggerated deliberation. "Let me show you something, Rollie," he said, his voice brimming with enthusiasm. "You'll love this!"

After a few swipes, he straightened in triumph. "Here we are!" He stood, placing the phone on Rollie's desk, the screen displaying a picture.

Rollie leaned forward, his expression neutral. "What am I looking at, Denver?" he asked, picking up the phone.

"That's me in front of the Hume statue in Edinburgh! Can you believe it? I'm actually related to *that* Hume! Haw haw!" Denver's excitement spilled over as he gestured animatedly.

Rollie regarded the photo, tilting the phone slightly for a better look. The image showed an exuberant Denver, his brilliant white teeth gleaming as he posed in front of a statue of a seated man engrossed in a book. The letters *H U M* and *E* were prominently carved into the stone base.

"Good Lord," Rollie murmured, raising an eyebrow. "I know that statue. It's on the High Street, just down from the castle."

Denver corrected him quickly, "It's the Royal Mile, actually. But yeah, just down from the castle. What do you think? Do we look alike? Haw haw!"

Rollie's lips curved into a faint smile, his tone light. "Yes, indeed, Denver. The resemblance is uncanny. A spitting image of your predecessor – and I shouldn't doubt, an equally enlightened philosopher?"

Denver roared with laughter, slapping his thigh. "Haw haw! I like you, Rollie! You've got my sense of humour! We're going to get on well."

Rollie placed the phone back on the desk, his polite smile remaining firmly in place. "Well, Denver, it's clear you come from distinguished stock."

"Now then, Denver," Rollie said, handing the phone back with a deliberate air, keen to guide the meeting back to its purpose. "Have you been introduced to everyone yet?"

Denver turned to glance at the seated group behind him, his grin widening. "No, I haven't, Rollie. *But –*" he leaned back theatrically, flashing those impossibly white teeth – "how about I take a crack at guessing who they are? I'm good at this kind of thing! What do you say?"

Rollie's smile remained polite, his sharp eyes betraying his disbelief. "As you wish, Denver."

He leaned back slightly in his chair, observing Denver's fearless enthusiasm with a faint curiosity. Those dazzling teeth, Rollie thought, seemed to shine as much from confidence as from polish.

Denver stood and turned to face those seated behind him, spreading his arms theatrically. "Hell, this is like performing at the Hollywood Bowl! Haw haw!" His booming laughter filled the room as he strode over to Harry, extending a firm handshake. "You must be the younger sibling, Harry?"

Harry chuckled, playing along with Denver's flamboyance. "That's a lucky guess," he said, shaking Denver's hand with a grin.

Denver moved to the two sons seated in the middle. He paused dramatically, scanning their faces with mock seriousness. "I reckon you're Nigel," he said, pointing to one, "which makes you Jamie!" He clasped their hands in turn, each handshake as forceful and exaggerated as his personality.

Continuing to the third set of chairs, Denver stopped in front of Les. "And you must be the older brother, Les?" Les nodded curtly, his expression unreadable, but he didn't extend a hand. Denver hesitated for a fraction of a second before pivoting back toward the others, his grin unshaken.

Finally, Denver gestured toward Alan. "But I'm stumped on this one. Who's this sitting with your brother Harry?"

Harry interjected smoothly, "This is Alan – my personal security."

Alan stood, his handshake firm but measured as Denver clasped his hand enthusiastically. "Security," Alan thought to himself, his sharp eyes studying Denver up close. "No longer the succession plan."

As Denver returned to his seat, Alan's gaze lingered on the man's head. The closer he got, the more certain he became: the striking blonde hair was a *syrup*.

"How did I do?" Denver asked, his grin wide, confidence brimming.

"Very well, Denver. You did very well," Rollie replied, his tone measured. "Now, perhaps you can tell me what role Ciara plays?"

Denver's jovial manner shifted in an instant, his smile vanishing. His voice turned sharp and cutting as he almost spat, "If you must know, she's the one who conducted the analysis that brought us here today. But she's a tool I don't need anymore. She won't be part of the ongoing work." He waved dismissively in Ciara's direction, not bothering to look at her. "She does her best work flat on her back with her legs open, and we don't need those services anymore. We'll put the bitch to work back in Boston."

A flicker of surprise crossed Rollie's face as his eyebrows rose slightly. Denver, unbothered, pressed on, gesturing dismissively. "Don't be fooled by that innocent act, Rollie. She's just like all those 'blackfaces' –" he waved his hand dramatically over his face, miming a mask, "– only out for what's in it for her."

Rollie's expression tightened almost imperceptibly, his composure unshaken. "Mr. Hume," he said coolly, "two of my four former wives were of African descent. I'd greatly appreciate it if you could show a little more respect, both to Ciara and to the company you're in."

Denver shrugged dismissively, leaning back in his chair. "Yeah, yeah, as you like, Rollie. I thought you'd only had three wives?"

Rollie inclined his head slightly, acknowledging Denver's observation. "You've done your homework, Mr. Hume. Maximilian might agree with you. I was married in The Gambia some years ago, and we were never entirely sure if the documentation would hold up under British law."

Denver erupted into laughter, his booming voice filling the room once more. "Haw haw! You've been quite the lad in your time, haven't you?"

Rollie didn't respond immediately, letting Denver's laughter echo before quietly replying, "Perhaps."

"You live in Beantown, then, Mr. Hume?" Rollie asked, his tone casual but probing.

"Beantown?" Denver repeated, then chuckled as understanding dawned. "Ah, Boston. My boss is based there, so I split my time between Boston and New York."

"The city that never sleeps," Rollie replied with a small smile. "I imagine your personality fits right into a place as lively as that. Are you from New York originally, Mr. Hume?" he asked, his sharp eyes studying Denver as though assembling a puzzle piece by piece.

Denver's grin widened. "Not bad, Rollie, not bad at all! I'm actually from Albany, but hey, you're pretty damn close."

Rollie inclined his head slightly, as though storing the information for later. "Well then, shall we get down to business, Mr. Hume?"

Before Denver could respond, Jamie's muttered, "About time," cut through the moment, drawing a quick glance from Rollie but no comment.

Denver adjusted his position, his demeanour shifting noticeably to something more businesslike. "Well, Rollie, it's quite straightforward," he began, his tone now measured and professional. "I represent a competitor based out of Boston, with operations spanning the entire Eastern Seaboard. My specialty is M&A – mergers and acquisitions," he added, proudly glancing around the room to gauge the response.

"We've had a look at your operations from afar and we like what we see. We'd like you to open your books to us," Denver continued, leaning forward slightly for emphasis. "Our operation is on a much grander scale than yours, and we already have strong ties into London through our Irish partners. We see significant synergies between our organisations. Pending a thorough review of your financials, we're prepared to offer a substantial price to acquire the rights you currently hold."

He paused deliberately, scanning the room for any immediate questions. None came, though the air bristled with unspoken reactions.

Denver pressed on. "The corporate restructuring would be seamless. Our aim would be to boost your local market share, drive growth, and enhance your competitive advantage. We believe our influence could also strengthen your supply chains and create new opportunities for expansion."

He sat back, his expression confident, as though awaiting an inevitable agreement.

Finally, Jamie spoke up, his tone sceptical. "Hold on a minute, Denver. That all sounds impressive, but why do you think we'd be interested in giving up what we've worked hard to build? We're not about to roll over to the Irish Mob!"

Denver didn't flinch. "Jamie, may I call you Jamie?" he asked smoothly, continuing undeterred by the challenge. Jamie gave a curt nod.

"We're not the mafia," Denver continued, his voice steady. "Not even close. We're an enterprise just like yours – an honest one, meeting the needs of a population that's become dependent on a steady supply chain, not just for recreation, but for survival. And as for 'why,' let's just say we'll compensate you well. If you decide to stay on in the new organisation, senior roles will be available to you."

Rollie raised a hand, signalling for the conversation to pause. "My son tends to speak out of turn, Mr. Hume," he said, his tone firm but measured.

Denver's eyes flickered to Jamie before responding, his voice cutting, "Your son believes he's next in line, Rollie. He's frustrated with the wait. He needs to realise that times have changed."

Rollie's gaze sharpened. "Enough," he said, his hand still raised. The room fell silent as he rubbed his chin thoughtfully, as if contemplating the absence of a beard. After a long pause, he spoke again. "Well, Mr. Hume, I'm willing to let you work with Maximilian to start. I see no harm in that. Then we can regroup and discuss the way forward, if there even is one, once you've completed your due diligence."

Denver flashed a wide grin. "Excellent! That's great news. I think this will work out well for everyone. Now..." He paused, his expression turning playful, as though enjoying the moment. "There is one small caveat."

Rollie raised an eyebrow, intrigued.

Denver leaned in slightly, a mischievous gleam in his eye. "I need you to give up your driver, Bruce Thompson."

Rollie's face remained a picture of feigned surprise. "Why on earth would you be interested in Bruce, Mr. Hume?"

Denver's grin widened, but his tone sharpened. "Look, I don't want to sound, how do you say… like a 'pork chop,' but Bruce caused my team a lot of trouble. He's got a few things to answer for."

Rollie met Denver's gaze without flinching. "I see," he said coolly. "Well, Mr. Hume, I think it's time for a short break – about fifteen minutes. Maximilian can arrange for some refreshments. Meanwhile, I'd very much like to spend a bit of time with Ciara. I trust you don't mind?"

Rollie rose from his seat, and October stepped forward as if to assist, but Rollie waved him off.

Denver didn't seem pleased. "I don't think Ciara will have anything to offer you, Rollie," he protested.

Rollie's smile didn't waver. "I'll be the judge of that, Mr. Hume." He gestured to a puzzled Ciara. "Come along, dear," he said, guiding her toward one of the anterooms without waiting for further comment.

A Plan

The anteroom mirrored Rollie's grand office, its dark wood panelling exuding the same timeless authority, though on a far more intimate scale. Rollie gestured for Ciara to take a seat, then pulled a chair to face her. Settling in, he glanced toward October and said, "Leave us, please." October hesitated before nodding reluctantly and slipping out.

"May I call you Ciara?" Rollie asked, his tone courteous but firm.

She gave a small nod. "Of course."

"Thank you. I have a proposition for you."

At this, Ciara's expression shifted – from lugubrious to wide-eyed surprise. Rollie chuckled heartily. "Ha! No, no, my dear, you've misunderstood. I'm not asking you to become the fifth Mrs. Monroe! As lovely as you are. Now, perhaps if I were twenty years younger?"

Ciara's lips twitched, and for the first time since their meeting, she smiled. The sight pleased Rollie immensely. "Actually," he added with a wry grin, "maybe ten years younger might do it!"

He leaned back, the chair creaking softly. "You know," he continued, "young people these days flock to old houses – drawn to their patina, their age-worn charm. But I doubt young women feel the same about old men. And trust me, my dear, they don't come much more patinaed than me!"

His self-deprecating humour seemed to break the tension, and Ciara's posture softened. "But I digress, I aim to remove your fetters, not to replace them with some of my own," he said, waving a hand dismissively.

"Ciara, tell me about my business," Rollie said, his voice steady but inviting, like a teacher testing the waters of a promising student's knowledge.

"I… Well, I'm not sure what to say." Ciara shifted in her seat, avoiding his eyes momentarily.

"Relax," Rollie said with a warm smile, leaning back in his chair. "This isn't an interrogation. I just want to understand what you know – just the basics. Start where you like."

Ciara hesitated, then nodded, drawing a steadying breath. "Alright... Where should I start?" It was a rhetorical question.

Rollie smiled again, this time with more encouragement, like a gardener coaxing life from delicate seedlings.

"Okay, uhmm..." Ciara began tentatively, her soft Irish tone gaining confidence as she went on. "You operate at the highest end of the market. After your brother's death and the consolidation of your assets, you briefly tried to compete with the general market – which was expanding rapidly at the time. But you were too smart for that."

Rollie tilted his head slightly, intrigued but silent.

"Initially, you cut your imported product with benzocaine," Ciara continued, glancing at him for a reaction. "Procured legally through a dental license – very clever, by the way. You kept experimenting with different ratios, testing the market constantly. You were way ahead of your time when it came to measuring the customer experience."

Rollie's lips curved in a faint smile, his eyes gleaming with approval.

"And," Ciara went on, her confidence visibly growing, "you made friends in the police force. You supported some of their high-profile campaigns to bring down other, less... ethical players. It was expensive but brilliant. It earned you allies and made you look like the good guy. Of course, that's when you moved your importing operations to Scotland. You wanted a complete disconnect between your products and your 'friends.'"

Rollie's expression didn't change, but there was a flicker of interest in his eyes. He looked skywards for a moment before meeting Ciara's eyes. "You know my dear, I've always thought justice should be for sale, I've never understood why it isn't. I mean, what's so special about justice? Some judges are even willing to accept a payment plan, they're not naïve."

Ciara nodded before carefully adding, "I will say, though, I think there's a risk with the Leith operation, but... that's another conversation. And then there's your brother Harry – he's a constant liability." She stopped abruptly, a faint blush rising in her cheeks. "Sorry, have I overstepped the mark?"

Rollie chuckled, a low, rumbling sound that filled the room. "Not at all, my dear. I did ask for your frankness. Please, continue."

Encouraged, Ciara leaned forward slightly. "At the same time, you never stopped looking outward – always keeping an open mind for opportunities. For instance, you were the first in the UK to import mescaline directly from Peru. That was bold."

Rollie arched an eyebrow, impressed despite himself.

"But the thing you understood better than anyone else," Ciara said, her tone sharpening, "was not to overreach. You stayed in your lane, perfected your segment of the market. That's when you made the decision to focus solely on the highest-end users. They had the money, the discretion, and the loyalty you wanted. And of course, you stopped cutting your product altogether, selling it pure. You even let your dental license lapse. You didn't need it anymore. As far as I can tell, you make a very good profit from what you do, but you're also not shy of spending on security – in whatever form that takes."

Rollie laughed again, this time louder, the sound rich with admiration. "Well, well, Ciara. You've done your homework. And here I was, thinking I was a mystery wrapped in an enigma."

Ciara allowed herself a small smile. "You asked for the basics. I thought I'd give you a little extra."

"Ha, very good!" Rollie said, his laughter rich and genuine. He leaned forward, resting his elbows on his knees. "Let me tell you something, Ciara – the essence of every great leader, in every era, is that he is, or was, a lonely man."

"Or woman?" Ciara interjected smoothly, tilting her head ever so slightly.

Rollie paused, then laughed again, this time softer, more reflective. "Ha, yes, of course. Quite right, my dear." He stopped himself abruptly, shaking his head with a rueful smile. "There I go again. I shouldn't call you 'my dear.' It's a relic of my age, I'm afraid."

Ciara gave him a small, knowing smile. "That's alright, Mr. Monroe. It doesn't bother me."

He studied her for a moment, as if searching for hidden meaning in her words, before nodding. "Well, I'm glad. I try to keep up with the times, but some habits cling like ivy on old stone."

Ciara leaned back slightly, her expression thoughtful. "For what it's worth, my first impressions are that you are a good leader. And I imagine it is truly a lonely place where you sit."

"Ciara, please just call me Rollie. I would like to offer you a job, are you willing to help me?" Ciara listened intently. "What Mr. Hume proposes is a *fait accompli*, that is to say, if I refuse, I'll be driven out regardless." Ciara opened her mouth to reply, but Rollie raised a hand, gently cutting her off before she could say more. "Hear me out, please. I know you're a resourceful young woman, and I'm fairly certain you believe you can outmanoeuvre whatever fate Mr. Hume has in store for you. Unfortunately, this time, I fear your confidence may be misplaced."

Ciara's brows knitted together, a flicker of uncertainty crossing her face. "And how could you possibly know all of this?" she asked, her soft Irish lilt a stark, welcome contrast to the sharp, grating volume of Denver Hume.

Rollie chuckled softly, leaning back in his chair. "Call it a hunch, my dear. Let's just say I have a knack for reading people. And I know that you possess knowledge – very valuable knowledge – about the way the predatory organisation which Mr. Hume represents... operates. Who is who, how the pieces fit together. That's what I'm after. I want you to work for me – on *this* side of the transaction."

Ciara hesitated, her expression a mixture of apprehension and confusion. Sensing her hesitation, Rollie pressed on. "You're likely thinking, 'What's in it for me?' A fair question. My answer is simple: I will ensure your safety. Mr. Hume and his cronies won't be able to touch you under my protection."

Her eyes narrowed slightly. "Why would you do this for me?" she asked, her voice cautious but tinged with curiosity.

Rollie's gaze softened, and for a moment, he seemed almost disarmingly candid. "As I said, you have something I need – knowledge I don't possess. But beyond that, I'm not in a position to deny Mr. Hume outright. He has the upper hand, for now. With your help, though, I can manage this situation and perhaps even turn the tables."

He leaned forward, fixing her with a steady, searching look. "So, Ciara, I'll ask you plainly – can I trust you? Will you help me?"

There was a beat of silence as Ciara studied him, her emerald eyes bright with thought. Finally, she nodded, a spark of determination igniting in her gaze. "Gladly, Rollie."

"In that case, I can tell you – I know about your relationship with Bruce."

Ciara opened her mouth to deny it, but Rollie raised a hand, silencing her.

"No need, my dear," he said smoothly. "I understand completely. A man like Bruce, drawn to a siren like you? It makes perfect sense. And while I should fault him for sharing some of his knowledge with you, I'll forgive him for that lapse. But now, I need your help. Bruce must be protected from Mr. Hume."

Ciara's brow furrowed. "Mr. Hume? Why is Bruce in danger?"

"As I mentioned, I cannot refuse Mr. Hume's request. For all that he's a *Pasquinade*, he is a dangerous one."

"I'll do anything I can, Rollie," Ciara said earnestly. "But why is Bruce so important to you?"

Rollie's expression softened, the faintest hint of emotion breaking through his composed exterior. "Bruce is… unique to my operation. A single point of failure, as they'd say in business. But it's more than that. I feel protective of him – like a third son." He paused, his voice thickening slightly.

Then, regaining his composure, he added, "As a great President once said, you and I have a rendezvous with destiny."

Integrating Ciara

The group resumed their seats, and Rollie wasted no time taking control. He acceded to Denver Hume's requests but insisted on recruiting Ciara, brushing aside Denver's objections. Jamie and Nigel exchanged incredulous looks before voicing their astonishment. Rollie dispatched Max and Denver to the anteroom he had just vacated, instructing them to begin the planning immediately.

As soon as the door closed behind Denver, Jamie was the first to break the silence. "Dad, are you serious about this woman?" He jabbed a finger toward Ciara. "She's young enough to be your granddaughter!"

Nigel chimed in, his tone as sharp as his brother's. "This is insane, Dad. You can't be serious."

Rollie leaned back, his expression impassive. "Ciara is here to advise us on how to deal with the Americans. She's lived among them, worked with them, and understands their ways. I'm not inviting her; I'm integrating her. I intend to avoid a Carthaginian peace, and I'll do whatever it takes to keep this family alive and intact."

Jamie wasn't done. "And where exactly is she going to stay, Dad?"

Rollie hesitated, caught off guard by the practical question. Ciara's brow furrowed slightly, as though the thought hadn't occurred to her either. "There are plenty of empty guest rooms here," Rollie said after a moment. "She'll stay in one of them."

Jamie threw up his hands in exasperation. "For crying out loud, this is embarrassing!"

Across the table, Alan stifled a grin, clearly enjoying the brothers' discomfort. He caught Les's eye, but Rollie's younger brother remained unmoving, a shadowy figure whose silence added to the tension in the room.

It was Harry who broke the awkward pause, his tone mocking yet soothing. "Don't worry, boys. Uncle Harry's got you. You can lean on me if this gets too much."

Rollie shot his brother a sharp glance, keeping his voice steady. "Harry, your concern is touching, but unnecessary. We'll manage."

Straightening, Rollie turned his attention back to his sons. "Let me be perfectly clear. We are going to negotiate with Mr. Hume, and you will embrace Ciara as part of this family. To support me, she needs a comprehensive understanding of our operations. That means full cooperation from all of you." His eyes swept the room, landing briefly on Jamie, Nigel, and Harry, who now looked like sulky schoolboys. "And just so there's no confusion – this is an order, not a request."

Standing, Rollie signalled that the meeting was over. "October," he called, glancing toward the ever-efficient security guard, "please show Ciara to the second guest suite."

Maxy-boy

Max was growing weary of Denver's larger-than-life personality. The American's loud, jocose manner clashed sharply with his own quiet restraint. Still, Rollie had entrusted him with the task of guiding Denver through the process, and Max was determined to remain professional.

"He's quite the character, your boss!" Denver declared, his voice booming as if the walls themselves might respond. "He's wrong about that Irish bitch, though. But hey, it looks like he'll have to figure that out the hard way. You need to watch her. He's got gravitas, sure, but is he for real, or what?"

Max inhaled deeply, willing himself to keep his composure. "Rollie is exactly as he appears, Denver. In Spain, they'd call him a *caudillo*."

"A what now?" Denver frowned, his energy momentarily dampened by confusion.

"A leader who commands both respect and loyalty," Max clarified. "To Rollie, no man is inherently a villain."

"No *person*, Maxy-boy! You need to get with the programme, haw haw!" Denver chuckled and delivered another playful thump to Max's shoulder.

Max suppressed a wince and pressed on, eager to steer the conversation back to business. "Rollie has approved your due diligence. My role is to assist in identifying potential risks and act as the intermediary, within the liminal space so to speak, between you and the Monroe family. I'll manage the contractual provisions on both sides, including indemnification clauses. Does that make things clear?"

Denver threw his head back and roared with laughter, startling Max with its sheer volume. "You're a riot, Maxy-boy! I haven't understood a word, but I like you!" He punctuated his statement with yet another shoulder punch, harder this time.

Max's patience was wearing thin. He glanced at the clock, silently willing the day to end.

The Stiletto

Alan and Max had chosen their second-favourite haunt, the Coach and Horses, for a quiet debrief. Harry had been insistent they join him and his nephews at The Court Club, but both had reached their limit with the Monroes for one day.

Denver Hume had officially begun his due diligence, though Max had confided to Alan that "diligence" was a generous description of the man's efforts. The one consolation, particularly for Max, was Denver's imminent return to the U.S. after only a few days. The prospect of his departure felt like a breath of fresh air.

Later that night, Alan stepped out of the taxi in front of number 37, slipping a note to the driver before shutting the car door. The pub's warmth lingered faintly in his senses as he turned toward the house – only to stop in his tracks.

There, perched on the doorstep, was a small, unmistakable figure: Audrey Hepburn.

A jolt of surprise hit him, followed quickly by a wave of unexpected delight. The intensity of the emotion caught him off guard, as if a long-forgotten chord had been struck deep within him.

"Are you coming in for a drink?" Alan asked as he approached the door, his voice casual, though his gaze lingered on Audrey's hunched form at the doorstep.

"Yes, please," Audrey replied softly, their voice trembling, a fragile strength barely holding them together.

Alan unlocked the door and gestured for them to enter. "Set up the whiskies, would you? I'll be right with you," he said, keeping his tone light as he headed to the bathroom.

When he returned, Audrey was seated on the armchair, the room bathed in the soft, golden glow of the standard lamp. Alan paused, noticing the telltale glimmer of tears streaking their face. Their usually immaculate hair – styled in homage to their namesake – hung messily, partially obscuring their features. But it couldn't hide the bruises.

Alan's heart tightened as he crossed the room and knelt beside them. Gently, he brushed their hair aside, revealing the full extent of the damage. The sight sent a surge of protective anger through him.

He leaned in, cradling their head against his chest. "Was this your father again?" he asked softly, his voice a careful balance of tenderness and fury.

Audrey barely nodded, their breath shaky. "I only went home to get some clothes," they murmured. "He said if he sees you again, he'll hurt you. I don't want you to get hurt." Their voice wavered, fear lacing every word. "I'm sorry, but I think he knows where you live."

Alan's jaw tightened, the anger brewing beneath the surface threatening to spill over. "You don't need to worry about me," he said firmly. "I can handle myself." His hand rested reassuringly on their shoulder, though his knuckles were white with restrained rage. "What a bastard he is," he muttered, the words heavy with suppressed fury.

"Can I stay tonight, please?" Audrey implored, their voice wavering with a quiet desperation.

"Of course," Alan said without hesitation. "The spare room is made up." He paused, weighing his next words carefully. Finally, against his better judgment, he added, "I'll give you a spare key. Stay as long as you need."

Audrey's eyes glistened with relief. "Thank you," they whispered, the sincerity in their voice underscored by a fragile vulnerability.

Boffin, ever attuned to the room's mood, leapt gracefully onto Audrey's lap, curling up and purring softly. Audrey's hand absentmindedly stroked her fur, the gentle motion a small solace in the quiet tension of the evening.

They alternated between sipping fine whisky and delicate lines of cocaine, the room steeped in a heavy, shared silence. Words felt unnecessary, their mutual exhaustion speaking volumes. By the time the bottle ran dry, they were too tired to lift another glass, let alone speak.

***

Three years had passed since Guatemala City, yet the rot still hadn't set in. Alan felt no remorse, no empathy – nothing. It was just a job. *A dirty job*, he told himself, though the words carried no weight, no conviction.

A soldier, he had learned, is little more than a machine built to obey orders. Not a mindless machine, but one that moves with purpose under the guidance of leadership. Reasonable, perhaps, but stripped of the luxury of hesitation.

He remembered one of the many operational briefings, where they'd spoken of *Weltanschauung* – a person's worldview or guiding philosophy. The instructors had emphasised its importance, saying he needed to believe he was performing a necessary service for the world. Yet even then, he'd been numb to the idea.

Looking back, he realised it had probably been a test. They weren't gauging his conviction but his indifference. He hadn't understood that at the time.

And now, standing on the brink of another nightmare, he wondered if that indifference had become permanent – or if it would one day destroy him.

Alan flew into RAF Akrotiri for the operational briefing, though he already had a clear idea of the task ahead. It was his third visit to Cyprus, a country he found himself increasingly comfortable in. He had always appreciated its subtropical climate, which seemed to strike a pleasant equilibrium between heat and coolness – or perhaps he'd simply been lucky during his previous visits.

The base, part of the British Sovereign Base Areas, was a key asset for the Royal Air Force, with a storied history of covert surveillance operations under NATO's sanction. Such activities were conducted carefully from UK sovereign territory to avoid offending Cypriot sensitivities. Alan's arrival, like the base itself, operated discreetly, raising no eyebrows.

Hospitality on the base, however, was predictably strained. The RAF maintained a long-standing rivalry with their Army counterparts, and outsiders were rarely welcomed with open arms. Alan had grown accustomed to being called a "Brown Job" but bit back the temptation to retaliate with the Army's favoured nickname for the RAF: "Crabs."

He kept himself to himself and his focus on the task ahead, eager to get through the briefing quickly and leave the base behind. The operation awaited, and Alan preferred action over the petty politics of inter-service rivalries.

In 2012, during Alan's visit, the local Communist Party was aggressively campaigning for the removal of the UK military presence from Cyprus. This development deeply concerned NATO, as it risked creating a strategic opening for Russia amidst lingering Soviet-era influence. Addressing this geopolitical challenge was central to Alan's mission.

The briefing outlined the brewing financial crisis, its acrimonious aftermath deliberately engineered to destabilise the region's political landscape. The Russians, who stood to lose the most, would see their influence diminished, and the fallout was expected to weaken the ruling Communist Party's grip on power.

Alan listened closely, absorbing the details, though his thoughts were focused on his immediate task. He trusted the architects of the operation to have their rationale in place and saw no need to wade into the ideological waters of anti-Communist rhetoric. For him, this was another mission – a piece in a larger puzzle that he had no interest in solving, only executing.

Alan relocated from the base to a hotel in Limassol, just a few miles away on the island's southern coast. Though he spoke no Greek, he carried false British ambassadorial papers, which allowed him to blend in effortlessly as another unassuming tourist. The timing of his arrival was deliberate - it coincided with Limassol's ten-day carnival, ensuring the streets were alive with revellers and distractions.

Dressed to fit the part, Alan wore shorts and a garishly bright Bermuda-style shirt, his camera slung around his neck and a rucksack emblazoned with a bold *Canon* logo hanging from one shoulder. He spent the day playing the role of an enthusiastic sightseer, starting with the Limassol Castle, a centuries-old landmark rich in history. He framed shot after shot with practiced precision, pausing occasionally to consult the camera equipment tucked in his bag.

From the castle, he moved to the bustling '28 October Avenue,' a seaside promenade transformed by the carnival's revelry. The avenue was a kaleidoscope of colour and sound: flamboyantly adorned floats paraded by, featuring themes ranging from ancient mythology to modern pop culture. Performers in elaborate costumes danced through the streets, their energy infectious, while vendors hawked everything from souvenirs to sweet treats. Alan captured it all, each click of his camera lending authenticity to his cover.

At the appointed hour, Alan arrived at the target hotel, an inconspicuous yet strategically placed building along the avenue. He double-checked the time and his surroundings, his casual bearing belying the calculated precision of his movements.

Alan strolled casually through the hotel lobby, blending in effortlessly with the stream of guests. He stepped into a lift, pressing the button for the specified floor with an air of unhurried ease. When the doors opened, he exited and located the room with little difficulty.

Knocking twice, he waited. Silence. No response. Fishing the keycard from his pocket, Alan slid it into the reader. A soft click signalled success, and he pushed the door open, a quiet relief washing over him as he confirmed the room was unoccupied. So far, the intelligence had been precise.

The suite was tastefully appointed, its centrepiece a wall of glass offering an unobstructed view of Akrotiri Bay and the shimmering expanse of the Mediterranean. For a fleeting moment, Alan let his gaze linger on the horizon before turning his attention back to the task at hand.

In the bathroom, he methodically unpacked his Canon bag, laying out its concealed contents. He began with the ankle holster, securing it in place and sliding his Micarta-handled hunting knife into its sheath – his backup blade. Next came the shoulder holster, snug against his torso,

271

holding a compact push dagger as his secondary fallback. Finally, he retrieved his favourite stiletto knife, the blade gleaming faintly under the bathroom's sterile light. He gripped it in a reverse hold, testing its balance, the motion instinctive and precise.

Again, there were no firearms – a deliberate measure to ensure complete silence. The room, the knives, and Alan himself were instruments of calculated precision.

When "Viktor" entered the hotel room, Alan's heart rate barely ticked above its resting pace.

He waited, motionless, until the target came into view. Then, in a single fluid motion, Alan stepped out from the bathroom's shadows and drove the stiletto blade upward, piercing the hyoid bone with surgical precision. That should have been it. Months of planning, days of travel, all distilled into five critical seconds. Five seconds that eliminated one of the most influential Russian financiers in Southeast Europe – a man whose assassination might tip the scales toward a Cypriot financial crisis.

But fate had other ideas.

As Viktor crumpled silently to the floor, Alan's peripheral vision caught movement – two others had entered the suite with him. Comrades. Armed, no doubt, and now wide-eyed with shock. The operation, meticulously planned for precision and minimal mess, descended into chaos.

Alan moved swiftly, his instincts honed to lethal efficiency. The first man lunged, and Alan sidestepped, pivoting as he drove the push dagger deep into the assailant's torso. Blood spattered the pristine hotel walls as the man collapsed, gurgling.

The second attacker was quicker, pulling a blade of his own. Alan's Micarta-handled hunting knife was already in hand. A parry, a twist, and the knife found its mark – a brutal arc across the throat. The man staggered, choking, before collapsing in a heap.

Alan stood over the bodies, his breathing steady despite the violence. He glanced down at his bloodied tools, silently grateful for their reliability. This hadn't been the surgical strike he'd envisioned, but the result was the same: mission accomplished.

Alan methodically took the requisite photographs of his 'kills.' There was no macabre fascination in the act – just the cold, practical need for proof. The images served as irrefutable documentation, verifying the success of the mission and providing crucial evidence for those tasked with identifying any secondary players. In this line of work, every detail mattered.

The room, however, quickly became suffocating. The metallic tang of fresh blood mingled with the acrid stench of bodily release as the muscles of the deceased gave way. The miasma thickened, clawing at his throat and making each breath more laboured.

Alan moved quickly to the window, sliding open the glass door to the balcony. The rush of fresh air hit him like a wave, cooling his skin and clearing his senses. The balcony, with its sweeping view of the Mediterranean, was a luxury he neither noticed nor had time to appreciate. In that moment, it was simply a sanctuary – a brief reprieve from the stifling aftermath inside.

As Alan cleaned and packed up in the bathroom, a wave of faintness crept over him. He sank onto the closed toilet seat, bowing his head between his knees. It wasn't that the additional two 'kills' had disrupted the plan – unforeseen complications were part of the job. But these were real lives, real human beings, with families and histories of their own. Likely decent people, possibly innocent. That thought, though fleeting, added weight to the task. Two more faces would linger within the charnel house of his dreams, his conscience heavy with their memory.

While he caught his breath, he examined his favoured stiletto blade, the Damascus pattern catching the light. Handcrafted by a master, it was a thing of undeniable beauty – almost artistic. He admired its craftsmanship for a moment, then, with practiced care, wrapped the blade in its sheath and returned it to his bag.

Slipping into a fresh shirt from his kit, Alan draped the room's bed linens over the bodies, attempting to absorb as much of the blood as possible. The effort was symbolic, at best. He exited the suite, hanging the "Do Not Disturb" sign on the door – glad to escape the suffocating mephitic atmosphere of the hotel room.

Though he'd left behind traces of himself, Alan knew his DNA was untraceable. His brother, the only living relative, had already disappeared into the shadows, and any trail would lead nowhere. The garments he'd discarded in his original hotel room would be abandoned without a second thought – a final act of detachment from this place, from the operation.

His plan was clear. He'd head back to the RAF base, wrap up his business in Cyprus swiftly, fly out today, and never look back.

The operation was a success. The financial crisis unfolded as intended, the Communist Party bore the blame, and the Russians were left seething – frustrated by the cost and their bruised pride. Alan, however, felt nothing. He was indifferent to the fallout, his focus already shifting to the next task, the next mission.

***

Alan woke in a cold sweat, the remnants of a nightmare lingering in his mind. He realised he had shouted, "I'm sorry!" but was uncertain how loudly. His heart raced, the arrhythmia a familiar, unwelcome companion. He forced himself to take deep breaths, willing his pulse to steady and his frazzled nerves to calm.

The silence of the room felt disorienting. He glanced at the bed, noting Audrey's presence beside him. He wasn't sure how long she had slept in the spare room, but at some point, during the night, she had sought comfort in his company, ending up in his bed. The thought brought an unexpected warmth, though he quickly pushed it aside. Thankfully, his outburst hadn't roused her; the tumult of the day had been heavy enough for both of them.

The emotional turmoil of their day had somehow drawn them closer, forging an unspoken bond neither had anticipated nor quite understood. A connection born from shared vulnerability, a silent understanding of the weight they each carried. Neither of them had planned for this, but it was there – quiet, fragile, yet undeniable.

Opening the Books

Over the following weeks, Ciara threw herself into understanding every detail of Rollie's sprawling business empire. She meticulously studied its inner workings, leaving nothing to chance. Her unwavering commitment fostered a strong rapport with Max, who, in turn, grew to respect and trust her. The expected resistance from Rollie's sons, Jamie and Nigel, was evident, but even they couldn't resist her charm and acumen. It quickly became clear that Ciara was no naive 'bimbo,' as Denver Hume had once dismissed her. Her intelligence, often underestimated, not only caught them off guard but impressed them both. However, they attributed their father's approval to mere luck, dismissing her abilities as coincidence rather than foresight.

In Bristol, while working with Nigel, Ciara gained a deep understanding of the operations under his control. Yet, the trip left a sour taste – Nigel's unwanted advances were a persistent irritation, and Ciara had to rebuff them firmly, leaving a tension that lingered after she returned.

Back in Brighton, Ciara focused on reviewing the accounts of Harry's bars, drawing on her experience managing a lap-dancing club in Ireland. The subtlety of the money laundering schemes fascinated her, even if it was disheartening to see so much revenue literally poured down the drain. She suggested ways to improve trade to Harry, but her ideas were quickly dismissed. He belittled her, calling her a "pretty little thing" and insisting she leave the business to the men. Max, who saw through Harry's attitude, offered an apology on his behalf, recognising the underlying misogyny. But Ciara, seasoned by similar encounters, took it all in stride. She was accustomed to the male-dominated world she moved through and wasn't easily deterred.

Her relationship with Bruce proved to be more complex. The weight of his expectations was ever-present, and the fear of letting him down hovered over her actions. It became a delicate balancing act, one that required patience and discipline. As she always did, Ciara approached it with methodical control, focusing on the long game and avoiding any impulsive moves.

In contrast, Rollie found Ciara to be an absolute delight. She quickly endeared herself to him, stepping into the role of the daughter he had never had. Her place within the Monroe family's intricate web of business and relationships was firmly cemented, she had become an indispensable part of Rollie's world in a short time.

Reporting Back

Denver Hume thrived in the vibrant energy of Boston, a city that felt far more attuned to his lively spirit than the frenetic chaos of New York or the sometimes stifling atmosphere of the UK. His return to the United States had rekindled a sense of belonging, a place where his dynamic persona was not only accepted but celebrated. It was here he could embrace his carefree, independent approach to relationships, unencumbered by the more rigid expectations of elsewhere. The American soil seemed to resonate with his confidence, as though it were the perfect backdrop for his charismatic take on life.

Before settling in Boston, he'd made a brief stop in Albany, his hometown, to visit his parents. His father, a man seasoned in high-ranking political circles, was a tough nut to crack. If Denver's ego was as expansive as New York State, his fathers was nothing short of national. Expectations were always sky-high, and their conversations – long, drawn-out affairs – often felt like bureaucratic exercises, leaving Denver with the constant sense that he was falling short. It was this complex dynamic that had fuelled his ambition, driving him to succeed on his own terms. Sharing the latest strides of his burgeoning business empire in the UK was both a moment of personal triumph and a quiet plea for his father's elusive approval.

Back in the bustling streets of Boston, Denver cruised through the city in a sleek, charcoal-coloured Ford Mustang GT – a car as bold and dynamic as his own personality. The engine roared to life beneath him, its power seeming to echo his own exuberance. The polished exterior gleamed in the sunlight, reflecting the surge of confidence building within him, a perfect symbol of his vibrant, unstoppable energy.

On the surface, the meeting with his bosses had been a disappointment. Denver had passionately made his case for acquiring Exotic Food Imports Limited, a UK-based venture in Brighton. Where he saw untapped potential, his bosses saw nothing but risk. Where he envisioned soaring revenue, they fixated on the company's poor financial performance, as presented by Denver. Where he saw a solid supply chain, they saw outdated, inefficient operational processes. The contrast in perspectives was jarring.

The bottom line was clear: they wanted nothing to do with this deal. But Denver, undeterred, made a bold proposition. He asked for the opportunity to pursue the venture on his own, ready to take on the risks and eager to augment his own experience. He assured them he wouldn't encroach on their territory, a small price to pay for his independence. It was a gamble, one his bosses vehemently advised against. Grateful for their counsel, he maintained a mask of respect, then, with as much subdued determination as he could muster, informed them that he intended to go for it – alone.

As Denver left the meeting, a surge of elation coursed through him. Sure, Ciara had written 95% of the presentation, but it was *he*, the great Denver Hume, who'd had the foresight to tweak the numbers – just enough to obscure the true value of the deal.

The exchange had gone better than he could've hoped. His bosses had walked straight into his trap, hook, line, and sinker.

Tomorrow, he'd set his sights on Bruce Thompson. Rollie might believe he'd secured some hollow victory by keeping Ciara in the fold, but that was irrelevant now. Bruce was going to pay, and Denver would make sure of it.

Tonight, he planned to revel in his newfound empowerment. The evening would be a showcase of his opulence, an indulgence in his penchant for juvenile girls, a way to assert his influence and control, to show them who the real boss is. His passion for seizing life's pleasures was undeniably at its peak, an expression of his ambitions and desire for success.

All In

Bruce couldn't make sense of it. In his mind, he and Ciara shared a magnetic connection – an unspoken bond that felt undeniable. To him, it wasn't just a casual 'thing'; it was something deeper, vibrant, and real. With Ciara now settled in Brighton and working for Rollie, it seemed like the perfect chance to explore the connection further, to see where it could lead.

Romantic relationships had never been Bruce's forte. It wasn't that he couldn't understand women – he understood them well enough. It was relationships themselves that confounded him. He saw them in binary terms: they either worked, or they didn't. And what he had with Ciara? That worked. Without question. If a relationship faltered, Bruce was pragmatic – he let it go without a backward glance. But when it thrived, he was all in.

That's why Ciara's insistence on "taking things slowly" didn't compute. He wasn't expecting whirlwind declarations or rushed plans for marriage, but he did expect momentum. Progress. More than sporadic Saturdays and fleeting moments together. His work often kept him away for days, but he craved something steadier, more meaningful.

Yet Ciara remained distant, citing her workload and the need to focus on Rollie's business dealings. The excuses felt endless, leaving Bruce in limbo – waiting, wanting, and growing ever more frustrated at the glacial pace of their relationship.

Saturday had arrived faster than Bruce anticipated, and with it, his anticipation swelled. He picked through his more recent wardrobe additions, opting for a look that struck the right balance between laid-back and polished. His gaze kept drifting to his phone, waiting for Ciara's call. She'd mentioned working at Rollie's house that morning but promised to ring and arrange their afternoon plans: drinks, a trip to the cinema, dinner, and, as she'd teasingly added, *"who knows where we could end up."* It was that last part Bruce was most looking forward to.

When his phone finally buzzed to life, his eagerness almost got the better of him. He moved to answer immediately, expecting Ciara's lilting Irish voice, only to pause at the sight of an unknown number. Hesitating, he let it go to voicemail.

Three minutes later, the notification pinged. Curious but wary, Bruce played the message.

The voice, American perhaps, was slightly muffled but dripping with a chilling confidence that sent shivers down his spine.

"Bruce Thompson, we have Ciara."

A scream erupted in the background – high-pitched, raw, unmistakably feminine.

"We're going to make a right mess of her," the voice continued, followed by a chilling laugh. "I'll send you an address, and you can come pick up the pieces. Enjoy your movie."

The message cut off with a click.

Bruce stared at the phone in stunned silence, his pulse racing. A new text had already appeared, listing an unfamiliar address in central Brighton.

He played the voicemail again, hoping he'd misheard, but the sinister tone was unmistakable. The scream lodged itself in his mind, as sharp and vivid as a knife.

Was this a sick prank? Who would go to such lengths? And how did they know about the cinema? Or his phone number?

Panic surged through Bruce like a tidal wave, crashing through his thoughts and propelling him into action. He fumbled with his phone, opening the map application and pasting the address from the text message. Less than two miles away. Too far to run swiftly, but he could make it quickly on his motorbike. He snatched his crash helmet and dashed towards the exit, intending to call Rollie on his way. The gravity of the situation was sinking in, and urgency propelled him into action.

A Call Amongst The Cauliflower

Sarah had been spending more time at Rollie's place lately – a refuge from the gnawing uncertainty surrounding her husband Peter's disappearance. Taking control of their finances had been necessary, and Peter's estate agency still supported her, though she doubted how long that would last.

Rollie welcomed her increased presence and insisted on compensating her for the extra work, a gesture she was reluctant to accept. On this particular Saturday morning, she had thrown herself into a task she'd normally avoid – a deep cleaning of the carpet in Rollie's office. It was a significant undertaking, but the distraction was welcome amidst her emotional unrest.

The shrill ring of Rollie's desk phone startled her. Without thinking, Sarah picked it up and answered. Moments later, cordless phone in hand, she hurried into the garden where Rollie was crouched between rows of potato plants.

"Excuse me, Rollie," she said, carefully stepping through the neat rows, trying not to disturb anything.

Rollie looked up in alarm. "Please be careful, Sarah! I've planted cauliflower between the potato rows." Sarah handed him the phone, awkwardly lifting her feet to avoid disturbing the planting. "You see, the cauliflower has a shallow root system that won't compete for nutrients with the more deeply rooted potatoes." Rollie noticed Sarah appeared flustered. "Is everything okay, Sarah?"

"I'm sorry I didn't mean to interrupt. Someone named Bruce Thompson is on the phone, and he sounds frantic!"

"Bruce?" Rollie stood, brushing dirt off his hands, and took the phone. "Bruce, what's going on?"

"Rollie! They have Ciara!" Bruce's voice was frantic, barely coherent amidst the roar of traffic in the background.

Rollie's brow furrowed. "Slow down, Bruce. Who has Ciara? Where are you?"

"They sent me an address – I'm heading there now to get her. Oh God, Rollie, I hope I'm not too late!" Bruce's words tumbled out, heavy with desperation.

"Bruce, wait! I think you might be mistaken. Ciara's here – she should be here somewhere. Let me check first!" Rollie's calm tone clashed with Bruce's rising panic.

"No, Rollie! I heard her! I heard her scream! If they've hurt her, I'll kill them!" Bruce's voice cracked, his anguish clouding his judgment, making it impossible for him to listen.

Rollie glanced around the garden, as though the solution might be hidden among the plants. "Bruce, stop for a moment and give me the address," he said firmly, his mind racing.

An Industrial Staircase

Bruce's desperation burned into a white-hot fury. Whoever had crossed him was about to face the full force of his wrath – they would regret ever daring to involve Ciara. The navigation app guided him through the intricate web of Brighton Lanes, an area known to locals but unfamiliar to him.

He pushed his motorbike hard, weaving through the maze of narrow streets with precision. Crashing was not an option; getting there intact was his only priority. The app's twists and turns felt like a cruel taunt, dragging him deeper into the labyrinthine lanes. The roar of his engine echoed through the alleys, bouncing off worn cobblestones as he sped past boutique shops and shadowy alcoves.

Finally, he arrived at the address.

Bruce dismounted, hooking his crash helmet onto the handlebars without a second thought for security. Time was too precious to waste. He scanned the surroundings, puzzled by the sight before him – a shuttered second-hand clothes shop. The dimly lit storefront seemed out of place, exuding an unsettling air of secrecy.

As he looked up, his breath caught.

The building's first floor was adorned with an awe-inspiring stained-glass window that stretched the entire width. It depicted a radiant sunrise, its mosaic of reds, oranges, and golds casting an ethereal glow onto the street below. The intricate artistry portrayed the sun cresting the horizon, its beams reaching out in a symphony of light, creating a surreal, mesmerising, almost celestial ambiance.

But Bruce had no time to marvel.

The shop stood at the end of a charming terrace of other stores. Adjacent to it was a sturdy metal fire escape, offering a means of access to the first floor. The structure stood in stark contrast to the brilliance of the façade, its metallic surface reflecting the surrounding light, accentuating its sharp angles and clean lines.

Without hesitation, Bruce sprinted toward it, bounding up the metal steps two at a time. Urgency fuelled every movement; every heartbeat echoed the gravity of the moment. Ciara's fate depended on him, and he couldn't afford to falter.

Who's Ciara?

Sarah had never seen Rollie so unsettled. His usual calm composure was replaced by hurried, disjointed movements.

"Is there anything I can do to help?" she asked, her voice steady but her heart racing.

"Uhm, thank you, my dear," Rollie said, momentarily frozen, his gaze darting around the garden. "Can you find Ciara for me? She's likely in her room."

Sarah hesitated – *Who's Ciara?* she wondered. Rollie quickly corrected himself, snapping out of his distraction. "Apologies, my dear. She's in the second guest suite. Please ask her to meet me in the office immediately. There's no time to waste."

As Rollie shuffled off to his office, Sarah turned toward the guest rooms. But before she could get there, Ciara appeared at Rollie's desk, her expression sharp and alert, sensing trouble in the air. Meanwhile, Sarah silently began packing away the carpet cleaner, an uneasy weight settling in her chest. Something serious was happening.

Rollie wasted no time explaining Bruce's harrowing call, his words spilling out in an uncharacteristically rushed manner.

Ciara's face turned pale, her horror unmistakable. "Oh my God, Rollie, it's a trap! You have the address, don't you?"

Rollie nodded. "Yes, Bruce sent it."

"Then I'll go down there myself," Ciara declared, already moving toward the door.

"No, absolutely not!" Rollie said, his voice firm but strained. "It's far too dangerous. I'll call someone from security to handle it." His gaze flicked around the room, seeking a solution. "October will be on his way home. But November – he might be nearby. I'll ring him."

"Rollie, there's no time!" Ciara's voice cracked with urgency, her hands trembling. "This is my fault. What have I done?"

"No, dear, it's not your fault." Rollie sank into his oversized office chair, fumbling with his phone. His frustration boiled over. "Damn this contraption!" he muttered, stabbing at buttons on the unfamiliar device.

Sarah cleared her throat, stepping forward cautiously. "I have my car," she offered, her voice quiet but steady.

Ciara turned, as though suddenly remembering Sarah's presence.

"I can drive you," Sarah added, glancing at Ciara with quiet determination.

"Thank you, Sarah, but no." Rollie's tone softened but remained resolute. "I won't risk putting either of you in harm's way."

Ciara watched Rollie, his fingers fumbling over his desk phone, his persistence noble but painfully slow. Her jaw tightened, her resolve hardening.

"Thank you, Rollie," she said, her voice firm now. "If you can get through to November, send him to the address. But I can't wait." She turned to Sarah. "Let's go."

The two women exchanged a determined glance. Without hesitation, Sarah grabbed her keys, and they moved as one, urgency driving them into immediate action.

Am Empty Room

At the top of the fire escape, a heavy metal door stood ajar, its hinges creaking softly as Bruce pushed it open. He stepped cautiously inside, unsure of what awaited him.

The room he entered was vast yet enclosed, dominated by the towering stained-glass sunrise that spanned the entire right-hand wall. The masterpiece cast a kaleidoscope of vivid hues – reds, oranges, and golds – onto every surface, flooding the space with an almost otherworldly glow. The light seemed alive, shifting subtly as it refracted through the intricate glass, filling the room with a warm yet surreal ambiance.

As the door clicked shut behind him, Bruce instinctively turned to test it, but the handle was gone – only a smooth, featureless surface remained. It had locked automatically, sealing him inside. His stomach tightened as he faced the room once more.

The space was almost entirely bare. The walls, once painted white, had faded to a dull, uneven grey, their age evident in the peeling paint and cracks running like veins across the plaster. The low ceiling, however, reflected the stained-glass brilliance, amplifying the light in a way that gave the room an oddly reverent quality.

Opposite the door he had entered was another, almost identical in appearance: plain, heavy, and resolute. Bruce crossed the room, his new shoes echoing faintly against the hardwood floor. He pressed against the second door, but it too was locked tight.

Above each door, modern security cameras were mounted, their sleek design at odds with the antique charm of the stained glass. A faint red light blinked steadily from one of them, its unblinking gaze fixed on him.

Bruce stared into the camera, his jaw tightening. A cold shiver ran down his spine as a voice broke the silence, echoing from hidden speakers embedded in the walls.

"Step away from the door, Mr. Thompson," the voice commanded, calm but edged with authority.

Bruce froze, his breath catching. He recognised it instantly: the same unmistakably American voice that had delivered the voicemail earlier.

The room seemed to shrink around him as the words hung in the air. The voice carried an unsettling confidence, its tone a calculated mix of menace and control.

Yet, as unsettling as it was, it steeled Bruce's resolve. Whoever this was, they were watching him, playing games – but they had Ciara, and he would do whatever it took to get her back.

Thelma & Louise

Ciara's mind was a storm of racing thoughts and growing suspicions. As the gates to Rollie's estate swung open, a chilling possibility hit her like a punch to the gut: *Could this be a double bluff?* Denver Hume was more than capable of such treachery.

The moment Sarah eased her BMW 1-Series through the gates onto Withdean Road, Ciara's gut screamed for action. "Stop the car!" she ordered, flinging the passenger door open before Sarah could fully respond.

Ciara sprinted to the gate controls, her pulse pounding in her ears. With a sharp press of the button, the gates began to close, their metallic clang reverberating through the air. Her eyes darted around, scanning for any lurking threats. The stillness beyond the gate felt ominous, but nothing moved – not yet.

Back in the car, she rattled off the address, her voice edged with urgency. The tension between them was palpable, heavy like an impending storm.

Sarah nodded briskly. "I know the area. It's in the Lanes, near the sunrise window."

"The sunrise window?" Ciara echoed, frowning.

"You'll see. It's impossible to miss," Sarah replied, weaving the car through Brighton's midday traffic with deft precision. Her tone was confident, almost reassuring, but the weight of the situation pressed down hard on Ciara's chest.

Ciara exhaled sharply, fighting to steady her nerves. Anxiety clawed at her, each passing second feeling like an eternity.

"Don't worry," Sarah said firmly, eyes fixed on the road. "I know the side streets; we'll be there soon."

As the car navigated tighter streets, Ciara pulled out her phone and dialled Rollie. Her voice was steady, but her words carried unmistakable resolve. "Rollie, listen carefully. When November gets there, keep him with you. This could be a trap. Stay put."

Rollie's reply crackled through the line, a mix of protest and concern. "Ciara, are you sure –"

"I *am* sure," Ciara cut in sharply, her tone leaving no room for debate. "Do *not* leave the estate. Keep everyone close until I update you."

The finality in her voice silenced Rollie's objections, leaving him with little choice but to comply. Even through the chaos, Ciara's unwavering composure and command were striking, her determination cutting through the uncertainty like a blade.

The clock was ticking, and the stakes seemed higher than ever.

Seconds Out…

Bruce took a cautious step back as commanded, his muscles coiled with tension. A sharp buzz signalled the door's release, its mechanism clicking ominously before the heavy steel panel creaked open. The behemoth figure of his *nom de guerre* Goliath stepped through, his entrance as commanding as it was unsettling. The door sealed shut behind him with mechanical finality, a chilling reminder of the unseen eyes orchestrating this twisted spectacle.

Goliath was an intimidating presence, living up to his name in every conceivable way. At six feet and seven inches, he loomed like a monument to brute strength, his physique a sculpted testament to years of gruelling discipline. A former professional wrestler from Ghana, his reputation for dominating the ring now translated to a more dangerous arena.

The speakers crackled to life, the same taunting voice dripping with smug amusement. "Ah, Mr. Thompson, I thought it fitting you two finally settle your score. I'm going to enjoy the show."

Bruce's fists clenched as the voice faded, leaving behind a charged silence. Whoever was behind this was revelling in their own sadistic production, but Bruce wasn't about to let them control the outcome.

Ciara's words about Goliath's strength echoed in Bruce's mind as he studied the man before him. Goliath's presence was nothing short of overpowering. His ebony skin gleamed under the glow of the stained glass, the vibrant colours playing across his sinewy muscles. The tight blue T-shirt and shorts he wore seemed almost superfluous, merely framing the massive bulk of a man built for combat.

Goliath's steps were deliberate as he moved to the centre of the room, the floor seeming to tremble beneath his weight. His intense gaze locked onto Bruce, his expression unreadable but brimming with quiet menace.

The room seemed to shrink in the face of Goliath's overwhelming presence, as if struggling to contain the energy surging within him.

Bruce stood his ground, every muscle tensed, his heart pounding in his chest as his eyes locked onto the patch on Goliath's left thigh. The cloth barely concealed the scar of their shared history – the stab wound Bruce had inflicted months ago. It was a silent testament to their brutal past, a grudge that had festered and now materialised in this ominous confrontation.

Determination surged within Bruce as he glanced towards the door he had entered through. He sprinted, hoping without hope for an escape route, but it stood resolute and locked.

In a flash of desperation, Bruce turned to the security camera mounted above the door. A potential weapon, a tool he could use to his advantage. He sprang, his body straining with every muscle, but the height of the camera was a cruel obstacle. His fingers brushed the edge, but it was too far. Frustration ignited a fierce resolve within him. He couldn't afford to waste time; improvisation was his only chance.

The room felt suffocating as Goliath stood there, an immovable monolith, his grin wide and unsettling. His confidence radiated through the air, thick with menace, further amplified by the terrifying difference in size between them. Bruce felt small under Goliath's gaze, the weight of the situation pressing down on him like a crushing vice.

The walls seemed to close in, the dim orange glow from the stained-glass window casting long, eerie shadows across the barren room. No allies, no weapons, no escape. Bruce was alone, cornered, his only recourse the martial skills he had honed over the years. They were all he had left, and as the gravity of the moment settled on him, he knew they had to be enough.

Determination surged through Bruce's veins as he seized the initiative, launching his first strike with the intent to catch Goliath off guard. Though nearly a foot shorter, Bruce knew that in the right circumstances, this height disparity could work to his advantage. He moved quickly toward the centre of the room, dropping into a low stance, targeting Goliath's formidable torso, ready to exploit any opening.

But Goliath was no mere brute; he was a seasoned fighter, sharp and calculating. As Bruce closed the distance, Goliath feigned a step back, baiting him into committing. Bruce, sensing a moment of weakness, pressed forward – only for Goliath to explode into motion, his speed shocking. The massive man's fist landed with brutal force, knocking Bruce off his feet and sending him crashing to the floor.

Instinctively, Bruce rolled away, every muscle primed for another strike, his eyes locked on Goliath's massive form, ready for the stomping blow he feared was coming. But to his surprise, Goliath didn't advance. Instead, he stood rooted to the spot, his chest heaving with deep, guttural laughter that reverberated through the room.

Bruce's mind raced. He had expected brute force – but not this. Goliath's agility was unnerving, a testament to his years of training. The sheer speed and finesse of a man with such an imposing frame sent a cold shiver through Bruce. It was a sobering realisation, one that flickered a moment of doubt in his chest. This was no easy fight. Goliath, driven by youth and raw power, was a force to be reckoned with.

Goliath revelled in his dominance at the room's centre, the familiarity of the wrestling ring echoed in his bearing. It was a cruel dance where Bruce was the reluctant partner, forced to circle the behemoth with a sense of subjugation. He adhered to the cruel choreography, moving warily, never losing sight of the immense threat that loomed before him. He crouched low, a coiled spring of determination, ready to pounce at the right moment.

With each attempt to close in, Bruce encountered the cruel reality of Goliath's overwhelming reach. His strikes were futile, like a desperate insect trying to pierce an impenetrable shell. Goliath's blows landed with crushing force, sending Bruce reeling, desperately evading the onslaught. The room felt suffocating, the walls seemingly closing in as Goliath tightened his grip on the battlefield.

Bruce tried to regain control, seeking an opportunity amidst the relentless storm of attacks. He aimed for Goliath's legs, a tactic to undermine the titan, but his efforts were futile. He was pushed back, battered, and thwarted at every turn. The blows were relentless, a brutal reminder of the immense power possessed by Goliath.

As Goliath advanced, Bruce felt a surge of panic, the room shrinking around him. He attempted the door once more, clinging to the hope of escape, but it remained obstinately jammed. In a desperate gambit, Bruce lunged forward, executing a forward roll to slip beneath Goliath's reach. The room momentarily stilled as Bruce found a brief respite, but Goliath's sinister grin signalled the relentless pursuit of their deadly tango.

Bruce lunged into the fight once more, a mix of desperation and determination driving him. His strikes landed, but they seemed insignificant against Goliath's gargantuan frame. Goliath retaliated with another clubbing blow, only catching Bruce with a glancing hit. Bruce rolled, evading capture yet again. The dance continued, Bruce catching his breath, Goliath enjoying the cruel game. Time was running out, and Bruce knew that his resilience could only carry him so far against this colossal adversary.

Goliath's malevolent advance continued, his grin widening with a twisted delight that sent shivers down Bruce's spine. It was as if this vicious combat was nothing but a morbid game to the towering adversary. Bruce, on the other hand, knew the stakes were high and the outcome held dire consequences. He continued to evade, a dance of survival at the edges of the room, desperately staying out of the giant's lethal grasp.

In the chaos of their battle, a flicker of hope ignited within Bruce – a glimmer fuelled by the memory of Goliath's old wound. A wound Bruce had inflicted during their encounter at the motorway service station. Perhaps fate had orchestrated this moment, granting Bruce a sliver of advantage.

Goliath swung with the force of a wrecking ball. Bruce sidestepped, narrowly avoiding the crushing blow, his back now pressed against the room's cold, unforgiving wall. He found himself face-to-face with the mesmerising stained-glass window, its intricate patterns momentarily capturing his attention as he braced for Goliath's assault.

As the massive foe closed in, preparing for an onslaught, Bruce steeled himself, mustering every ounce of courage. He moved towards Goliath, a combination of determination and dread swirling within him. Summoning all his strength, he directed a powerful punch at the stab wound.

The blow landed, but Goliath's retaliation was brutal, a heavy hit that momentarily threatened Bruce's consciousness. The room tilted around him, yet he refused to yield. Undeterred, Bruce pressed on, unleashing a fierce kick aimed at the same wound. He moved swiftly, attempting to exploit the vulnerability further. Goliath's reaction hinted at pain, a groan escaping the behemoth as Bruce persisted, attempting to gouge the wound.

The giant faltered, showing a flicker of weakness. He let out another groan, shoving Bruce away, granting a momentary respite in the relentless clash. The tide of the battle had shifted, if only slightly, and Bruce seized this opportunity to gather his strength and plan his next move.

Bruce stood to catch his breath; as he breathed deeply to clear his head, he watched as his opponent seemed to stagger to his left side, clutching his wound. As he lifted his hand from the wound Bruce could see the adhesive bandage had taken on a shade of red.

"Good," he thought, "I've opened the wound." Finally, he may have found a weakness, a chink in the armour.

Bruce's next move was an eruption of pure audacity, born of desperation and instinct. In the weeks that followed, as he replayed this pivotal moment in his mind, he struggled to trace its origin. It felt like an act beyond logic, a split-second leap into chaos that defied reason. Reflecting later, he doubted whether he'd have taken the same risk had he been in his right mind.

Driven by an unstoppable surge of adrenaline, Bruce hurled himself forward, his body and will aligned in a singular, desperate act. His left arm shot beneath Goliath's massive right leg, seeking to further destabilize the giant, while his right arm wedged under Goliath's left armpit. Fuelled by raw necessity and the latent strength honed through years of weight training, Bruce heaved upward. To his astonishment, he lifted the behemoth clear off the ground – a Herculean feat so improbable it felt surreal, even in the moment. The sheer force of his effort reverberated through his body, every fibre screaming in exertion.

Momentum became Bruce's ally as he staggered forward, his burden a staggering 240 pounds of raw muscle and menace. Goliath's hulking frame writhed in his grasp, the tension between them a battle unto itself. Bruce's eyes locked onto the stained-glass window, its vibrant hues blurring into a target. His hope, fragile and fleeting, clung to the idea that the window might shatter, granting him an escape.

But the window didn't yield. Instead, it resisted with unrelenting strength. Bruce collided with the glass, the impact jarring him to his core. Rebounding off its surface, he was propelled backward, Goliath's weight threatening to drag him to the floor. Every muscle in his body screamed as he fought to remain upright, his right foot instinctively mimicking the weightlifters he'd watched in awe – the stabilising movement of a lifter's "jerk," desperate and precise. His stance wavered, but he held, a trembling anchor in the maelstrom.

Time seemed to stretch unbearably thin. Goliath thrashed, his colossal sternocleidomastoid bulging in defiance, his guttural growls mingling with the mocking voice that had haunted Bruce throughout this ordeal. The seconds bled together, an eternity condensed into agonising heartbeats.

With a final, primal roar, Bruce summoned the last vestiges of his strength. Muscles already pushed to their limits screamed in protest, his lungs burned, his vision narrowed – but he surged forward once more. The window loomed ahead, its unyielding surface an implacable judge of his resolve. Bruce's final dive was an act of sheer willpower, a desperate attempt to break free.

In that fleeting moment, as Goliath's weight bore down on him, Bruce thought he heard a low chuckle – a cruel echo of victory. Yet even in the face of that mockery, Bruce clung to his hope, refusing to yield to defeat. If the glass would not break, he would find another way – or die trying.

Broken Glass

Sarah and Ciara used the short drive to forge a tentative connection, curiosity and shared urgency drawing them together. Sarah longed to delve into Ciara's enigmatic background, but the clock was against them.

Navigating Brighton's bustling Lanes, Sarah skilfully maneuvered her compact BMW through the tight streets. Lunchtime revellers spilled from lively bars into the narrow roads, forcing her to honk repeatedly. Ciara, tension sharpening her Irish brogue, let loose a stream of nearly unintelligible curses at anyone who failed to move fast enough. There was no time for niceties – Bruce was in danger, and every second counted.

They finally arrived, slamming the car doors in unison. Shoppers and tourists moved around them without a second glance, their urgency lost in the hum of the busy street. Ciara gestured to a shop with a faded sign above the door, its windows dark and uninviting.

"That's the place," she said, her voice tight. "But it looks shut – empty even!" She rushed to the window, cupping her hands against the glass. "There's no one in there!"

Stepping back hastily, she nearly collided with a pedestrian and stumbled, catching herself just in time. As she steadied, her eyes widened, transfixed by the stained-glass window above the shop.

"Wow," she murmured, awe breaking through her frustration. "You were right, Sarah. You couldn't miss that."

Sarah's gaze shifted to a motorcycle parked nearby. "Could this be Bruce's?"

"Yes," Ciara confirmed, tension thickening her accent. "That's his. So, where the hell is he?"

Sarah nodded toward the fire escape on the side of the building. "What about up there?"

Ciara approached the metal staircase, its cold, industrial aesthetic stark against the quaint surroundings. The weight of the moment pressed down on her as she placed a foot on the first step.

Before she could climb, a deafening crash shattered the ordinary murmur of the street. Startled, she spun toward the shop just as shards of coloured glass cascaded to the cobblestones below.

Sarah stumbled back, shielding her face. Around them, shoppers froze, then scattered, their screams piercing the air. Ciara's gaze locked on the chaos, her breath catching.

"That's Goliath!" she cried, alarm clear in her voice.

Amid the glass shards lay two tangled bodies. Ciara rushed forward, heart pounding as she recognised Bruce, his frame entwined with Goliath's in a grim tableau of broken glass and blood.

"And that's Bruce!" she yelled, motioning to Sarah, though there was no mistaking him. The shattered glass framed the two men in cruel splashes of red and yellow, a macabre mosaic on the street.

"Quick, help me get him!" Ciara urged.

Together, they hauled Bruce upright, his weight heavy between them. His eyes fluttered open but remained unfocused, his lips struggling to form words. Ciara gently cradled his head as they eased him into the back seat of Sarah's car.

"Bruce, can you hear me? Do you know where you are?" Ciara's voice was soft but urgent, her worry palpable.

His silence was unnerving. Onlookers had started gathering around Goliath's prone form, some pointing at Sarah's car. The crowd's interest added to the tension.

"Let's go – back to Rollie's," Ciara said, her voice trembling with urgency as she dialled her phone. "I'll call him."

In the back seat, Ciara kept a protective hand on Bruce's head as the call connected. "Rollie, it's me," she said quickly. "Bruce is hurt – badly. He fell. He's out of it, can't even speak." Her words tumbled out, raw with emotion.

A moment later, she hung up and turned to Sarah. "Rollie says he'll sort medical care at his place. Just drive!"

Sarah didn't hesitate, focusing on the road while Ciara stayed with Bruce.

"Rollie's got a fully stocked first aid room," Sarah offered, her tone calm despite the situation. "I've cleaned it before – it's top-notch."

Ciara nodded, relief flickering across her face. Yet, beneath the surface, a gnawing unease grew. The fall, the glass, Goliath – none of it felt random.

As the car sped toward Rollie's, Sarah's thoughts churned. The day's events veered dangerously close to outright chaos, and the weight of her involvement hung heavy. She only hoped this wouldn't spiral into something they couldn't undo.

The Bungled Exit

Denver Hume followed his assistant, Rob Gates, through the fire exit at the back of the shuttered clothes shop. The chaos they'd left behind demanded haste. Goliath's fate would have to be a problem for someone else – whatever authority eventually scraped him off the pavement.

The two men had worked quickly, yanking cables free and cramming the laptop and other critical equipment into a worn rucksack. They had the footage, but it wasn't the triumphant display they'd hoped for. Goliath's domination hadn't been captured – just a chaotic, muddled confrontation. The best outcome Denver could hope for now was that Bruce Thompson was just as incapacitated as their own man.

Around the corner, they scrambled into a nondescript hire car. Rob, his arm still encased in a cast from his own encounter with Bruce, slid awkwardly into the passenger seat, leaving Denver to take the wheel.

"You botched it, you fat idiot," Denver snapped, venom dripping from his words as he threw the car into gear.

Rob flinched but said nothing. He knew better than to engage – Denver's sharp tongue and towering ego weren't worth the fight. Besides, Rob had seen the cracks in the plan from the start but pointing that out now would only add fuel to Denver's fury.

The car sped away, the rucksack shifting uneasily in the back seat, a silent reminder of how far their grand scheme had fallen short. Denver gripped the wheel tighter, his mind racing for the next move, while Rob stared out the window, resigned to the fallout yet to come.

Bruce's Concussion

After hanging up with Ciara, Rollie immediately called Dr. Crawley, the Monroe family's trusted medic. The doctor, known for his wealth of expertise and discretion, wasted no time firing a series of pointed questions. Rollie, unprepared for the flood of medical jargon, stumbled over his answers, unable to provide the level of detail the doctor sought.

Sensing Rollie's frustration, Dr. Crawley quickly adapted, his tone softening. Years on a generous retainer from the Monroes had honed his ability to manage crises with calm efficiency. "Don't worry, Rollie. I'll be there as soon as I can," he assured, estimating it would take him about an hour to arrive.

In the meantime, Crawley offered a stopgap solution. "I'll send a local nurse – someone I trust. She'll get there much faster and can stabilise things until I arrive."

Relief flickered across Rollie's face. Dr. Crawley's reliability was precisely why the Monroes had kept him close all these years.

The nurse arrived with remarkable alacrity, trailing Bruce's arrival by only five minutes – a relief to everyone present. Rollie's security guard, November, stepped in to assist, helping Bruce into the first aid room and easing him onto the waiting bed. Though Bruce was murmuring incoherently under his breath, he remained unexpectedly calm.

Without wasting a moment, the nurse began her assessment, simultaneously calling Dr. Crawley to report Bruce's condition: noticeable head swelling, disorientation, confusion, and persistent dizziness. Dr. Crawley, listening intently, instructed her to monitor Bruce closely and to alert him immediately if his condition changed. He also expressed the need for a micro-CT scan at the earliest opportunity and promised to make the necessary arrangements. The cost was not a problem.

Throughout it all, Ciara stayed resolutely at Bruce's side, her unwavering presence a quiet testament to her concern. Her watchful eyes never left him, even as the nurse worked methodically.

True to his word, Dr. Crawley arrived nearly to the minute, bringing with him a calm, authoritative presence that seemed to lighten the tension in the room. Shortly after, the promised micro-CT scanner arrived. To Ciara's surprise, its name belied its complexity – it was anything but compact. Alongside the scanner came a full suite of equipment: a dedicated computer, monitor, and keyboard, all essential to the diagnostic process.

As the scanning began, Dr. Crawley took a moment to pull Rollie aside. "A proper hospital would be better for him," he said gently, his tone careful not to overstep. Yet he understood the Monroe family's preference for discretion and chose not to press the point.

The results confirmed what Dr. Crawley had suspected: Bruce had suffered a concussion and a linear skull fracture – a serious but manageable injury with the right care. He prescribed paracetamol for the pain and set up an intravenous drip of propofol for sedation and left with a promise to return the next day to reassess Bruce's condition. The nurse accepted a lucrative retainer to stay bedside to monitor.

As the tension in the room began to ease, Ciara exhaled softly, her hand resting briefly on Bruce's shoulder. For now, he was stable, and that was enough.

Anticipating the challenges ahead, Rollie asked about Bruce's chances of resuming his driving duties. Dr. Crawley's response was measured but firm: Bruce would need at least a month of recovery before even considering getting behind the wheel. The news presented Rollie with a serious dilemma, as he quickly began calculating the logistical and operational setbacks this would cause. For now, the question wasn't just about finding a replacement driver – it was about ensuring the entire operation didn't grind to a halt.

Shifting Gears

Rollie sank heavily into his office chair, the fatigue etched in his face betraying the toll of the day's events. Across from him, Ciara watched with concern, noting the weariness in his posture. Beside her, Sarah sat quietly, cradling a large Courvoisier brandy bowl, her hands trembling slightly.

"How are you both holding up, my dears?" Rollie asked softly, his voice warm despite the tension in the room. The clock read only 10 p.m., but the weight of the day made it feel like the early hours of the morning.

"I'm fine," Ciara replied, her tone steady enough to convince him. "But I'm worried about Sarah." Reaching out, she gently rubbed Sarah's arm, a small gesture of reassurance.

Rollie shifted his focus to Sarah. Her tear-streaked cheeks and the way she clutched the glass spoke volumes. "Sarah, I'm so sorry you got pulled into this," he said earnestly. "You must stay here tonight. It's the very least I can offer."

Sarah nodded, her expression distant but compliant. Rollie turned to Ciara. "Could you pour her another brandy? Actually, pour one for me as well."

As Ciara moved to refill their glasses, Rollie leaned forward, pinching the bridge of his nose. Ciara caught the subtle tremor in his hand.

"What is it, Rollie?" she asked, her voice soft but probing.

He sighed deeply, lowering his hand to pick up the brandy bowl Ciara had set in front of him. "I hate to bring this up so soon, but Bruce is out of action for a month – doctor's orders. And we have a delivery scheduled next week. I don't have a driver."

Rollie leaned back into his chair, swirling the amber liquid in his glass. The reality of Bruce being their "single point of failure," as Rollie had once described it, was hitting harder than Ciara had expected.

"Is there really no one else?" she asked, though she already suspected the answer.

Rollie shook his head, the stress visible in his eyes. "We could hire a driver," he said reluctantly, "but trusting someone new, someone outside the family, is a massive risk."

Ciara understood immediately. Rollie wasn't just worried about competence; he was worried about exposure. "What about using a different vehicle?" she pressed. "Something smaller?"

Rollie leaned forward again, considering the idea. "In theory, yes. But in practice, the operation is optimised for the van – sorry, the truck. Changing that adds significant risk. And regardless of the vehicle, we still need a driver. The cargo won't fit in a car."

Ciara frowned, her mind racing. "Could we postpone the delivery? Just long enough to buy us some time?"

Rollie shook his head firmly. "That's not an option. The window to delay has already closed." He took a long sip from his glass, the tension in his shoulders barely easing.

"What type of vehicle is it?" Sarah asked, her quiet voice cutting through the tension and startling both Rollie and Ciara. They had nearly forgotten she was even in the room.

Rollie blinked, caught off guard. "Um, well, my dear, it's… a large one," he replied hesitantly, unsure where she was going with this.

Sarah leaned forward, undeterred. "Yes, but I meant, what kind of license is required to drive it?"

Rollie frowned, glancing at Ciara, who shrugged, equally unsure. "Does it have a detachable trailer?" Sarah pressed.

"Hold on a moment, my dear," Rollie muttered, rummaging through a desk drawer. After a few moments, he produced a photograph of the vehicle – the same one he'd used when hiring Bruce. He slid it across the desk toward Sarah.

She studied the picture briefly, then looked up. "I can drive that."

Rollie blinked again, utterly perplexed. "I'm sorry? You can what?"

Ciara straightened in her chair, suddenly intrigued.

"I can drive that truck," Sarah repeated, pointing at the picture. "It has a rigid body base. I'm licensed for it."

Rollie's confusion deepened. "I... I don't follow."

Sarah set her brandy glass down, her voice calm but firm. "My parents owned a freight business. My sister and I were trained to step in if a driver let them down – which happened a lot. I used to have a Class 1 HGV license, but when I last renewed it, I switched to a Class 2 for simplicity. That license still lets me drive any rigid vehicle without a trailer. This lorry," she said, tapping the picture, "fits the criteria. And I renewed my license four years ago, so it's still valid."

Rollie and Ciara exchanged stunned looks.

"That's incredible!" Ciara said, breaking the silence, her admiration clear.

"It is quite remarkable," Rollie admitted, though his tone carried a note of caution. "But absolutely not, my dear. I deeply appreciate the offer, but I can't let you do this."

Ciara leaned forward, excitement lighting up her face. "Hang on, Rollie. Let's not dismiss this so quickly. It could solve our problem. I could go with Sarah – I know the route. This might just work!"

Rollie shook his head firmly. "No. It's far too dangerous, and I won't put Sarah at any further risk. We need to explore other options."

Ciara sighed but didn't back down, her mind already turning over the possibilities. Sarah, meanwhile, leaned back in her chair, waiting for the inevitable argument to play out, her resolve unwavering.

<u>Girl Power</u>

Rollie felt cornered, grappling with the weight of the decision to let Sarah take the wheel of the lorry heading north. It was the only viable option, but that didn't ease the gnawing anxiety building within him. His concern for both Sarah and Ciara festered each potential risk playing out in his mind. Yet Ciara's confidence was strangely reassuring, her steady words cutting through his doubt and sowing a reluctant sense of calm.

Rollie's protective instincts flared as he considered sending security to accompany them on their journey to Edinburgh. The thought of ensuring their safety was paramount. Ciara, however, was adamant against the idea, insisting they could handle things alone. After much debate, she conceded to having security shadow them on their return to Brighton, when the lorry and its cargo would be most vulnerable. Even then, she viewed it as unnecessary.

"Low profile is key, Rollie," she emphasised. "One vehicle, no extra attention. A convoy or security tail would just put a target on us. Stealth is our safest bet."

The plan came together with meticulous precision. Sarah and Ciara would drive to Edinburgh in a single day, leaving the lorry at the Port of Leith for safekeeping. They'd spend two nights in the city, retrieving the loaded lorry early on the third morning for the drive back to Brighton.

To ensure added security without drawing attention, Rollie's team members August and November would fly to Edinburgh on the second day. They'd rent a car to follow Sarah and Ciara at a discreet distance on their return journey, ready to intervene if needed. Every move was calculated to minimise risk and maximise the mission's success.

As dawn broke, Sarah guided the white Mercedes lorry out of its storage facility on the outskirts of Brighton. Initial apprehension over handling an unfamiliar vehicle melted away. The lorry's modern design featured a 7.1-litre, six-cylinder engine with nearly 300 brake horsepower, making it surprisingly smooth and responsive. It was a far cry from the clunky freight vehicles Sarah had driven in the past.

Behind the seats, she noticed a compact but thoughtfully organised space: a pillow, sleeping bag, a set of dumbbells in one corner, and a flask in another. A setup clearly tailored for Bruce, though Sarah privately preferred the comfort of hotels.

She glanced over at Ciara, seated in the passenger seat with effortless poise. Despite the early hour, Ciara looked impeccable in a sleeveless, knee-length summer dress, her makeup flawless and her aura radiant. Sarah couldn't help but compare her own jeans and loose blouse, feeling suddenly frumpy. She'd spent less than five minutes on her makeup, while Ciara's polished look hinted at hours of preparation.

Ciara, engrossed in her phone for a few moments, finally glanced at Sarah with a bright smile. "Wow, Sarah, you're seriously rocking this monster truck! Proper girl power!"

Sarah chuckled, keeping her eyes on the road. "It's not exactly a monster truck, but thanks. I've driven plenty of these for my parents' company. This is nothing new for me."

"Well, according to my app, we've got about eight hours ahead of us – that's without stops for refuelling this beast or us." Ciara grinned, leaning slightly toward Sarah. "So, there's plenty of time for you to tell me everything about yourself. Starting with how you became a pro at driving these lorries!"

Sarah smiled, amused by Ciara's enthusiasm. "It's not as glamorous as you might think," she began, her hands steady on the wheel. "But if you're curious, I guess we've got time."

And with that, the journey began, the road stretching out before them, laden with both challenge and opportunity.

The Surprise Package

Max had received Rollie's call the previous evening, summoning him to the office at precisely 6 a.m. He was instructed to pack an overnight bag and extend the same request to his friend Alan. Though Max was no early riser, he knew Rollie was, and Rollie's tone left no room for negotiation. Max didn't question the timing or suggest an alternative – he understood that when Rollie called, you showed up.

Uncharacteristically, Rollie had arranged coffee, and bacon rolls for the meeting, which took place at his long table rather than his usual perch behind the desk. The informal setup only heightened Max's curiosity. As Rollie laid out the plan for Ciara and Sarah's upcoming trip to Edinburgh, Max nearly choked on his coffee. The audacity and risk of the operation weren't lost on him.

Then came the favour, and Rollie prefaced it with the rare acknowledgment that Max could refuse – but they both knew that wasn't an option.

Rollie wanted Max to tail the women on their journey, accompanied by Alan. The request caught Max off guard. Why not delegate this to the security team? Rollie waved off the question with a vague explanation: "Not an option this time." His tone made it clear that pressing the matter further would be futile.

Rollie handed Max details of a tracking app that would monitor the women's progress and emphasised the utmost secrecy. No one else in the family was to know about the mission. Concerned, Max asked about potential threats, but Rollie downplayed the risks, insisting it was a precautionary measure to safeguard Ciara and Sarah.

Max drained his coffee, left the table, and phoned Alan to brief him and ensure he packed for the overnight trip. Arriving at Alan's flat, number 37, Max stayed in the car, glancing impatiently at the front door. Alan appeared in the doorway, mid-conversation with someone Max hadn't expected – a young woman.

Frustrated by the delay, Max lowered the passenger-side window. "Alan, can we move it along? We're on the clock!"

Alan waved dismissively, exchanged a few more words with the woman, and then approached the car with his case. As he loaded it into the boot, Max noticed something odd – there were two cases. Before he could comment, the young woman walked briskly to the car and climbed into the back seat.

"Alan," Max growled, his patience wearing thin, "we can't afford detours. I don't have time to drop anyone off."

"I'm not asking you to," Alan shot back, irritation in his tone. "They're coming with us."

Max blinked, dumbfounded. "What the hell are you talking about? Who is she?"

Alan slid into the passenger seat, shutting the door with an air of finality. "I'll explain on the way, and it's 'they', not 'she'. Let's just get moving."

Max stared at him for a beat, then glanced in the rearview mirror at the woman, who sat silently with their hands folded in their lap. Petite, with neatly styled dark hair, they wore a dark polo neck and light wide-legged trousers – a picture of composure amidst the chaos.

Grinding his teeth, Max started the car and pulled away. He didn't like surprises, and this one promised to complicate an already precarious situation.

Half Way There

Sarah found herself enjoying the conversation with Ciara, even if she mostly played the role of listener. Hours had flown by during their journey, but she felt a surprising sense of fulfilment. She had shared so much of her life – stories she rarely discussed – with Ciara, almost baring her soul. Yet, she realised she knew very little about Ciara in return. It struck Sarah how effortlessly Ciara navigated the art of conversation, drawing her out with skilful questions and genuine curiosity. Ciara's breadth of experience felt vast, almost intimidating, and by comparison, Sarah saw her own life as sheltered, cocooned in the familiar routines of her small cleaning business. Still, Ciara's sincere interest in her work left Sarah pleasantly validated.

Ciara, for her part, was equally enjoying Sarah's company. She saw in Sarah a woman of integrity and unvarnished honesty, qualities Ciara admired. While Sarah was in charge of the lorry, the rhythm of their conversation naturally placed Ciara in that driver's seat, steering the topics and deciding what fragments of her own life to reveal. She was used to controlling the narrative and found comfort in that. Despite her typical command of the situation, she was genuinely impressed by Sarah's adept handling of the massive lorry. Hours had passed without a single complaint from Sarah or a request for a break.

Their connection deepened with every mile, shaped by a shared understanding that their journey was more than just a drive – it was an unspoken step toward something unknown.

As the road stretched on, Ciara glanced at the passing signs, sensing the growing need for a pause. A green sign appeared ahead, reading *"Wetherby Service Station – 2 miles."* Ciara took the initiative, further cementing her role as the leader of their duo.

"How about we pull into the next stop?" she suggested, her tone carrying a hint of authority. "Quick pit stop for me – loo and a coffee – and I'm sure you could use a break. We're about halfway there, so it's perfect timing."

Sarah felt a wave of relief. Five hours on the road had begun to wear on her, though she hadn't wanted to be the one to call for a stop. Her instinct to follow rather than lead in their dynamic kept her silent until now.

"Sounds good to me," Sarah replied, her voice tinged with gratitude.

As they approached the service station, Sarah appreciated the balance Ciara brought to their journey – her assertiveness offering a structure that Sarah was happy to follow.

<u>Max's Chagrin</u>

Max had spent most of his driving years behind the wheel of BMWs, each successive purchase a calculated step up the ladder of luxury and performance. His current 7-Series was the pinnacle of his collection – powerful, opulent, and unflinchingly comfortable. Though he and Alan had left Brighton two hours after the lorry, Max had already managed to close the gap by an impressive 30 minutes. Glancing at the tracking app, he noted that Ciara and Sarah had stopped at a motorway service station. Encouraged, he was confident the distance between them would continue to shrink.

What unsettled him, however, was the quiet, almost spectral presence of Audrey in the back seat. Alan, seated beside him, had provided a vague explanation of how they'd met Audrey, a story strange enough to pique Max's curiosity but too incomplete to satisfy it. When pressed for details, Alan had been evasive, leaving Max frustrated. This was his car, after all, and he was the one navigating this peculiar situation. With hours still ahead of them, the tension in Max's chest grew as his questions about Audrey remained unanswered. Alan might be a trusted friend, but even that trust felt tested by the oddness of their current predicament.

Audrey, for their part, offered little to bridge the gap. Their silence had stretched on for so long that Max had given up trying to engage them in conversation. Whether their muteness was due to shyness or indifference, Max couldn't tell, but he decided not to waste any more effort figuring it out.

Alan, perhaps sensing Max's simmering frustration, shifted his focus to the tracking app. "It'd work in our favour if the ladies hung around at the service station for a bit. We'd catch up in no time."

"True," Max replied. "Just remember, they can't know we're following them."

Alan frowned. "I still don't understand that part. Why all the secrecy?"

Max's grip tightened slightly on the wheel. "Rollie's orders. Ours is not to reason why." His tone was clipped, a clear signal he didn't want to delve further into Rollie's reasoning. Alan, sensing the conversation had hit a wall, let the subject drop.

The atmosphere in the car was heavy, a quiet tension Max wasn't used to feeling around Alan. Seeking to lighten the mood, Alan fiddled with the radio, settling on a mellow playlist. The soft strains of music filled the cabin, providing a temporary reprieve from the discomfort of unspoken questions and the unsettling presence in the back seat.

Pit Stop

The sun shone brightly over Wetherby, and Ciara and Sarah sat at a picnic bench, enjoying sandwiches and coffee. The warm rays on their faces added to the sense of calm as they refuelled for the second leg of their journey. Stocked up on water and snacks, they were ready to hit the road again. After a restful 45-minute stop, Ciara suggested it was time to get moving. She decided to freshen up one last time while Sarah prepared for their departure.

As Ciara strolled back to the lorry, she absentmindedly massaged moisturising cream into her hands, savouring the perfect driving weather. The instruction to park away from the service station buildings had puzzled her, but the short walk back had been pleasant. She smiled at her luck, thinking, *We've been fortunate – ideal weather and no hiccups.*

But fortune turned cruel in an instant.

The sound of hurried footsteps behind her snapped Ciara from her thoughts. She turned, but before she could react, a heavy blow to the side of her head sent her sprawling to the ground. Dazed, she barely registered her hands being zip-tied in front of her before she was yanked upright and slammed against the cold fiberglass side of the lorry. Her heart pounded as her vision cleared just enough to see Denver Hume's grinning face.

"Well, fancy meeting you here, bitch!" he sneered, his Albany accent dripping with mockery.

Ciara's gaze darted past him to the lorry's cab, where the unmistakable figure of Rob Gates struggled to hoist his bulk onto the driver's seat.

"Denver, stop!" she pleaded, trying to keep her voice calm despite the panic rising in her chest. "This is a huge mistake!"

"Haw haw!" Denver's loud, jeering laugh echoed around them, unconcerned with any potential witnesses. "And why's that, Ciara?"

"We're on the same side!" she insisted desperately.

Denver's smile widened, but his eyes hardened. "I don't think so." He turned to someone she didn't recognise behind her and barked, "Gag her and throw her in the back of the car."

Before she could respond, a rope was pulled tightly across her mouth and knotted behind her head. Her protests were muffled as she was half-dragged, half-lifted toward a waiting car. The back door was already open, ready to receive her.

From inside the cab, Sarah's panicked voice rang out. "Who the hell are you? Get out of here!" Her defiance turned to a scream as Rob Gates brandished a gun, its cold menace silencing her immediately.

"Shut up and listen," Rob growled, his voice low and threatening.

Sarah's chest heaved as she stared at him, terror freezing her in place. "What do you want?" she stammered.

"Do what you're told, and no one gets hurt," Rob replied coldly.

Denver confidently climbed the step to the passenger seat, his confidence radiating as he glanced at Rob. "Everything under control here?"

"Just dandy," Rob replied, his lip curling into a sneer. He turned back to Sarah, levelling her with an icy glare. "Now, listen closely. We've got someone else who can drive this thing, so don't think for a second you're irreplaceable. If you try anything stupid, I *will* kill you. Understand?"

Sarah nodded, her throat too tight to speak.

"Good. Get back on the motorway. Take the next exit – junction 50."

Tears welled in Sarah's eyes as she gripped the steering wheel, her hands trembling. Denver leaned back in his seat, grinning smugly as if this were just another day. In the rearview mirror, Ciara's captors loaded her into the car.

The lorry roared to life, pulling away from the service station, the idyllic afternoon now a nightmare of fear and uncertainty.

The Chase

Less than an hour behind the lorry, Alan studied the shifting icon on the tracking app. "They're leaving the service station," he announced, his tone calm yet focused. Max, gripping the steering wheel, didn't respond, his attention fixed on the road ahead. The BMW hummed under his command as he edged past the speed limit, walking a fine line between urgency and legality.

Meanwhile, some 250 miles away in Brighton, Rollie sat in his stately office chair, his eyes glued to the tablet resting on the polished mahogany desk. The tracking app displayed a simple car icon rejoining the motorway, its movements slow and uneventful. Yet, to Rollie, the unassuming graphic belied the far more complex and volatile reality of the situation. He drummed his fingers lightly on the desk, his mind racing through contingencies, the weight of unseen threats pressing heavily on his thoughts.

Off To The Races?

Sarah's mind raced, scrambling for any semblance of a plan, any faint hope of survival. Every moment felt precarious as she drove, deliberately easing her speed in a quiet act of defiance. If she could just slow down enough, perhaps she'd find an opening to call for help. Her small rebellion didn't go unnoticed.

Rob Gates, silent until now, lunged forward, pressing the cold barrel of his gun against her thigh with brutal force. "Speed up, or I'll shoot you," he snarled, his voice low but saturated with a chilling certainty that froze Sarah to her core.

Heart pounding, Sarah tried to reason with him, her words trembling. "You know, we're on the same side," she ventured, hoping to find even the smallest crack in his resolve. "I'm just the cleaner. I shouldn't even be here." Her voice wavered as she added, "Please, I'll do anything. Just don't hurt me."

Rob's response came as a venomous sneer. "Shut up and drive. Do that, and you might make it out of this alive." After a pause, he barked, "Exit at the next junction and follow the signs for Ripon Racecourse. I'll tell you where to go from there."

For a fleeting moment, Sarah felt a sliver of relief. *Just follow his orders,* she thought. *Do what he says, and maybe he'll let me go.* Clinging to that hope, she dared to ask, "Where's Ciara?"

Rob's cruel laugh cut through the air like a blade. "Don't worry about that Irish bitch. She's caused us enough trouble. You won't be seeing her again."

The cold finality of his words sent shivers down Sarah's spine, her relief giving way to a hollow dread. A pang of sorrow gripped her for Ciara, but there was no time to dwell on it. She focused on survival, on steering the lorry through this unfolding nightmare.

As they approached Ripon Racecourse, Rob directed her down a narrow B-road. The lane was ill-suited for such a large vehicle, forcing her to slow down further to navigate the tight bends and oncoming traffic.

Her hands clenched the wheel, knuckles white with tension, as the anxiety within her tightened its grip.

Soon, the path turned rougher, devolving into a dirt track. Vast fields stretched endlessly on either side, isolating them further. In the distance, a clearing emerged. Gravel crunched under the lorry's tires as she approached what appeared to be a makeshift compound. On the left loomed a massive shed, large enough to house the lorry. To the right stood two portable cabins, weathered but functional, the kind typically seen on construction sites.

"Park by the shed," Rob ordered sharply, his tone brooking no argument.

Sarah obeyed; her breath shallow as she maneuvered the vehicle into position. In the rearview mirror, a black sedan crept closer, its dark silhouette a harbinger of whatever lay ahead. She suspected Ciara was inside, and the thought twisted her stomach with dread.

As the lorry came to a halt, the oppressive silence of the isolated clearing enveloped her. The gravel beneath the tires whispered ominously, mirroring the tension that filled the air. This was the destination – but Sarah couldn't shake the feeling that it marked the beginning of something far darker.

The Diversion

The phone in Max's car jolted to life, its ring echoing through the vehicle. Glancing at the dashboard, Max's eyes darted to the caller ID – Rollie. A surge of anticipation mingled with dread as he answered, putting Rollie on speaker phone, mindful of the grim circumstances.

"It's just you and Alan, isn't it?" Rollie's voice, calm but strained, filled the car through the Bluetooth connection.

"Um, yes, just the two of us," Max confirmed, consciously ignoring Audrey's presence in the backseat. "I assume you're calling about the diversion Ciara and Sarah have taken?" He aimed to steer the conversation back to the urgent matter at hand.

Rollie's reply was urgent and laced with concern. "Oh good, you've seen that too. I can see you're not too far behind them. I've tried calling both of the ladies, but their phones are switched off. Max, Alan, I am worried for them."

Alan leaned forward, his tone steady but reassuring. "Mr. Monroe, um, Rollie, I mean, it's Alan here. I see they've stopped now – we're maybe fifteen, twenty minutes behind. Don't worry; we'll figure this out. It could just be an innocent detour."

Alan turned to Max, his expression grim. "I doubt it too. You'd better put your foot down."

Max nodded, his jaw tightening as he pressed harder on the accelerator. The tension in the car was palpable, the sense of urgency mounting with every mile.

Fifteen minutes later, they reached the entrance to a narrow dirt track. Max eased the car to a stop, the crunch of gravel under the tires the only sound in the stillness.

Max's knuckled whitened as he gripped the steering wheel, his gaze fixed on the ominous scene before them. He could feel the weight of responsibility pressing down on him, the burden of choice that could shape their fate.

"So, what do we do now?" Max's voice wavered, a thread of determination cutting through his anxiety.

Alan scanned the area, his eyes narrowing as he took in the scene. To the left stood the white Mercedes Atego, its bulk casting long shadows. Behind it, an open shed yawned emptily, while to the right, a sleek black executive car sat ominously still. Two portable cabins loomed in the background, their windows dark. The silence was suffocating, as if the entire scene were holding its breath.

A flicker of resolve crossed Alan's face as he turned to Max, urgency etched in his features. "There's no option. Drive up and park to the left-hand side of the lorry. We'll at least be hidden from those cabins. Just prey they don't hear us."

Max nodded, the gravity of the moment driving them both. As the car lurched forward, they braced themselves for what lay ahead.

As instructed, Max guided the BMW into position, aligning it strategically behind the white lorry, shielded from view of the portable cabins. The car came to a halt, its engine ticking softly as tension coiled around them.

Alan exhaled sharply, his voice steady but low as he turned to Max and Audrey. "Listen carefully. Stay in the car. If anything feels wrong – anything – drive out of here fast. Don't wait for me. Got it?"

Max met his gaze, his expression hardening. "Got it."

Alan stepped out of the car, moving swiftly toward the front of the lorry, using its bulk as cover. Each second dragged, the silence amplifying every sound as he scanned around the nearest cabin for signs of movement. Nothing.

Keeping low, he darted toward the closest portable cabin. Both cabins were identical in design – one door in the centre flanked by square windows. His arthritic knees protested as he crouched to the first window, but his view was blocked by a blind. He moved to the opposite side of the door, only to find the second window similarly obscured.

Gritting his teeth, Alan pushed onward to the second cabin, every nerve alert for the faintest hint of activity. At the first window, it came –

a burst of voices, followed by raucous laughter. The sound was chilling, an almost taunting echo in the quiet afternoon.

Alan flattened himself beneath the window, his heart pounding as he crept to the space between the window and the door. Taking a steadying breath, he rose slowly and peered inside.

The scene hit him like a blow.

A wooden park bench dominated the room's foreground, where Denver Hume sat with his back to the window, his laughter rumbling like an unpleasant melody. To the left, a portly man with a goatee clutched a gun in his left hand, his right arm immobilised in a sling, his face alight with manic fervour as he chanted like a crazed football supporter.

And then, to the right, his gaze landed on an old metal desk – and the sight that froze him.

Ciara was bent over the desk, her dress yanked up over her waist, her underwear gone. A hulking man, well over six feet tall, stood behind her, his trousers pooled around his ankles, his hands at the waistband of his boxer shorts.

Alan's breath caught in his throat, his body locking in place as the brutal reality of the scene seared into his mind. Every instinct screamed for action, but for a moment, he was paralysed, grappling with the sheer horror of what was unfolding before him.

Alan's mind raced, frantically calculating the odds in this perilous game of chance. He knew that time was slipping through his fingers like sand and berated himself for not being better prepared, for not anticipating the dire straits they now found themselves in. A flash of regret surged through him, wishing he had armed himself, at least with a knife from home.

His eyes swept the area, searching desperately for anything that could serve as a weapon. Beneath the cabin, a line of stones caught his attention, likely placed there for drainage. He snatched up the nearest one, its rough surface biting into his palm. It was barely the size of a tennis ball, its weight pitifully light. Alan clenched his jaw, scanning for something better, something heavier, but the other stones were even smaller.

Time wasn't on his side. The stone would have to do.

Alan gripped it tightly, feeling its rough edges press into his skin as if grounding him to the moment. His plan crystallised: he had to reach the gunman first. If he could close the distance, the man's hesitation – his weaker left hand, his injury – might give Alan the split second he needed.

He took a deep, shuddering breath, forcing his heartbeat to steady itself. The weight of the situation bore down on him: Ciara's safety, the lives hanging in the balance. There was no room for error.

Alan charged through the cabin door, adrenaline roaring through his veins. He braced for resistance, expecting the door to hold firm – but it swung open effortlessly, nearly throwing him off balance. He caught himself, surging into the room, his focus locked on the man with the goatee and the gun.

Denver Hume barely had time to flinch as Alan brushed past him, the sickly stench of sweat and cheap cologne hanging in the air. The gunman hesitated, raising the weapon too slowly. Alan didn't.

With brutal precision, he slammed the stone into the man's face, the impact cracking against his eye socket with sickening force. The goatee man crumpled to the ground, the gun skidding across the floor in the opposite direction.

Alan spun, his attention snapping to the half-naked man looming over Ciara. The man froze for a split second, startled by the chaos, but quickly turned to face Alan, fists clenching. Alan couldn't risk a kick – too much room for error. Instead, he drove his fist with ferocious accuracy into the man's exposed groin.

The result was immediate. The brute let out a strangled gasp, doubling over in agony. Alan followed up with a powerful shove, sending him sprawling backward. The man crashed into the wall, collapsing in a heap, his trousers tangled around his ankles.

Alan's breath came in ragged gulps as he scanned the room, the shift in momentum palpable. But there was no time to revel in the advantage. Every second counted.

He turned, ready to press the attack – and froze.

Denver Hume stood before him, the gun now steady in his grip, its barrel aimed squarely at Alan's face.

"You're quite quick for an old man, haw haw!" Denver's grin stretched unnaturally wide, his teeth flashing stark white in the dim light. It wasn't just amusement – it was malevolence, raw and unnerving.

He shifted the gun, pointing it downward toward Ciara, who was slumped by the metal desk. Her trembling hands, locked together by a cable tie, adjusted her dress in a futile attempt to preserve her dignity, her gaze locked on the floor.

"Or should I finally get rid of Miss Ciara first?" Denver's taunt hung in the air, a sickening reminder of their vulnerability in this macabre dance of fate. Every nerve in Alan's body screamed at him to act, but the cold, hard reality of the gun's barrel held him in its paralysing grip.

The cabin door emitted an eerie creak, groaning under the strain as it inched open. A figure emerged, and the room seemed to hold its breath in response to the unexpected arrival – Audrey Hepburn.

Denver's eyes widened in surprise, and he spun around, raising the gun in his grasp, prepared for a new adversary. But as he took in Audrey's visage, a mocking grin etched across his face, he lowered the weapon in disbelief. "Haw haw! Who is this little girl?" he taunted, underestimating the peril that now stood before him.

Audrey advanced, a determined glint in their eyes, their right hand discreetly concealed behind their back. Denver, oblivious to the threat she posed, taunted further, "What do *you* want, sweetie?"

Audrey's response was silent and swift. In one fluid motion, their hand emerged, revealing a gun. Before Denver could react, the weapon was raised, aimed, and fired.

The gunshot roared through the cabin, deafening in its finality. Denver staggered, his mocking grin replaced by a stunned expression as the bullet struck true. He collapsed to the floor in a graceless heap, his reign of terror brought to an abrupt, decisive end.

For a moment, the cabin stood still, the echoes of the shot fading into silence. Audrey exhaled slowly, lowering the weapon, their steady composure masking the tremor in their hands.

A heavy silence blanketed the cabin, broken only by the faint ringing in their ears from the gunshot. The acrid tang of gunpowder lingered, sharp and bitter, mingling with the sweat and fear that hung thick in the air.

Ciara moved first, shaking off the shock that gripped her. She rose unsteadily, her movements deliberate and retrieved the gun Denver had dropped. Her gaze shifted to Audrey, gratitude flickering in her tired eyes. "Thank you," she said, her voice steady despite the tremor beneath it. "Are you with Alan?"

Audrey nodded, their calm composure belying the intensity of the moment.

Ciara exhaled deeply, her focus sharpening. She turned to Alan, who still seemed caught in the aftermath of the chaos. "Why don't you and Audrey go next door and get Sarah?" she said firmly, as if reclaiming control of the situation gave her strength.

Alan nodded, though his movements were sluggish, the shock of Audrey's action still anchoring him.

"Denver will have a switchblade," Ciara added, her tone brisk and practical. "It'll be in one of his socks. You'll need it to cut Sarah loose. And –" she held out her wrists, the crude bindings cutting into her skin – "could you deal with this first?"

Alan blinked, the request jolting him into action. "Of course." He knelt beside her and worked quickly, cutting through the ties with his pocketknife.

As he finished, Alan glanced toward the unconscious assailants sprawled on the floor. "What about these two?" he asked, his voice low. "Want me to tie them up?"

Ciara's expression hardened, a fierce determination gleaming in her eyes. "I'll deal with them," she said, her tone leaving no room for argument.

Alan hesitated for a moment but then gave a curt nod. The urgency of Sarah's plight outweighed the risk of delay. The atmosphere in the room remained taut, a volatile mix of uncertainty and resolve, as they braced for what was still to come.

The man Ciara knew as Rob Gates lay quivering on the floor, his bravado shattered, desperation in his voice as he pleaded for mercy. Ciara looked down at him, "Just shut up, I'm only going to tie you up."

However, Ciara's first port of call was her attempted rapist. Standing over him, she delivered her words with a sharpness that matched the pain she had endured. "You don't look so aroused now?" she stated, her voice laced with defiance, staring down at the man's groin.

The man looked back in panic; his arrogance reduced to mere fragments. "Let's make sure you can't do that again, eh?" Ciara fired a single shot into his crotch, the man passed out immediately.

Rob Gates now lay prostrate, tears streaming down his face, begging for mercy. Ciara kicked at him, rolling him onto his front and then scanned the room in search of cable ties, her eyes darted around, but the restraints proved elusive. She had a dilemma, if she tried to tie him up, she'd need to put the gun down. If she did that then he could overpower her. Ciara had no choice; she pointed the gun at the back of one of his knees and fired.

"Sorry, not sorry," she quipped, her words a defiant retort, as she swiftly exited the cabin.

<u>Saving Sarah</u>

Standing outside the cabin, Alan gazed at Audrey and gently inquired, "Are you alright?" He couldn't help but notice that their expression had remained unchanged from the moment they had left the apartment earlier that morning.

Audrey's response came softly, a delicate crack in their usual poise. "Oui, ça va bien merci," Their voice carried a hint of fragility, a subtle tremor that Alan couldn't ignore.

Perplexed by her choice of language, Alan accepted it gratefully. At least they had responded, even if it was in French. "Bien," he replied, offering a simple acknowledgment.

Without further delay, Alan moved toward the door of the adjoining cabin. His first attempt at the lock proved futile, its resistance defying his urgency. Setting his jaw, he delivered a decisive shoulder thrust. The door gave way with a protesting creak, swinging open to reveal a space steeped in darkness.

Alan stepped inside, his eyes straining to adjust. He rushed to one of the windows, his hands fumbling with the blind in his haste. The brittle mechanism resisted, and with one forceful tug, it tore free from its fixture. Sunlight burst into the room, illuminating rows of grey metal filing cabinets, their utilitarian bulk dominating the space.

In the room's centre, Alan's gaze fell upon Sarah. She was bound to a chair, her wrists and ankles tethered by tight cable ties, her movements restricted, and her head slumped forward.

Gunfire echoed faintly from the cabin next door, a grim reminder of the danger still present. Alan moved quickly, kneeling beside her and cutting through the restraints with precise efficiency. As the ties fell away, Sarah shifted, testing her freedom before raising her head. Alan carefully removed the gag that had silenced her, his touch gentle.

Sarah's relief was palpable as she slowly unfolded her body and stood, embracing Alan with gratitude. "Thank you. I can't tell you how pleased I am to see you."

Alan returned her embrace, his words infused with reassurance. "You're safe now."

Sarah pulled back slightly, her gaze locked on his. "I can't believe you're really here." Her voice faltered, carrying a mixture of disbelief and overwhelming relief. Then, with a sudden surge of emotion, she leaned in and kissed him softly. "I love you," she whispered, her words intimate and sincere.

Alan froze for a heartbeat before the warmth of the moment overtook him. "I love you too," he replied instinctively, his tone earnest and unguarded. The tender moment, however, was interrupted by a flicker of movement at the edge of his vision, Audrey had silently witnessed the tender embrace from the doorway. Catching their gaze, he sensed their withdrawal, as they turned and rapidly exited the room.

Doughnuts

Alan gathered the group near Max's car, their weary faces bearing the marks of the trials they'd endured. Max, still brimming with unease, voiced the concern weighing on them all.

"Are we really safe?"

Alan glanced around, his demeanour calm but watchful. "I did a quick scout – no sign of anyone else. We're clear for now."

Before the reassurance could fully settle, Ciara stepped forward, her voice cutting through the tension with a steady, no-nonsense tone. "Listen up. I've spoken to Rollie. He's arranging a team to clean up this site."

Max hesitated, raising a cautious hand. "Wait, Ciara – Rollie doesn't have people here. Are you sure he said that?"

Ciara nodded firmly. "Yes. He said, and I quote, 'Doughnuts will be with you shortly.' Does that mean anything to you?"

Max blinked, then burst into laughter – deep, unrestrained, and oddly cathartic. "Oh, you're in for a treat. You'll *love* Bobby Doughnuts!"

Ciara shook her head, exasperation flickering across her face. "Right. Focus, Max," she said sharply, before turning to Sarah, who stood apart, shoulders slumped under the weight of exhaustion and grief.

"Sarah," Ciara said gently but resolutely, "you and I are going to finish the job. We'll deliver the lorry to Leith." She paused, catching Sarah's hesitation. "Come on. We've got this – girl power, remember?"

A faint smile tugged at Sarah's lips, though her exhaustion lingered.

Ciara pivoted back to Max, her tone regaining its authority. "Rollie wants you to meet Doughnuts and then follow us up, just to be cautious. The immediate danger seems to have passed, but let's not take chances." She tried to inject a note of optimism. "Once we're all clear, we'll check into a posh hotel on Rollie's tab and enjoy an overpriced meal. That sound good?"

A reluctant murmur of agreement rippled through the group. Despite their weariness, the promise of an end in sight – and a bit of luxury – was enough to move them forward.

Ciara's gaze hardened as she looked directly at Max. "One more thing: radio silence with the rest of the family. No exceptions. We can't risk anything leaking."

Max nodded, his earlier amusement giving way to a solemn understanding.

The group started to disperse but a white transit van pulled onto the gravel track stopping them in their tracks.

The End is in the Beginning

A wave of relief washed over Rollie; a sensation akin to a heavy burden being lifted. The fate of the ladies had teetered on a precipice, leaving him profoundly thankful for Alan's crucial intervention. Knowing that everyone was safe now was a balm to his worried soul.

Ciara's tone during their call had carried a fiery determination, almost a ferocity that he hadn't witnessed before. He allowed a brief chuckle to escape, vowing silently never to find himself on her 'wrong side'. Humour aside, Rollie admired Ciara's resilience; she was undoubtedly a 'survivor,' a force of nature who seemed capable of facing down any storm.

He was equally thankful for the Baileys, old friends he trusted implicitly. They were en route to clean up the scene, and there was no one better suited for the task. Rollie took solace in knowing the job would be handled with precision and discretion.

In the quiet confines of his office, dimly lit and absent of the usual security detail, Rollie weighed his next moves with careful consideration. The forthcoming three to four days would not only define his retirement plans but also the trajectory of his entire organisation. He reclined in his expansive Chesterfield chair, brandy in hand, lost in contemplation.

A wistful smile graced Rollie's lips as he recalled the words of Samuel Beckett, embracing their resonance. *"The end is in the beginning, and yet you go on."* Rollie was standing at the cusp of his own new beginning, one that would start with a rare phone call to his older brother, Les.

But there would be no room for what Beckett had called *"impossible mourning."* Rollie's resolve was ironclad. Whatever challenges lay ahead, he was ready to meet them head-on. The future was his to shape, and he intended to leave no stone unturned in securing the legacy his family had worked a lifetime to build.

Irish Cream

The white Transit van rattled up the gravel drive, coming to a stop near the group. Max blinked in surprise at how quickly they'd arrived. The passenger door creaked open, and out stepped a wiry man in his sixties, his cropped white hair catching the light. Slightly stooped but full of energy, he strode toward Max, his grin wide and familiar.

"Max! Jaysus, it's been far too long, so it has!" The man's rich Irish brogue boomed across the yard.

"Bobby Doughnuts!" Max exclaimed, his face lighting up with a genuine smile for the first time in what felt like days. "How've you been, you old rogue?"

Bobby glanced around the group, his eyes twinkling. "And which one of you fine folks might be Ciara?"

Ciara stepped forward, cautious but intrigued. "That'd be me. Nice to meet you, Bobby."

Without hesitation, Bobby pulled her into a firm embrace, surprising her. "Ah, from the home country, no less! What a blessing, so it is!" He stepped back, giving her an exaggerated once-over. "Don't worry, love, you're perfectly safe with me. My Bruce is in the van behind us, so he is."

Ciara turned just in time to see a colossal man struggling to extract himself from the driver's seat of the van behind them. The vehicle seemed to sigh with relief as the man finally heaved himself out, muttering curses under his breath. He was a mountain of a man, with a moustache that could have housed several small animals, and a frame that easily tipped 400 pounds.

Max leaned toward Ciara, grinning. "That's Bruce 'The Bear' Bailey – Bobby's husband. Bit of a legend."

Ciara's eyebrows shot up as she took in the scene. "He's... larger than life," she murmured, unsure what else to say.

Bobby clapped his hands, rubbing them together eagerly. "Right then, you'll be wanting to scarper, so you will. What are we dealing with?"

Ciara, still processing, pointed to the second portable cabin. "Three bodies – one, maybe two, still alive – and we need the black sedan gone. Quickly."

Bobby's expression didn't falter as he nodded briskly. "Got it. We'll take care of the lot. You just leave it with us." He turned and waved a hand at his husband, who was lumbering toward them with a duffel bag of tools. "Second cabin, love! I'll join you in a tick."

Bruce paused mid-stride, his deep voice rumbling like distant thunder. "Not until I've had me lunch baguette. Not lifting a finger 'til then."

Bobby rolled his eyes, muttering something in Irish under his breath, then shot Ciara an apologetic smile. "What can I say? He's got the appetite of a bear too."

As Bobby and Bruce disappeared into the second cabin, Ciara turned to Max, her face a mixture of disbelief and bewildered amusement. "Did that actually just happen?"

Max burst into laughter, nodding. "Oh, it happened. Welcome to the world of the Baileys."

The End of a Long Drive

The drive to Leith felt endless, stretching over four gruelling hours. By the time Sarah carefully manoeuvred the lorry into the cramped port-side garage, exhaustion had taken a firm hold. The biting chill of the North Sea mist – what the locals called the *haar* – seeped into her bones, making the distant memory of Brighton's sunshine feel like a cruel joke. Fourteen long hours had passed since they'd left the south coast.

Outside, Ciara was in her element. Sarah watched through the windshield as she effortlessly directed the port crew, her confident gestures and crisp instructions leaving no room for confusion. She managed them as if she'd been running ports her entire life. It was impressive – intimidating, even – but also strangely reassuring.

Moments later, Ciara swung open the driver's door and flashed a grin. "Come on, let's get a drink."

"Now you're talking!" Sarah replied, her spirits lifting at the thought of a quiet spot to unwind, maybe even a decent glass of wine.

In the taxi, Ciara gave the driver a clear destination: The Balmoral Hotel. Sarah raised her eyebrows, impressed. The Balmoral was no ordinary stop – its name carried weight, a symbol of elegance and indulgence.

"The Balmoral?" Sarah said, unable to hide her surprise.

Ciara smirked. "We've earned it, haven't we? And the boys will meet us there soon enough." She shifted slightly, her tone becoming more casual. "Speaking of which... what's the story with Audrey? You ever met them?"

Sarah frowned, the name catching her off guard. "Nope. They seem to be a friend of Alan's, but honestly? He's never mentioned them. I didn't even think he *had* friends, well, apart from Max of course."

Ciara laughed, leaning closer to nudge Sarah playfully. "Don't sell yourself short, hon. He's got you, too."

There was a warmth in Ciara's words, a sincerity that cut through Sarah's fatigue like a ray of sunlight. Despite everything – the danger, the cold, the long hours – Sarah felt a flicker of comfort. They were in this together, and that connection made all the difference.

Waverley

The valet expertly whisked Max's BMW away from the bustling Princes Street as the imposing façade of The Balmoral Hotel loomed above. "Wow!" Max breathed, turning in a slow circle to take it all in. The grandeur was overwhelming – the intricate carvings, towering spires, and meticulous details of the sandstone exterior epitomized Scottish Baronial elegance.

"This place is incredible!" he added, his awe evident.

Alan's attention, however, was elsewhere. He noticed Audrey lingering just outside the grand entrance, their posture tense and hesitant. "Go on ahead," he said to Max, gesturing toward the marbled steps. "I'll catch up."

Max gave him a quick nod, his excitement carrying him toward the hotel's golden-lit lobby.

Alan approached Audrey, his voice soft but steady. "You alright?"

To his surprise, Audrey turned toward him, their face crumpling as they buried their head in his shoulder. Their voice was small, almost lost in the noise of the Princes Street. "I want to go home, Alan."

He tightened his arm around their shoulders, pulling them close. "We will go home, Audrey. But not yet – we're booked for two nights. Don't you want to enjoy this place, even for a little while? It's one of the finest hotels in the country."

Audrey tilted their head up, their eyes glistening, a single tear sliding down their cheek. "I don't belong here, Alan," they whispered, their voice trembling. "I'm just a no-name slob, belonging to nobody, nobody belonging to me. I just want to go home." They hesitated, biting their lip. "Can I use your credit card to get a train?"

Alan recognised the echo of a familiar movie line in their words, and it tugged at something deep within him. He cupped their face gently, his expression a mix of sadness and understanding. "If that's what you really want, of course you can. But..." His voice softened, a plea hidden beneath. "I wish you'd stay, Audrey. Just for a little while. You might find this place isn't as bad as you think."

"Thank you. There's a sleeper train in an hour – I'll catch that," Audrey said, their tone steady but distant.

Alan nodded, hesitating for a moment before asking, "By the way, where did you learn to shoot like that?"

Audrey turned to him, their expression unreadable but faintly amused. "Why do you assume I've had lessons?"

"Because you flipped the safety off like a pro," Alan replied, a wry smile tugging at his lips. "I was worried the gun might not fire, and Denver would beat you to the punch."

Audrey let out a small, almost reluctant laugh. "I learned in France."

Alan raised an eyebrow, intrigued but knowing better than to pry for further details.

"You know you've never not done the right thing, don't you?" Audrey said softly, their words catching Alan off guard.

He turned to them, frowning slightly. "How do you mean?"

"These dreams you have…" they began.

"Nightmares," Alan interjected, his voice low.

Audrey nodded, conceding. "Alright, nightmares. But they're not your fault. You were following orders. The burden you're carrying – it doesn't belong to you."

Alan looked away, his jaw tightening as he mulled over their words. "I could have said no," he said quietly, the weight of those four words hanging heavy in the air.

"You don't need to atone," Audrey said gently.

"What are you now, a priest?" Alan shot back, his tone half-joking but edged with discomfort.

"No," they replied with a smirk, "and you're not some modern-day Savonarola either."

Alan pulled a credit card from his pocket and pressed it into Audrey's hand. "I'll miss you," he murmured, his voice unsteady, perplexed by the intensity of his own feelings.

337

Audrey looked up at him, her expression neutral, free of any bitterness. "You've got Sarah for company tonight," they replied.

"It's not like that," Alan said quickly, a defensive edge to his voice.

"Not yet," Audrey countered, a faint smile playing at the corners of their lips as they gently eased themselves from his embrace. "The station's just here. I'll grab a ticket, some food, and then sleep on the train."

"Alright, my Huckleberry friend," Alan said with a forced lightness. "Keep me posted on your progress. You'll need the PIN for my card. And I'm taking the gun from you."

"I know your PIN," Audrey replied with a wry grin. "And no, I'm keeping the gun."

They stood on tiptoe, pressing a kiss to his cheek. "See you soon."

With that, they turned and descended the stairs into Waverley Station, conveniently positioned next to the hotel. As they reached the bottom, Audrey glanced back, their lips forming the words "Au revoir, mon amour," before they disappeared into the crowd.

Alan's hand remained on his cheek, where the warmth of the kiss still lingered. He chuckled softly to himself, bemused by how Audrey had managed to learn his PIN. And the gun – he wanted to protest, to remind them of the danger, but the words died in his throat. He knew better than to push it.

Taking a steadying breath, Alan turned and made his way into the hotel's grand reception. The weight of the day hung heavy on him, and he could feel a stiff drink calling his name, something to soothe the whirlwind of emotions churning inside him.

Comfort in a Bottle

True to her word, Ciara had reserved five rooms at The Balmoral. The staff were gracious when she cancelled the fifth, particularly after learning the group had booked into the hotel's most exclusive restaurant. The dining experience was exquisite, with Max sparing no expense on some of the finest wines the menu had to offer – confident that Rollie would cover the bill.

Yet, the day's harrowing events had taken their toll. Ciara and Sarah excused themselves after dinner, retreating to their rooms for much-needed rest. Alan and Max lingered in the whisky bar, enjoying drams from obscure distilleries, some of which they had never even heard of. The warm amber liquid provided a brief respite, but weariness soon claimed them too.

Alan ordered one last whisky to take back to his room, a solitary indulgence to close the night. While his psychological training had dulled the sharper edges of the day's trauma, the fatigue remained insistent. He drifted off within minutes of lying down, only to be roused less than half an hour later by a gentle knock on the door.

Instantly alert, he crossed the room and peered through the peephole. Relief washed over him at the sight of Sarah on the other side, clutching a bottle of red wine.

"Looks dangerous," Alan joked, eyeing the bottle of wine in Sarah's hand.

"I can't sleep," she admitted, stepping into his room without waiting for an invitation.

Alan chuckled lightly. "Well, you'd better come in, then!" he said, though she was already rummaging around for wine glasses. He grabbed his bathrobe. "Hope you don't mind if I make myself decent."

"Nothing I haven't seen before," Sarah teased, adding with a sly smile, "And this time, I really mean that – from when I looked after you in your Bristol apartment."

Alan groaned theatrically. "I'll always be grateful for that, of course, but for now, just pour the wine."

As Sarah uncorked the bottle, the light banter faded, replaced by a weightier silence. Recent events had left her shaken – the mystery of her missing husband, the shock of firing a gun, the helplessness of being bound and gagged. These were alien, unwelcome traumas that buzzed in her mind, keeping sleep far out of reach.

The first glass loosened the tension in her shoulders. By the time the bottle ran dry, Alan had already called room service for another. They talked about lighter things, avoided the darkness for a while, and slowly, the combination of wine and the steady presence of a trusted friend began to dull the edges of her anxiety.

As the hour grew late, Sarah set down her glass, her eyelids heavy but her voice still tentative. "Do you mind if I stay here tonight? I just… I feel safer with you."

Alan nodded, his expression softening. "Of course. Get some rest. I'll look after you."

It wasn't long before Sarah drifted off, reassured by Alan's quiet presence. For the first time in what felt like days, she felt secure.

***

Sarah was startled awake, the oppressive stillness of the room broken by a palpable tension. In the dim light, she saw Alan sitting bolt upright, his fingers gripping the bedsheet like a lifeline. Beads of sweat glistened on his ashen brow, and his laboured breaths filled the silence, rasping and uneven, as if he were fighting for air.

"Alan!" Sarah gasped, scrambling upright beside him. Her eyes locked onto his, wide and searching. "What's wrong? Are you okay?" Her voice quivered with urgency.

Alan didn't answer immediately, his chest heaving as he wrestled with the storm inside him. When he finally spoke, his voice was barely audible, trembling under the weight of his distress. "Just a bad dream," he managed, though the torment etched into his features told a deeper story.

Sarah's heart ached at the sight of him, his strength momentarily stripped away. Tears pricked her eyes as she reached for him, her hands brushing against his trembling arm. "You're shaking," she murmured, her voice soft but unsteady. "Can I get you something? Water? Tea?"

Alan let out a faint, humourless chuckle. "A whisky might help," he muttered, the ghost of a smile flickering and vanishing just as quickly.

"Tell me about it," Sarah pressed gently, her hand resting on his arm, offering a small island of warmth and comfort. "The dream – what happened?"

Alan hesitated, his gaze distant, as though staring into the remnants of the nightmare itself. When he spoke, his words came slowly, each one a struggle. "I saw my wife," he began, his voice brittle. "But not as she was. She was pale… almost spectral. Like a ghost."

Sarah's breath hitched. The realisation struck her like a blow, shattering her assumptions about Alan's past. "Is she dead?" she whispered, the question escaping before she could think to soften it.

Alan's nod was almost imperceptible, but the weight of it landed heavily between them. "Yes," he said quietly, the single word laden with grief. It was a confession, not just of loss, but of the lingering sorrow that still gripped his soul.

For a moment, silence enveloped them, broken only by the faint sounds of their breathing. Sarah tightened her hold on his arm, a silent promise that he didn't have to bear the burden alone.

Alan's trembling form sank onto the bed, his strength drained. Sarah followed, wrapping her arms tightly around him as though her embrace alone could shield him from the storm within. "I meant it, you know?" she whispered into the quiet, her voice trembling with unspoken emotion. Her heart lay bare, vulnerable in the dim light.

Alan didn't respond, the chaos of his emotions rendering him mute. His gaze held hers, searching for answers he couldn't articulate. When her lips met his in a tender, deliberate kiss, the world seemed to pause. In that fleeting intimacy, they found a fragile refuge, clinging to each other as if the connection might keep the darkness at bay.

When morning arrived, Alan woke to an empty bed. The absence of Sarah's warmth was a sharp contrast to the memory of the night before. Regret crept in, heavy and oppressive, settling over him like a shroud. He scanned the room, searching for any sign of her, but found only the faintest echoes – a wine glass left on the nightstand, a fragile reminder of the passion and vulnerability they had shared.

His head throbbed, the hangover a cruel physical reminder of the night's tumult. The ache in his heart was far worse, a relentless replay of torment, regret, and fleeting solace. His eyes landed on the half-empty bottle of wine perched on the small table in the corner of the room.

Desperation overcame him. He reached for it with shaking hands, seeking the numbness it promised. A fleeting escape, he knew, but one he couldn't resist. As the wine burned its way down, it dulled the edges of his anguish, even as the shadows of regret lingered, refusing to fully release their hold.

The Shopping Trip

With a free day in Edinburgh, Ciara, radiant and brimming with enthusiasm, invited Sarah to join her for a shopping spree. Though "invited" might have been too soft a word – it felt more like a command than a suggestion.

When Ciara arrived at Sarah's room, she looked effortlessly stunning, as always. Sarah couldn't fathom how she managed it, especially after everything they'd been through. The designer jeans hugged her frame as if custom-made, and the Gucci-printed blouse seemed to have leapt straight from a fashion spread to her wardrobe.

Sarah offered weak protests, claiming fatigue and a need to rest, but Ciara was undeterred. "Harvey Nicks and the St. James Quarter are just a short walk away," she declared. "You know, the place with that odd roof – it looks like swirly steel ribbons." Ciara didn't add her private thought that it resembled something far less glamorous.

Relenting, Sarah suggested they make a detour along George Street's boutique shops. "And obviously, darling," she added with a sly grin, "we'll stop for wine along the way."

Sarah couldn't quite understand how it had happened, but perhaps it was Ciara's infectious energy – or sheer determination – that led her to allow Ciara to spend what felt like a small fortune on new clothes for her. As they paused for coffee, Sarah stirred her cappuccino absentmindedly, still adjusting to the whirlwind of Ciara's shopping spree.

Ciara, ever the conversational instigator, leaned in with a curious glint in her eye. "So, what actually happened with Audrey? Did you send them packing?"

Sarah frowned, caught off guard by the question. "I don't know what you mean," she replied, her tone edged with unease at the suggestion.

Ciara's lips curled into a playful smile. "Oh, come on. There's only room for one strong woman – or non-binary person – in Alan's life." She winked, clearly enjoying the provocation.

343

Sarah sighed, shaking her head. "You've got the wrong idea about us." She took a sip of her coffee, steadying herself. "Besides, I spoke to Alan. He mentioned that… *they* – he referred to Audrey as 'they' – just wanted to get home."

Ciara smirked, already knowing the details. She'd asked Alan herself, of course, but her curiosity about Sarah and Alan's dynamic wouldn't let her drop it just yet. "Mmm-hmm," she hummed knowingly, a teasing note in her voice.

Sarah shot her a pointed look, but Ciara simply clapped her hands together. "Right! Finish your coffee. The faster we get through the rest of this shopping, the faster we can reward ourselves with some wine!"

***

Alan and Max sat in a cozy bar on the quieter side of Princes Street, a place steeped in the same timeless charm as their grand hotel. The interior was a warm blend of polished wood, gleaming brass, and large windows that framed the city's soft afternoon glow. Max leaned back, taking in the surroundings, and couldn't help but smile.

"I could get used to Edinburgh," he remarked, his voice tinged with genuine admiration.

Alan nodded, though his enthusiasm was noticeably muted. "Yeah, it's a nice place," he replied, standing abruptly. "I'll get us another round."

Max watched him with a slight frown. "I've got a long drive tomorrow, Alan. I should probably take it easy."

"Fine," Alan said, his tone resolute. "I'll get myself another one."

When Alan returned, pint in hand, he took a slow sip before cutting through the afternoon's pleasantries. His voice was steady but edged with tension. "Max, where the fuck did that gun come from?"

Max shifted in his seat, tugging at his shirt – a size too snug, as usual. "It's the same one. The one Sarah fired. The one that shot you."

"Yes, Max, I figured that much," Alan replied sharply, his patience thinning. "But how the hell did it end up in Ripon?"

Max hesitated, looking down at his hands as if the answer might somehow appear there. "It's been in my glovebox since Bristol," he admitted, his voice low and laced with guilt.

Alan stared at him, his disbelief palpable. "You're telling me you've been driving around with a gun loaded with live rounds? You're a solicitor, Max! Do you have any idea what would've happened if the police stopped you?"

"I know, Alan," Max said, his tone defensive but tinged with remorse. "It was a mistake. A lapse in judgment. I... I forgot it was even there."

Alan shook his head, the weight of Max's admission settling heavily on his shoulders. "Jesus Christ," he muttered, rising from his seat. "I need a whisky to process this. You want one?"

Max nodded, his expression subdued. "Yeah, I think I do."

As Alan headed to the bar, Max stared into his glass, the consequences of his carelessness unravelling in his mind. The afternoon, once steeped in Edinburgh's charm, now carried the uneasy weight of unresolved tension.

***

At first light, Max retrieved his car from the valet at the hotel entrance, the morning air crisp with the promise of a new day. He drove Ciara and Sarah to Leith, where the women picked up the laden lorry. Meanwhile, he and Alan embarked on a slow journey south, shadowing their every move.

For Alan, nursing the effects of the previous night's whisky, it was a long and uneventful day – a small mercy, given the circumstances. Unseen but ever-present, Rollie's security detail also trailed Ciara and Sarah, their vigilance ensuring the pair were never truly alone.

But while the day passed without incident, trouble was brewing further south in Brighton. A storm loomed on the horizon, one carefully engineered by the darker recesses of Rollie's calculating mind.

Street Knowledge

Alan wearily stepped into Number 37, the weight of the long journey clinging to him despite his modest role as Max's co-pilot. The week had stretched him thin, its unrelenting demands evident in his sluggish gait.

The apartment greeted him with silence and darkness. Flicking on the lights, Alan scanned the space, his primary concern finding Audrey – but the apartment appeared empty. Boffin, ever attuned to his presence, pressed against him with a soft whine. Alan knelt to stroke her fur before dutifully filling her food bowl, her gentle purring a small comfort in the stillness.

Continuing his search, Alan's gaze landed on the fridge. A note was tucked beneath a new magnet – a playful parody of the "Straight Outta Compton" logo, now reimagined to read "Straight Outta Edinburgh" in bold monochrome. He allowed himself a faint smile before plucking the paper free.

The note was brief, written in Audrey's familiar hand:

Dear Alan,

I'm staying with a friend. See you on Sunday. I'll cook us a roast.

Aud. xx

Alan stared at the words, the ache of unanswered questions gnawing at him. He resisted the impulse to call or message Audrey, especially about the gun. Such a move could be reckless – a misstep that might complicate matters if the situation ever reached a courtroom.

With a resigned sigh, Alan accepted that there was little he could do until Sunday. For now, patience was his only option. He grabbed a cold beer from the fridge and sank into the lounge, craving the brief solace of stillness after a relentless week.

A Great Catch

Jamie tapped the answer button on his phone and greeted his brother with mock cheer. "Hello, dear brother of mine. Care to bet I can guess the reason for your call on the first try?"

Nigel's voice came through, clipped and joyless. "Oh, please, do entertain me. And while you're at it, enlighten me – where exactly are you right now?"

"I'm fishing for trout," Jamie replied, utterly content. He leaned back in his chair, the rhythmic babble of the stream adding to his tranquillity.

Nigel's response dripped with sarcasm. "As long as it keeps you busy. You're turning into Dad more and more each day, not that you'd ever admit it."

Jamie smirked, deliberately keeping his tone light. "What's on your mind, Nige? You're scaring the fish."

Nigel didn't bite at the deflection. "Why has Dad called for this meeting now? Isn't it too soon?"

Jamie cast his line with practiced ease, a note of mischief creeping into his voice. "Too soon? If you ask me, it's long overdue. Things are looking up for us, Nige. Your wealth and influence are about to soar – though, of course, not quite to my level."

"Ha bleeding ha," Nigel muttered, unimpressed. After a beat, his tone grew serious. "Do you think the old man knows?"

Jamie chuckled, low and menacing. "I'd stake my catch on it – he hasn't got a clue. A week from now, he'll be out of our hair for good. And honestly? I can't wait."

"Amen to that," Nigel replied, a dark satisfaction evident in his voice. "I'll see you tomorrow."

The call ended, leaving Jamie to his fishing rod and private thoughts, his smile stretching wider as he imagined what lay ahead.

One Last Time

Max had already given Alan the heads-up, stressing the urgency of assisting Rollie once more. Now, seated across from him in the lounge at Number 37, Max sipped his tea thoughtfully, contemplating the path ahead.

"Remind me, Max," Alan asked, peering over the rim of his cup, "why should I keep helping Rollie? The Monroe family has done nothing but bring me trouble so far."

With a heavy sigh, Max leaned back in his chair, weighing his words carefully. "It's not just about Rollie, Alan. It's about helping me. And let's not forget – Rollie trusts you. He could be an asset to your own plans down the road."

Alan stared into his teacup, his thoughts swirling with the same patterns. "Max, my friend, I've had more than enough of the Monroe family's drama. I've been in crossfire for over twenty years. All I want is peace. No future plans, no more mess. I'll help you this time – but that's it. Don't ask again."

Max nodded, his expression sympathetic. "Fair enough, Alan. I appreciate it. Now, do you have the camera?"

Alan's eyes narrowed, the question hanging in the air. "Yes, I've checked it. It's in working order. But we're supposed to leave our phones behind?"

There was a quiet tension between them, as if the weight of what they were about to do was pressing down. "Do you even know what we're walking into?"

Max gave a nonchalant shrug. "Alan, I'm as much in the dark as you are. All I know is that it's a closed meeting of the brothers."

Alan raised an eyebrow, a wry smile tugging at his lips. "For such an intelligent guy, you can be really clueless sometimes."

Max's eyes sparkled with amusement. "Where's Audrey, by the way?"

Alan shook his head, pushing himself up from his seat. "Come on, we need to move. We don't want to be late."

The two friends exchanged a look, uncertainty and resolve mixing in the air between them as they prepared for whatever lay ahead.

Arriving at the Court Club, Max was surprised to find the bar closed and securely locked. He rattled the door, frustration mounting as it remained steadfast. Just as he turned to address Alan, the distinct click of the door's lock echoed.

Trevor, the resident barman, swung the door open. "Come in, gents," he beckoned, ensuring the door was locked securely behind them.

Alan followed Max inside, his gut coiling with unease. The room felt different charged, like the air before a thunderstorm. He'd sensed trouble brewing and wasn't about to be caught off guard. Beneath his jacket, two knives rested, carefully concealed but ready at a moment's notice.

"We're waiting on the brothers," Trevor said, moving behind the bar. "Care for a drink?"

Alan surveyed the dimly lit surroundings, his senses heightened. "Two G and Ts, please, Trev." Alan gestured subtly toward one of the security cameras, noticing the usual pin-sized blinking light was now dimmed. "Has that camera been disabled?"

Trevor was visibly impressed. "You're quite sharp this afternoon, Alan. Yes, the entire system has been offline for over an hour, by orders of the management."

Alan's stomach tightened further. He kept his expression neutral, but the words lodged like splinters. The club's tension wrapped around him, cold and heavy, as if the walls themselves were holding their breath.

Something was wrong – very wrong.

***

Alan and Max settled into seats off to the side, the arrangement reminiscent of theatregoers waiting for a show to begin – except the stage remained empty, and the actors were nowhere in sight. Twenty minutes ticked by before Alan signalled Trevor for another round.

"Closed all day, Trev?" Alan asked, his tone light but probing.

Trevor, pouring with practiced efficiency, shrugged. "Just following orders, mate."

The soft clunk of the lock turning drew their attention. The door swung open to reveal Harry, striding in with his usual gruffness.

"Showtime," Trevor murmured with a smirk as Harry stomped to the bar.

"Am I the early bird today?" growled Harry, a rhetorical question since he clearly was the first brother to arrive. "Trev, a pint," he demanded. Then he turned to Alan, frustration evident. "Ridiculous, isn't it? Rollie says jump, and we're all supposed to ask how high."

Before Alan could respond, a knock reverberated through the room.

"We're closed!" Harry barked, but Trevor was already unlocking the door. Les stepped inside, the eldest of the brothers carrying himself with a deliberate calm that seemed to irritate Harry even more.

"Oh, it's you," Harry said, voice dripping with sarcasm. "Still waiting on His Majesty to grace us with his presence."

Les ignored the jab, brushing past him with a placid air that only deepened Harry's scowl.

Alan eased back into his seat beside Max, their drinks refreshed, as his attention shifted to Les. The eldest brother moved slowly toward a table near the bar, his every step laboured. Les leaned heavily on a weathered walking stick, the rhythmic *thud* of its tip on the floor the only sound in the room. Over his shoulder hung a soft black vinyl snooker cue case, its weight pulling slightly at his stooped frame. Alan's instincts pricked – he doubted it held anything as benign as a snooker cue.

"Off to play snooker, are we, Les?" Harry quipped; his tone laced with mockery.

Les paused, a thin rasp escaping his lips as he fought for breath. His gaze, sharp despite his frailty, pinned Harry in place. "Fetch me a drink and sit down," he wheezed, his words commanding despite their laboured delivery.

Harry smirked but turned to Trevor. "A glass of tap water for our Les," he said, the mockery lingering. Trevor obliged without comment, sliding the glass across the bar.

Les raised a hand, stopping Trevor mid-turn. "And a whisky," he added, his voice steadying. "Neat."

Harry waved a dismissive hand. "Make it a neat malt, Trev," he barked before pulling out a chair opposite Les.

The room seemed to tighten around them, the faint hum of tension amplifying. Alan took in the scene: Les, frail but unyielding; Harry, brash yet oddly subdued. There was an unspoken charge in the air, as if the room itself braced for what was to come.

Trevor delivered their drinks without a word, retreating to his stool behind the bar, his movements careful and deliberate, as if sensing the storm brewing in the quiet.

Les shifted in his chair, his movements slow and deliberate, each one betraying the pain he was enduring. "Rollie won't be joining us," he said, his voice strained but steady. His head remained bowed, as if even the effort of looking up was too much. "Is that Max and Alan over there?"

Alan exchanged a glance with Max, the question hanging in the air. Les's frailty was unsettling, a stark contrast to the commanding presence he once had.

"You old fool, of course it's them," Harry shot back, his voice dripping with scorn. "So, what now? Meeting's off, is it? No show without Punch."

"Shut up, Harry," Les snapped, the words cutting through the tension like a blade. With visible effort, he raised his head, his gaze locking on his younger brother. "The meeting is just the two of us."

Harry chuckled, brushing off his brother's revelation. "Just us, eh? Well then," he said, leaning back with feigned ease. "Guess I'll need another drink to survive this farce. Trev! G&T!" he bellowed, his voice echoing in the room.

Les placed the snooker cue case on the table with deliberate care, then lifted his whisky for a slow, measured sip. Moments later, a coughing fit overtook him, his frail frame shuddering as he clung to the edges of the table for support, anchoring himself until his breathing steadied.

"Now, Harry," he said, his voice thin but firm. "I don't want to repeat myself. Do you understand?"

Harry exhaled sharply, shaking his head in exasperation. "Yes, Les, I understand. Just get on with it."

Les's expression hardened, his gaze piercing. "I'm dying," he began, only for Harry to cut him off with a dismissive wave.

"Yes, I'm aware, Les. You've had prostate cancer for years. You'll probably outlive us all at this rate!"

Les raised a hand, silencing him. "I said listen, Harry." The steel in his voice left no room for argument.

"The cancer has spread," he continued, his words deliberate, each syllable carrying a grim weight. "To my bones. To my lungs. They can slow the bone cancer, but my lungs are failing. It's too far gone to treat."

Harry's smirk didn't fade.

"In a month, maybe less, I'll be on a ventilator and pumped full of painkillers. I won't be able to get to a toilet on my own. Hell, I probably won't even know I've been to the toilet." Les's voice was eerily steady, stripped of emotion. He had clearly made peace with his fate, even if his words carved unease into the room.

Alan watched the exchange unfold, surprised – and unsettled – by Harry's reaction. He had expected at least a flicker of sympathy or concern for his brother's grim news. Instead, Harry shrugged, casually signalling Trevor to refill his glass.

"Well, this is quite the dramatic revelation, Les," Harry said, his tone light, almost mocking, though the weight of the moment hung heavily in the air.

Les suppressed another cough, this one less violent but no less draining. He took a sip of water, regaining some composure, then reached for the snooker cue case. Alan's instincts sharpened as Les unzipped it, confirming what he'd suspected.

From the case, Les carefully pulled out a stubby rifle, its dark finish glinting faintly in the dim light. He held it up with practiced care, his frail hands steady as he examined the weapon's craftsmanship, the faintest hint of reverence in his expression.

Across the room, Max stiffened, his hand twitching toward the table's edge. Alan placed a firm but calming hand on Max's arm, leaning in just enough to whisper, "Don't worry," his voice low and measured.

Harry, however, didn't flinch. He leaned back in his chair, swirling his drink as though the rifle were nothing more than an antique trinket. His lips curled into a faint, bemused smile.

"What's this about, Les?" Harry asked, his tone casual, though his eyes betrayed a flicker of curiosity.

Les cradled the rifle with care, his fingers gliding over its surface as though it were a treasured heirloom. His voice was slow and deliberate, every word weighted with meaning.

"Harry," he began, "I know you've never been one for anything larger than a pea shooter, but this – this is a beauty. An original De Lisle carbine, 1944." He glanced at the rifle, his expression a mix of pride and nostalgia. "It's in remarkable condition, save for the suppressor. Unfortunately, those wear out quickly with regular use."

He looked up briefly, catching Harry's eye. "Even now, it's one of the quietest firearms ever made. That's why it was a favourite of the British Commandos – and mine. Rollie and I used to take it out hunting deer and fox in Ashdown Forest."

Les's voice softened, a hint of warmth creeping in as he added, "The venison from those hunts was something special."

He paused, a dry, rasping cough forcing its way up. Setting the rifle down with care, he reached for his water and took a slow sip, the act offering him a moment of relief.

"And yet," Les continued, his tone wistful, "I never understood why you didn't follow in mine and Rollie's footsteps with hunting. Always had to carve out your own path, didn't you, Harry?"

Harry chuckled dryly, swirling the gin in his glass. "Is this going anywhere, Les? Or are we here for a history lesson?"

Unfazed, Les ran a hand over the rifle, his fingers tracing its contours like an old friend. "This piece," he said, almost to himself, "was made at the Ford plant in Dagenham. Imagine that – going from producing specialised World War Two weaponry to rolling out Ford Capris. Funny, isn't it? A shift from shaping tools of war to everyday machines." His lips twitched into a faint smile, though his eyes never left the firearm.

He pressed on, his voice carrying the weight of memory and expertise. "Of course, there's always a trade-off when you want silence. To keep the sound down, the round leaves the barrel at a slower speed. No sonic boom, but you sacrifice range. And it's bolt-action." He chuckled, the sound low and self-deprecating. "These days, I'd be lucky to get off five rounds a minute. Not exactly a rapid-fire affair."

Les laughed softly at his own limitations, then added, almost as an afterthought, "The magazine holds seven rounds. I've got a larger one somewhere at home, buried under all that clutter."

Harry set his drink down with a faint clink. "So, what's it worth, Les?" he asked, his tone half-curious, half-dismissive.

"They only made about 130 of these," Les replied, a spark of pride flickering in his voice. "To the right buyer, it'd fetch a tidy sum." He placed the rifle on the table in front of him, his movements deliberate, almost reverent.

Harry leaned back, folding his arms. "Fascinating," he said, though his sarcasm undercut the word. "But what's that got to do with me? You want me to sell it for you?" His patience was clearly wearing thin.

Les's lips curled into a faint smirk. "I imagine Colonel Alan over there enjoyed the story," he said, raising his voice as he called out, "Didn't you, Colonel?"

Alan straightened slightly in his seat, caught off guard. "Yes, indeed," he replied, his voice steady but noncommittal. He hesitated, sensing it might be wiser not to elaborate.

The air in the room shifted, the atmosphere growing heavier. Alan glanced at Max, whose shoulders had tensed, mirroring the unease Alan felt.

"What's your motivation, Harry?" Les's question landed like a sudden blow, unexpected and direct. Harry paused, his eyes narrowing as he considered his response.

"I can tell you what gets me through the night – booze, broads, or the bible. Ain't that right, Colonel Alan?" Harry's grin widened as he threw a glance Alan's way, clearly enjoying the moment of shared mischief.

"Well, it was according to Kris Kristofferson," Alan replied with a chuckle, clearly amused by the exchange. He was warming to the banter.

Les wasn't swayed. "No, seriously, Harry," he said, his tone sharp. "I've never understood your motivation. You seem to love playing John Barleycorn."

Harry raised an eyebrow, turning to Max but still keeping his gaze locked on Les. "What's that mean, Max?" His voice rang with challenge.

Max, unfazed, replied dryly, "I think it means you've got a drinking problem."

Harry's lips curled into a smirk, and he threw his head back in laughter. "What, are you suddenly, the temperance society?" He exhaled a puff of cigarette smoke, his eyes still locked on Les. "At least I'm not a quitter, Les. That's why I never gave up smoking."

Les ignored the jab, his focus sharpening as a fit of coughing clawed its way up his throat. He fought to suppress the reflex, his chest heaving as he battled to regain control. After a moment, he managed to steady himself and poured a touch of water into his whisky, swallowing slowly to calm the irritation rising in his throat. He fixed Harry with a piercing gaze, his voice quiet but loaded.

"Tell me about Denver Hume, Harry."

Harry shifted uncomfortably in his chair, clearly on edge. "He's the loud American from the board meeting," he replied flippantly, raising his hands as if to say, *what more do you want from me?*

Les's patience thinned. "Cut the crap, Harry. I don't have time for your games. You've been working with Hume for a while now, haven't you?"

Harry's smile faltered, and his voice turned sharp. "I don't know what you're talking about, Les. Are you sure that cancer hasn't spread to your brain?"

Alan, who had been silently observing, raised an eyebrow at the dismissive tone in Harry's voice. There was a shift in the air, a weighty tension settling between the brothers.

Les's hands moved deliberately back to the rifle, his fingers tracing the wood of the stock with a tender, almost intimate touch. One hand played with the bolt handle, the motion deliberate and purposeful. To Alan, the message was clear – this was no idle conversation.

"Whatever deal you've made with Hume," Les said, his voice low and measured, "it's done. Agreed, right?"

Harry shook his head slowly, his lips curling in disbelief, but the unease in his eyes betrayed his bravado.

"Listen, Harry," Les said, leaning forward, his voice laced with more determination, "I'm not asking *if* you've struck a deal with Hume. I'm asking *why*."

"*Why?*" Harry shot back, his voice rising in anger, momentarily silencing the room. He took a long gulp of his gin and a drag from his cigarette before continuing, his words coming fast, "I'll tell you why, Les. Rollie should've retired years ago. He's yesterday's man. For Christ's sake, I'm 77 – *I* should be retired by now! And Rollie? He's a bloody antique!"

He paused, looking to Les for a response, but none came. His frustration mounted as he pressed on. "The organisation needs fresh blood, new ideas. It needs someone who cares more about the business than his damn garden!"

Les's gaze never wavered. "And you think you're that person, Harry?"

"I *deserve* my chance," Harry snapped, his anger rising to a boil. "I've earned that much!" His fist clenched around his drink, the tension in his voice unmistakable. "I was only going to run it for a few years before handing it over to Jamie and Nigel. That's what I've agreed with Denver."

Les raised an eyebrow, his voice cool and direct. "And what part was Hume supposed to play in all of this?"

Harry's response was swift, though laced with impatience. "Very little. He was going to advise, help with supply – use his contacts. I'd pay him a retainer."

"And was kidnapping Ciara and Sarah part of that plan too?" Les asked, his voice calm but carrying an edge. Harry's surprise was evident; he hadn't expected Les to know.

Harry's smile never wavered. "You gotta break a few eggs to make an omelette, Les."

Les's expression hardened. "You were willing to sell out the family for your own gain. You've been a pathogen to this family for as long as I can remember." His voice dropped lower. "Have you heard from Hume in the last couple of days?"

Harry's eyes flicked away, but his tone remained defiant. "You always did think the worst of me, Les."

Les's reply was razor-sharp. "Yeah, and I was rarely disappointed."

Harry's face flushed with frustration, his voice rising. "I was trying to *save* the family, Les!" He leaned forward, his fists clenched. "And no, I haven't heard from Denver. But I expect I will soon enough."

Harry scrambled to regain control of the situation, his voice tight with forced confidence. "Anyway, Les, you keep talking like this is all in the past, as if it's not going to happen. But it is. Whether you and Rollie like it or not."

Les's hand tightened around the carbine, raising it slowly until it pointed toward the ceiling. His voice was cold, unyielding. "Would it surprise you to learn that Hume is dead, Harry?"

Harry's face twisted in disbelief, his eyes wide as he shook his head. "You're a fucking liar, Les."

Les didn't flinch. He held Harry's gaze, then turned toward Max. "Am I a liar, Max?"

Max's response was quiet but firm. "No, Les."

"You sold us out, Harry. Or at least you tried to." Les slid the bolt into place with a deliberate, menacing click, the sound of the firearm cocking echoing through the room like a warning.

Harry, still reeling from the revelation, stood his ground, trying to mask his unease. "Oh, put that down, Les. You wouldn't shoot your own brother."

Les's eyes darkened as he levelled the carbine at Harry, his voice low and cold. "I'm dying, Harry. Not months – weeks. My family's taken care of. I'm at peace. You, though... you're a disease, a blight on everything we've built. Why wouldn't I shoot you?"

Harry's reply came with a hollow, forced chuckle, trying to mask the fear. "Put it down, Les. You don't scare me. Stop acting like a bloody pork chop."

Les's grip tightened, his finger pressing slowly against the trigger. The weight of the moment hung heavy, suffocating the air. He pulled.

Two Bullets

The Scenes of Crime Officer (SOCO) would eventually find one of the .45 ACP cartridges lodged deep into the concrete wall behind the bar, where it had taken an impressive, if somewhat reckless, journey.

On its trajectory to its final resting place, the bullet had torn through the flimsy aluminium back of a beer fridge, slashing through two bottles of lager like a disgruntled teenager smashing bottles at the beach. It didn't stop there. The double-glazed front of the fridge shattered into a mess of glass, just for good measure. Had Trevor still been occupying his stool behind the bar, it's safe to say the projectile would have found a new home in his thigh bone. But Trevor, always a step ahead, had wisely taken refuge in the adjacent kitchen.

Before reaching the fridge, the bullet had punched through the bar panel. In keeping with The Court Club's retro vibe, the panel was made of inexpensive sapele wood, which, like most things in the '60s and '70s, had aged poorly. The wood was a modest 26 mm thick, just enough to slow the bullet down but not enough to prevent it from creating a hole the size of a golf ball.

Before breaching the bar, the bullet had already made a stop at the backrest of Harry's chair. True to Harry's penny-pinching ways, the chair's backrest was composed of two layers of Formica, each a wafer-thin 2.2 mm. It offered as much resistance to the speeding bullet as a piece of wet cardboard.

Despite his declining health and advanced age, Les's marksmanship remained razor-sharp. Though, as Les would no doubt have attested, from a range of only a few feet, even the most incompetent marksman would have had a hard time missing. The bullet came remarkably close to Harry's sternum, threading its way through his rib cage and clipping his heart – quite literally. The last few moments of Harry's life were spent in a surreal, agonising silence as the projectile took the scenic route through his insides before meeting the unyielding embrace of the concrete wall. In that brief, tragic second, his life was extinguished.

Les swiftly re-cocked the carbine, the mechanism clicking with a precise, almost mechanical finality. The spent brass casing ejected with a sharp snap, shooting about five feet to his left like a discarded playing card in a game of poker. He turned the carbine towards himself, the weapon's compact, stubby length fitting neatly in his grip. Exiting through the back of Les's head, the trajectory of the second cartridge took it deep into the timber framework, burying itself so expertly within the ancient wooden beams that it became nearly impossible for the Scenes of Crime Officer (SOCO) team to unearth it. The ceiling's dusty, cobweb-streaked plaster seemed to absorb the evidence as if to hide it from prying eyes and sharp instruments.

Ten Minutes

Alan scrambled to his feet and rushed over to the lifeless bodies. There was no need for a coroner's inquest to confirm their fate – both victims had succumbed to gunshots. As tempting as it was to inspect the De Lisle carbine, a legendary model, Alan resisted the urge. Now was not the time for admiration or sentimentality.

He knew the next few minutes were crucial. Turning to Max, he ordered, "We should go, we can't afford to be found here. Go and wait in the car. Be ready to leave as soon as I join you." Max hesitated, on the verge of asking a question, but thought better of it. Alan shouted into the kitchen for Trevor to come out, then hurried back to the table he had been seated at, grabbing the gin glasses they had used.

Alan placed the glasses on the bar, his eyes locking on Trevor as the bartender emerged, his face a mask of shock at the grim sight. Stepping into Trevor's line of sight, Alan's voice was firm, cutting through the panic. "Trev, don't look at that. Focus on me and listen carefully. Do exactly as I say, and you'll be fine."

Trevor's nod was slow, his expression one of profound disbelief. "Where's your glass washer?" Alan pressed, not waiting for the shock to settle.

Trevor pointed to the small kitchen he'd just left. Alan's tone sharpened. "Go there. Half-fill it with glasses, including these, and set it for the quickest cycle. Got it?"

"Yes," Trevor replied quietly, the word barely escaping his lips.

While Trevor attended to the task, Alan returned to the table for his camera, quickly photographing the bodies, desperately hoping the faces wouldn't haunt his own dreams.

Trevor returned to the bar, his hands shaking slightly as he confirmed the glass washer had started. Alan wasted no time. "Where's your phone?"

Trevor fumbled it from his pocket. "Is there a clock in the kitchen?"

Trevor nodded, still dazed.

Alan's instructions were concise, his voice steady. "Place your phone on the bar. Then go hide in the kitchen. Stay there for ten minutes. When you come out, call the police. Max and I were never here. Everything else – cameras off, door locked, all of it – will remain as it happened. You'll be asked why you waited to call. Simple answer: you heard one gunshot, thought Les was still here, and left your phone on the bar. You were afraid and believed you were in danger. Understand?"

Trevor's eyes widened, but he nodded, the weight of the plan sinking in. "Yeah... got it."

Alan clapped him on the shoulder, his voice softening. "Alright. I'll be in touch soon. Good luck, mate. And don't worry – you're basically telling the truth."

Alan slid into the front passenger seat of Max's BMW, the door slamming shut behind him. "Max, I need you to take us back to number 37, but we've got to avoid as many traffic cameras as possible. Got it?"

Max didn't hesitate. "Got it. We'll have to cross the railway track, though, and there's a camera there we can't bypass. But the rest of the route is clear."

Alan nodded, already thinking ahead. "Stop at the convenience store just before the tracks. I'll grab something quick. If we get questioned, that'll cover our movements."

Max flicked the turn signal, his focus sharpening. "Understood."

Finally, back at number 37, Alan poured them each a generous measure of whisky. "That's a Dalmore 15-year-old," he said with a hint of pride, letting the amber liquid settle in the glass.

Max, however, would have settled for a cheap blended brand at that moment. He tossed the whisky back in one go, his face betraying the rawness of what he'd just witnessed. Holding out his glass, he silently asked for a refill.

"Easy, tiger," Alan chuckled, topping up Max's glass with more whisky.

"That was just horrible, Alan," Max muttered, shaking his head. He looked haunted. "Why did Les have to go that far?"

Alan's face grew more serious. "Les had nothing left to lose, Max. I mean, they're hardly likely to arrest him now."

He savoured a sip of the whisky, letting it roll over his tongue. "Very nice, this," he said to Max, then added, almost thoughtfully, "Les wasn't wrong about the gun. It sounded different, quieter. Very effective."

Max, still processing everything, shook his head, his disbelief apparent. "It was plenty loud enough for me."

<u>The Vintage Gardener</u>

Alan had sworn to distance himself from the Monroe family, but yesterday's encounter at The Court Club had shattered that resolve – at least for now. Change was in the air, and with it came an undeniable pull to protect Max. He couldn't ignore the fact that Sarah, too, was now caught in the same web of danger. This time, he would be prepared. He wasn't about to repeat past mistakes. Alongside the two knives concealed on his person, he now carried a retractable cosh cleverly hidden in a discreet pocket of his trousers. The device was unassuming: a slim metal cylinder resembling a small telescope. A single button extended it threefold, transforming it into an efficient, brutal weapon.

The call from Rollie the previous night had left Max visibly tense. The police had descended on The Court Club, grilling Trevor with unrelenting questions. Their conclusion? This was sibling rivalry taken to an unprecedented extreme. Outwardly, Rollie had expressed shock and dismay at the events, a performance Superintendent Richards – his most trusted ally in the force – had subtly aided. The investigation was in its infancy, and while a press blackout had been enforced, Rollie knew it wouldn't last. By afternoon, the lid would come off, necessitating a midday meeting in his office.

Inside Rollie's domain, Alan positioned himself near one of the double doors, a silent sentinel with a clear view of the room and the main entrance beyond. The office, doubling as a boardroom, exuded authority: dark wood panelling, an imposing table, and high-backed chairs. On one side of the table, Jamie and Nigel sat like mismatched chess pieces – each poised to strike in his own way. Rollie took his seat opposite them, his face betraying none of the tension simmering beneath the surface.

Standing at attention near the table's far end were two of Rollie's trusted enforcers. October, the towering Sikh with a calm, unyielding presence, contrasted sharply with August, his shorter but powerfully built Greek counterpart. Both radiated an air of quiet menace. A laptop, tethered to a large monitor at the far end of the table, awaited its turn in the proceedings. Max, seated nearby, was ready to operate it when needed, though his hands rested uneasily on the desk, betraying his unease.

Nigel broke the heavy silence, his voice cutting through the tension like a blade. "Where's your new Irish sidekick, Dad?" The sarcasm in his tone was unmistakable.

Rollie didn't miss a beat. "You tell me, son," he replied dryly, his expression unreadable.

Nigel elbowed Jamie, and the two exchanged a smirk, their suppressed laughter betraying a shared joke at their father's expense.

"Will Harry and Les be joining us?" Nigel asked, his voice taking on a sharper edge, the question carrying a subtle challenge.

Alan watched Rollie shift uncomfortably in his standard office chair. It was a stark contrast to the grand Chesterfield he normally occupied – a throne that suited him far better than this utilitarian seat. Rollie adjusted himself again, a faint grimace crossing his face.

"No, son," Rollie said at last, his tone measured but heavy. "Unfortunately, Harry and Les are no longer with us—"

Jamie cut him off, his irritation boiling over. "Oh, stop with the theatrics, Dad. They're shareholders. If they're not here, then you're wasting our bloody time." He gestured toward Nigel, exasperation clear. "You dragged him all the way up from Bristol on short notice for *this*?"

Not waiting for an answer, Jamie turned back to Rollie, his frustration turning venomous. "For fuck's sake, you're such an antique. Maybe if you spent less time fussing over your bloody garden and more time running the business, we wouldn't be in this mess."

In the charged silence, Rollie glanced toward Max and gave a barely perceptible nod. Max adjusted his spectacles, opened the laptop, and tapped the keyboard, bringing the monitor to life. For a moment, the flickering screen stole the room's attention, the tension shifting toward whatever was about to be revealed.

Jamie groaned audibly, his impatience boiling over. "What now? Stop messing around, Max!" He shot a glare at him, shaking his head in frustration.

Unfazed, Max moved the wireless mouse with precision, his focus entirely on the laptop screen. A few clicks later, the monitor displayed an image that froze the room.

Nigel gasped, his face draining of colour as his eyes locked on the monitor. "Is this some kind of sick joke?" he asked, his voice shaking with disbelief.

Jamie opened his mouth to speak, but Rollie silenced him with a raised hand. "Wait," he said firmly, his tone leaving no room for argument. "Max, show them the next one."

The room held its collective breath as Max clicked again. Another image filled the screen, even more grotesque than the first. Nigel recoiled, his voice rising. "What the hell is this, Dad?"

Rollie leaned forward, his eyes hard as steel. "Boys," he began, his voice steady but heavy with meaning, "yesterday, your Uncle Les shot your Uncle Harold. Then he turned the gun on himself."

Jamie shook his head in disbelief, his mind racing to catch up. "Why? Why the hell would he do something like that?"

"Harold was a quisling," Rollie began, his voice calm but laced with disdain. "He was colluding with Denver Hume to undermine our organisation. We uncovered the betrayal and resolved the matter accordingly." He paused briefly before continuing, "Unfortunately, Les was terminally ill. He made a unilateral decision to use the opportunity to end both their lives. It wasn't an action I sanctioned."

Rollie allowed himself a small, bittersweet smile. "Les had become the quintessential old curmudgeon in his later years," he said with a hint of melancholy. "But when we were younger? He was almost *Panglossian* in his optimism."

Nigel shifted uneasily in his chair, the weight of the revelation pressing down on him. It was Jamie who broke the silence, though his usual bravado had dulled. "How did you find out about all this... collusion, Dad?"

Rollie ignored the question, his gaze sharpening as he studied his sons. "When did you last speak with Denver?" he asked, his tone deceptively mild. His eyes moved between them, waiting for their answers with an unsettling calm.

Jamie's bravado had drained away, leaving him exposed. "We've only met him once, Dad," he said quietly, his voice lacking its usual edge. "At the board meeting. In this very room."

Rollie shifted his attention to Nigel, his gaze unrelenting. "Does James speak for you as well?"

Nigel hesitated, feeling the confidence seep out of him. "Um… yes, Dad. Yes, he does."

Rollie's tone hardened, cutting through the room like a blade. "This is your final chance, Nigel. Does James *truly* speak for you?"

A chill ran through Nigel, his heart pounding. Sweat prickled at his skin as he stumbled over his response. "Y-yes, Dad," he managed, though his voice wavered with uncertainty.

Rollie leaned back slightly, a faint smile tugging at his lips. "Fair enough, son. Now, allow me to shed some light on the matter." His tone was calm, composed, yet brimming with quiet authority. "Denver Hume was in contact with Harold before our board meeting. Long before I ever laid eyes on Mr. Hume."

Jamie stirred, opening his mouth to speak, but Rollie stopped him with a raised hand. The gesture was firm, leaving no room for interruption.

"Denver and Harold had already crafted a proposal to present to Denver's superiors well before our board meeting," Rollie began, his voice measured but tinged with discomfort. "Their plan deliberately understated our organisation's true capabilities, painting us as a poor investment. Mr. Hume designed it that way – he wanted to kill any interest from his bosses before it even started. The orotund Mr. Hume," Rollie added with a faint smirk, "had an unshakable belief in his own brilliance."

Jamie frowned, shifting in his seat. "Why would Denver do that, Dad?" he asked, unease creeping into his tone.

Rollie's expression darkened. "Because Mr. Hume coveted our organisation for himself. He offered the obsequious Harold a prominent position in his imaginary version of things. But the truth? Denver would've tired of Harold in weeks. I doubt your uncle would've lasted a month."

Jamie hesitated, the weight of the revelation pressing down on him. "How do you know all this, Dad?" he asked, his voice faltering now.

Rollie rose slowly to his feet, a slight wince betraying his age. October stepped forward, offering a steadying arm, which Rollie accepted with a small nod of gratitude.

"How indeed," Rollie said, his tone almost teasing. "Especially when all my focus was on my garden." He glanced at October, the faintest trace of a smile softening his features, before returning his gaze to his sons, his composure as sharp as ever.

Rollie continued, methodically unravelling the web of deceit. "Firstly," he said, his tone razor-sharp, "Mr. Hume used a peculiar phrase – calling someone a 'pork chop.' Harold was the only person I've ever known to use that irritating expression."

Nigel shifted uncomfortably, the implications sinking in. Rollie didn't give him time to dwell.

"Secondly," he pressed, "Ciara spent weeks conducting due diligence on our organisation, meticulously gathering details. Yet Mr. Hume claimed to have done the same in a single weekend, based solely on discussions with Max. That's not just improbable – it's impossible."

Nigel's stomach churned, the weight of realisation bearing down on him. His composure was slipping fast.

"And finally," Rollie said, his voice now quieter but no less commanding, "Harold didn't have the broad understanding of our business needed to provide Mr. Hume with the detailed insights he used. That information had to come from someone else. It had to come from *you both*."

The Photos

Rollie's revelations brought the room to a standstill. Nigel and Jamie exchanged uneasy glances, each silently wishing they were anywhere but under their father's unrelenting scrutiny.

The tension shattered as August, the blond Greek security guard, suddenly erupted. "That's it! I've had enough of this – I'm out of here!" He turned on his heel, striding purposefully toward the door.

Alan moved swiftly, stepping into his path.

"Get out of my way!" August barked, his frustration boiling over.

Alan raised his hands in a placating gesture, trying to diffuse the situation. But August was having none of it. He threw a punch, fast and hard. Alan deflected it with practiced ease, but August pressed on, his attacks relentless.

Alan gritted his teeth as he absorbed a few blows, silently cursing himself for engaging with someone so much younger and fitter. *This isn't good for your health, old man,* he reminded himself grimly.

Then, with practiced precision, Alan reached for the retractable cosh hidden in his trousers. In one fluid motion, he extended the weapon and struck August low on the hip, halting his momentum. The brief pause was all Alan needed. He followed up with a calculated blow higher up, knocking August to the floor and ending the assault.

Alan barely had time to catch his breath before the imposing figure of October moved into view. The towering Sikh security guard closed the distance with alarming speed, his expression unreadable. Alan braced himself, already weighing his odds. *If it comes to it, I'll need the knives,* he thought, grimacing.

But before October reached Alan, he effortlessly scooped August off the floor like a rag doll. In a single, devastating motion, he delivered a bone-rattling blow that sent August crashing back down, unconscious.

Alan stood frozen in astonishment as October, calm as ever, dragged August's limp body across the room. Pulling a cable ties from his pocket, October secured him firmly to one of the heavy table legs.

Alan exhaled, his tension easing as relief washed over him. He couldn't help but marvel at October's display of raw strength. *Thank God he's on my side,* Alan thought, silently vowing to avoid crossing him at all costs.

"Thank you, October, my most trusted friend," Rollie said, his voice steady but heavy with meaning. He remained standing, his hands gripping the back of his chair at the long table. Turning to Alan, he offered a nod of appreciation. "And thank you, Colonel Alan."

Alan touched his tender cheekbone, wincing slightly at the blossoming pain. He could already feel the bruise forming.

Rollie's attention shifted back to his sons. His gaze, filled with disappointment and frustration, settled heavily on them. "Boys," he began, his voice low but cutting, "you'll no doubt be interested to learn that I've had to terminate both November's and August's employment. Though, I suspect you'd already anticipated that – given the promises you made to them."

Jamie's face paled, and he leaned forward, his words spilling out in a rush. "Dad, you've got it all wrong. This wasn't our idea – it was Harry's! He's the one who wanted your position. Nigel and I," he gestured toward his brother, seated stiffly beside him, "we just went along with it because we thought it was best for the company."

Rollie's expression hardened, his disappointment deepening into something colder. "You went along with it?" he repeated, his tone sharp enough to cut. "Neither of you thought to consult me? Did you assume I was too preoccupied with my garden to care?"

Nigel stepped in, his voice wavering as he tried to placate his father. "Look, Dad, we didn't mean any harm. Honestly, we wouldn't have let anything happen to you. You're our father!"

Rollie's eyes darkened with disdain, his expression leaving no doubt about his disappointment. Without a word, he turned to Max. "Next photo, please."

Max, his hands steady despite the tension in the room, moved the wireless mouse. The monitor flickered, revealing the next image: Denver

Hume's bloodied, lifeless body, crumpled in a grotesque and unnatural position on the cold ground.

Jamie recoiled, his face draining of colour. "Oh no... no, no," he stammered, his voice trembling. Beside him, Nigel buried his face in his hands, his body shaking, whether from shock or shame was unclear.

Rollie's voice cut through the silence like a blade, sorrow and accusation mingling in his tone. "This photograph was taken in a deserted builder's yard near Ripon Racecourse. Does that location ring any bells for either of you?"

Nigel kept his face hidden, his hands clenched tightly as if trying to shut out the world. Jamie, barely managing to compose himself, croaked out a response. "No, Dad. We... we don't know it."

Rollie's piercing gaze remained fixed on them, unrelenting. "This," he said, gesturing to the image on the screen, "is where Ciara and Sarah were taken after Mr. Hume, and his men kidnapped them off the M1. Tell me – were you aware this was going to happen?"

He didn't wait for an answer. His head shook slowly, disappointment etched in every line of his face. "Of course, you were," he said bitterly, the weight of his words sinking into the air like stones into deep water.

Rollie pressed on, his disappointment thick in the air. "It was Mr. Hume who met his end that day, not Ciara. Not Sarah, for that matter. Did you even care about what happened to Sarah? She was just an innocent bystander in all this deceit."

The challenge in Rollie's voice hung like a dark cloud, his words cutting through the room with brutal clarity.

"No, of course, you didn't care," Rollie continued, his tone now laced with bitter accusation. "Your only concern was your own selfish desires." He shook his head, sorrow etched deeply across his features.

Rollie glanced toward Max, his gaze weary and laden with unspoken exhaustion. "Max, please, turn that off. It's making me feel quite ill just looking at it."

Max, without hesitation, closed the laptop. The screen faded to black, leaving an oppressive silence in its wake.

Jamie's voice broke through the quiet, desperation lacing his words. "Please, Dad…"

But Rollie, resolute, raised a hand to silence him. "Enough, James. I've heard more than enough from you both." He stood for a moment, as if gathering his strength, before taking a deep breath.

"I need a short break," Rollie added, his voice controlled but firm. "Both of you stay here."

With that, Rollie turned and slowly made his way to the door opposite Alan, the weight of his emotions evident in every step he took toward the anteroom. Each stride seemed to carry the heaviness of the revelations that had just unfolded.

Retirement (at last)

"So, what do we do now?" Nigel's voice cut through the silence, his challenge hanging in the air, thick with unease.

Jamie shot him a sharp look, his patience wearing thin. "Just quieten down," he snapped, his eyes flicking to Max, desperation creeping into his tone. "Max, do you have any idea what Dad's planning? He wouldn't do anything reckless, would he? We're family, for God's sake." The words spilled out in a rush, his voice wavering with a mix of anxiety and hope.

Max, eyes flicking between the two brothers, shook his head. "I honestly don't know, Jamie. Half of what's been said today is news to me," he admitted, his voice steady but tinged with confusion.

The tension in the room thickened as Jamie rose to his feet, his unease growing with every passing second. "Where the hell is he going with this?" he muttered to himself, frustration building.

"Your father told you to wait," October's voice boomed, firm and unyielding. The authoritative tone caught Jamie off guard, sending a ripple of surprise through him.

Jamie's gaze locked onto October, instantly aware of the shift in power dynamics. Where once he held sway over the man, October now commanded respect, his loyalty to Rollie and his physical presence a clear signal that he was no longer a subordinate. "I'm just getting some water. Is that alright?" Jamie asked, trying to mask his discomfort with a feigned calm.

October's expression remained unreadable, but he nodded once, granting Jamie permission.

Nigel pleaded with Max, "Can you do anything, Max?"

Max replied, "I'm sorry Nigel but you've perjured yourself many times over, cede to your father's will and express remorse and he's sure to go easy on you, after all, you are his son."

The door to the anteroom creaked open again, but this time it wasn't Rollie who stepped through – it was Ciara. Alan couldn't suppress a wry smile, barely stopping himself from letting out a laugh. Max had been right; when it came to playing the game, no one outmanoeuvred Rollie.

"What the hell do you want?" Jamie's voice was sharp, his frustration boiling over.

Nigel, slowly lowering his hands from his face, mirrored the sentiment, his tone dripping with exasperation. "Just what we needed…"

Ciara flashed them a grin as she slid into the chair where Rollie had just been. "Well, that's a warm welcome, boys," she teased, her gaze flicking from one brother to the other, amusement dancing in her eyes.

"Our father is sitting there," Jamie muttered, bitterness seeping through his words.

"Your father *was* sitting here," Ciara quipped, her tone light and unbothered, the sharpness of her response cutting through the tension.

Jamie stood, but before he could fully rise, October's commanding voice froze him in place. "Sit down!" The command rang out, unyielding. Jamie hesitated, his jaw clenched, grappling with the shift in power, but finally sank back into his seat, his frustration palpable.

Ciara, her voice smooth and upbeat, laced with her distinctive Irish brogue, continued as if nothing had happened. "Denver shocked everyone when he kidnapped us on our way to Edinburgh. I mean, honestly, why steal an empty lorry?" She didn't wait for a response. "I was lucky to have Alan and Max with me," she added, nodding toward them. Both Alan and Max gave brief acknowledgments.

"We figured the kidnapping would happen once we were loaded up," Ciara went on, glancing toward the brothers. "I'm sure you did, too." When neither of them responded, she grinned, savouring the moment. "Well, my good luck turned into bad luck for Denver, of course," she said, her voice full of relish. "And, as it turns out, bad luck for both of you."

Before either brother could protest, Ciara launched into her next question with a quickness that left no room for deflection. "Do you know who Dominic Di Prima is?"

Nigel, his voice subdued, answered, "Um, yes, he is… he was, Denver's boss, back in Boston."

"Correct!" Ciara replied, her tone bright with amusement. "Your father's been in talks with Dominic for the past few weeks."

"I don't have to listen to this," Jamie muttered, his voice thick with embarrassment as he shook his head, the weight of the situation pressing down on him.

Ciara's tone shifted, sharp and commanding. "No, you don't, Jamie. You can either listen to me, or you can face October. What's it going to be?" Jamie clenched his fists, the frustration evident in the way he seethed in his seat.

"Max, could you please bring up the video feed?" Ciara asked, her voice cutting through the tension.

"Of course," Max replied calmly. He opened the laptop with practiced ease, quickly navigating to the right application and starting the feed. The image flickered to life on the monitor.

"What now?" Nigel's voice cracked slightly, his uncertainty and dread clear as the reality of the moment settled in.

The live feed flickered to life on the monitor, and for a moment, everyone was silent, trying to make sense of what they were seeing. Alan, unable to stand the uncertainty, stepped away from the exit and moved closer to the screen. The camera showed two plush, limousine-like car seats, bathed in soft lighting. The faint hum of indistinct voices filtered through the background, adding to the uneasy atmosphere.

Then, Rollie appeared, carefully settling into one of the seats, his movements slow and deliberate. Hands reached in from off-camera to assist him, and his voice could be heard, offering a brief thank-you to the unseen helper. As he adjusted himself, Rollie glanced around, appearing to take in his surroundings, though he seemed unaware of the camera's presence.

Suddenly, another figure slid into the seat next to him – a man with dark, slicked-back hair, a lean, athletic frame, and piercing, intense eyes.

"Rollie, Dominic, can you hear me?" Ciara's voice rang out, sharp and demanding from the monitor.

Rollie looked around, his expression comically confused as he tried to locate the source of the voice. It was the man beside him who spoke first, breaking the silence. "Hi, Ciara. Yeah, we can hear you, but we can't see you. Can you hear us?"

Alan's ear caught the unmistakable "Noo Yawk" accent, a sharp edge of Lower Manhattan that was all too familiar. He half-expected to hear an Irish lilt, but instead, it was all New York.

"Loud and clear, Dominic. Good to see you again," Ciara responded, her voice cool and controlled.

Rollie, growing impatient, demanded, "Where is she?"

Dominic, amused, chuckled softly. "Why, she's in your office, Rollie."

Rollie's face lit up with a small grin, though his confusion remained. "She is? Oh, that's good," he replied, then turned to what he thought was the camera. "Ciara, dear, is everything okay in there?"

The sound of Dominic's chuckle filled the car. "Rollie, the microphone's right there," he pointed, gesturing off-camera. "You can use your normal voice."

"Oh, I see," Rollie said, his tone shifting. "Yes, thank you, Dominic." He cleared his throat and addressed his sons. "James, Nigel, I know you can hear me. I'm in a car with my friend Dominic, who's kindly offering me a lift to Heathrow. Listen carefully, please. I want to make this short and sweet, and I don't intend to repeat myself." He paused, letting his words sink in.

Rollie's tone was calm, but there was a finality to his words. "You're both out. No harm will come to you or your families, but from today, you're both unemployed. Now, don't try to argue – this is all on you. You've both done well for yourselves, we know that, but I can't trust you anymore. As for your shares in Exotic Food Imports Limited… they're null and void. Max can fill you in on the details once this call is over."

Rollie paused for a moment, and a hand from off-camera passed him a glass of champagne. He accepted it with a nod. "Thank you, dear," he said to someone unseen, his voice softening just for a moment.

Jamie's confusion boiled over. "What is this?" he asked, his voice edged with disbelief. "What's going on here? What kind of charade is this?"

Rollie's gaze shifted back to the camera, his expression now one of quiet resolve. "This isn't a game, son. Ciara will take over as CEO, and Dominic will support her from Boston. Sarah will relocate to Bristol to manage our Southwest operation, taking over from you, Nigel. Max will remain as our Legal Counsel. And as for my loyal friend, October... are you there?"

"I am, Rollie," October replied, stepping forward into view, his stature imposing as ever.

"Good," Rollie said, his voice warm yet authoritative. "October, I need you to show Ciara the same loyalty and care you've always shown me. I'll ensure you're handsomely rewarded, directly from my own pocket. And when the time is right, I'll host you and your family at my villa."

"Of course, sir... um, Rollie, I mean," October replied, his voice thick with emotion. Alan couldn't help but notice the tightness in October's throat, the unspoken bond of loyalty and respect between the two men palpable. It was clear that the giant Sikh's admiration for his now-former boss ran deep, and this moment of change hit harder than any of them had anticipated.

"Dad, is there anything I can say, anything I can do to fix this?" Jamie's voice trembled, desperation clear in his words. "I mean, Sarah in Bristol? She's your bloody cleaner!"

Rollie's expression hardened, his voice unwavering. "I've had to slice through the Gordian knot you and your brother tied, James. There's no turning back now. Sarah is far more resourceful and trustworthy than you or your brother could ever be, sad though it is for me to admit about my own sons." His gaze sharpened. "Now, go and enjoy the early retirement I never had the luxury of, while you still have time."

He shifted focus with practiced ease. "Colonel Alan, I trust you'll spend some time in Bristol with Sarah, at least to help her with the transition. She'll need your support in the beginning." Rollie paused, his brows furrowing slightly as he scanned the room. "Is Alan even there?"

"Yes, Mr. Monroe, um, Rollie, I'm here," Alan replied, his voice betraying a hint of unease, but firm, nonetheless. "And yes, I'll be there to help."

Rollie gave a small nod of satisfaction, but his mind seemed to drift again. "Ciara, a few final words before I sign off." He waited for her acknowledgment, though he couldn't see her. "Look after Bruce, dear. He's invaluable. Don't wear him out, though," he added, a chuckle escaping his lips as he delivered the pun. "Now, where was I? Ah yes, as Keats said in *To Autumn* – it's time to gather the fruits from the garden and preserve them for the long winter ahead. Well, something to that effect. Don't let my garden become overgrown, my dear."

"I won't, Rollie, I promise," Ciara assured him.

"Thank you," Rollie replied softly. He took a sip of his champagne, savouring it for a moment. "If you need me, you – *and only you* – know how to reach me. I'll always be here for advice on the garden." He paused, a thoughtful look crossing his face. "And now, I finally step into retirement. While I can't slow my own aging, I want to let the passage of time slow down. Goodbye."

With that, Dominic leaned forward and shut off the camera feed, the screen flickering to black.

Practicalities

The week that followed the meeting in what was once Rollie's office was a blur for Max and Alan, as the whirlwind of events they'd endured continued to unfold. Their usual refuge – drinking – had become a distant memory. The days had been filled with practicalities, leaving little room for leisure.

Max found himself buried in paperwork, overwhelmed by the complexities of the recent changes. The pubs were now under new ownership, with Trevor from The Court Club taking over as licensee. Exotic Foods' shareholding had been meticulously restructured. Max had also ensured Sarah's mortgage in Brighton was settled and helped close her cleaning business. The deeds to the Withdean Road mansion had been transferred, and he was now preparing to drive Sarah to Bristol to start her new life.

The revelation of Sarah's pregnancy had been a surprise, but the news that Alan was the father, while shocking, was less of a revelation than one might expect.

Alan's reaction had been a mix of shock and fear. Sarah had reassured him, making it clear that she had no expectations of him stepping into a father's role. Still, Alan was unwavering in his commitment. He'd promised to be there for Sarah and the child, whatever the future held.

For Sarah, the news brought her a deep sense of happiness. While secretly hoping for a closer relationship with Alan, she understood that even without becoming a couple, she would still have what she'd always wanted: stability, security, and the promise of a new life. Bristol represented a fresh start, a chance to leave behind the weariness of Brighton and begin anew. With the changes that were coming, she would have financial stability, a new sense of responsibility – and most precious of all, a baby. She hoped the city would offer her the rejuvenation she longed for, something that had long been absent from her life in Brighton.

Sarah opened the wardrobe in Alan's bedroom, her eyes scanning the outdated clothes inside. "Just how old are these?" she asked, pulling a wrinkled shirt from the rack.

"Very old," Alan replied with a dry smile, his attention split as he hastily packed a suitcase.

Sarah closed the wardrobe with a sigh. "Right, that's it. We'll get you a new wardrobe in Bristol."

Alan raised an eyebrow. "If it means we can stop talking about clothes for the rest of the day, then I'm all in," he said, zipping up the suitcase with a snap. Just then, the front door opened and closed, followed by the sound of footsteps climbing the stairs.

"Audrey?" Alan called out.

Audrey Hepburn appeared at the top of the stairs, moving with her usual elegance. "Hi, Alan. And hello, Sarah!" she greeted, her gaze briefly drifting past Alan to the open door of his bedroom.

Alan's face lit up at the sight of her. "Where have you been staying?" he asked, eager to catch up.

"Give them some space, Alan," Sarah teased, stepping forward to embrace Audrey. "I never properly thanked you for what you did for us back in Ripon."

Audrey shrugged it off, her modesty apparent. "It's what anyone would have done. No thanks needed."

"I disagree," Sarah countered with a grin. "I don't know anyone else who would have done what you did. Well, maybe Ciara!" She shot a playful smile at Alan.

Audrey glanced at the open suitcase. "You're packing?"

"Yes, Sarah's moving to Bristol, and I'm going down for a few days to help her get settled," Alan explained.

"A few days!" Sarah exclaimed, feigning shock. "I'm hoping it'll be a little longer than that!"

"Alright, a week or so," Alan said with a shrug.

"A week!" Sarah repeated, raising an eyebrow. "What's he like?"

Audrey gave Alan an exaggerated eyeroll. "Just dreadful," she said with a smirk. "Alan, can I have just two minutes of your time?"

"Of course," Alan replied, glancing between the two.

"Let me take another look through those wardrobes," Sarah suggested, taking charge. "You two can use the lounge while I sort this out."

Alan closed the lounge door behind him, concern etched across his face. "Audrey, are you okay?"

"*Sarah est enceinte,*" Audrey said softly, her gaze fixed on the floor as she switched to French.

Alan frowned, momentarily thrown. "Your French is better than mine, but... do you mean pregnant?"

Audrey nodded, her eyes flickering up to meet his briefly before falling again. "Yes."

"Why the sudden switch to French?" Alan asked, his voice a mix of confusion and irritation.

"*Confidentialité,*" Audrey replied quietly.

Alan let out a small sigh, running a hand through his hair. "Right. Fine. Or, uh, *d'accord,* I suppose," he muttered, deciding not to push her on it.

Audrey took a steadying breath, her voice trembling slightly as she continued. "*Sarah est enceinte. Es-tu le père de son enfant?*" [Sarah is pregnant. Are you the father of her child?]

Alan's brows shot up, the question hitting him like a punch. "What? *Pourquoi me demandes-tu cela? Pourquoi est-ce important?*" [Why are you asking me this? Why is it important?]

Audrey's shoulders seemed to fold inward as she lowered her gaze again, her voice barely above a whisper. "*Parce que je suis aussi enceinte, et tu es le père.*" [Because I am also pregnant, and you are the father.]

The revelation hit him like a steam train. "Oh, uh…" He faltered, the words slipping through his grasp. "I'm sorry, Audrey." It was all he could manage, his mind a whirlwind of confusion and guilt.

Audrey frowned, her confusion evident. "You don't need to be sorry," she whispered, reaching out to lightly touch his elbow. The gesture was subtle but grounding, a fleeting moment of reassurance.

Alan blinked, struggling to keep up as Audrey continued, her tone measured. "Listen, I've met someone. Her name is Rita."

His emotions spiralled, ricocheting between shock and unease. He blurted out the first thing that came to mind, a clumsy, half-formed reference. "Does... does their perfume smell sweeter?"

Audrey tilted her head, bemused but determined to stay on track. "Uh, anyway," she said, ignoring his stumble, "Rita knows about the baby. She's just as excited as I am. Can she move in with me?"

Alan struggled to find his footing. "Wait... they or she?" he asked, tripping over the words.

Audrey raised an eyebrow, exasperated but patient. "Does it matter?" she countered. "I'm young. I'm still figuring things out."

"You keep telling me you're not so young," Alan muttered, rubbing the back of his neck. "But no, of course it doesn't matter. I'm sorry." He paused, collecting his thoughts. "I'll move out. Give you both some space."

Audrey's expression softened. "Alan, you don't have to—"

"No, it's fine," he interrupted. "Boffin will be thrilled. She likes you better than me anyway. Give me a fortnight, and the place is yours... Rita's too, of course." He hesitated, then added, "I'll hire someone to convert the box room into a nursery."

Audrey shook her head, a small smile playing on her lips. "Stop fussing," she said, though the gratitude in her voice was unmistakable.

Alan shrugged, his voice quieter now. "I just... I want to get this right. I've made too many mistakes before."

"Thank you," Audrey said softly, and she meant it. Rising onto her toes, she kissed him gently on the lips – a gesture of forgiveness, understanding, and something unspoken.

Loose Ends

Ten days later, Alan emerged from St. Andrew's churchyard, his footsteps slow and deliberate as he headed back to Number 37. The evening with Max had been exactly what he needed – a brief escape from the tangled web his life had become. They'd drunk too much, laughed too loudly, and for a few fleeting hours, the weight of his responsibilities had lifted.

In Bristol, Alan had thrown himself into helping Sarah settle in, handling the practicalities with quiet determination. He didn't mention Audrey's revelation; it didn't feel right to burden Sarah with that – not yet. Instead, he focused on the small victories, ensuring she felt supported and secure.

Back in Brighton, Alan had set to work arranging the nursery and packing up his belongings. His "goods and shackles," as he wryly called them, were either donated, binned, or sent to storage. He'd wanted to spend more time with Audrey, to offer more than just logistical support, but they'd brushed him off, claiming, "the timing wasn't right." It stung, though he told himself it was their way of keeping their independence – something he admired, even if it left him feeling redundant.

Still, Alan was resolute about the move to Bristol, even if it wasn't permanent. Audrey's news had hit him like a lightning strike, but he was determined to be part of their life, he wouldn't abandon his responsibility, however old fashioned that might appear.

Max had promised to keep an eye on things and report back on Audrey. It gave Alan some peace of mind, knowing someone he trusted would be there. Max, of course, would expect updates in return – how Sarah was settling in, and managing her new role.

After all, he told himself, Bristol wasn't so far.

Tonight had been a welcome reprieve from the usual stresses – a simple evening with an old friend, filled with laughter and the kind of light-hearted nonsense that seemed impossible to find in their everyday lives. As Alan walked out of the churchyard, the cool night air greeted him. He crossed the road and headed for the wide alleyway, his usual route home. It was the same path where he'd first met Audrey, a memory that, despite the circumstances, always brought a smile to his face.

But tonight, the familiar comfort of the alley was shattered. A figure stepped out from the shadows, blocking his way. The silhouette loomed closer, and Alan's heart sank as he recognised the man.

Audrey's father.

"Alright, old man? Let's see how tough you are now, without the element of surprise," the man growled, his voice low and menacing. Alan heard the distinct sound of a switchblade flicking open.

"For crying out loud, not now," Alan muttered under his breath, his hand instinctively reaching for the cosh tucked inside his coat.

THE END